THE
FOOTPRINTS
OF SATAN

The Footprints of Satan

by

Norman Berrow

RAMBLE HOUSE

Third Ramble House Edition

ISBN 13: 978-1-60543-194-9

ISBN 10: 1-60543-194-X

Published: 1950
Reprinted: 2005 by Ramble House
Cover Art: Gavin L. O'Keefe
Preparation: Fender Tucker

Foreword

ONCE UPON A TIME—ON THE NIGHT OF THE 8th February 1855, to be exact—the Devil visited England. At least that was the widely accepted theory, and to this day the theory has not been disproved. It must have been His Satanic Majesty, for his peculiar tracks—the marks of *hooves*—were found in the snow the following morning in and around a number of towns in the south of Devon. Moreover, they were seen in such physically inaccessible places as on the tops of high walls enclosing private gardens and on the steep roofs of houses, and it was apparent that the visitant possessed the power of passing through solid substances.

You don't believe me? I refer you to the account (quoted elsewhere in this book) published in the issue for the 16th February 1855, of that most conservative and realistic of newspapers, *The Times*. I refer you also to various reports and articles appearing in issues of the *Illustrated London News* between the 24th February and the 17th March of that year. This *is fact*—not fiction. . . .

Even *The Times,* in cautious language, touches on the possibility that the impressions in the snow may have been the marks of Satan himself; and in the minds of hundreds of Devonshire folk, and perhaps thousands of other Britons, the marks of Satan they were.

A short while ago, in the year of the Big Snow, it appeared that he again visited the land, this time descending upon the outskirts of the small country town of Winchingham. Again he left his own peculiar tracks in the snow, corresponding to those of almost a century ago; again they were seen not only in the private gardens of inoffensive citizens, but also in such apparently physically inaccessible places as on the tops of the enclosing walls and on the steep roof of a house; and yet again it seemed that the visitant possessed the power of passing through solid substance.

But this time his motives were not so obscure, and an investigation of the phenomenon was undertaken by a sceptical—and intelligent—C.I.D. officer attached to the Winchshire County Constabulary, one Detective-Inspector Lancelot Carolus Smith.

The investigation was crowned with success—and yet . . .
yet, at the end of it, Lancelot Carolus was left in unnaturally
sober and meditative mood, left wondering whether, in
terms of the Absolute, the Dispenser of Evil had not in truth
been there and left his mark among the habitations of men.
For, if Evil directs a medium or works through a channel,
would you say it was the channel acting of itself? Or would
you say it was the Overlord of the Lost manifesting himself?

The Footprints of Satan

PART ONE

The Spoor of the Unknown

"Stay as long as yer like," Jake Popplewell invited his nephew in an hospitable roar. He flung out his right arm in an expansive gesture, and knocked the clock off the mantelshelf. "The place is yours. Stay as long as yer like, do what yer like. Be it ever so humble there's no place like old Jake Popplewell's ivy-covered cot. The abode of conscious though unostentatious licence. The last stronghold of freedom."

"Thanks, uncle," smiled Gregory Cushing, bending down and picking up the fallen clock. He was head and shoulders taller than his uncle, and far more presentable; but away deep in his eyes was the shadow of a great sorrow. "But there's no need to wreck the place—this has stopped."

"It's been stopped these fifteen years," said Mr. Popplewell proudly. "I only keep it up there to remind me of the days when a stinkin' little timepiece governed me life. Ha! Well, now that yer settled in, what about some prog? An' mebbe a little drop o' somethin' to keep out the cold?"

"Prog?"

"Grub, chow, eats—food, damme! But not on an empty stom-ach—d'ye drink?"

"In moderation," admitted Gregory Cushing.

"Huh!" snorted old Jake. "Moderation. The curse of the cultured classes. The masochistic impulse to knock off just when yer be-ginnin' to enjoy yerself." His expression altered. He screwed up one eye and leered at his nephew. "It's not generally known, me boy, that I manage to snaffle a drop of mountain dew now and again. Wait there—an' chuck some more wood on that fire."

He stumped into his little kitchen and came out a moment or two later with two generous portions of whisky in two household tumblers. To Gregory Cushing they looked like small flagons.

"Here y'are, Greg. Down the hatch with it."

Gregory took a tumbler from one gnarled hand and sniffed at it. "Is this neat?"

"Of course it's neat!" bellowed old Jake belligerently. "Better for yer that way. Much. What d'ye want to water it down for? Are you a man or a flippety bit of a wench? And none of yer cold-blooded, la-di-da sip—sip—sip—here, Greg. Toss it down, an' let the warmth of it spread through yer guts like the blessin' of God."

"Oh, well," sighed Gregory resignedly. "Here's to you, uncle, and many thanks for your welcome and your kindness."

"*Nitchevo,*" returned uncle Jake. "Here's to you, me boy. An' damnation to the petticoat."

He raised his glass, and a split second later it was empty. Gregory did his best to emulate his uncle, and then fought for breath while the old man smacked his lips.

"That'll warm the cockles of yer heart. Now for a bite of dinner. Come on into the kitchen an' I'll show yer where things are kept. Or where they're supposed to be kept. . . . Bachelor's Hall this, Greg me boy," said Mr. Popplewell jovially, pushing his nephew before him into the kitchen, "an' by the livin' Lord Harry, Bachelor's Hall it'll remain! Here, take these."

He thrust plates and knives and forks into Gregory's hands. "If yer want a cloth on the table ye'll find one somewhere in the parlour. Me, I don't bother—only have to wash the damn thing."

"But isn't there a laundry—?"

"Laundry, me glass eye! I do things for meself. If I can't do 'em I go without. Independent—that's me." He lifted the ring in the old-fashioned stove, threw in some more wood and moved the kettle to cover the flame. "So yer wife's left yer, hey?" he called through the door.

"Yes," replied Gregory Cushing briefly. "Some time ago."

"Ha! Mine left me fifteen years ago. Best day's work she ever did. I sold up everythin', settled a lump sum on her—*she* saw to that—and started wanderin' about here, there an' everywhere. An' then one day I happened to be passin' through these parts an' saw this crib up for sale. Goin' beggin' it was. I liked the look of it. I saw that it 'ud suit me. 'This,' I said to meself, 'is it. This is Jake Popplewell's castle. Within these four walls shall dwell liberty, equality, fraternity an' goodwill to all men—an' never the breath nor the shrill complainin' voice of a woman shall poison the atmosphere. So I moved in with me books an' stuck that clock up there."

Gregory glanced round the little room literally cluttered with books in all degrees of decrepitude, and then at the mantelpiece.

"The books I can understand, but the clock—"

Old Jake gave a snort of sardonic laughter. "That wasn't put up there to tell time, that was put up there to mock at time. Besides, it comes in handy for throwin' things at—it relieves me feelin's."

Gregory Cushing smiled to himself and completed the not very intricate business of preparing the Bachelor's Hall banqueting table. The old man came in from the kitchen a few moments later with a battered old Britannia metal teapot in his hand.

"But books now—ah! there's a different pair o' shoes. Readin', says old Bacon, maketh a full man; an' only the full man can properly appreciate the God-given blessin' of solitude. I don't hold much in the communion o' Saints, but in the noble company of good books a man is in intimate communion with the choicest spirits of the earth."

Descending from this lyrical note to a more practical one, he dumped the teapot on the table and looked a trifle apprehensively at his nephew. "No danger of yer wife comin' back, is there, Greg? No fear of her trackin' yer down here?"

Gregory shook his head curtly. "Oh, no. She's dead."

"Dead? When did she die?"

"A couple of months ago."

"But, rot me! she was only a young woman. What ailed her? What did she die of?"

"Suicide."

"*Suicide?* You mean she killed herself?"

"The police," said Gregory wearily, "picked her body out of the river. I had to go with them and identify it. She told me she was going to do it, but I didn't believe her. You see, I'd refused to take her back—"

"Quite right," said Jake Popplewell vigorously.

"No, quite wrong. But I was sore and angry with her—and stupid. . . ."

Uncle Jake turned away abruptly and hooked up a chair to the table. "Greg, me boy, I ask no questions. For as long as yer like this is yer home now. But don't sour the pride of yer youth in lamentin' over spilt milk. The past is past an' dead, an' a wise man puts all dead things behind him. Now, sit yerself down an' tuck into it."

He sat down himself and began to "tuck into it" with gusto.

*   *   *

Old Jake Popplewell's cottage still stands at the foot of The Rise, a small hill on the outskirts of Winchingham, and at almost the exact point where the bitumen ends and Old Chipping Road narrows to become The Rise. It is the last dwelling on that side of the road, standing by itself some hundred yards or so from the last newly-built neat bungalow. On the other side of the road, up the slope of The Rise, are the homes often or twelve well-to-do and mostly retired gentlefolk; and on the summit is the house of Mrs. Pendlebury, where dwells also Mrs. Pendlebury's sister, Miss Emmeline Forbes, who had quite a lot to do with and to say about the footprints of Satan. . . .

In the valley of the miniature river Winch on the other side of The Rise lies Steeple Thelming, which is itself a mystery in that Steeple Thelming is more a geometrical figure than a geographical place. It is a location without being a settlement. There has never been a steeple there within the memory of man—except the Steeple Inn, which doesn't really count—and no one has any idea of the meaning of the word "thelming," if indeed it ever had any meaning. Jake himself scratched a living from two acres of ground, the flat part of which he worked desultorily as a market garden, and the hillside part of which had been planted in fruit trees. In person Jake was short and stocky. His face was seamed and wrinkled as a walnut; he had fierce chin-whiskers, an unshakable contempt of and abhorrence for women, and a painful weakness for potent liquor. In character he was generally held to be an offence to the righteous and a blot on the town's escutcheon. The more censorious referred to him as "that old scoundrel," or alternatively as "that drunkard"; the more tolerant dubbed him a character. By which they really meant he was out of character; for whereas Jake had originally come of very good family he had since gone a long way from it. In later years he had shed all refinement and grown coarse and uncouth. But the substratum of culture was still there.

*   *   *

"An' how," inquired Mr. Popplewell of his nephew at the conclusion of their simple meal, "is the hoppin', the steppin' an' the jumpin'?"

Gregory Cushing was an over-tall stringy young man in his thirties, who had been a notable exponent of this particular athletic feat, and at one stage of his career had come within call of representing his country at an Olympiad. But now he merely shook his head and smiled a little ruefully and replied that it had been a long time since he had done any serious practice.

"Getting too old for it," he murmured.

"Old!" scoffed uncle Jake. "Married life, mebbe. Domination by the petticoat." He sniffed and waxed philosophical. "Though what possesses a feller to take up this peculiar and slightly ludicrous form of sport beats me. But life is full of odd little mysteries like that. One feller goes hop, step an' jumpin' through life. Another spends most of his time in an orchestra starin' at a piddlin' little metal triangle an' whanging it about twice a fort night—"

"You're behind the times, uncle. The drummer does that now."

"Does he? In my young days it was a full-time job. . . . Then there's the feller who spends most of *his* life luggin' round a damn great bull-fiddle an' solacin' his soul with lugubrious plunkin' an' boomin' noises. . . ."

"Oh, well," said Gregory tolerantly, "I suppose you sort of graduate to these things from other things. I know I started out as a long jumper."

"Now *that*," retorted Jake, "I can understand. That's a natural development with practical uses, besides bein' an expression of man's rebellion against the crampin' an' restrictin' clutch of Mother Earth. But this hopscotch business—"

He stood up, stacked his cup and saucer on top of his plate and carried them through into the kitchen. Gregory followed suit, and the table was soon cleared. Jake emptied the kettle into the sink, washed the dishes while Gregory dried, swabbed the tiny bench and sink and wrung out and hung up his dishcloth like a tidy old bachelor. After which he produced, filled and lit a short stubby pipe and invited his nephew to come outside and be shown the demesne.

"Come on out for a smoke an' a stroll an' view the broad acres of Bachelor's Hall."

A thin wooden door with a latch to it opened directly out of the kitchen and on to a long narrow path that Jake had sown with cinders and bordered with broken bricks. Gregory stood on the path with his hands jammed in his pockets to keep them warm, and looked about him. The broad acres—both of them—were unkempt and haggard under the leaden winter sky, the leafless trees shivered in the biting wind that blew across the upper slopes of the hill.

"Cold as organized charity," rumbled old Jake, cocking an eye at the lowering sky. "A hard winter, me boy—an' there's snow in the air." But the first fall of snow was more than a week away yet.

At the end of the path, which ran between rows of currant and gooseberry bushes tastefully decorated with portions of Jake's washing, was a crumbling wooden shed.

"Can't do anythin' in the garden this time of the year, y'understand, Greg," said Jake over his shoulder as he stumped down the path. "It's me off-time. Consequently it's Boomer's off-time as well."

"Boomer?"

Jake cackled, showing yellow teeth. "A friend of mine. He lives in here."

He opened a door in one side of the shed, disclosing a little open cart with sloping sides, something like an overgrown wheelbarrow, a jumble of tools and implements, some bales of hay and two or three bags of oats. Then he opened the other door and introduced Gregory to Boomer. Boomer was a small, grey, shaggy donkey.

"But why Boomer?"

Old Jake grinned and stepped into the stall. A thick layer of straw had been strewn on the earth floor, a homemade manger stood at the far end and harness hung on the wall. "Short for Boomerang. 'Cos he always comes home—*always* . . . ."

He slapped the animal affectionately and resoundingly on its shaggy rump, and bellowed its name. The donkey flapped its great ears and looked round lethargically.

"Finished yer grub, Boomer? Like to go out an' forage in the orchard? Hey?"

The donkey turned its head round and butted Jake in the waistcoat.

"Come on then," said the little old man encouragingly. And Boomer turned round neatly in the narrow stall, much more neatly than any horse would have done, and followed his master outside.

"Watch this!" cried Jake proudly.

Boomer plodded sedately on his tiny hooves to a little wooden gate set in a low wall that had been made of boulders from the hillside. He muzzled free the latch of the gate, nosed it open, passed through and began to amble slowly and aimlessly up through the fruit trees.

"Not," observed Jake, watching his four-footed friend, "that that gate serves any useful purpose other than givin' the moke somethin' to play with. . . . He'll come back when he gets cold, which shows that he has more intelligence than some of yer highly-bred blood horses."

"You sound fond of him," murmured Gregory.

"I am," said Jake simply. "More than I am of the so-called lords o' creation round here. The donkey—people call him an ass. They're the asses! A donkey is an intelligent an' resourceful beast. Like meself he's had the supreme intelligence to simplify his life an' shed his inhibitions."

"But did he ever have any? And aren't all animals like that?"

"The donkey is more so," thundered old Jake aggressively. "Twice in the recorded history of the world the donkey has stood out head an' shoulders above all livin' four-footed creatures as a monument of patience an' sagacity. There was Balaam an' his ass. Balaam was the ass there! The donkey had the intelligence to stop in the face of danger, an' the patience to take the beatin' that fanatical half-wit Balaam gave him. Though it passes me comprehension why he didn't pitch the two-legged ass off his back an' kick the livin' daylights out of him!"

Gregory made soothing noises. "And the second instance?"

"The second instance was when a man named Jesus of Nazareth went ridin' into Jerusalem. Did he go dashin' in on a fiery charger? Did he drive in like a rushin' wind in the equivalent of the modern motor-car? He did not. He chose that most appropriate symbol, the intelligent, the patient, the philosophical donkey. As slow, sure, certain an' inexorable as his teachin'—which the priests an' parsons have done their best to mangle an' disguise from that day to this."

Gregory laughed outright at old Jake's vehemence. "All right, uncle, I'll believe you."

"Rot me! Isn't it true . . .? They say donkeys eat thistles. Mebbe they do, though I've never seen old Boomer chewin' them. But if that's a sign of asininity what would you say of so-called intelligent human bein's who eat—from choice, mark you, an' deliberately—eat snails an' the legs o' frogs? An' I've known grown-up men who drink"—Jake's voice sank to an awe-struck whisper—"*Cocoa.* . . . Cocoa! Makin' their guts sluggish an' fillin' their bones with ash!"

He gazed into the grinning face of his nephew towering above him, and little by little the lines of aggression faded out of his own.

"I s'pose yer think I'm barmy, hey? But I'm not the only champion of the ill-used an' much-maligned donkey. Remember Chesterton's magnificent poem? 'Fools!' shouted Chesterton, an' with plenty of reason. 'One far fierce hour an' sweet.' Ah! Every dog an' every animal has its day, but the donkey's was the greatest day of all."

"Why, uncle," said Gregory, still grinning. "I didn't know you were a religious man."

"I'm not," retorted old Jake devastatingly. "I'm an intelligent man." He changed the subject with a suddenness that made Gregory blink.

"What d'ye say to a little constitutional? Over The Rise to Steeple Thelmin' an' back again. Hey?"

2

They sauntered up the hill. That is, the long-legged Gregory sauntered: Uncle Jake stumped along beside him at his usual dogged gait, which was faintly suggestive of that of a determined duck. Gregory's black felt hat was well down on his head, and the collar of his overcoat turned up against the wind. Jake was enveloped in one of those stiff weatherproof farmer's riding coats that seem all straps and buckles. His feet were shod in stout boots, and an old tweed cap sat jauntily on his perky head, contrasting rather oddly with his jutting fringe of whiskers. He glanced with disfavour at his nephew's thin city shoes.

"Those dinky little dancin' pumps o' yours are no good for country roads, Greg me boy. An' just between ourselves, an' not meanin' any offence, what with that black hat an' yeller coat yer look a bit of a spiv."

Gregory shrugged his shoulders carelessly. "Think so, uncle? Not nearly wide enough. Anyway, it wasn't my choice, it was Pauline's."

"Pauline?"

"My wife. My late wife," he added with bitterness in his voice.

"Oh! Ha! Yes. . . . Well, now," said Jake briskly, constituting himself a sort of tourist guide, "all this land round here on the other side of these houses an' me own little place is farmin' land. Sheep, crops, a few cows." He laid a finger against the side of his nose in a Drury Lane gesture. "I know where I can get a bit of meat an' a drop of milk when I want it! . . . That house at the bottom there, almost opposite me own, belongs to a feller named Jacques. Jacques one side of the road, Jake t'other. Ha! But I've never laid eyes on him. Poor devil's bedridden. So much for bloated wealth, Greg . . . Next one up is Mayhew's. Mayhew is practically subhuman, but he has been known to say 'good-day' to old Jake Popplewell, which is more'n I can say for most of the others up here . . . . That's Croxley's, an' this one is Weldon's."

"They all seem to be pretty well in," observed Gregory, casting a roving eye over well-tended grounds and comfortable-looking houses.

"They are. Money here, me boy."

"What do these people do?"

"Do? They don't do anythin'. Retired wolves most of 'em, livin' on the proceeds of a lifetime of fleecin' the lambs. But all very virtuous an' respectable now. They're welcome to their money—it don't seem to make 'em any happier."

Gregory Cushing pointed to the last row of fruit trees showing above the tall hedge on the other side of the road. "I take it that's the end of your property, uncle?"

"That's it. Rest of it, down to Steeple Thelmin', is part of old Silver's farm. Now, he's human. He an' I do a bit of business together now an' agen. We might run into him down below."

"From what I can see of his land it seems to be all rocks and boulders."

"Well, now, that's a feature of The Rise. Me own place must 'a' been like that once, only the energetic cuss who had it before me picked most of 'em up an' built those stone walls with 'em."

"You didn't?" asked Gregory mischievously.

"Rot me, no!" retorted old Jake indignantly. "Life's too short to fuss about like that." He turned his attention to the house they were passing on the other side of the road. "Funny thing, I dunno who lives there. Never have known, an' don't care enough to find out. Y' never see anybody movin' about in there. Y' get a furtive glimpse of a man an' a woman in a big car now an' then, but that's all.

"Now, this place"—pointing with his stubby pipe at the next house up—"this belongs to a feller named Maltravers. Mister Lionel Maltravers. Y' ought to see his phiz, Greg. If ever Cohen or Isaacstein was written on a feller's mug, it's on our Mr. Maltravers's. They play croquet in there in the summer-time. Croquet!" repeated Jake in disgust. "The amount of money that old bloodsucker must 'a' spent in order to be able to shove little coloured balls through iron hoops on a billiard table lawn would 'a' housed a fair-sized family. . . . That thing there peepin' above the wall, that thing that looks like the roof of one of those Eastern pagoda things, that's what he calls his pavilion."

"I wouldn't mind half his complaint," murmured Gregory, craning his neck in an attempt to see more of the pavilion behind the six-foot brick wall.

"Pavilion is right!" growled the old man. "Pavilion'd in splendour, an' girded in forty per cent compound on money lent on note of hand alone!"

The next house was the last on The Rise. Through wide-open double gates Gregory caught a glimpse of a solid home standing four-square almost on the very summit of the hill. Then his view was cut off by tall trees, and thick shrubs ranked behind a low brick wall surmounted by an iron railing. The grounds of this place didn't seem to him to be quite as well tended as all the others, and he commented on it.

"They lost their gardener some time ago," Jake told him. "Now they haven't got one, not a regular one. I come up here meself now and agen when I can spare the time an' do a bit for 'em, but it's too big for one man workin' only casually at it."

He stopped to relight his pipe, shielding the match scientifically in cupped hands. He made sibilant sucking noises, and when the pipe was drawing to his satisfaction he went on with a chuckle in his rusty old voice.

"I can tell yer somethin' about this place, Greg. Old Mrs. Pendlebury lives here along with her sister, Miss Forbes. There's a son, but he got into some sort of a scrape about the time the gardener died an' he don't live here now. I think the old lady's put him to some useful work somewhere. The sister's an old maid with funny ideas, funny religious an' philosophical ideas. But she does treat me like a human bein', an' we have some great old chats together."

"Oh, you do, do you?" said Gregory, smiling. "I thought you were a confirmed woman hater?"

"Emmy Forbes is different," replied old Jake placidly. "So are her ideas an' her conversation. A little while ago it was all karma an' reincarnation; now it's somethin' she calls phenomena."

"Phenomena? That means—er—things, doesn't it? All this." Gregory waved an arm that took in the entire visible universe.

"Well, yes an' no," said Jake, moving on again slowly and meditatively. "It means, in Miss Emmy Forbes's mind, questionin' the reality of things. Which is what physicists have been doin' since Rutherford split the atom, an' what philosophers an' metaphysicians have been doin' for centuries. She talks learnedly—or what she hopes is learnedly—of the objective an' the subjective. Dead keen on what they're now callin' physical phenomena."

"Who are 'they'?"

Jake cackled amusement. "The psychical researchers, me boy. The professional ghost hunters. An' what they mean by physical phenomena are physical things an' actions not produced by ordinary physical means."

"Good Lord! Spooks—"

"No, no. Emmy Forbes isn't one of those poor fish who hold hands in the dark an' listen to the departed spirit of their Aunt Fanny—or the falsetto voice of some swindlin' medium—natterin' about how beautiful everythin' is an' how happy she is. Give the old gal her due. She's got a little more intelligence than that. She approaches the problem rationally an' scientifically—as far as any woman can be rational an' scientific. But she don't go far before she loses herself—"

"Yes, but what's the problem?"

"Phenomena. The question of the reality of things seen an' experienced. Fact or fantasy. Objective or subjects. We swap books on the subject, but I reckon it's got too much for her. Just now she's studyin' poltergeist manifestations."

"Oh," commented Gregory. "Back to spooks again—isn't that what it amounts to? But I didn't know that you—"

"I told yer," said Uncle Jake irrelevantly, "once we got this side o' The Rise we'd leave the wind behind us." He hadn't said anything of the sort, but Gregory forbore to comment. Uncle Jake sucked reflectively and happily at his foul pipe.

"Point that worries the Emmy Forbes's o' this world is this: do we see an' experience anythin' that has any real existence, or do we see an' experience what the mind creates for us?"

"Are you asking me?" inquired Gregory humorously, gazing down at this surprising uncle of his.

"The physicists say that the universe is nothin' but a collection of atoms an' electrons an' fields o' force—intangible, abstract conceptions. Some of 'em refuse to go as far as that an' say that what is really there can only be expressed in mathematical equations. . . . Once upon a time God was a Big Man with benevolent miracles in one hand an' thunderbolts in t'other. Then He became all pervadin' Spirit—like a sort of super-ether with personality. Now He's a mathematician. Any day now He'll turn into the Red King—"

"*What?*"

"You've read *Alice Through The Looking Glass,* haven't yer? Somebody tells Alice in the book that none of 'em really exist, they're only characters in the Red King's dream. When he wakes up they won't *be.* That's about what modern philosophy is leadin' to. . . . Anyway, that's what the physicists say is out there"—Jake waved a careless hand at the world around him to indicate what he meant by there—"mathematical equations, symbols. An' a man don't see or feel anythin'; his brain merely receives electromagnetic waves of varyin' lengths—equally abstract an' theoretical. Where then do we get our sensations of substance an' colour an' form an' all the rest of it? Does the mind translate the symbols? Or does it create a gigantic illusion?"

"You're getting out of my depth," complained Gregory. "What's this got to do with what you call poltergeist manifestations?"

"One contains t'other. The Emmy Forbes school investigates minor illusions within the Great Illusion, an' question whether they can grant 'em the same or a similar certain measure of apparent but satisfyin' objectivity.

"Anyway," roared old Jake suddenly, "what the hell does it matter either way? The Preacher—old Ecclesiastes—put it in a nutshell. 'Vanity of vanities,' he said, 'all is vanity.' All is emptiness, all is speculation. That covers it goin' an' comin', an' it's as much a mathematical equation as any the physicists think up. Man is a creature, an' life is a gift. An' a sensible creature, like old Boomer down there, makes the most of it an' enjoys the gift while he's got it. It's only man, the ass, who worries his soulcase out wonderin' about the unknowable."

He took the pipe out of his mouth and pointed with it to the crossroads at the foot of the hill. "That's Steeple Thelmin'. . . ."

3

Once over the brow of the rise and a little way down the slope on the other side, the wind died away, and Jake's pipe merely fumed without leaving a trail of sparks. The thick hedge on their right hand continued to the bottom of the hill without a break, but the one on their left, that had sprung up beyond the boundary of the Pendlebury home, was thin and choked with gorse, with gaps in it here and there large enough to allow a full-grown man to pass through.

"What's Steeple Thelming?" inquired Gregory.

"That is," said Jake.

"I don't see any steeple. In fact I don't see anything except a crossroads, a couple of little stone bridges and the back of some derelict house."

"That, me lad," said Jake with an anticipatory gleam in his eye, "is the Steeple Inn. Aside from which no one's ever heard tell of any steeple. An' those three bridges—there's another one just round the corner—are a prime example of old English rural road makin'. The Winch goes under 'em. An' why they couldn't 'a' built one bridge on this side an' had the roads crossin' on t'other is known only to the gentry who built 'em two, three, four hundred years ago. . . . Old man Silver lives round there a little way"—indicating the road that meandered away to the north—"an' between him an' the crossroads is the only other buildin' in Steeple Thelmin'. See that clump o' trees, there?"

"Yes?"

"In there is the country house of a feller named Mason, Just an ordinary house, Greg, not one of yer thirty-six bedroom, huntin', shootin' an' fishing castles—"

"Mason?"

"Yeh."

"Not Montague Mason?"

"That's the feller. . . . Hey!" Jake peered up at his nephew. "D'ye know him, Greg?"

"Oh! So that's his place, is it? . . . No, I don't know him, uncle, I only know of him. That is, if it's the same man. Do you know him?"

Jake waggled his chin whiskers. "I've seen him about. Little feller, 'bout me own size. Looks like a ferret. I dunno what he keeps that place for, he's hardly ever here. But yer know when he is here—y'can hear the welkin ringin' a mile away. He comes here for a few days now an' agen at odd times, an' brings parties of stockbrokers an' chorus gals with him—"

"Racketeers and black market operators, you mean," said Gregory moodily. "Yes, it sounds like the same man; I knew he had a hide-out somewhere round here."

"Whaddyer mean, hide-out? Is this feller a crook?"

"I don't know. He's like your people back there on The Rise, he doesn't do anything, other people do it for him. He lives in a big house in the West End of London; he has a damn sight more money than is good for any man, but no one seems to know how he makes it."

"Ha! Ever had anythin' to do with him, Greg?"

"Oh, no. I don't move in such exalted circles. But I've heard of him—most people have—and I know he has a shady reputation in ordinary business circles, and a damn bad name where women are concerned."

"More fool him!" commented Mr. Popplewell tersely, and dismissed Mr. Montague Mason from his mind.

By now they had reached the crossroads at the foot of the slope and were in the heart of Steeple Thelming. On their immediate left stood the one solitary visible building, a small and rather desolate-looking structure like an overgrown farm labourer's cottage. Four grimy windows, two on either side of a plain wooden door, bore the laconic legend, *Ales.* On the lintel above the door was painted in small black letters, with the same economy of phraseology, *G. Borwell, Lic.* And above that again, jutting out from between a couple of bedroom windows, a weather-beaten sign proclaimed to the world that this was the Steeple Inn. North and south over their little stone bridges ran narrow winding lanes; westward and straight ahead of them the road rose gently from the third bridge to thread its way across undulating country.

"Savoury looking dump," was Gregory's comment on the Steeple Inn.

"Mebbe," said old Jake tolerantly, "but it *is* a tavern o' sorts. An' I suggest, me boy, we take advantage of the fact an' pop in an' take a drop o' somethin' to kill the cold."

"I'd like to have a look at that place of Mason's," muttered Gregory, staring curiously along the northing road at the belt of tall trees.

"Plenty o' time for that. Stroll along that way presently—c'mon in now an' have a drink with yer uncle Jake."

Against his own inclination, but feeling it would be churlish to refuse, Gregory followed his uncle into the public bar of the Steeple Inn, which, besides being small, was dim, dingy, dirty, damp and depressing. From beyond a half-open door behind the bar came a dull mutter of voices, which ceased abruptly as uncle Jake, who seemed to be quite at home in this hovel, hooked one foot in the unpolished brass rail and bellowed for "George."

A man came shuffling in, a shabby, flabby, bulky man with a bullet head, several unshaven chins and a sullen moon face. His shirt, innocent of collar and tie, was fastened at the neck with a protruding brass stud, and from his corpulent belly depended a coarse filthy apron.

Jake greeted this unprepossessing person as a welcome friend. "G'day, George."

The man nodded curtly.

"This," said Jake, "is me nephew Gregory Cushing. Lemme introduce yer to George, Greg—Honest George Borwell."

Gregory grinned uncertainly at Honest George Borwell, and Honest George favoured him with the same curt unemotional nod he had bestowed upon old Jake. Then, compliments having been exchanged, he stretched out a languid hand for a pewter mug and filled it nearly to the brim at the beer handle, turned his back on his customers and fumbled with a bottle, turned round again and set the mug on the bar in front of Jake. Then he looked meaningly at Gregory.

"Give him the same, George," said Jake, tossing some money on the counter.

In the same deliberate silence Mr. Borwell filled another pewter mug, going through the same performance, planted it in front of Gregory, swept the money off the counter, returning some change to Jake, and then began mechanically to wipe the bar with a cloth that was anything but clean.

"Always drink out of pewter," uncle Jake advised his nephew, "when yer can get it. This is the only pub I know round Winchingham where yer can get it, an' that's why I come here."

To Gregory it didn't seem to matter much whether the vessel was pewter, earthenware or glass, since the plurality of ales advertised on the windows all seemed to come from the same tap.

"Down the hatch," said uncle Jake, lifting his mug. He drank, sighed appreciatively and contentedly, and watched Gregory's face. Gregory sipped, put down his mug, stared at it and then stared at the publican.

"What is this?" he demanded.

Honest George Borwell spoke for the first time. "Beer," he said in a defensive growl. " 'Olesome beer."

"With a dash o' rum," added Jake, grinning like a hyena.

"Rum? Good Lord! Beer and rum."

"Beer," said Jake oracularly, "wholesome beer, as me friend George observes, nourishes an' sustains the body. Rum kills the cold an' fortifies the system. Both together in harmonious companionship they titillate the palate."

"Harmonious!" Gregory shook his head in a kind of helpless admiration. "You're an amazing man, uncle Jake."

"I am," said uncle Jake modestly. "We'll drink to that. . . ."

"Well," said Gregory some minutes later, "I suppose we'd better have the other half."

"Spoken like a true Popplewell!" crowed Jake—which Gregory Cushing was not.

"Same again, please, Mr. Borwell. Leave the rum out of mine this time."

"Please yerself," rumbled Jake, "but I think yer makin' a mistake. An' don't call him Mr. Borwell, call him George . . . Thank'ee, me boy. Down the hatch . . ."

Then, of course, they had to have a third. Jake insisted on it. Couldn't just walk in and have one apiece and walk out again; Honest George would be offended. Gregory wanted to argue, but Jake showed unexpected stubbornness. Honest George replenished the mugs and Gregory began to realize the mistake he had made in coming in in the first place. For by now the true nature of Jake's "constitutional" was becoming apparent, and the little nuggety old man had attached himself like a limpet to the bar.

They had a fourth. Gregory let his pewter stand on the counter.

Jake sipped and entered into conversation with the honest Mr. Borwell.

"Cold outside, George."

"Ah," agreed Honest George, swabbing decks automatically.

"Hard winter, an' goin' to be harder."

"Ah."

"Shouldn't be surprised to see snow any minute."

"Ah."

Jake took a pull at his tankard. "Got someone stayin' here, George?"

This time Mr. Borwell contented himself with a nod of his bullet head.

"Guest of the house? Or a friend?"

"Friend," mumbled George, showing an unexpected command of the English language.

"Ha! Any friend of me friend George," said Jake with alcoholic goodfellowship, "is a friend o' mine."

"Ah," observed Honest George, and left it at that. . . .

*   *   *

Some time later, when Gregory was beginning to feel muzzy and miserable from the thin beer, another man came in from outside. He was a big burly man in breeches and leggings and a coat similar to the one Jake was wearing, and his face was a round, jolly, beaming, good-humoured mask. This was Farmer Silver, and he was the kind of man who is instantly liked by everybody; a quality which, admirable in itself, does not necessarily betoken integrity and stability: beneath that smiling, good-natured mask the acute physiognomist would have detected something sly and secret, and perhaps unscrupulous. Jake greeted him rapturously.

"Jim, me boy, I was near prayin' for yer comfortin' presence to come among us. . . . Greg! Hey, Greg—where are yer?"

Gregory, who had been staring aimlessly out of the window, returned to the bar.

"Ha. . . . Greg, meet me old friend, Jim Silver. Jim, this is me nephew, Gregory Cushing."

"How do you do?" said Gregory politely.

"Fine. How's yourself?" responded Mr. Silver, crushing Gregory's hand in his own, and nodding to Honest George Borwell. "Well, Jake?"

Jake, a little wild of eye, a thought thick of speech, turned back to the bar.

"Wassail, George. Three more for yer three best customers."

Gregory accepted another tankard of beer without protest, but allowed it to stand on the bar and gradually lose its sparkle. But Jake downed his as if it had been his first, and Mr. Silver kept him company. After which Jake craved the favour of a word in Jim Silver's ear, and the pair of them withdrew a little way from Gregory. Jake stood on tiptoe and whispered sibilantly, and Gregory guessed that some transaction not involving the use of ration books was being discussed. He gazed gloomily into his pewter mug, while George waddled round from behind the bar and poked the miserable, ash-choked fire.

"Toosd'y," observed Jake loudly, "it is then. . . . Whaddyer dreamin' about, Greg? C'mon, me boy, down the hatch with it."

But Gregory, wondering how he was ever going to get his uncle away from this place, shook his head firmly. "I can't keep up with you. You and Mr. Silver go ahead, I'll sit this one out."

"Sit it out, me glass eye!" roared Jake, suddenly incensed. "Yer mean yer won't drink with yer old uncle, hey?"

Gregory lifted his mug. "I am drinking with you," he said mildly. "I merely can't keep pace with you. Can't—not won't, uncle."

Jake stared at him in disgust, while Jim Silver beamed over the little man's shoulder. Suddenly he struck an exaggerated attitude and declaimed:" 'Come, y' virtuous ass, y' bashful fool, must yer be blushin'? . . . What a maidenly man-at-arms are yer become! Is it such a matter to get a pottle-pot's maidenhead?' "

"We're off!" chuckled Jim Silver.

Honest George spoke up from behind the bar. "That don't make no sense," he complained.

"Sense?" bellowed Jake fiercely. "It makes sense to a gennel-man. 'I am a gennelman; thou art a drawer.' Fill 'em up agen—drawer!"

George filled them up again—after that one drink of beer Jim Silver went on to whisky, of which the Steeple Inn appeared to have no stint. He moved along to take up Gregory's mug, but the latter shook his head. George gave his usual curt nod of under-standing, and mumbled: " 'E sez it's Shakespeare, but it still don't make no sense to me. Goes on for hours."

"Can't you leave the rum out of his beer?" asked Gregory in a whisper.

A shake of the bullet head. " 'E'd pick it immediate."

Jake had hoisted his own tankard over his head and was gazing at it with shining eyes. It was no longer a piece of dull and dis-coloured pewter to him, but the battle standard of Old England.

"Once more unto the breach, dear friends, once more;
Or close the wall up with our English dead!
In peace there's nothin' so becomes a man
As modest stillness an' humility:
But when the blast o' war blows in our ears. . . ."

Jake Popplewell, as Mr. Silver had remarked, was off. His amazing memory for Shakespeare, stimulated rather than dimmed by rum-and-beer, kept pace with his rusty, naturally aggressive sounding voice. Jim Silver leant easily against the bar and fiddled with his nip of whisky, his big round face one expan-sive jackal grin. Honest George gaped at the orator and shook his head from time to time like a slow baffled bull. Gregory, the lamb in this menagerie, listened with grudging admiration. Jake, the tiger, pausing once to haul down the battle standard and drain it dry, snarled on to the conclusion of the famous speech.

"I see yer stand like greyhounds in the slips,
Strainin' upon the start. The game's afoot:
Foller yer spirit; an', upon this charge
Cry ` God for Harry! England an' St. Geooorrge!"

He finished on a long-drawn, nerve-tingling yell, and demanded of the other George to fill 'em up again.

*   *   *

Time passed by. The ale and whisky flowed. Jake, egged on by Silver, gave his opinions on Shakespeare as a man and philosopher and a poet, and struck attitudes and quoted extensively from his works until the edges wore off his words.

"Ter be," pondered old Jake solemnly but sloppily—

"Ter be, or norra be: 'a'sa queshun:
Whether 'tis nobler in the min' ter suffer
The slings an' arrers of outrageous forshun. . . ."

" 'Amlet!" announced Honest George Borwell, recognizing familiar phrases. " 'Im what 'e calls the Great Dane."

"Yes," said Gregory morosely, "and something is rotten in the state of Denmark. How long does this go on?"

"Hours," replied George succinctly. "Mebbe more. Mebbe less."

"Can't you do something about it? Can't you refuse to serve him with any more drink?"

"Why should I?" demanded Honest George, and became startlingly loquacious. " 'E ain't doin'no'arm. If a man wants 'olesome likker, an' 'as the money to pay for 'olesome likker, so long as 'e be'aves 'isself, 'olesome likker 'e gets." And then added darkly and somewhat contradictorily: "But yer better get 'im away before 'e starts seein' the Blue Woman."

"Seeing the *what?*"

"Arter 'e gets through Shakes-a-pearianizin'," the stolid George told him, " 'e'll begin talkin' about the Blue Woman."

"Who the blazes is the Blue Woman?"

Mr. Silver, rubicund face aflame with whisky, air of jollity even more pronounced, slid along the bar and joined the other two. Behind them Hamlet stalked—unsteadily—the battlements at Elsinore and tried to make up his mind whether or no to shuffle off this mortal coil.

"There's an old story hereabouts," said Jim Silver, twisting his glass round and round in his sausage-like fingers. "I don't know whether there's any truth in it, and I don't know what's in old Jake's mind, but there may just be something to it. There's a paddock along there on the other side of that house—"

"Is that Mason's house you're meaning?" interrupted Gregory.

Silver shot him a quick, keen glance. "That's the one. Well, there's an open paddock there with one dead oak tree slap in the middle of it. All that land used to belong to a titled gent couple of hundred years ago, and this titled gent—Lord Something-or-other —was dead set against poaching. The story goes that he caught a woman poaching there one night, and he lost his temper so bad that he decided to make an example of her and he had her hung on that dead tree. I don't know why they Call her the Blue Woman; p'raps she wore blue, or something; but she was supposed to be a witch. Witch or no witch," said Mr. Silver, laughing at the jest of it, "that old lord fixed her! Now they say her ghost walks Steeple Thelming on certain nights; and they also say that the oak was live and hearty then and that it began to die the minute after the Blue Woman was hung up there."

"Um. That's a damned unlikely story."

"Oh, I know that," admitted Silver, with another fat laugh. "I'm only telling you what the story is. And, as George says, Jake certainly does seem to see a Blue Woman."

"It must be somethink fair 'orrid," ruminated Honest George. "I've seen 'im near orf 'is chump wiv funk."

Gregory began to grin. "I'm not surprised. After the amount of rum-and-beer I've seen him throw down his neck this afternoon I wouldn't be surprised if he saw pink elephants. . . . What do *you* think of this yarn, Mr. Silver? Think there's any slight degree of truth in it?"

"I couldn't say."

"Has anybody else besides uncle Jake ever seen the Blue Woman?"

"Not to my knowledge."

Here Hamlet overbalanced and tumbled off the battlements and fetched up all-standing against the bar, with his whiskers jutting out at a challenging angle between Gregory and Jim Silver.

"How about coming home now, uncle?" asked Gregory reasonably.

"Get thee to a nunnery!" was the fierce and somewhat inconsequential retort. " 'You jig, you amble, an' y' lisp, an' nick—*hic*—nickname God's creashures, an' make yer wan'onness yer ignoransh—' " He broke off and glanced a trifle nervously first over one shoulder and then over the other.

" 'Ere she comes," muttered George with foreboding.

But "she" didn't come, not that day or night. It must have been one of her days off. Jake's bleary eye fell on the empty mug he was still clutching. He held it up, gestured gracefully with his other hand to draw attention to it, and addressed Honest George in feeling accents.

" 'Alas! poor Yorick. I knew him, Horatio; a feller of infinite jest, of most ekshellent fanshy—*hic*—fancy—' Le's drink to poor Yorick; fill 'em up agen, Horatio."

But Jim Silver, to Gregory's huge relief, shook his head. He drank off his whisky and set down his glass with an air of finality.

"All very well for some people, but I've to go home and feed the stock before it gets dark—"

Jake smote himself a resounding slap on the forehead. "Boomer!" he exclaimed remorsefully. "Poor ol' Boomer! Must go home meself an' feed ol' Boomer." He stared at Gregory as if he had never seen him before. Then his wrinkled brow cleared. "Ha! Yeh. C'mon, me boy—mush go home." He lurched away to the door, where he turned and raised his arm in a theatrical gesture of farewell, and then stumbled over the threshold and out of the Steeple Inn.

The raw, cold air hit him like a hammer. But it didn't silence him. Hamlet had relinquished his tenancy of Jake's meagre frame, had apparently been left behind in the inn, but his place had been taken by Macbeth. Gregory let him babble and assisted him up the hill; and by the time they had reached the top Macbeth had murdered Gawdor, Duncan and sleep, and was playing exceedingly unmusical chairs with the ghost of Banquo.

Just over the brow of The Rise, standing in the gateway of Mrs. Pendlebury's drive, were two old ladies. They were eminently respectable ladies, they were chatting peaceably together and doing not the slightest harm to anybody or anything in this world or in any other. But the sight of them seemed to sting old Jake to unreasoning frenzy.

"How now!" he thundered at them. "How now, you secret, black an' midnight hags!"

"For Heaven's *sake!*" gasped Gregory, appalled.

"It's Popplewell," observed the slightly younger of the two ladies placidly, screwing up her eyes. What light the grim winter afternoon had carried was now fast fading.

"Beware Macduff!" bellowed Jake Popplewell. "Beware the Thane of Fife!"

"Shut *up!*" hissed Gregory, and laid violent hands on the little man. As he dragged him past the gate he grabbed at his hat and said desperately: "I'm terribly sorry. I apologize most humbly and sincerely for my uncle—"

"Uncle?" repeated the lady who had previously spoken. "Really? Your uncle? . . . Oh! Oh, that's all right. The man's drunk. No one with any intelligence takes the slightest notice of the ravings of a drunken or otherwise mentally deranged person. The psyche is astray. The machine is out of order."

Gregory mumbled something and passed on down The Rise with his burden, guessing, rightly, that uncle Jake had just been smartly set aside, docketed and put in his place by the redoubtable Miss Forbes.

For the rest of the way down to the cottage Jake was practically asleep on his feet. Once there, however, he woke up and insisted upon feeding Boomer with his own hands. He strapped on Boomer's cover, which that sagacious beast invariably attempted to roll out of during the night, stumped into the parlour, fell into a battered old arm-chair in front of the dead fire, and promptly went soundly to sleep.

Gregory let him sleep. He rebuilt and relit the fire, made himself some tea and then browsed among his uncle's books. He checked up on his Hamlet, flipped from one book to another, and finally came across the story of Borley Rectory. He lost himself in this while Jake slept on, snoring every now and again with odd little whistling noises.

The hours slipped by while every conceivable thing to haunt the senses of man and plague his wit happened at Borley Rectory, and when he at last put the book aside Gregory was ready for bed. He gazed thoughtfully down at the slumbering Jake, put some more wood on the fire, threw a rug over the unconscious man and went upstairs to his own bed.

4

Gregory was awakened the next morning by the sound of his uncle moving about down below crooning a little dirge to himself. Grey dismal daylight filtered through the diamonded window-pane, and the weather was still bitterly cold; but there was a savoury, nostalgic aroma pervading the cottage that gave him a sudden fresh zest for life, and made him think of green fields and sunlight glinting on water and a galloping pony. . . . He sprang out of bed, donned his overcoat in lieu of dressing-gown and padded downstairs to the bathroom, a primitive affair, being merely a lean-to built on to the kitchen.

Jake was pottering about in the kitchen, which was warm from the stove.

"The Moorish king rides up and down,
  Ay! de mi alamo. . . ."

Gregory surveyed him quizzically. "Dressed, and in his right mind!"

"Ha! Hullo, me boy, breakfast's ready."

"How's the head this morning?"

"What should be wrong with me head?" demanded Jake.

"Well, you ought to know." Gregory moved on a few steps to the origin of the savoury smell, the frying pan on the stove. "Bacon!"

"Yeh."

"And eggs!"

"Yeh."

"And fried bread!"

Jake grinned at him. "I got me friends," he said smugly. "Y' could count 'em on the fingers of a one-armed man who'd had his hand caught in a circular saw, but all the same—"

"Jim Silver?" inquired Gregory.

Old Jake's hyena-like grin widened. "Take what the gods provide, an' ask no questions. . . . An' get a move on, will yer? I'm ready to dish up."

Gregory vanished into the bathroom. As there was no hot water laid on anywhere in the cottage—the tin bath had to be filled by bucket from a boiler outside that had once done duty as a bran-mash tub—he had to wash himself in icy cold water and postpone his shave until Jake had done with the kettle. Jake was juggling with plates.

"Crescent shadows Christian cross,
  Don Roderick trembles for his crown;
  Ay! de mi alamo—"

"Hey, Greg!"

"Hullo?"

"D'ye drink coffee?"

"Drink anything."

Jake grunted satisfaction, and by the time Gregory emerged from the bathroom his bacon and eggs were waiting for him on the parlour table. He sat down and basked in the warmth of the bright fire leaping and dancing on the open hearth.

"Goin' to clear," announced Jake, chin whiskers moving rhythmically up and down.

Gregory glanced out at the lowering sky. "How do you know that? It doesn't look much like it at present."

"It'll clear," repeated Jake confidently. "I can tell by the moke's hide. Sun'll be out be midday. You see."

"I hope you're right. I'd like to see the sun again."

"Umph. What are yer goin' to do with yerself, Greg? I'll be goin' up the hill this mornin'."

"I'll be all right. I'll take a stroll through the thriving city of Winchingham and see if I can pick up any cigarettes." He gazed thoughtfully at his uncle. "What exactly do you mean by 'going up the hill'?"

"Got a job of work to do in Mrs. Pendlebury's garden."

"Oh! . . . Uncle!"

"Huh?"

"Do you remember coming home yesterday afternoon?"

"Well, yes," said uncle Jake, but not altogether confidently, "in a manner o' speakin'."

"Do you remember meeting two old ladies outside Mrs. Pendlebury's?"

Jake screwed up his face and shook his head slowly from side to side. He put down his knife and fork, lifted his coffee cup and cradled it in his hands, and then executed a flank attack.

"I told yer yesterday, Greg, that this was the last strong hold of liberty. Y' do what yer like here, an' no one questions yer. Similarly no one questions *me.* I may have been enjoyin' meself in me own quiet way, but I do no harm to any livin' soul—"

"Quiet way! Do you remember what you said to those two old ladies?"

Jake shook his head again, even more slowly and more uneasily. "What did I say?"

"You said—in fact you yelled: 'How now, you secret, black and midnight hags!'"

Old Jake stared at him over the cup. "Get out!"

"You did. Fact, uncle. I had to apologize grovellingly for you."

"What the perishin' purple hades did I say that for?"

"Well, you were under the impression that you were Macbeth, and the crown of Scotland was sitting a bit uneasily on your blood-stained head. The fortunate part about it was that they didn't seem in the least upset or offended. One of them, whom I take to have been your Miss Forbes, merely said, 'Oh, that's all right, the man's drunk and you don't take any notice of drunken persons.'"

"Ha!" exclaimed Jake, vastly relieved. "*Nitchevo,* Greg—Emmy Forbes is all right."

Gregory said hesitantly: "There's something else. . . ."

"Hey?" Jake's uneasiness returned to him. "Somethin' else I said, or did?"

"No-o, not last night. But—uncle Jake, who or what is the Blue Woman?"

Jake put down his coffee cup and stared uncomprehendingly. "Whaddyer talkin' about now?"

"The Blue Woman?"

"Who the Sam Hill is the Blue Woman?"

"That's what I'm asking you."

"*I* don't know. Beelzebub's sister, by the sound of it. Rot me! why ask me?"

"Because—" Gregory scratched his head in puzzled fashion. "Your Mr. Silver was telling me about it in the Steeple Inn yesterday afternoon. The story goes—"

He told the story as he had heard it from Farmer Silver, but it didn't appear to mean anything to old Jake.

"First I've heard about it," he rumbled. "Jim Silver's never said anything about it to me."

"But he told me you'd seen her. Your friend, Honest George, backed him up: he said he'd seen you scared out of your wits by her."

"Scared out o' me wits!" bellowed Jake, annoyed. "I tell yer, Greg, I dunno what yer talkin' about. Seein' Blue Wimmen! Me! Give yer me solemn word I've never seen a Blue Woman in me life. An' if I ever did see one"—with a final indignant roar—"an' she started plaguin' me, I'd send her to the right-about pretty smartly." He calmed down, cackled and added more quietly: "Old Jim Silver's been pullin' yer leg, me boy."

He seemed to be so obviously telling the simple, literal truth that Gregory dropped the subject.

*   *   *

Jake went away up The Rise, and later on in the morning Gregory sauntered out in the opposite direction and prowled about the narrow, old-world streets of Winchingham. As Jake had prophesied the weather cleared gradually, the leaden sky split and parted and the clouds massed in ranks and tiers allowing strips of wan and watery sunlight to shine through—a "streaky-bacon" sky, old Jake would have called it.

The old man returned for lunch shortly after midday, and his wrinkled, whisker-begirt face lit up with pleasure when he saw the table already prepared. Gregory, coming in from the kitchen with two plates in his hands, noticed the book under his arm.

"Hullo, uncle, what have you got there?"

Jake cackled, tossed the book carelessly on to a small and rickety table under the window, and sat down to his meal. "Book of Emmy Forbes's, me boy. All about physical phenomena. What you and I, out o' date, would call psychic phenomena."

"I gather," murmured Gregory, sitting down himself, "that all is still well between you and Miss Forbes."

"An' why shouldn't it be? A'course it is. . . . She's been hard at work on that book for the past couple of years. Calls it her scrap-book. Full o' newspaper clippin's, magazine articles, extracts from here, there an' everywhere, collected an' typewritten by herself. Says I must read it. 'Popplewell,' she says," quoted old Jake in shrill falsetto, " 'this is not a book I would allow anybody an' everybody to have, but you are an intelligent man.' Well, y' can't say fairer than that, can yer? . . . This looks good, me boy."

"I'm no cook, uncle, but I can always dish up cold meat and potatoes and make a pot of tea. In the days when eggs were eggs I used to be able to scramble quite a tidy egg."

"Eggs," said Jake mysteriously, "are still eggs hereabouts. Greg, have y' come across anywhere in this mess"—he flung out a hand at the mess. Unfortunately his fork was still in his hand, and the piece of meat impaled on its tines broke loose and went flying across the room. He got up leisurely and casually kicked the morsel into the hearth. "Have y' come across a copy *of Barley Rectory?*"

"Funny you should mention that one," smiled Gregory. "I came across it last night."

"Ha! Did y' read it?"

"Yes, while you were—" He checked himself abruptly.

"While I was havin' forty winks," said Jake with undisturbed aplomb. "Yeh. . . . Whaddyer think of it?"

"I'm damned if I know what to think. 'There are more things in heaven and earth than are dreamt of in your philosophy, Horatio.' " He added thoughtfully: "That's one you missed yesterday afternoon somehow or another."

"An' you got it wrong," returned Jake calmly. "Horatio goes after that word 'earth' . . . Where's *Borley Rectory?*"

"On top of that pile behind you."

Jake screwed his head round to see for himself. In doing so his eye alighted on a strange object on the mantelshelf.

"What the hades is that?"

"Portable wireless. Little battery set of mine—"

"Wireless?" repeated Jake.

"Yes."

"Wireless!" snorted Mr. Popplewell. "Wherever I go I hear wireless sets moanin' an' yappin' an' squealin' an' dronin'—"

"All right, all right," said Gregory hastily and soothingly. "If you don't like it we won't have it on while you're around; you won't hear a peep out of it."

"Umph. It's not that I object to music—good music. But these bellyachin' crooners, an' the plummy-voiced announcers, an' those damnably patronizin' talkers . . . I like readin' about things, not bein' talked at be some half-baked complacent ass who insists on addressin' yer as if yer were ten years old an' backward at that. An' furthermore," roared the little old man in a final burst of indignation, "I don't give a three-cornered damn whether the time is eleven hours Greenwich Mean, or a million hours Colney Hatch!"

Gregory grinned at him. "All right, uncle. I said you wouldn't hear a peep out of it."

"Urrr—hmf! Thank God the Steeple Inn don't have one. The only civilized, Christian inn left in these parts."

Gregory eyed him a trifle apprehensively. "What are you doing this afternoon, uncle?"

"Well, I hadn't intended to, but I'll be goin' up to Pendlebury's agen—gotta take that book to Emmy Forbes Mebbe I'll do some more work for 'em, mebbe I'll go for a constitutional. It depends."

"Oh!"

"Whaddyer mean—oh?" demanded old Jake suspiciously.

"Nothing. Nothing at all. I only meant I'd like to stay here and sit in front of the fire and read and relax. . . . if it's all right with you."

Jake nodded his head in approval. "A'course it's all right with me. Yer do just whatever yer like here—short o' burnin' the place down. Rot me, I don't have to keep tellin' yer, do I? . . ."

*　　　*　　　*

The "streaky-bacon" sky had closed up again, and the grim and lowering day was sullenly drawing on its hood of darkness when Jake returned to his own home that evening. Gregory, flushed and somnolent from the cozy warmth of the cheerfully untidy little parlour, was pleasantly surprised to find him sober: apparently uncle Jake had decided against taking his "constitutional" and had spent the afternoon pottering about in Mrs. Pendlebury's garden and discussing the mysteries of the universe with Miss Forbes.

He said as the old man came into the room: "I've fed Boomer, uncle, and put his blanket on. Thought it would save you a job."

"Ha! Thank 'ee, me boy, thank 'ee. So it will." Jake sat down heavily in the basket chair and began to unlace his boots—where another man would have taken his boots off, Jake merely unloosened his and clumped about the cottage with the laces flapping and trailing.

"But I didn't quite know what to do about tea," went on Gregory. "I didn't know whether you could look cold meat in the face again—"

Old Jake looked up. "Didn't y' find the rabbit stew?"

Gregory stared back at him. "Did you say—rabbit stew?"

"Yeh. In the pot under the sink."

"Rabbit stew! You do yourself well, uncle Jake."

"A'course I do meself well," roared Jake. "Why shouldn't I? Whaddyer think I live here for?"

"All right, all right. Pot under the sink—I'll fix it."

Jake got to his feet. "You stay here, me boy, I'll 'tend to it. I know me way about better than you do. Rot me! I been doin' it for fifteen years."

He went into the kitchen, lace ends striking his boots like little bullets, put the pot on the stove and came back again with a bottle and two tumblers. "Whaddyer say to a little snort to kill the cold?"

"Well . . . not too much of a snort, uncle. Make it a sigh . . . That rabbit stew—Santa Claus Jim Silver again?"

Jake cackled. "Not this time, me boy. Honest George Borwell this time. . . ."

When they were sitting down to their tea Jake grinned across the table at his nephew and said: "Y've made a conquest up the hill, Greg."

Gregory looked up from his rabbit stew long enough to ask what he meant by conquest.

"Emmy Forbes. She says to me, 'Popplewell' "—Jake's rusty voice, as it always did when quoting Miss Forbes, soared up to a villainous falsetto—" 'Popplewell, who was that most presentable young man who was with you yesterday afternoon?' 'That was me nephew,' I told her. 'I know that,' she says, 'but his name? An' what is he doin' here?'"

"Nosy old bitch!" said Gregory unchivalrously.

"Now, now." Jake defended her warmly. "Emmy Forbes isn't like that, Greg, not like some women. Emmy Forbes is all right. Anyway I told her yer name an' said yer were a stranger in a strange land. 'Convalescing' I says on the spur of the moment. 'We must remedy that, Popplewell,' she says. 'Y' must bring him up here some time, me sister an' I will be very pleased to make him welcome.'"

"Well," said Gregory dubiously, "it sounds all right, but what exactly does it mean? Tea in the kitchen with Miss Forbes standing by patronizingly? Or a lecture on metaphysics in the potting shed?"

"Both, mebbe," chuckled Jake. "I dunno. Anyway y' don't have to go if yer don't want to."

Tea over, the table cleared and the washing-up cloth folded neatly over the tap, Mr. Popplewell began to show signs of restlessness. Gregory in a chair in front of the fire, idly browsing through Miss Forbes's scrap-book, watched him out of the corner of his eye. Eventually the old man sat down in the basket chair, and began lacing up his boots.

"Greg!"

"Yes, uncle Jake?"

"Think I'll go for a constitutional."

"I thought that was coming," sighed Gregory, but in too low a tone for his uncle to catch.

"Hey? What was that?"

"Nothing. I only said it was a filthy cold night for it."

"That's when it does yer good. Gets yer blood movin'."

"Um. . . ."

"Y' don't have to come with me if yer don't want to. If yer happy here, stay here, me boy."

"I'll admit the fireside is pulling, uncle. You won't think it ungracious of me—"

"Lor' love yer, no. If yer'd rather stay an' wallow in this fug, stay be all means. But me, I think I'll stretch me legs."

He got up and went into the kitchen, reappearing a moment later with his old tweed cap on his head and his stocky little body enveloped in the O.S. weatherproof coat. He said cheerily: "See yer at breakfast, if not before," and stumped out into the night.

*   *   *

It was a few minutes after eleven when he returned from his "constitutional." Gregory, in his own bed the past hour, heard hurried floundering footsteps approach the little garden gate. He heard the click of the gate and the ringing of iron-shod boots on the short brick path to the front door. The door burst open and slammed shut, and then there was nothing to be heard but quick, laboured breathing. Then uncle Jake let out a roar, a vicious yell carrying an undertone of fear.

"The Devil rot yer, yer blue-faced hag!"

This was followed a minute or two later by a tinny crash. "That," thought Gregory, "is the clock." He sat suddenly bolt upright in bed. "Or my radio! Hell, I hope he hasn't hit *that!*"

A few moments later he heard Jake clamber up the ancient and protesting stairs and go into his own room. And after a little while there was silence, broken only by lusty snores. Gregory snuggled down under the blankets, and went to sleep again.

5

Uncle Jake still denied all knowledge of any Blue Woman. He denied it vehemently and contemptuously. And either he was lying, or memory failed him utterly in moments of drunkenness. Gregory came to the conclusion that the latter was the correct state of affairs.

The first snow fell a week later. It began to drift down late in the afternoon, thickened as the darkness closed in, but ceased altogether an hour later. It froze on top of that, but during the night the weather cleared, and in the morning the streets of Winchingham were a mess of slush. By nightfall nothing remained of it. The next three days were fine and dry; but then the weather thickened again and the B.B.C. began broadcasting snow warnings all over the country.

During that week old Jake remained remarkably sober. Twice he harnessed Boomer to his little open cart and went abroad on certain nefarious expeditions; returning on the Tuesday with mysterious packages from some equally mysterious source— "Tuesday," thought Gregory to himself, "Tuesday . . . Jim Silver"—and on the Thursday with a load of firewood that had definitely not been purchased through any legitimate channel. And at other odd times he put in some honest and remunerative work in Mrs. Pendlebury's garden.

Gregory Cushing spent his time in orienting himself and learning to recognize his neighbours on The Rise. He went for three or four long exploratory rambles in and around Winchingham and Steeple Thelming; and he also made the acquaintance of Miss Emmeline Forbes. The upshot of this was that he began to accompany his uncle "up the hill"; and while that estimable if somewhat unconventional old gentleman did all the work, Miss Forbes showed him all round the place in detail, chatted with him on a variety of topics, including her own pet subjects, and, learning that he was but lately widowed and in such tragic circumstances, made much of him.

Then, on the Saturday, the snow clouds crowded in on the kingdom from the north and east; and all that day, as the snowfall crept down from the northern counties, dire and baneful prognostications were sent out over the air and were caught and retailed by the little portable wireless set on the mantelshelf—which had escaped a damaging blow by a hair's breadth the night Jake had flung his boots at the clock.

That afternoon Jake fell from grace once more.

That evening the heavens opened and the snow fell thick and fast.

And that night the Devil came to Winchingham, specifically to The Base and Steeple Thelming. . . .

*   *   *

With regard to the first of these separate phenomena it was close upon half-past four when Gregory heard the noise outside. He had arrived home before his uncle, and was in the kitchen at the time building up the fire in the stove—for, as Jake had gone out earlier in the donkey cart, he confidently expected him back before dark, particularly in view of the threatening weather.

It was a kind of grating thud, and going out to investigate he found that Boomer, true to his name, had returned home. But uncle Jake had not. Boomer, turning in his own gateway at too narrow an angle, had fouled a post, catching it between the nearside wheel and the body of the cart. Gregory found him waiting patiently, like Balaam's ass, for the obstacle either to remove itself or be removed, and he guessed what had happened. Uncle Jake had got stuck into the rum-and-beer at the Steeple Inn and the passing of time had ceased to be to him a matter of any importance whatsoever; and Boomer, outside, had grown first cold, then hungry, and finally impatient and had pushed off home for the feed he was accustomed to receive at a certain definite time.

Gregory cogitated for a few minutes. Then he went back into the cottage for his hat and coat, came out again, backed the cart free of the gatepost and drove the extremely reluctant Boomer up The Rise through the gathering darkness and down to the Steeple Inn.

He found Jake insensible on the floor of the bar, with the stolid George standing over him and scratching his cropped head in perplexity. There had been another man with Honest George, but he had vanished inside with suspicious celerity upon the entrance of Gregory, and the latter caught only the merest glimpse of his retreating back. George greeted him with his usual curt, unemotional nod.

" 'E," said Honest George, referring to the prone Mr. Popplewell, " 'e come rushin' back in 'ere yellin' out the Blue Woman was arter 'im, an' then 'e falls down—*wump!*—like that."

"Stinko again, I suppose," said Gregory shortly.

"Ah. I've slapped 'is face an' dropped a dash o' brandy down 'is gullet—wot ain't bin paid for yet—an' I've tickled 'is ear wiv a fevver—"

"Tickled his ear?"

"Ah. I've 'eard tell it brings 'em round sometimes. I done everythink, but 'e won't come round."

Gregory said nastily: "You didn't think of refusing him any more drink when you saw what state he was getting into, did you? All right, I'll take him home—he won't wake up for hours now."

He scooped up the unconscious Jake as a child picks up a doll, and slung him over his shoulder. At the door, struck by a sudden thought, he asked: "Was Mr. Silver here with him?"

Honest George Borwell shook his bullet head. Gregory went out with his burden, dumped it into the cart, untied Boomer and drove back to the cottage. Boomer, anxious to get home and to the eats, made light work of the hill.

Gregory carried his uncle inside and flopped him down in the basket chair. Then he went back to the shed, unhitched the cart with clumsy, inexpert fingers and followed Boomer who had walked smartly into his stall the moment he had felt himself free. He took off harness and bridle, strapped on the donkey's cover and filled the manger with a generous hand. Boomer butted him appreciatively in the chest, and then snorted happily into the hay and oats.

Returning to the warmth and light of the parlour—the only even comparatively modern amenity in Jake's cottage was the electric light, and that was to fail before morning—he found the old man just as he had left him, dead to the world but breathing satisfactorily, if stertorously. And after a few moments' indecision he carried him up to bed and tucked him in, boots and all.

Downstairs once more he glanced absentmindedly at the battered clock on the mantelshelf—which had stopped fifteen years ago at 3.40 A.M.—and then at his own watch, and went back into the kitchen to get himself some tea.

*   *   *

With regard to the second and third of these phenomena, which were bound up in each other, the snowfall reached Winchingham round about eight o'clock. It snowed on and off for five hours and then ceased altogether, when the sky cleared and the stars shone out and the air seemed suddenly to have lost its bone-chilling cold. But people returning home from picture theatres and dance halls had to grope their way through a soft, silent, blinding fury. The residents of The Rise, however, hardly ever went to picture theatres at night time, certainly not on Saturday nights, and never to dances. Nor, with one or two exceptions, were they early risers; and even the exceptions never seemed to leave the warm comfort of their well-appointed houses, or appear outside their gates, before ten o'clock at the earliest.

This much is certain: that that night, while old Jake Popplewell snored intermittently and gustily and slept the deep sleep of the drink-sodden, and Boomer the donkey, outside in his cozy stall, stood unmoving on the flat of three hooves and the tip of the fourth, apparently having fallen peacefully asleep in that position; that night the people on The Rise huddled round their firesides and listened to their radios, and at decent and respectable hours filled their hot-water bottles and went to their beds; while all up and down the hill, and in and around Steeple Thelming, the snow gathered undisturbed and lay in one vast unbroken expanse. Yet in the morning—

6

It was Gregory, up and dressed at an unusually early hour by reason of the strange light and the uncanny hush in the world, who first saw the marks in the otherwise virgin mantle of snow. And what he saw sent him out quickly for a closer inspection.

The second witness on the scene, at the foot of The Rise, that is, was Mr. Stanley Mayhew—that Mr. Mayhew who had been slanderously described by old Jake as being subhuman. His house was opposite but one from Jake's cottage and on a slightly higher level, and he had seen the marks in the middle of the road from his wife's bedroom. For whereas Mr. Mayhew was a pillar of his particular church and had risen early, for him, to attend Communion, Mrs. Mayhew was not and had not. She was still abed. Entering her room to wish her good morning, Mayhew had noticed the marks in that dazzling carpet that had covered the world overnight; and, in his lamentable fashion, had begun to titter with amusement, having connected them in his own mind with that rascal Popplewell's donkey. But as he had continued to gaze out of the window with its fussy, frilly curtains, he had abruptly stopped tittering, darted from the room and plunged out of the house to investigate what appeared to be an utterly impossible phenomenon.

By the time he joined Gregory there were three extra but reassuringly human series of tracks in the snow. Gregory had made these himself. He had, he told Mayhew, come out for a closer and more detailed view, disbelieved the evidence of his own eyesight and gone back into the cottage to rouse his uncle. But uncle Jake had not yet "got over it," and Gregory had been unable to wake him. He had merely muttered incoherently without opening his eyes, and had refused to take the slightest interest in any matters mundane—or extramundane. So Gregory had left him to his hoggish slumbers and come out again.

And now the two men stood in the snow, careful to avoid those other tracks that were soon to be known as the "devil marks," and stared in mounting bewilderment and incredulity. . . .

They began at the bottom of The Rise a little way the other side of Jake's cottage: subsequent measurement showed the actual distance to be thirty-seven feet. They started abruptly and inexplicably in the middle of the road and stretched away up the hill, turning in and out of various garden gates on the way. They were the imprints of hooves and they might have been made by Boomer—but only if Boomer had walked on his hind legs all the way and, in addition, had possessed the power of levitation. Judging by eye and literally rule of thumb, the impressions were four inches by three inches in size, and were almost in a dead straight line one behind the other.

It was Mr. Mayhew who spoke first. "I suppose," he said with a nervous titter, "it really couldn't have been your uncle's donkey?"

"Look at them," said Gregory simply. "I've only been out here a few minutes, but I've already seen two or three things about these marks that are, on the face of it, flatly impossible in nature. No donkey, no four-footed creature known to man, could have left *that* trail. Or any two-footed creature either. When any animal walks, no matter how many legs it has, its paws or hooves fall on either side of a central line. You walk like that yourself—have a look at your own tracks coming down the side of the road there. But look at *these* tracks. . . . And look at the distance between them—it's only a matter of some ten or twelve inches. Whatever it was that left this trail, it can't have been very big."

He glanced back along the untrodden snow towards the centre of the town, and then at the first of those mysterious prints. Mayhew said feebly: "Perhaps the animal only had one leg and—and had to hop. I've heard of such cases—birds caught in traps, for instance. . . ."

"It must have been a mighty big first hop," retorted Gregory, waving his arm at the blank expanse of snow stretching away behind them. "Where did it hop from? . . . Birds, yes; but this thing had *hooves*. And things with hooves don't fly. So will you tell me how in the name of all that's unnatural and abnormal these hoof-marks come to start here, from nowhere, bang spang in the middle of the road! Was the—Thing standing here when it began to snow, and did it stand here on this one spot all last night waiting for the snow to stop? Or—"

"Or what?"

"Hell, there isn't any alternative! I give it up—let's see where they go to. . . ."

The trail led in a straight line in the middle of the road past Jake Popplewell's humble cottage on the one side and Mr. Jacques's fine house on the other, and up The Rise past Mayhew's own residence. But not quite in a strict, mathematical straight line: here and there were very slight but perceptible waverings and kinks, places where a hoof had landed a trifle off centre. Afterwards the distances between a number of impressions were measured, and the stride found to average a bare ten inches.

Outside the next house up, which belonged to a Mr. Croxley, occurred the first deviation. Here, for some reason or another, the tracks left the road and turned in at the gate; which, as was the rule on The Rise, was seldom if ever closed and invariably opened on to a drive that led down a gentle declivity to the house. Still keeping well clear of the prints Mayhew and Gregory approached this gate, and there Mayhew hesitated. But Gregory was not in a mood now to be worried by normal, everyday scruples.

"Come on," he said shortly, leading the way down the drive. "No harm in entering a man's garden—not like breaking into his house."

"But look," said Mayhew, pointing. "They come out again."

"I can see. But I want to know where they go to in here."

The tracks didn't seem to go anywhere particularly. They merely led straight down the drive to the front door of the house, turned away again and doubled back in the same unswerving path out on to the road.

"What did it do that for?" asked Mayhew in a whisper.

"Search me," muttered Gregory.

"Do you think it went inside?"

"It doesn't look like it. It looks as though it just walked down here, stood outside the door, turned round and went back again.

But," he added, scanning the marks directly outside the door, "it settles something for us; the thing had two legs." He glanced up at the bedroom windows. "These people sleep late—and they sleep soundly. Or aren't they at home?"

His question was answered almost immediately. A window overhead was flung open and a man thrust out his head and shoulders. The man was still in his pyjamas, he was almost completely bald, he had a strong beard that must have needed shaving twice a day, and he was wearing heavy horn-rimmed spectacles on his pudgy nose.

"What goes on?" he demanded.

"I say, Croxley," called out Mayhew eagerly, "are you all right in there?"

"Of course we're all right! What the—Oh, hullo, Mayhew! What are you doing—?" Then he saw the tracks. "What the blazes is that?"

"That," replied Mayhew with his nervous, ingratiating titter, "is what we want to know. They start down at the bottom of The Rise and come in here and out again—"

"It's that damn donkey of Popplewell's!"

"No, it isn't," said Gregory curtly. "You never saw a donkey walk like that in your life—not unless he stood on his hind legs and was a tight-rope walker into the bargain."

"No-o," mused Croxley, studying the marks. "No, b'gosh," he added briskly. "You're right. Here, wait a minute till I slip on some clothes, I'm coming out with you."

But Gregory shook his head. "There's something altogether too queer about this. We're going on to see if we can catch up with the thing. If you're going to follow us, don't mess up the prints."

"I'm not going to mess them up," retorted the bald-headed Mr. Croxley. "I'm going to photograph them while they're still there."

"That's an idea, and a good one," said Gregory approvingly, but turning away all the same.

Out on the road again they found the visible population of The Rise increased by three. A little way down from the top, earnestly studying the line of prints, were three people, one lady and two gentlemen, all elderly. Gregory recognized the lady as Miss Forbes and one of the men as Mr. Lionel Maltravers, but the second man was a stranger.

"Miss Forbes," observed Mayhew, pointing out the obvious. "And Maltravers. Let's go up—"

"Wait a minute." Gregory caught hold of his arm. "Let them come down to us, I want Miss Forbes to see the start of this trail."

That lady had already caught sight of them and begun to halloo. Gregory waved for her to come down and join him and Mayhew, and waited patiently while the three of them walked down the side of the road, dodging hoof-prints as they came.

Miss Emmeline Forbes was a tallish, thinnish woman approaching her sixtieth year. She wore spectacles set in honey-coloured frames, which was quite the wrong colour for her grey hair and faded complexion, and her clothes sense was nil; but her eyes were still bright and her mind alert and inquisitive. She began talking to Gregory some little distance off.

"Aren't they peculiar marks, Mr. Cushing? What do you make of them? . . . Oh! Good morning, Mr. Mayhew. . . . They're all over our garden. We've been examining them, but we can't make out . . . But, of course, you don't know one another yet, do you?" She turned to the second man of her trio. "Colonel, this is Mr. Cushing—Popplewell's nephew." Gregory was "Mr. Cushing" to her; poor old uncle Jake was merely and baldly "Popplewell." "And this is Mr. Mayhew. Colonel Gormsby, gentlemen, who has been staying with us overnight."

The men shook hands all round, and Mr. Maltravers, whose dark eyes were hidden behind even darker sunglasses, bade Mayhew and Gregory a curt good morning. And then asked Gregory: "Was that donkey of your uncle's loose last night?"

"Look here," began Gregory wearily; but Miss Forbes cut him off.

"You know, Mr. Cushing, I thought myself at first it might have been the donkey, but Colonel Gormsby said no—"

The colonel, grey, compact, well-groomed, well-shaven save for a little white moustache, shook his head firmly. "Out of the question, ma'am. No donkey dropped by a she-ass ever made those marks."

"Thank you, sir," said Gregory warmly. "I was getting tired of defending poor old Boomer. I see you've spotted it."

"Yeh." The colonel clipped his words and spoke in a tone and fashion that reminded Gregory forcibly of his uncle—as old Jake must have spoken before he had fallen so low in the social scale. "Yeh. Whatever left this spoor had only two legs; but if you can think of anythin' that goes on two legs and has *hooves,* you're a better man than I am, Gunga Din. Never seen spoor like this in all me days."

"We've got something queerer still to show you," Gregory told him. "Something that absolutely baffles imagination. That's why, Miss Forbes, I rather rudely waved for you to come down to us.

You'll be interested in this with a vengeance! Come on down to the bottom."

He led the way down to the flat where the spoor of the unknown commenced.

"Those tracks, those three to and from the cottage, they're mine." He explained once again how he had come to make them, and Miss Forbes clicked her tongue distressfully and muttered something about "that wretched Steeple Inn." Gregory grinned at her and went on: "The others are Mr. Mayhew's. But *these*—Well, you tell me, sir, how they come to start here, suddenly, like this, coming from nowhere, starting abruptly in the middle of a great bare unmarked spread of snow. . . . That's what Mr. Mayhew and I saw a little while ago from our windows—isn't that right, Mr. Mayhew?"

Mayhew nodded assent.

And after a moment Colonel Gormsby raised his head and plucked at his little white moustache. "But, good gad, this is impossible!"

"Not impossible, Colonel," said Miss Forbes, whose bright, darting eyes were filled with a wild excitement. "There they *are,* staring us in the face. But incredible, if you like; incredible, that is, by normal material standards."

"This," said Mr. Maltravers glumly, "beats my own show—and heaven knows that's queer enough. These same tracks come into my place—"

"Saw that," grunted the colonel.

"Yes, but what you didn't see was them coming out again. They don't."

"Hold on! They must—they're all over Mrs. Pendlebury's garden."

"I tell you they don't. They go straight across the lawn to the pavilion and end slap up against a blank wooden wall. They end, I tell you, suddenly—like that!" And he pointed one long finger at the first mysterious, incredible, impossible hoof-print.

It was at this juncture, while they were all staring stupidly at each other, that Mr. Croxley came bounding down towards them. His bald head was now covered, and he was muffled up to the eyebrows. The colonel gazed thoughtfully at the camera in his hand.

"Ha! Now that's a good idea."

"Yes," said Mr. Croxley enthusiastically. "This snow will melt and the tracks disappear, but these pictures won't."

"Ha!" exclaimed the colonel again. "Hum. Mr. Mayhew, have you a telephone in your place?"

"Why, yes."

"May I use it? I want to ring up the police station."

"Police station?" echoed Gregory. "You don't want a country cop in on this, you want a native tracker, or a psychical researcher!"

Colonel Gormsby smiled a fleeting frosty smile. "Nevertheless I think I'll ask my inspector to come along. . . . Now, all of you, please remain where you are until I come back, and whatever you do avoid trampling on these prints."

He went away with Mayhew, and Gregory stared after him.

"Autocratic old buck. 'I'll ask my inspector to come along.' . . . Miss Forbes, just who and what is this Colonel Gormsby of yours?"

Miss Forbes told him. And that was when Gregory Cushing learnt that he had been hobnobbing with the chief constable of the county.

7

The police car arrived some fifteen minutes later, stopping, at the colonel's warning hand, some little distance short of the mystery prints. Three men got out: Superintendent Blackler, Detective-Inspector Lancelot Carolus Smith, and Detective-Sergeant Poynter. Superintendent Blackler is a tall spare quiet man with a curiously self-effacing manner; while Inspector Smith, not quite so tall but with the same elegant leanness, is deceptively casual and whimsical, and not at all self-effacing. The chief constable has been heard to observe that there are times when his inspector is a trifle too flamboyant for a conventional police officer. Loosely speaking, Superintendent Blackler plays Alexander to the inspector's Montgomery. The sad-faced, mournful-tongued Bill Poynter is the police photographer and fingerprint expert, and the inspector's right-hand man.

"Good morning, sir," said Superintendent Blackler briefly.

"Good morning, sir," said Mr. Smith, looking about him. "Where's the body?"

Detective-Sergeant Poynter said nothing. He was lugging his camera out of the back of the car.

"No body," chuckled the colonel. "No criminal action or intent so far as I can see, but—" He was suddenly serious again. He pointed an accusing finger at the inspector. "You've got us into some damn rummy things in your time, an' I thought you ought to be in on this lot. This is right up your alley."

Mr. Smith grinned at him. "Bit hard on me, sir, so early in the morning. What is it this time—the trail of '98?" He jerked his head at the tracks stretching up The Rise.

"Yeh. I'd like to know what you make of 'em. Also I want Sergeant Poynter to take some good clear photographs while the prints are still fresh an' sharp. Now, I'll bring you up to date with us." The colonel began to effect one-way introductions. "This is Mr. Cushing, who first saw the marks from that cottage over there. This is Mr. Mayhew, who lives this side of the road two houses up, and who saw the marks at about the same time. Mr. Croxley, his next-door neighbour. Miss Forbes, of course, you know."

"Yes, sir. I remember. The Case of the Bishop's Sword," said Mr. Smith in capital letters. He smiled at the lady. "Merry Christmas, Miss Forbes."

"Good hunting, Inspector," returned Miss Forbes significantly. "I think you'll need it."

"Mr. Cushing," said the colonel crisply, "tell the inspector what you saw out here from your bedroom window."

"That line of hoof-prints," responded Gregory briefly. "That—and nothing else. Not another single mark anywhere in the snow."

"There are plenty now," murmured Mr. Smith.

"We made those," the colonel told him impatiently. "Mr. Mayhew?"

"Y-yes?"

"Tell the inspector what *you* saw."

"I saw the same thing, from my wife's bedroom window. And Mr. Cushing standing just there staring at them."

"Right!" barked the colonel, "They couldn't make anythin' of 'em. We can't make anythin' of 'em. What do you make of 'em?"

"Well"—the inspector screwed up his eyes against the glare—"at first sight they look like the tracks of a pony or donkey. At second sight they don't. At third sight they don't look as though they'd been made by anything—natural."

Miss Forbes gave a little crow of pleasure. "I think you're right, Inspector; I don't think they were made by anything natural, meaning of material form or origin."

Mr. Smith glanced at her quizzically. "I thought you'd say that." He squatted down on his heels and studied the first two or three impressions long and earnestly. "Give it up, sir. Where's the catch?"

"This isn't a joke," said Colonel Gormsby sharply. "I'm deadly serious about this, Inspector, an' I've got some very queer things to show you higher up. But at this end—well, you see the impossibility of it?"

"This sudden mysterious beginning, you mean? Oh, yes, sir? That's why I asked where the catch was. But you mean to say—?"

"I most seriously and solemnly do."

"Gadzooks! We're in it again, Super."

"Yes," agreed the puzzled superintendent. "It's beginning to look like it, Smithy."

Mr. Smith stood up and followed with his eye the line of footprints returning to the cottage. "Old Jake gone inside again?"

"He hasn't been out," replied Gregory. "You know uncle Jake?"

"Uncle? . . . Oh, yes," said the inspector carelessly. "Yes, everybody in Winchingham knows old Jake Popplewell—and his donkey cart."

"Oh, Lord!" groaned Gregory. "Are you still trying to drag poor old Boomer into this?"

"No. Those tracks weren't made by any donkey. I just said so. But these—?"

"They're all mine. I came out and went back for uncle Jake, but I couldn't rouse him. He's still—er—"

"Still sleeping it off," the inspector finished for him calmly. "I know."

"We all know Popplewell," added Miss Forbes, with an undertone of impatience and indignation in her voice. "He'll wake up at midday, roaring, and if you tax him with having been drunk last night he'll deny it flatly and probably blasphemously."

"Well?" asked Colonel Gormsby of the inspector.

"Well, as you say, sir, it's impossible—on the face of it. And as I say, for the moment, I give it up. Where do these tracks lead to?"

"That is what we shall all proceed to find out now. . . . You get to work with that camera, Sergeant. I want a close-up of one or two, and then a line of them if you can get 'em in."

"Yessir," murmured Poynter.

"Close-up of two in sequence, please, Bill," added the inspector. "Also measurements, detailed and accurate measurements."

"Okay, Inspector."

The party moved off with the colonel and Inspector Smith leading the way, and Superintendent Blackler escorting Miss Forbes. Croxley, the amateur photographer, lingered behind for a few moments to discuss angles, exposures and other technical details with the professional.

*   *   *

When they came to the front door of Mr. Croxley's house, by which time Croxley himself had caught up with them, the inspector's hand went to his head.

"Why this little visit? Why come in here just to go away again?"

"But," asked Miss Forbes, "*did* it go away again?"

"What do you mean by that?"

"Perhaps it didn't just turn away. Perhaps it went inside."

"It couldn't have got in," objected Croxley. "That door was locked all night, and we weren't disturbed—"

"My dear man," said Miss Forbes severely. "A locked door wouldn't have stopped *this* thing. And it may not have wanted to disturb you."

"Gawd!" ejaculated Mr. Croxley with hanging jaw.

"Let us," suggested Mr. Maltravers, breaking a long silence, "let us just take Mr. Croxley's word for it for the present. Let's get on—this is nothing to what you're going to see in my place."

The trail, returning to the middle of the road, passed by the next house but turned in again at the one after that.

This was the house wherein dwelt that furtive couple whose name was still a closed book to old Jake. It turned out, according to Miss Forbes, that the name was Jackson and that the couple were a quite respectable, though somewhat retiring, man and wife. The tracks again ran straight down the drive and along to the front door, turning away as they had done at Croxley's house; but this time they cut diagonally across a snow-covered lawn to the low privet hedge fronting the road. The Rise, perhaps it should have been explained before this, had not as yet been favoured with any paved footpath.

"Doesn't seem to be anyone at home," murmured the inspector, glancing up at the windows with their drawn blinds.

"I think they're away," said Miss Forbes. "They went out yesterday morning in their car, and I haven't seen it come back yet."

"Let's get on," grunted Colonel Gormsby impatiently; and the party moved off across the lawn, following the line of tracks to the privet hedge.

This was low enough for anybody, except perhaps an elderly lady in long skirts and the stiff-jointed Mr. Maltravers, to step over without disturbing the ledge of snow that lay along the top of it. And this was the route the Thing had taken—they were all thinking of it as the "Thing" now—for the trail continued on the other side without a break. Almost literally without a break. For the Thing hadn't stepped *over* the privet; it had stepped *on* to it, stood on it, and then stepped down the other side.

On top of that flimsy hedge, which would not have supported a newly-born kitten, were two clearly defined hoof-prints side by side.

"*I* don't believe it!" gasped Gregory in such a comical tone of expostulation and dismay that Mr. Smith cocked a quizzical eyebrow at him. "I mean to say, judging by the length of its stride, it can't have been very big, but it must have had *weight*!"

Miss Forbes laughed at this, a delighted, knowing little laugh.

"Yes," sighed the inspector. "The same thought had occurred to me."

He moved a little way from the prints and, standing on one leg, placed his other foot on the hedge. It left a good clear impression, but the instant he put any weight on it his foot went through into the hedge and snow began to fall off. He took his foot away quickly.

"People," observed Miss Forbes sapiently, "believe only what they *want* to believe, what they've been accustomed to believe. What's in your mind now, Inspector?"

"Bogles, ghosties and things that go bump in the night," replied Mr. Smith unhappily. "Things that go on two legs and have hooves and can apparently gain or lose weight at will." He stepped over the hedge and yelled down the road for Bill Poynter. Five of the party stepped over after him, Miss Forbes and Mr. Maltravers going out again by the gate through which they had come.

The black figure at the foot of The Rise, which had now been joined by a little group of curious and excited spectators, looked up and obeyed the inspector's wave. When he came up to him Mr. Smith showed him the marks on the hedge. "See those, Bill?"

"I see 'em," said the lugubrious Poynter. "And I'll believe anything now."

"An observation of which Miss Forbes will no doubt heartily approve. . . . Get those in your camera as well, will you, Bill? As they are there, both together. . . . Are those people down there getting in your way?"

"Not now. I've finished there. Wish I could take a plaster cast of these, but of course that's impossible in snow."

"We'll have half Winchingham out here in a minute," grumbled the chief constable.

"Well, sir," said Superintendent Blackler, "we can't very well stop them. We can keep them behind us, I suppose; but apart from that it's an open road."

"We've seen the marks," said Miss Forbes sharply, "and photographs have been taken of them. They're an evanescent phenomenon, and considering their nature I should say the more people who see them while they're still here to be seen, the better."

Poynter focused his camera. Mr. Croxley also took a photograph of the marks on the hedge, and a long shot of the trail across the lawn for good measure. The party moved on up the hill.

Again the tracks returned to the middle of the road, passing the next three houses and turning in at the gate of the fourth, which was Mr. Maltravers's. This was the last house but one from the summit, and here the tracks seemed to leave The Rise for good. And again they led straight down the drive and along the side of the house to the front door. On both sides of the trail, in fact all over the place, but never touching it, were Maltravers's own footprints.

"This," said that gentleman, advancing his black goggles to the lead with Colonel Gormsby, "is where they end. Maybe they begin again next door, but they end here—and you can make what you can of that."

No one made any reply to this. They had all grown very quiet, sunk in their own mystified thoughts. From the front door the prints turned away, crossed diagonally a stretch of snow that Maltravers said was his croquet lawn and led up to a small pavilion set in the angle of two high brick walls. And there, as Mr. Maltravers had said, hard up against the blank wooden side of this pavilion, as abruptly and inexplicably as they had begun—the tracks ended.

The walls were both of the same height: six feet, two inches, as determined by subsequent measurement. One ran along the frontage of Maltravers's property, and the other was the dividing line between his and Mrs. Pendlebury's gardens. The pavilion, a pale-green wooden hut with a central door in the front of it, flanked by two small windows, had a high-pitched roof of reddish-orange tiles that curved suddenly outwards to the gutter that ran all round it. Two small spires, or cupolas, perched at either end of an ornamental ridge-piece; and the whole effect was curiously reminiscent of some miniature, transplanted Eastern pagoda. Which was presumably the effect Mr. Maltravers had striven for and, also presumably, satisfied his aesthetic fancy.

It had been built with its back to the wall facing the road, and its far side against the side wall. But not hard up against the walls; there was a space all round between walls and pavilion of approximately two feet. Even in this sheltered and confined space enough snow had fallen to have taken the impressions of anyone, or anything, walking on it. But there were no impressions in it; no hoof-prints or any other kind of marks marred its smooth, virgin surface. The last of the hoof-prints ended eight inches from the wooden wall of the near side of the pavilion.

"Well?" inquired the black-goggled Mr. Maltravers.

No one said anything for a moment or two. Croxley began to take more photographs. Mr. Smith, requesting that no one should move until he returned, went for a tour round the pavilion, looked in at the tiny windows and tried the door.

"That's locked," said Maltravers quietly. "Want it open?"

"Oh, no," sighed the inspector. "No, thanks—it's not in there." He came back to them, took off his hat and thrust his fingers through his thick dark hair.

"Inspector Smith!" said Miss Forbes. Her eyes were very bright behind the honey-coloured spectacles, but her normally crisp and confident tones were a shade uncertain.

"Yes, Miss Forbes?"

"Have you noticed something that I think I've noticed about these marks?"

"If you mean they were shod hooves, yes."

"Shod?" queried Mayhew—who should have been well on his way to church by now.

"The hooves had shoes on," explained Croxley gruffly. "Horse-shoes. Like Popplewell's donkey."

"Like Mr. Popplewell's donkey," agreed the inspector gravely. "And yet not like Mr. Popplewell's donkey. Not at all like it."

"No, no," said Miss Forbes. "That's obvious. No, I meant something else. Doesn't it seem to you, Inspector, that the hooves might have been—*cloven?*"

"Oh, now, now! You'll be giving the Thing horns and a tail yet!"

"But look at the marks! Look at them closely."

"I have been looking at them, you know," said Mr. Smith mildly. "And I think I have a vague idea of what's growing in your mind, but—oh, no! I think it's merely that the snow has packed in the concavity of the hoof tinder the shoe, and lifted a bit here and there."

"Damme!" snapped the chief constable, never the most patient of mortals. "Cloven or whole, what's the answer to *this?* They appear again next door all over the show."

"I don't know, sir," replied Mr. Smith frankly. "I don't pretend to have any answer to the question. I merely suggest we go next door."

8

The party retraced their footsteps out through the gate and back on to the road. Here they met Detective-Sergeant Poynter—and not only Poynter, but about a dozen curious and excited hangers-on. More were following them up The Rise.

Colonel Gormsby growled his annoyance. "They'll mess up the spoor, confound 'em!"

"I don't think they will, sir," said the superintendent soothingly. "They'll be too interested."

"Will it really matter very much now if they do?" asked Miss Forbes. "We've all seen them, *they're* seeing them, and we'll have photographs. Besides, the marks won't last for ever, and I still say the more who see them, the better."

The inspector was talking to Poynter, "You could take some more photos in there, Bill. Follow the trail—you'll find it leads slap up against the wall of that pavilion thing."

"Okay, Inspector," replied the unemotional Poynter, and took himself and his camera into Mr. Maltravers's garden.

"Not you people," roared Colonel Gormsby at the crowd, which showed every intention of following. "That's private property, an' you can't go in there without the owner's permission. An' if y're goin' to hang about here, keep clear of those hoof-prints."

" 'Oo sez?" demanded an indignant voice.

"I say so. The chief constable of this county."

"And I say so," added Mr. Maltravers. "I'm the owner of the property."

The indignant voice promptly labelled the one a bleedin' Fascist, and the other a pot-bellied, blood-sucking capitalist; but neither its owner nor anyone else attempted to trespass on the private property of the said capitalist.

Mr. Smith moved on to where Maltravers's high wall ended and Mrs. Pendlebury's began. It was one continuous wall, but whereas Maltravers's was six feet in height, Mrs. Pendlebury's was only half that: an exact three feet, to be precise. But it was surmounted by an iron railing; and here, between that thin railing and the edge of the bricks, the tracks appeared again.

The inspector regarded them in a thoughtful silence.

"Oi!" called out the Voice. "What made these perishin' marks? What are we chasin'? A ruddy performin' goat, or somep'n?"

"That man," observed Miss Forbes, without bothering to lower her own clear, cultured tones, "might be nearer the truth than he imagines!"

Mr. Smith smiled to himself, and his eyes travelled up to the top of the wall, five inches above the level of his vision. He glanced round his own party clustered about him, and his gaze fell on Gregory.

"Mr. Cushing, you're young and strong. I want to have a look at the top of this wall; will you give me a back?"

Gregory obligingly braced himself against the brick and allowed the inspector to stand on his bent back.

"Odds blood!"

"What is it?" said the chief constable, bustling forward. "Here, let me see."

Gregory bent down again and the colonel hopped up.

"Gad, they're up here!"

"*Wot's* up there?" demanded the irrepressible Voice.

The colonel very properly ignored him, but Mr. Smith answered with careless courtesy: "More of those same tracks. . . . Keep off them, will you, like good chaps. Don't mess them up."

"Okay, chum," replied the self-appointed spokesman affably. "An' no offence meant, but 'oo might you be?"

"Police," returned the inspector briefly.

"Lumme! Wot's up?"

"That's just what we don't know. That's what we're trying to find out. And you'll help us by keeping out of the way a little."

"Okay, okay." The Voice—for the moment—lapsed into silence.

Colonel Gormsby had returned to earth, to Gregory's relief, and was saying: "They run along the top of the wall from behind that pavilion thing, beginnin' again at a point exactly opposite where they stopped on the other side, an' they step down here—"

"Some step!" Gregory interrupted him, eyeing the drop from one wall to the other. "A thing that size never *stepped* down from there. It jumped; and it would be a damned ticklish jump, if you ask me."

"And how," inquired Maltravers blandly, "do they happen to be on the top of that six-foot wall? How did the Thing get up there at all? Answer me that!"

"I'll tell you how it got up there," said Miss Forbes. More backs were now being bent against the wall in question, and more people were seeing for themselves. "Levitation!"

"Levitation?" repeated Mayhew. "What does that mean?"

Mr. Smith told him. "It means," he said solemnly, "that although the tracks come to a sudden end on the other side of that pavilion, the Thing didn't. Like Felix, it kept on walking. Only it walked on the empty air. It walked upwards on the empty air, passing through solid matter, until it reached the top of the wall where the marks of its hooves become visible again to mortal eyes."

Miss Forbes smiled approvingly.

"But that—" protested Mayhew shrilly, "that's *silly!*"

Mr. Smith grinned at him. "Oh, I know. But that's Miss Forbes's explanation. Have you any alternative?"

Mr. Mayhew's reply to this was no answer to the question. But he was the first person to voice aloud the opinion that was to be held by a number of persons in Winchingham—and, indeed, by a vast number of persons throughout the country—who should perhaps have known better.

"I don't like this," he muttered in scared tones. "This is devil's work!"

*   *   *

The original group of investigators, joined once more by Sergeant Poynter, moved on into Mrs. Pendlebury's drive, down which the trail of the unknown ran clear and straight. Inside the gate, Miss Forbes turned and addressed the camp followers.

"If this were my own place I'd invite you all in. But it isn't, it's my sister's home; so I'm afraid I'll have to ask you to stay outside. I'm sorry, but I'm sure you'll understand." She smiled apologetically at them.

"That's all right, mum," said the Voice heartily. "We'll 'ang abaht 'ere an' sing carols till yer gets back."

But neither Miss Forbes nor any of her party came back to that spot. For the trail, following what now appeared to be a prescribed pattern, led them down the drive, taking a short cut across a circular box-edged flower-bed—which gave the drive its run-round—and up to the big wide porch before the front door. Here, yet once again, it turned away, ran along the front of the house to the corner, rounded the corner and on to a terrace, stepped down into the rose garden and went along a narrow path between neat rectangular beds to a summerhouse. And there, as they had done at Mr. Maltravers's pavilion, the tracks ceased abruptly.

"Airborne again," muttered the inspector. "I'm beginning to agree with Mr. Mayhew; this is so damned impossible it's getting silly!"

"Are you getting afraid of the evidence, Inspector?" asked Miss Forbes. "It's really there, you know, we can't all be dreaming it."

Mrs. Pendlebury's house was situated on the highest point of the hill, and this summerhouse was therefore actually over the brow. It looked out over the other side down a boulder-strewn grassy slope to the little river Winch at the bottom. Once, in that squat stone house on the river's bank, there had dwelt a self-styled philosopher with a retinue of Chinese servants, or disciples; but he was there no longer, his departure having been effected by Detective-Inspector Smith—one of the inspector's more recherché cases, which has already been chronicled under the title of *The Bishop's Sword*. The grass was hidden now under the snow, and the boulders showed up grey with little white caps on their heads.

The summerhouse was an octagonal wooden structure with a high conical roof. In summer-time it was open all round to a height of some three feet, with a convenient ledge for resting the arms upon while lounging in this retreat; but during the winter months it was boarded up from the inside and the door locked. It was outside this door, at the end of the path, that the hoof-marks ended.

Mr. Smith gazed pensively at the dark wood. "Well, I don't suppose you've got it locked up in there."

"We haven't," said Miss Forbes drily. "We opened it up and had a look."

The inspector commenced to sidle round the summerhouse, while Mr. Croxley got busy with his camera once more. The summerhouse backed flush up against a tall, thick, rather over-grown privet hedge—the western boundary of the prop-erty—which, at this point, had been cut hard back with the level of the permanent wall, three feet from the ground, to allow of an unrestricted view. A narrow strip of ledge jutted out all round below the protective boarding, excepting, of course, at the doorway; and on this, save at one particular place, snow had fallen and clung. The one particular place was right at the back, where, protected by the body of the structure, the strip of ledge and the low part of the hedge immediately up against it was clear. Here no snow had fallen, or at any rate lain; but everywhere else it had; and everywhere else, with the exception of the path that led to the door, and round about the door itself, it lay smooth and dazzling and unmarked.

Mr. Smith edged his way round the summerhouse to the back and pushed his head through into the gap where the hedge had been trimmed. When he turned round again there was snow on his hat and on his shoulders, and a most comical expression of res-ignation on his good-looking features.

"The mixture as before," he observed. "The Thing just went right through, and kept on walking."

"Y' mean," cried Colonel Gormsby, "there are more tracks on the other side?"

"Yes, sir. And I suppose the only thing to do—Oh, Bill!"

"Yes, Inspector?"

"Better take a photograph or two of this ledge before we get through. Somebody's bound to brush some of this snow off, and we don't want any arguments later. . . . You know," he added a little grimly, "I'm getting my teeth into this thing. It's not only baffling me—I admit that frankly—it's intriguing and annoying me. I can't make head or tail of it. It's not only beyond all ordinary animal or even human behaviour; it's apparently beyond all natural, material explanation—"

"Isn't that just what I've been hinting all along?" asked Miss Forbes sharply.

"Yes, but even if I grant you your premise of some psychic visitation—which I don't, not without some considerable struggle—the *actions* of this Thing are still without any rhyme or reason. And surely even a supposedly materialized spirit—"

"Where the cause is unknown, unguessable, the effect is bound to be mystifying," said Miss Forbes composedly.

"But odd's sweet blood—!"

Gregory Cushing grinned to himself. Too bad uncle Jake wasn't here to be in on this.

"But even so," argued the inspector, "there must be some *meaning* to it somewhere. But this—this objectless first-footing, this aimless wandering about in the snow—that's as baffling in itself as the Thing's apparent passages through solid matter!"

"And how, my dear Inspector," inquired Miss Forbes crisply, instantly leaping on to her hobbyhorse, "just how solid is this solid matter in which you place such simple faith? You are an intelligent man, as I know from experience, and you should therefore be the first to agree with me when I remind you that it is not the ecstatic mystic who has destroyed the illusion of substance so much as the case-hardened, sceptical, material scientist. It is the physicist who has pulled the material world to pieces and found nothing in it; nothing discernible to any human sense, nothing to be grasped by any human intellect. He has taken far more from the phenomenon of material existence than *we* ever did. He has taken it all, and left in its place only mathematical formulae, symbols that are unintelligible even to himself. . . . But aside from that, *is* all this wandering in the snow aimless? It seems we haven't come to the end of the trail yet."

"That's true." Mr. Smith shot her a keen, respectful glance. "We haven't. . . . But as for all that other, well, the only thing I really know, and which I will maintain through hell and high water, is that you *cannot* move about in snow without leaving traces—even if snow is only a symbol, or a mathematical formula."

"But don't you *see?*" cried Miss Forbes earnestly. "That is because you and I and all created things are all victims of the Great Illusion. But this Thing may not have been!"

Gregory laughed unaffectedly at the expression on Mr. Smith's face. "Miss Forbes wins on points—how about pushing on, Inspector?"

"M'yes. . . . Finished, Bill?"

Bill Poynter patted his camera. "They're safe." Mr. Croxley had also been busy with his own camera, and had already used up one roll of film—before this queer business was over he was going to make a packet of money from the sale of his photographs to various newspapers and magazines.

Mr. Smith pushed his way between the privet and the back of the summerhouse, swung one leg over the cut-back part of the hedge and then the other, and stood in the snow on the other side. At Miss Forbes's request the other men followed suit. Gregory, however, held back, pressing the high, overgrown part of the hedge away from the summer-house.

"Thoughtful of you, Mr. Cushing," said Miss Forbes, settling her deplorable hat more firmly on her head, "but if that is the easiest and most efficient way over this hedge, you'd better go ahead with the rest. I should prefer not to have an audience—"

"As a matter of fact," said Gregory calmly, "it isn't the easiest and most efficient way. This is." And without more ado he caught her round the waist and under the knees, and swung her neatly and smoothly over the hedge.

"Oo!" cried the lady. "Oh. . . . God bless me, nobody's done that to me for thirty years and more!"

Gregory grinned at her. "Croxley missed that. He should have had that in his camera as well for the sake of posterity." Two easy, fluid motions of his own long legs, and he was standing beside her.

From this point, immediately behind the summerhouse, the trail led diagonally across the slope of the hillside to a gap in the gorse-choked hedge that lined the road leading down to Steeple Thelming, a distance of nearly a hundred yards. In all that bare expanse of snow only that single line of hoof-prints marred its unbroken, dazzling surface.

"This Thing," mused the inspector, squinting against the glare, "seems to have a weakness for advancing in echelon."

"Better get on," exhorted the quiet superintendent. "By the sound of it the mob's ahead of us."

9

The group of curious idlers had grown tired of cooling their heels outside Mrs. Pendlebury's gate, had shuffled forward over the top of The Rise and discovered that the mysterious tracks reappeared in the snow about a third of the way down on the other side. By the time Miss Forbes and Colonel Gormsby and their party had reached the gap in the hedge `through which the tracks passed, reinforcements had arrived and the crowd was milling about in the roadway asking itself questions and answering itself with wild guesses.

The Voice had a theory. The Voice maintained that the tracks had been made by a dawg. "A performin' dawg—I seen dawgs wot could walk on their 'ind legs fur bloomin' hours! An' wot else but a dawg, an' a big 'un like a S'n' Bernard or a Nalsation, coulda jumped on to that 'igh wall?"

"Dawg, nuffin'!" retorted one sceptic. "Dawgs don't 'ave 'ooves. An' them marks—"

But the Voice had a counter to this. "Ain'tcher never seen them little leather boots some people puts on their dawgs in mucky wewer? This dawg was wearin' 'em—that's why them marks look like 'oof-marks."

"Aw, nuts!" returned the sceptic contemptuously. "Dawg—I arsk yer! Gimme the name o' the dawg what coulda jumped up on to that wall—an' landed on one foot like a flippin' ballet dancer! Besides, this thing 'ad 'orse-shoes on, not fancy bootees. . . ."

"Dog, duck or dancing pony," struck in a third voice, a more educated voice; "have you chaps forgotten how they start—from nowhere—out of nothing—like a special act of creation?"

"That," murmured Detective-Inspector Smith to the superin-tendent walking beside him, "is the crusher!" He emerged on to the road behind Miss Forbes and the chief constable as the Voice inquired truculently of the third party who had asked *him* to chip in. . . .

"No," said Colonel Gormsby testily in answer to the importuning crowd, "we haven't found out yet what's been makin' these tracks—we don't know any more than you. And if you people are goin' to traipse along, please keep behind us and please keep clear of the prints."

The crowd good-naturedly fell in with the request, even the Voice remarking tolerantly: "Fair enough, mates, 'e did say 'please' this time. . . ."

And now the trail, once more in the middle of the road, led straight down to the bottom of the hill without a break. But once there, still apparently following some strange mystic plan, it turned to the left and went right up to the door of the Steeple Inn before turning away again and proceeding in the opposite direc-tion along the narrow road that ran past the country house of Mr. Montague Mason, and, farther on, the farmhouse of Mr. Silver.

Honest George Borwell was standing on the threshold of his inn as the investigators rounded the corner. He regarded them sus-piciously, but neither moved nor opened his mouth.

"Lumme!" cried the Voice. "Ole good King Wenceslas 'isself!"

"Is it open yet, chum?" inquired some thirsty optimist.

Honest George found a voice of his own. "No," he grumbled, "it ain't. An' 'oo's bin leadin' a norse up an' down 'ere, I should like to know?"

Various people told him. Their answers ranged from the Invisible Man to the Lion and the Unicorn, the Lion in this instance having been carried by the Unicorn on its shoulders. Gregory tugged at Inspector Smith's arm.

"You won't get anything out of this man," he said in a low tone. "He's solid bone from the neck up."

"You know him?"

"Unfortunately, yes. This is where uncle Jake gets his booze."

Colonel Gormsby overheard him and said to the superintendent: "This place looks as though it could do with a clean up, Blackler."

"We keep an eye on it, sir," replied the superintendent in that special soothing voice he kept for the chief constable. "Not an attractive pub, I admit, but the licensee says his trouble is staff. So far as we know, it's a law-abiding house."

"Humph! . . . What the blazes did this Thing come here for?"

"Why did it visit *any* of our houses?" put in Miss Forbes.

The Colonel shrugged his shoulders and turned away from the door, and began to follow the tracks once more. The crowd followed him, and after some lengthy silent communion with nature, Honest George shut his door and followed the crowd. Straight over the crossroads ran the line of prints and along the opposite road to a gap in the belt of trees that sprang up from the corner on the left-hand side. Here, in this gap, was a wide iron gate, now standing open to its fullest extent. A slight depression in the even mantle of snow showed where a wide path or a drive curved away towards the still invisible house.

"Who lives here?" inquired Colonel Gormsby, eyeing the line of prints that ran off at an angle through the gateway.

Normally that fount of information, Miss Forbes, would have answered his question, but she was staring at the gate in puzzled fashion. Gregory replied:

"According to my uncle, it belongs to a man named Mason. Montague Mason. But he doesn't live here; he's a Londoner, and he only comes down here on odd occasions."

"That's funny," murmured Miss Forbes.

"What's funny?"

"This gate being open. It's only open like this when Mr. Mason is here. But he hasn't been here for some months now, and when I last saw this gate, a few days ago, it was closed and locked."

"Perhaps," suggested Mr. Mayhew, with his nervous giggle, "the man has come down again unknown. He might be inside."

"Or," said Mr. Smith sardonically, "the Thing got tired of walking through solid matter—or mathematical formulae—and opened this gate for a change."

The colonel snorted at this. "D'ye know anythin' of this feller Mason, Blackler?"

"We know of him," replied the Superintendent cautiously. "We know he exists, and that he visits this place for a few days now and then. But that's about all."

"You don't happen to know how he makes his money, do you?" asked Gregory interestedly.

Three pairs of eyes immediately fastened on his face, and the "look"—the police look—came into the eyes: the chief constable's, the superintendent's, and Mr. Smith's.

"Do you?" countered the latter.

"No. And nobody else seems to, either. I'll bet the London police would like to."

"Do *you* know him, Mr. Cushing? Know him personally, I mean?"

Gregory shook his head. "Only by sight—I'm a Londoner myself, and Mason is a well-known figure in certain business circles—only by sight and reputation. And his reputation stinks."

"What of?" inquired Mr. Smith blandly.

"Oh . . . fish. You know—fishy fish." He hesitated slightly, shooting a quick glance at the one lady in the party. "He's got a bad name with women."

"Hum!" said the chief constable. "Ha! . . . Let's get on."

They advanced in one solid body; even Honest George had caught up now. And this time the crowd was not to be held back. It had scented a faint delicious odour of scandal. Tainted money—women—booze, probably lashings of it—"goings-on" . . .

As they marched down the curving drive the house gradually came into full view, facing them front on. And, as uncle Jake had told Gregory, it was not the usual "country house" of the aristocracy or the wealthy: it was a humble two-story building, little more than a cottage. The lower half of it was brick, the upper part half-timbered. The roof—but the nature of the roof was hidden beneath its blanket of snow.

It was Mr. Mayhew who first spotted what was on that blanket. "Good Heavens!" he squeaked, stopping suddenly to the embarrassment of the man immediately behind him. "Look at that!"

Everybody halted once more, and all eyes followed his pointing finger. The roof was a steep one, far too steep for almost anything other than a fly to retain a footing on it, and the whole covering of snow was already beginning to slide in one solid mass away from the ridge. *Yet on that steep, fluffy-smooth slope of snow was a ring of marks where something that had hooves had walked round and round in a wide circle.*

"How the hell did it get up there?" gasped Gregory.

"Like Santa Claus," hazarded the Voice. "Up the chimbley."

"What chimney?" asked Mr. Smith quietly.

"That there chimbley."

"That there chimney," said the inspector heavily, "is a good twenty-five feet from those prints, and the snow is still lying on it undisturbed. Nothing, not even smoke, has come out of that chimney since the snow fell on it."

There was a short bewildered silence.

"Wot price your jumpin' dawg now, mate?" inquired somebody at the back of the crowd. But the banter was dying out of the voices, and this was the last facetious, or semi-facetious, remark to be passed.

Mayhew expressed the growing sentiment. "I don't *like* it," he said nervously. "I think there's something really wrong, some-thing evil, in all this. That's no harmless ring of marks up there—the Devil's design is in that circle."

The voice of the orthodox churchman, thought Gregory. Miss Forbes began to chuckle.

"I didn't think *you'd* scoff at these things," he protested in-dignantly.

"My dear man," replied Miss Forbes, in her crisp, confident tones, "I'm not scoffing. Not at the phenomena. But I am intrigued by the contradiction. The full circle is the symbol of light, not darkness. The sun, the source of all light—the crown of the Godhead—the halo of the Christ. . . . It is the *broken* circle that is the devil-mark."

"Why?" asked Mr. Smith, interested.

Miss Forbes expounded. "The First Circle is the sun, the source of light, the giver of life. The first terrible sign to appear in the heavens—*out of a clear sky*—literally out of the blue—was the breaking of the First Circle. To us, of course, it is merely a tem-porary eclipse by the moon; but to the dawning mind of prehis-toric man it was a portent of unimaginable catastrophe. That, I fancy, is the origin of the belief that the broken circle is a symbol of bad luck."

"I didn't even know it was," said Mr. Smith simply.

"Didn't you? Go and have your tea-cup read sometime. If there's a little broken ring of tea leaves in it you'll be told you're going to have a quarrel with somebody, or that you'll hear of a broken engagement, or some other trivial unhappiness like that."

"I wasn't thinking of tea leaves, I was thinking of a horse-shoe. That's a lucky charm—"

"Maybe. But it isn't a circle. It never was, not even a broken one. It is a definite shape of its own: the arch. The same shape as the rainbow that comes out after the storm and brings comfort and delight to man."

"But, gadzooks, the arch is only a part of a circle; the arch of the rainbow is a perfect semi-circle—"

"Yes, Inspector—*perfect*. Unbroken. Continuous."

"Look here," said Colonel Gormsby testily. "Never mind the devil-talk—you people might be goin' ahead a little too fast. Whatever it was that left this spoor might have got on to the roof from inside the house, through a skylight, or somethin'. . . ."

But the inspector shook his head. "I hardly think so, sir. Consider. Obviously all these tracks were made after the snow had ceased falling, after it was all over and the weather had cleared. Now, if any skylight or trapdoor had been pushed up, or let down, it would have dislodged a patch of snow. But there is no such dislodged or even disturbed patch. The snow is unbroken, marked only where the Thing marched round and round and made that circle. And if there is a skylight in the other side of the roof where we can't see from here, and the Thing had got on to the roof that way, there would—or *should*—be a line of prints coming over the top and down to the circle. But, again, there isn't. The tracks don't come from anywhere, they don't go anywhere. They just begin—and end. . . . As a matter of fact there is no visible evidence that they even do that, since there is no beginning or ending to a circle. . . ."

"Then, damme, how *did* this Thing get up there? Did it fly up?"

"Yes," said Miss Forbes.

"What?"

"I said, yes!" repeated Miss Forbes firmly.

"Good gad!" said the colonel feebly.

* * *

They moved on again. Straight up to yet another front door ran the tracks; but on this occasion the unknown had not merely turned away again; it had, as shown by the prints disappearing round one corner and reappearing round the other, circled the house several times.

"Seven times round Jericho," murmured the inspector, running his eye along the snow. "Only the walls didn't fall down this time, so he tried the roof—"

"I've been thinking about that," said Gregory Cushing suddenly and clearly. "How about a ladder? A long ladder with, say, half a dozen or so rungs sticking up above the eaves. The ladder would not only stick up above the eaves, it would reach a little way over the roof itself. The—the Thing could have stepped down from a rung onto the snow, made that circle and stepped back on to the ladder. . . ."

His voice tailed off. Mr. Smith was shaking his head.

"Ingenious idea, Mr. Cushing, but there's too much against it. Find me your ladder. Then show me the marks in the snow down here where the ladder would have rested—they'd be about where Mr. Croxley is standing now, the lowest part of the circle is just above that window. And then find me any living creature, with hooves, that can *(a)* handle a ladder, *(b)* climb a ladder, and *(c)* stand on a roof as steep as that without sliding off. . . . Want any more? I can think of a few more snags."

"No," said Gregory, gloomily, "I don't want any more, there's too much already. This Thing not only has hooves—it walks upright on them on two legs!"

"And," added Superintendent Blackler with a dry chuckle, "when it feels like it, walks about on the empty air. I suppose that's how it got on to the roof—this is the daddy of the lot, Smithy!"

Mr. Smith gave him back a fleeting smile. "Yes, it's all that, Super. But even though it isn't, strictly speaking, our pigeon, I would like to know—"

"Yes," said Miss Forbes emphatically, "you'd like to know. You've still got your teeth into it, haven't you, Inspector? And I'm glad to hear it, because I'm taking this phenomenon seriously, if the superintendent isn't."

The inspector turned on her. "What I should like to know more than anything else is why this Thing was wearing *shoes*—horseshoes."

Miss Forbes looked at him gravely. "I don't expect you to understand this, but it is a philosophical truth. What we are following is an idea; and the horseshoes on the hooves are a part, a conventional attribute, of that idea."

Mr. Smith stared at her, as well he might. "Does an idea leave tracks in the snow?"

"But of course! The snow itself is an idea. The entire universe is an idea. Haven't I reminded you, Inspector, that it is the material scientist himself, the man who believed in the reality of substance and who went to work to investigate it, who has destroyed the material universe? All that exists does so only in *mind.* But there"—she smiled kindly at him—"I don't expect you to grasp all at once what I am driving at."

Gregory couldn't help it. He tapped the inspector on the shoulder. "As uncle Jake would say, old boy, you're only a character in the Red King's dream. When he wakes up, you won't *be.*"

And this was altogether too much for the chief constable, who, as he was wont to say himself, was a plain, blunt man with no time for high-falutin' misty theorizing. "What bl—hurrumph!—what infernal nonsense are you people spoutin'? All this argufyin'—besides, y' can't know much about horses, these marks are too small to have been made by any horse. Shetland pony, perhaps. Or donkey—"

"Huh!" snorted Gregory. "Back to Boomer, eh? That will be the day when old Boomer goes cavorting over roofs on his hind legs!"

"Who the hades is Boomer?"

"My uncle's donkey."

"*Oh . . .* come *on*—these tracks must end somewhere."

"They'll end," Miss Forbes told him with quiet confidence, "in the same way as they begin."

The chief constable said nothing to this, but walked to the corner of the house, followed by the others. Here he said "Ha!" and went on a little more quickly. Half-way along this side was another door, and from this door *two* lines of tracks stretched across to a gap in the laurel hedge that marked the end of the garden. One of these was the by how monotonously familiar spoor of the unknown, the other was obviously the footprints of a human being.

"Somebody ahead of us," grunted the colonel.

"That's what it looks like, sir. So our Mr. Mason must have been at home. Or else he has a caretaker—"

"He has no caretaker," put in Miss Forbes sharply.

"M'm. . . . Well, it looks plain enough. The Thing marched in here, but showed considerably more interest in this house than in any of the others it visited, and then pushed off again. Mason, I suppose, has seen the marks and gone to find out what it's all about."

"I hope he's had better luck than we have," growled the colonel. With a warning to the camp followers to keep off the tracks, he led the way to the gap in the laurel hedge. Beyond this was a wide track, or a narrow road, through the trees that led to the open field wherein stood the dead oak tree. As they passed through the gap, which was really a gateway without a gate, the marks veered together; the almost dead straight line of hoof-prints wobbled in two places and touched the foot-prints.

"Just a minute, sir," begged the inspector, whose eyes had been fixed on the ground. "I want to have a closer look at that."

The colonel halted obligingly and roared at the crowd to keep back. Mr. Smith squatted down in the snow, and when he got up again his face was troubled.

"This is—peculiar. The man wasn't following the Thing; the Thing was following the man.

"Hey?"

"Look at these prints here, sir—and those. You can see where the hoof-print is superimposed on the foot-print. The hooves trod on them—after them. . . ."

"By gad, yes!"

"Was this man—running?" asked Gregory.

"No-o, I don't think so. Judging by the length of the stride, he was walking. But—"

"But what?"

Mr. Smith ran his eyes along the tracks between the trees. "He doesn't seem to have been walking quite normally—there are places where he staggered. . . ."

"Drunk," said Gregory curtly. "I know Mason."

"Or pushed," put in the quiet superintendent. "This"—pointing to the hoof-prints—"may have been accompanying the man."

"Um. I don't think I like this . . . Bill!"

Detective-Sergeant Poynter pushed his way to the front.

"More photos, please, Bill. Both lots. . . . I think, sir," he said to the chief constable, "we'd better get a move on. Mason, or whoever the man was, went out there a long time ago—and he hasn't come back yet!"

"Push on," commanded the colonel urgently.

They pushed on, leaving Poynter and Croxley to take their photographs. They came to the end of the trees and emerged on to the bare, open field. And then they began running madly.

With but an occasional wobble and a stagger the two lines of tracks pointed straight as arrows to the tree that stood in the middle of the field; the normal foot-prints of a man, off-centre of a middle line; the abnormal hoof-prints of—something, one directly behind the other and less than a foot apart. And there they came to an end.

The man's prints ended because his feet had left the ground at this point. The feet were still there, but they were no longer in the snow. They dangled three or four inches in the air above it. And they dangled there like that, stiff and motionless, because the man's body was hanging from the lowest branch of the tree. There was a rope about his neck and he was stone dead.

The hoof-prints simply ended, as abruptly and inexplicably as they had begun at the foot of The Rise a mile away.

They had come to the end of the trail; and the end of the trail was a dead man hanging from a dead tree in the middle of a bare, empty paddock. And in all that gleaming expanse of snow had been only the tracks of the man himself, and the tracks of the Thing that had hooves; the Thing that had either followed him or accompanied him. Nothing else. Not another mark.

PART TWO

The Blue Hag

10

It hung there, a pitiable and repulsive object; the body of a small man with a face that in life had been thin and pinched with the sign-manual of avarice, with little green eyes that had been bright with cunning and false gaiety, and with thin flat hair the colour of Yarmouth sand. It was dressed in a neat grey double-breasted business suit, and—a little oddly—gumboots that were much too big for the small feet. A blue-grey negligee shirt made a quiet background for a brilliant tie, and the tips of a carefully folded handkerchief, the same colour as the shirt, peeped from the breast pocket.

An echo of old Jake Popplewell's rusty voice sounded in Gregory's ears. "Little feller . . . like a ferret. . . ."

But the description was no longer apt. For the face suspended between heaven and earth, and yet barely above the level of Gregory's own head, was now blue-black and swollen, and the sightless eyes were suffused with blood and starting from their sockets. The head was queerly twisted on its neck in an odd listening attitude, as if the man, deaf to all the noises of earth, were striving to catch something that could only be heard in the heart of silence.

The crowd reacted to the horrible sight in its various separate ways. Miss Forbes, coming up afterwards, after one quick shocked glance moved away and looked no more. Maltravers took off his black spectacles in a deliberate gesture, stared blindly for some moments, and then replaced them on his curving beak of a nose with an equal deliberation of movement, marred slightly by the trembling of his hands. Mayhew clutched at his stomach as if he had been mortally wounded, uttered a stricken moan and began chattering to himself.

"Oh, God! Oh, my God! This is devil's work—this is the work of the Devil! I should have gone to Communion—I should have gone to Communion—"

"What the hell good would that have done?" Croxley, rendered savage by shock, snarled at him. "What good would that have done *this* poor devil?"

Gregory Cushing, white and shaking and breathing quickly and unevenly, drew away and fought with himself to keep his gaze averted. But those bursting eyeballs seemed to exercise a terrible irresistible fascination over him, tugged at his own sick reluctant eyes, compelled him to look again and again. Someone behind him called out hoarsely, imploringly: "For heaven's sake, cut him down—cut him *down!*"

There is a vast difference between coming face to face with a dead man hanging on a tree—and reading about it in a book. . . .

A smooth, almost imperceptible change had come over Colonel Gormsby and his men. Before, they had been with the crowd; they had been the leaders, a kind of semi-official investigation party, but they had been *with* them. But now they were apart. They were policemen. Galvanized by that *cri-de-coeur* the colonel whirled about and spread his arms wide like a man trying to stop a rush.

"Back!" he roared. "Back on to the road outside—this is police work now!"

Superintendent Blackler stepped forward quickly and spoke to him in a low voice. Mr. Smith and Detective-Sergeant Poynter were already under the dead tree with its bare black branches overlaid with thin lines of snow, satisfying themselves that the thing that hung from the lowest and thickest branch was indeed beyond all human aid. The thin sandy hair was dry, the neat grey suit was dry, but the gumboots were still wet from the snow.

"Dead some time," muttered the inspector, and Poynter agreed with him. "Been here from the time it stopped snowing. . . . Mr. Cushing!"

"Yes?" said Gregory, a little breathlessly.

"You've told us several times you knew Mr. Mason."

"That's Mason."

"I can confirm that, Inspector," said Miss Forbes over the heads of the throng. "That was Mr. Mason."

Colonel Gormsby raised his voice again. "Listen, please. The police have now taken charge. With the exception of the following persons, everybody must go back on to the public road. Preferably you will all go back to your homes, but definitely you must leave these premises. The following persons will please remain here: Mr. Maltravers, Mr. Croxley, Mr. Mayhew, Mr. Cushing, Miss Forbes. . . ." He hesitated, and added in a softer tone: "It is not a request in your case, ma'am. . . ."

"Thank you, Colonel, but I think I'll stay."

"Very well, ma'am. The rest of you will go at once. And please avoid marring or obliterating these tracks. . . . Gad!" he groaned aside to the superintendent, "this'll bring all Winchingham out here!"

"I'll take them out," said the superintendent quietly. "I'll go with them. There's a telephone in that house, I noticed the wires as we came through. If it's still working I'll get hold of Dr. Scott. And I'll get some men out here. . . . Oh, Smithy!"

"Yes, Super?"

"Have you had a look in the pockets yet? Any keys on him?"

It was Poynter who felt gingerly in the pockets of that still well-pressed grey suit, and the sight of him fumbling with the dangling corpse seemed to cause the crowd to retreat more hastily than the chief constable's commands had.

"Bunch of keys in left trouser pocket," announced Poynter dispassionately, fishing delicately. "Loose change in right. Fountain-pen and pencil in upper left waistcoat pocket, gold cigarette-case in lower left, ditto lighter in lower right. Handkerchief in outside breast pocket—nothing in side pockets—wallet in inside breast. . . ."

"Give me the keys," said the superintendent.

Poynter handed them to him, and he went off quickly after the retreating crowd. The five civilians left behind gathered in an unhappy and mystified little group, and turned their backs on the tree and the strange fruit it bore. The colonel joined Mr. Smith and Poynter, gazed long and earnestly at the dead man, turned his attention to the trunk of the tree, and stared at the body again.

"What," he demanded almost petulantly, "what's his head turned like that for? What was he *lookin'* at?"

"He wasn't looking at anything," replied the inspector tonelessly. "Not then—not when that happened. . . ."

On the trunk of the tree, some two feet, six inches from the ground, was a large round excrescence: it looked for all the world as though the tree had started to grow a low stout branch just there, and had then decided against it. This excrescence was of such size and shape as to afford an easy foothold for any fairly agile man; and in the snow that had collected on the top side of it were impressions showing where a foot had rested flat on it, and the toe of the other had been wedged in behind. Between the spot where the body hung by a short piece of rope, and the join of the branch with the parent trunk, was a place where the snow had been dislodged.

"Well, Inspector?" said the colonel gruffly—though he knew one of the answers himself now.

"Well, sir," returned Mr. Smith deliberately, "it's rotten. It's incredible. It—it's *mad.* The marks in the snow tell us the story almost as plainly as words. Some time last night, after the snow had stopped, Mason left his house and came out here. He made straight for this tree, and he stood here close up against the trunk. He stood here a second—a minute—an hour—who can say? Then he hopped up on to this foothold, this wart thing in the trunk, and he tied—or started to tie—that bit of rope round the branch just here where you see the snow has been disturbed. But he saw that wasn't far enough out, so he moved the rope along to where it is now, tied it there, drew the noose tight round his neck—and stepped off . . .

"That was a rotten and a tragic business, and perhaps there was a little madness in the man's mind—for he must have been very cold-blooded about it, very determined. But it's not *incredible.* It's not even unusual. But as for the rest of it—"

Mr. Smith broke off and drew a long breath. When he went on again there was a hint of desperation in his voice.

"This is the story those other tracks have to tell us, a story that must be plain to us all. And this is a detective-inspector speaking, not a superstitious old woman, not a religious fanatic, not a half-mad holy hermit. . . .

"Some time last night, again after the snow had finished, some Thing came to earth at the foot of The Rise. It touched down there—like a bird from flight. But it was no bird. It had hooves, and it walked upright on two legs in a fashion unlike any creature known to man. And what is the most bizarre touch of all to me, it had *shoes* on its hooves—like horseshoes. It walked up The Rise, entering various private gardens on the way and, for some in-conceivable reason, approaching and turning away from the front doors of those people's houses. It stood with both feet, both hooves, on a flimsy privet hedge—and the hedge didn't give way beneath its weight. Yet there *was* weight, otherwise there would have been no impressions in the snow for us to read. It apparently walked clean through solid matter, rising up on the empty air until it gained the narrow top of a six-foot wall. It stepped, or jumped, down to a lower adjoining wall on which there is a central iron railing with dangerous spikes on it. It walked through solid matter once again—Mrs. Pendlebury's summerhouse—and so down to the foot of the hill, approaching and turning away from the Steeple Inn, and so on to here. Before coming out here—presumably before coming out here—it walked round and round Mason's house. It also walked round and round in a circle on a roof that is too steep to afford a footing for anything other than an insect, or perhaps a bird; gaining it apparently *like* a bird, by flight through the air, and leaving it the same way.

"And then—then it either accompanied Mason out here, and stood on and watched while the man hanged himself; or else it followed him later, came upon his dead body, stood under it, almost touching it, where those two last hoof-prints are, side by side. And there—it vanished . . . took *off* again into thin air. . . ."

The side door to Mason's house was unlocked, so Super-intendent Blackler had no occasion to try any of the keys taken from the dead man's pocket. And there was something above it that he hadn't noticed before: it was a horseshoe, and it had been nailed up there presumably to bring good luck, or to ward off evil—in which case it would seem that it had lost its efficacy. The superintendent opened the door and stepped through into a short passage that led to the hall. Immediately, on either hand, were two more doors; and opening the one on his right he saw that he was looking into a room that was obviously used as a study-cum-office. He also saw that which he was seeking, a telephone, which stood on a big desk by the window. He pounced on the instrument and called up the Winchingham Police Station.

Outside, the crowd which had so far behaved with surprising docility, was growing a little refractory. People prowled round the house peeping in at windows; other people hunted about at the back looking for a ladder long enough to reach the roof, and failing to find one; while others trampled all over the lawn and garden beds, gazed up at the ring of prints on the roof and advanced wildly impossible theories . . .

Superintendent Blackler put down the telephone, came out of the study and opened the door opposite. In the middle of this room was a long table with white lines on it, and beyond that, against the far wall, a long bar with half a dozen tall red-topped stools. This, it seemed, was a games room where the late Mr. Mason and his guests would first work up a thirst by a few games of table-tennis, and then proceed to slake the thirst. The room was quite tidy, but, like the study—like the whole house, in fact—was dusty and smelt stale.

Crossing to a door in the right-hand wall the superintendent opened it and found himself in the hall, where his eye was im-mediately caught by a peculiar pattern of light on the carpet. It came from the fanlight over the front door, an arch of coloured glass that in any place would have been an eyesore, but in a small private house was a monstrosity. It consisted of three fans of honey-coloured glass. The central and largest fan bore a castel-lated shield, the top fifth of it blue and the rest white, with a large red cross on the white ground. Surmounting the shield was a blue scroll decorated with alternate red and white rosettes. Similar scrolls adorned the panes of glass on either side.

The superintendent, noting this with impassive countenance, also noted that the stout door beneath was locked with the key on the inside. There was a cubbyhole in the hall, a place for the hanging of coats and hats and the washing of hands. But the old overcoat hanging in there, and the old tweed ribbonless hat were hardly those that the dapper Mr. Mason would have worn in the city; so the superintendent went stolidly on his way looking for the coat and hat that the dead man must have been wearing on his arrival.

He found them upstairs in one of the bedrooms, presumably Mason's own. The black hat had been tossed carelessly on to the bed, the grey overcoat lay on a chair directly under the window, with a travelling bag on the floor beside it. The bed had obviously not been slept in, the room tidy and undisturbed. Mason had not even started to unpack his bag.

The superintendent stroked his chin thoughtfully and went still higher. He discovered a small box room at one end of the landing, wherein a step-ladder stood open beneath a manhole in the ceiling. Mounting the steps he pushed up the little square door and poked his head through. Here, immediately under the roof, cobweb-festooned rafters stood out like the ribs of a skeleton, and it was very dark. But it was not a total darkness: a little way to his left, and some three yards down from the apex of the roof, there was a rectangular patch of pale light. There was a skylight there, and through its canopy of snow the daylight filtered in dimly. The superintendent stared at the skylight, stared at the rough bricks of a chimney some little distance from it, remembered the shape of the house and the route he had taken through it, and then cal-culated—correctly, as it turned out—that the skylight must be almost in the exact centre of the ring of hoof-marks on the roof. Stroking his jaw even more thoughtfully he descended the step-ladder and went back to Mason's bedroom.

Pondering a new problem, a little problem that had to do with Mason's bodily comfort while he had been in the house last night, he drifted to the window and gazed absently out over the side of the garden and the trail of prints that led out to the fateful tree. And then, suddenly, his eyes widened and fixed and focused themselves on the window-sill.

The window was closed and securely fastened on the inside, but on the outside, on that narrow snow-covered ledge, were two marks side by side—impressions
showing that some Thing that had stood there some time or an-other during the night or early morning—stood there and looked in. . . .

11

Police reinforcements had arrived, hustled the crowd off the premises and picketed the gates. Honest George Borwell had gone back to his inn and opened up and was doing a roaring trade. Dr. Scott, the police medical officer, had arrived just after the police, viewed the body, tersely pronounced it dead as frozen mutton and departed with it to perform an autopsy. And Colonel Gormsby, Detective-Inspector Smith and Detective-Sergeant Poynter had joined the superintendent in the house, leaving Miss Forbes, Gregory Cushing, Maltravers, Croxley and Mayhew to cool their heels outside.

"Why," grumbled Croxley, thinking of potential missed chances with his camera, "wouldn't they let us go in with them?"

"In case we mess up any clues, I suppose," said Gregory.

"What clues?"

"You tell me, and we'll both know."

Inside, in the hall, Superintendent Blackler said to the chief constable in his heavy, unemotional manner: "Nothing down here, sir. But there's something upstairs I'd like you to see."

He led the way up the stairs and into the dead man's bedroom, and showed them the hoof-marks on the window-sill. The colonel reacted satisfactorily, but Mr. Smith didn't make any comment. He looked curiously at the prints and he examined the window-frame carefully. Then he said simply: "Why?"

"Why what?" asked Colonel Gormsby.

"Why didn't it come in?"

"Why didn't it come in by either of those doors downstairs?"

The inspector smiled at that. "I think you'll find Miss Forbes has an answer to that. It's one we've heard before, by the way. But this window—I suppose you've noticed it's almost immediately above the door we came in by, Super?"

"Well, yes, but what about it?"

"Well, the Thing couldn't get in down there, so it hopped up here. But what stopped it here?"

The superintendent smiled faintly in his turn. "Your Miss Forbes might suggest that it wasn't stopped, but that it came right on in."

"I see. And took Mason away and made him hang himself on a tree. Yes, I wouldn't put it past her. But in that case, what about the prints on the roof? Why bother about the roof?"

"There's a skylight—" began the superintendent.

"Ha!" exclaimed the chief constable. "The devil there is! So I was right."

"In a way, yes, sir. Come along and I'll show you."

He took them out of the bedroom and into the little boxroom. "I didn't find that open," he told them, pointing to the manhole in the ceiling. "I pushed it open and left it like that. Careful when you get up there, sir; there are marks in the dust."

The colonel stared at him. "Here! Not—?"

"Oh, no. Normal human footprints this time. Mason's own, I take it."

Superintendent Blackler had procured a flashlight from somewhere. Armed with it, Colonel Gormsby mounted the step-ladder and scrambled through the little square aperture above. Mr. Smith followed him, and the superintendent followed Mr. Smith. Poynter, who had stayed behind for a moment to photograph the marks on the window-sill, came in and stood on the steps and peered through.

Floor-boards had been laid over some of the joists, so that walking was easy. The skylight was a little way to their left; that is, towards the front of the house. It was far enough up the slope of the roof to be above the heads of the three men, but low enough to admit of the chief constable, the shortest of the three, manipulating it quite easily. Foot-prints in the dust on the floor-boards showed that someone had been up there quite recently, had walked along to a point immediately beneath the skylight, and had gone down again. Below the skylight the dust had been scuffed up and the footprints had merged into each other, and just beside these marks was a long pole.

"Used for openin' the skylight," surmised the chief constable, flashing the torch this way and that. "Or for proppin' it open. Think Mason made these marks, Inspector?"

"I don't see who else it could have been, sir. The place, so Miss Forbes tells us—and she's the Intelligence Section in these parts—has been empty for months. The state of the house bears that out. It's more or less neat and tidy, it's undisturbed, but it's dusty. Mason came down here surreptitiously, arriving some time before the snow began to fall. He came up to his bedroom and left his things there. Then he came up here—"

"Why?"

"I don't know, sir. To open the skylight? Hardly, in that weather. To close the skylight, or to bolt it? Hardly again; it isn't very likely that he'd go away for months at a time and leave it opened or unfastened. To get something? Heaven knows. There's just one other answer."

"And what's that?"

"Well . . . you know what's up above us, sir?"

"Hey? . . . Oh, y'mean that ring of hoof-prints?"

"Yes, sir. This skylight must be somewhere about the centre of that ring. So the only other answer I can think of on the spur of the moment is that Mason came up here because he knew there was something on the roof—something walking about trying to get in."

"Looking for the skylight," added the superintendent. "You wouldn't see it beneath its covering of snow."

"And you wouldn't be able to open it without disturbing that covering. But the snow hasn't been disturbed. So obviously nothing has been in or out through this skylight since it started to snow . . . or has it?"

"Stop it!" snapped Colonel Gormsby. "We're headin' straight for the devil-talk again. Look, Mason came here to this house before the snow. He went out again hours later—after the snowfall. He didn't go to bed. What the blazes did he *do?*"

"No blazes, sir," said the superintendent easily. "No fire has been lit anywhere. So he can't have spent his time in destroying papers or documents or anything like that—not by fire, anyway. And if he left anything in the nature of a farewell note, I haven't come across it yet. Incidentally, though he must have been here for some hours, he doesn't appear to have given himself any heat. There are electric radiators downstairs, and of course he might have been down there, but there isn't one in his bedroom. So if he passed the time in there he must have sat about in his coat and hat."

"Ho!" said Mr. Smith quietly.

"Hey?"

"Yes, sir. The point had occurred to me also. It's not the usual thing for a man in his own house to take his overcoat and hat up to his bedroom with him. The usual thing is to leave them in the hall. But the answer is probably that Mason never took them off at all—not until he set out on that last grim walk of his. He kept them on for warmth. But *then* he wouldn't need them any more; they'd only get in his way. Let's go back to the bedroom—there might be something there. . . ."

Back in the bedroom the inspector opened the travelling bag, while Superintendent Blackler picked the hat up off the bed.

"Well, it's his own hat all right. Got his name stamped on the sweat band."

"Pyjamas, dressing-gown, slippers and toilet-kit," murmured the inspector, digging in the bag. "Monogrammed M.M. M'm. . . . Why bring these things if you don't intend to wear them?"

"The answer would appear to be," suggested the superintendent, "that he *did* intend to wear them."

"Maybe—maybe. But the bed hasn't been touched, and it didn't stop snowing until some time after one o'clock this morning. So he was up pretty late for a man on his own."

"He may have been busy."

"Yes—but doing what? He hasn't left any traces. . . . No papers in the bag, nothing that would give us a lead as to why he should have taken his own life." He snapped shut the bag and stood up. He picked up the grey overcoat from off the chair under the window. "Name on the tag in marking ink. Pair of gloves in the pockets—hullo, what's this?"

There was something under the glove in the right-hand pocket, something that felt like a necklace. He pulled it out and let it dangle from his fingers. It was a cheap rosary, with a little plain black wooden cross. He stared at it with a frown on his face.

"It's a rosary," said the chief constable, faintly sarcastic. "The man might have been a Roman Catholic. Nothin' very strange about it. Catholics often carry rosaries about with them."

"Um," said Mr. Smith, vaguely and unsatisfactorily. "I don't know. . . ." He dropped the coat back on to the chair, and his clouded eyes travelled from it to the hoof-prints in the snow on the sill the other side of the window-pane. "I don't know. . . . I think, sir, we're going to have a burst of what you call devil-talk.—Bill!"

"Yes, Inspector?"

"Pop down and ask Miss Forbes and Mr. Cushing to come up here."

"What d'ye want them for?" demanded the colonel, as Poynter went out of the room.

Inspector Smith said deliberately: "Those two, sir—and possibly old Jake Popplewell—are the only people in Winchingham who knew anything at all about the late Montague Mason. Cushing might be able to throw some light on this"—holding up the rosary—"while Miss Forbes, I fancy, has a theory. I'd like you to hear the theory, because it will probably be put forward by a lot of people all over the country, and it will probably cause us a deal of embarrassment, if not actual trouble. You see, I'm damned if *I* can see, at the moment, just how we are going to disprove it."

12

When Poynter came back with Miss Forbes and Gregory Cushing, the inspector took the two of them over to the window and showed them the hoof-prints. Miss Forbes's eyes brightened behind the shell-rimmed spectacles, but dimmed almost immediately and then she looked frankly puzzled.

"My reaction also," murmured the inspector, watching her quizzically. "Why didn't it come in? The fact that the window was fastened on the inside wouldn't have stopped it—would it?"

"No," said Miss Forbes clearly. "Nor the fact that those two doors downstairs were locked on the inside. I can tell you what stopped it down there. But this window—"

"Let it go for the moment. . . . Mr. Cushing?"

"Huh?"

"Would you have called Mason a religious man?"

Gregory's lip curled. "Like hell! That's the last thing I'd have called him, or anyone else who knew anything of him. Of course, there *are* whited sepulchres. . . ."

"Any idea what his religion was? By the sound of it he didn't practise any, but just about all of us are born into some sort of religion and baptised in some church or other."

"Not the faintest idea." Gregory shook his head firmly. "Why?"

"Because he was carrying this about with him." Mr. Smith held out the rosary. "It was in his overcoat pocket, there."

"In his pocket?" asked Miss Forbes quickly.

"Yes."

"And is that where you found the coat, on that chair just there?"

"Yes."

"Oh!"

Gregory was still eyeing the rosary. "You know, inspector, that doesn't look like Mason."

"I know. I know what you mean. If Mason had been a Catholic, even the most careless and loose living, and if he had got into the habit of carrying a rosary about with him, it wouldn't have been a simple, cheap little thing like this. It would have been a much more flamboyant article."

"I think so. He was a flamboyant type. Nothing but the best and most expensive for our Mr. Mason."

"M'm, yes, this hat and coat and bag seem to indicate that. And the things in this house. . . . By the way, Miss Forbes, we've been up under the roof. There *is* a skylight. But you wouldn't see it from the outside for the snow, you'd only know it was there by looking up at it from inside."

"Oh?" said Miss Forbes again.

Mr. Smith nodded. The superintendent silently brought a chair from the other side of the bed and poked it gently behind the lady's knees. Miss Forbes sat down thankfully. Gregory, who had had no breakfast, was beginning to feel leg-weary himself, and he sat down on the end of the bed.

"There's also dust up there," went on the inspector. "The dust of years. And in the dust are footprints. Marks, presumably, of Mason's own feet. It would seem that some time last night he must have gone up *to* the skylight. But we don't know why or what for. He didn't go to bed. He didn't light any fire or switch on any heater—not in this room as far as we can see. He must have sat in the freezing cold all that time, perhaps up here, for the superintendent tells us that nothing has been disturbed downstairs. Nothing has been what you might call disturbed up here, for that matter. . . . Of course we haven't really started to investigate yet; but—well, that's one side of this tragedy. There seems to be another."

He moved over to the bed and sat down beside Gregory and stuck his hands in his pockets in a characteristic action. "Shoot," he invited softly." Let's hear it. Let's hear the worst before all the spiritualists and psychical researchers in the country get at us."

Miss Forbes said, staring at him seriously: "You know, inspector, even I am beginning to feel a little uncomfortable over this business—and I think other people are going to be frightened. They're going to think along the lines that Mr. Mayhew is already."

"And what is he thinking?"

"That the Devil came last night—or sent one of his emissaries—for the soul of Montague Mason."

Colonel Gormsby was something more than scornful. "What? In these enlightened times—?"

"Are they so enlightened, Colonel? Doesn't all our scientific research seem to be leading to the conclusion that we really know and understand nothing? We dig down to the heart of matter, and find that it eludes us. We practise psycho-analysis, delving into the mysteries of mind, and find that it recoils upon ourselves—we can, as Joad has pointed out, push the views of the psycho-analysts to their *reductio ad absurdum.* And quite a surprising number of people still believe in the Devil. . . . I should like to point out to you, Inspector, once again, that it is not the *thing* that is significant, but what we *think* of the thing, consciously or subconsciously. In fact, subconscious thought—if I may be permitted the contradictory expression—*is* the thing. . . . Now, no matter what may be in your individual minds, it must be accepted that something very unusual, something unknown to man or to material existence, was abroad last night. And I, personally, don't think this Thing followed Mason—I think it *accompanied* him."

"Accompanied." Mr. Smith repeated the word gravely. "Uh-huh. Some Thing with hooves. Some Thing that wandered round and round this house, stood on that window-sill, walked about on the roof. Yes. But why? Why all this preliminary and seemingly unnecessary prowling about?"

"Looking for a place to get in by. To get *at* Mason."

"Why didn't it just walk in? There are a couple of doors down-stairs, and, according to your theory, a little thing like a locked door wouldn't have stopped it."

"Have you looked at those doors, Inspector? Really looked at them?"

"Go on," said Mr. Smith quietly. "I have an idea of what's in your mind, and I want the chief constable to hear the worst."

"Well," said Miss Forbes solemnly, "what else *can* we think, after what we've found, but that some Thing came looking for Mr. Mason? It found him here, in this house, perhaps in this room. It came up to the house, to the front door. But it couldn't get in by the front door; not because it was locked, but because there is something on the fanlight above it that bars the way to evil. That cross on the shield! No evil spirit, no elemental, can withstand the Cross. . . . Before you dub me a superstitious old woman let me remind you yet once again that evil and good, the pull of the Devil and the power of the Cross, exist only in mind—that mind that is common to man and which is strange, uncharted, mysterious territory. Mind creates that which it believes to be real. We, as individuals, are, as Emerson says, but inlets into that universal mind. . . .

"Barred, therefore, by the Cross over the front door, the Thing went round the house looking for another entry. It found the side door—"

Miss Forbes hesitated, and the inspector began to grin.

"And nailed up above the side door is a horseshoe. Is that what stopped it there?"

"I admit, Inspector, I'm not sure of my ground here. The horseshoe motif is rather in evidence, isn't it? The Devil is generally pictured—or, rather, used to be pictured—as having cloven hooves in addition to other picturesque attributes. But this Thing appears to have had whole hooves, and to have been shod."

Mr. Smith nodded confidently. "Wait till you see some of Sergeant Poynter's enlargements. I'll be able to show you the little indentations made by the sunken nail-heads—that is, the little holes into which the nails are driven."

"Where did you spot that?" asked Superintendent Blackler quickly.

"Oddly enough at this end of the trail. In that gap in the laurel hedge—the snow isn't quite so thick along there. All the way along, of course, the snow had clogged in the concavity of the hoof and the grooves or holes for the nails; clogged and fallen off again, clogged and fallen off. But just by that gap in the hedge are two or three perfect prints—I hope you've got those, Bill?"

"I've got them, Inspector."

"Good." Mr. Smith turned back to Miss Forbes. "But reverting to the horseshoe above the door—?"

Miss Forbes clasped her hands together thoughtfully. "I don't know what else to think but that that horseshoe, the symbol of good luck—which means, of course, spiritual welfare—also barred the way to this Thing. But if I put that forward as a theory, I must give some reasons for it.

"A little while ago I said that what we were following was an idea. Now ideas operate; things don't. Ideas are the realities; things are merely shadows. It seems to depend on the intrinsic vitality of an idea as to what sort of shadow it will cast, or whether it will—project a shadow, shall I say? Some shadows are transitory, others are permanent. Permanent, that is, by comparison with our own short existences. As an example of permanency take the rope with which Mason hanged himself. He didn't really kill himself with a rope, he killed himself with an idea—

"Wait! Let me explain. And remember it is not I who am dogmatizing thus, but your own materialistic, sceptical scientists. A rope is a piece of matter. The scientists have taken matter and reduced it to the atom, to the electron—and there they have lost it. They have got to the root of matter, and found it has no root. Out of nothingness—material nothingness—has everything been made that exists materially. Mason took a piece of nothingness and hanged himself with it. But Mason also was a piece of nothingness. So—he killed himself with an idea. One idea reacted on another.

"Now, as an example of a transitory thing or shadow, take the stigmata—you know what the stigmata is?"

The inspector nodded. "The marks of the nails that held Christ to the cross appearing on the hands and feet of some devout believer, generally young and generally a woman."

"That is so. There have been innumerable authenticated instances. An example of the projection of a shadow, or the materialization of an idea, consciously or subconsciously held, in certain favourable circumstances. *Just as in other certain favourable circumstances the belief in the efficacy of a cast-away horseshoe as a charm to ward off evil may also find actual material expression.* For, as the burnt child fears the fire, so the Devil dreads a horseshoe."

"But why?" asked the inspector, sitting up suddenly. "Gadzooks! Granting you all the rest of it, I can't see any possible connection—"

"Have you never heard of St. Nicholas?"

"Oh, yes. Our Santa Claus, or Father Christmas."

"Yes, yes, but the legend? Or, rather, one of the many legends associated with St. Nicholas. Don't you know that he once caught the Devil? By the strength of his own holiness—and, it is to be admitted, by judicious use of some holy water—he caught and held the Devil. And he stamped him with the seal of mastery. Of mastery of good over evil—the symbol of the taming of the wild. *He put shoes on the Devil's hooves!"*

"Good gad!" said Colonel Gormsby feebly. "I've heard some far-fetched stuff in my time—"

"It's all far-fetched," replied Miss Forbes calmly. "As Pilate asked, What is Truth? What is Reality? But reality and fantasy are only the inverse and obverse sides of a medal. . . . You wanted to know, from me, what prevented this Thing from entering by that side door. I have given you the only answer I can think of."

"All right," said the inspector pacifically. "What next?"

"Well, foiled thus from gaining access to the house down below, what did this Thing do?"

"It hopped up on that window-sill."

"That is as good a way of putting it as any. But here again it was foiled. What foiled it this time?"

"The Cross again," sighed Mr. Smith, and held up the rosary. "This."

"Precisely. It was, you tell me, in the pocket of that overcoat lying on the chair there. Immediately inside and underneath the window. Very small; but a symbol has no size, it is above dimension. Invisible to mortal eyes where it was, but still *there,* radiating its influence. And again the Thing was unable to pass by."

"Excelsior!" said Mr. Smith. "Onwards and upwards. It went higher. Hence the roof. Then what, Miss Forbes?"

"Then I don't know. Who does?" She added slowly: "You tell me Mason went up there somewhere under the roof, but you don't know why. Are we allowed to guess? Was it in a futile endeavour to bar the way? Or was it to answer a summons?"

"If," put in Superintendent Blackler, "if you mean to imply that the Thing gained access to the house by means of the skylight, I must tell you that it is patently obvious that the skylight has not been opened. But it *may* have been open when Mason arrived here, and he *may* have gone up at any time while he was here to close it, or to bolt it if it was already closed."

"My dear man," retorted Miss Forbes, "it wouldn't have to be either unbolted or opened. It wasn't the wood or the glass that prevented the Thing from entering—we already have evidence that it could pass through matter—but what was on or in or behind the wood and glass!"

And after that there was a long silence.

Gregory Cushing broke it by muttering something to himself.

"What was that?" asked the chief constable.

"Balaam's ass," repeated Gregory in a bemused tone of voice.

"What?" demanded Mr. Smith, who was sitting right beside him.

Gregory grinned. "I was thinking of something uncle Jake said, I don't quite know why. He was talking about Balaam's ass and saying how it could discern danger where no danger was visible to Balaam. Only, of course, this was no ass. Boomer is a genius to uncle Jake, but even Boomer couldn't two-step on window-sills and waltz over roofs."

Mr. Smith pushed his fingers through his hair. "You know, I was thinking of a Biblical incident too. But something quite different. I was thinking of Judas Iscariot. He fell into the hands of the Devil, and he went away and hanged himself on a tree. Now it's beginning to look as if Mason fell into the hands of the Devil—he also went away and hanged himself on a tree. . . ."

13

"Tree!" ejaculated Gregory, and gave a start that shook the bed. "Good Lord! That tree—!"

"Hullo!" said the inspector. "We're off on a new track."

"I don't know," said Gregory thoughtfully. "Miss Forbes might say it was part of the same pattern. Why did Mason trudge away out to that lone tree when he could have hanged himself quite easily anywhere in here?"

"Final flamboyant gesture in a flamboyant life," suggested the inspector.

"Possibly—but . . ." Gregory looked round the circle of faces. "Has anybody here ever heard of a Blue Woman?"

"Heard of a what?"

"A Blue Woman. No? You, Miss Forbes?"

Miss Forbes shook her grey head. "I've heard of Green Men and Women in White, but a Blue Woman—this sounds interesting, Mr. Cushing."

"Shoot," said Mr. Smith with resignation. "We might as well have all there is to have."

"Well . . . I only bring it up because it might have some bearing on this damned incredible business—it fits in with all the other devil-talk I've heard this morning. My uncle Jake seems to be haunted by a private ghost. No one else has seen this ghost, as far as I can find out, but two other people as well as myself can testify that uncle Jake sees a Blue Woman—which causes him great distress. The odd part about it is that the old man is only plagued by the Blue Woman when he's drunk: when he's sober he doesn't seem to have any knowledge of her, or any faintest recollection of having seen her; he doesn't seem to know what you're talking about.

"Now these two other witnesses are that innkeeper along there—Honest George Borwell," said Gregory sarcastically, "and Jim Silver, a farmer who lives farther along this way, and from whom I got the story. The last time uncle Jake saw the Blue Woman was only yesterday afternoon. He'd been hitting the booze again in the Steeple Inn, and I had to go after him. That was just before dark. I found him lying on the floor in the bar, dead to the world, out cold. He had actually gone out to go home, and found the donkey and cart gone, and had rushed in again screaming that the Blue Woman was after him. Then he passed out—either the Blue Woman, or the booze, or both, had been too much for him this time.

"Well, he won't tell me anything. As I say, when sober he has no recollection of any Blue Woman. But this is the story as told to me by Jim Silver.

"A long time ago all this land round here used to belong to what Silver called a titled gent, Lord Somebody-or-Other. It appears that Lord Somebody was a great autocrat and allergic to poachers. One night a woman was caught poaching on his preserves. Name, age and description of woman unknown, but referred to now simply as the Blue Woman. Maybe, as Silver suggests, she habitually wore blue. Lord Somebody was so peeved about it that he decided to make an example of the woman, and without waiting for the Law to step in and do it for him, he had her hanged there and then on that solitary oak tree. Now, according to Jim Silver, her ghost walks Steeple Thelming on certain nights; and as far as I can make out these nights seem to coincide with the nights on which uncle Jake gets plastered. This woman, by the way, was supposed to have been a witch; and hanging a witch on that tree doesn't seem to have done it any good. For I am told that the tree was hale and hearty then and full of life, but from the moment she was strung up there it began to die.

"Now," said Gregory, standing up, "I know this is a most unlikely story, particularly that part about the hanging, but the point is that uncle Jake definitely does see a Blue Woman, and it scares him senseless. And—well, something did kill the tree. . . ."

"Old age," murmured Mr. Smith. "M'm . . . I sense a faint suggestion of revenge in the story. The ghost of the murdered woman revenges itself on the present owner of what is left of the original estate. But I don't see—there's no suggestion, is there, that the Blue Woman has hooves instead of the conventional human feet?"

"Good Lord, no! . . . At least I don't think so. . . . Matter of fact, now you come to mention it, I don't know anything about her, except her colour—she might have anything."

"Dear me!" cooed Miss Forbes, and clapped her hands together softly. "But this is most interesting—*most* interesting. Don't you see? This might be a partial explanation. *'Blue meagre hag, stubborn unlaid ghost.'* . . ."

They stared at her.

"A quotation," she said brightly to Gregory. "Milton, if I am not mistaken; you'll find it in your uncle's copy. Dear me!" she repeated. "But this is fascinating. Don't you see, Inspector? Mr. Cushing has given us a possible explanation. The stubborn unlaid ghost is that of a woman reputed to have been a witch. Now witches are in league with the powers of darkness, and it would be perfectly possible for one who was adept to change her feet to hooves if she wished to do so for some particular purpose—

"Don't jump down my throat, Colonel! You *must* remember that that which seems so solid and real to you, so *natural,* is illusion. The world is ideal. Substance, material things, are the shadows of ideas, the projections of ideas into the physical plane. But *all* ideas exist in their own right on the psychic plane. Shakespeare knew that; that's why he said there were more things in heaven and earth than were dreamt of in Horatio's philosophy.

"Now a ghost is the physical shadow of a psychic reality, and under certain favourable circumstances can be seen as a physical thing. That is when it *becomes* a ghost. Certain favourable circumstances can include a state of intoxication—the man who 'sees things' while suffering from *delirium tremens* is actually giving psychic realities a temporary physical existence. . . . I have to use that word 'reality,' because I have no other to convey my meaning to you; but a psychic reality must not be confused with a psychic truth.

"Well then, here we have in existence what I can only call a state of mind. That is, a revenge idea existing on the psychic plane for a wrong done on the physical plane. That is perhaps the origin of the ghost and why the ghost walks. In certain circumstances, and perhaps because he is the only one who, by reason of his intemperance, is placed in these certain favourable circumstances, in a state of receptivity, Popplewell sees the Blue Woman. But I take it that she has been seen by others, since this Mr. Silver knows the story.

"There are two ways of putting what I have to say next. The first is to say that the Blue Woman's opportunity for wreaking revenge arrived last night, and that she hanged Mason, or caused him to hang himself, on the very tree on which she herself had been hanged—which conclusion will cause the chief constable to snort with tremendous indignation and scepticism; and the other way of putting it is to say that psychic influences so preyed upon Mason's mind that they reduced him to that state of melancholia in which the subject not only contemplates but commits the act of suicide—which conclusion may be more acceptable to the chief constable in that the imagery is more familiar to him. But both can mean the same thing. Psychic influences cause mental depression. They must do, when the subject is in normal health and there is no physical cause—by which I mean there are no material worries. There do not appear to have been any in Mason's case."

"Well, of course," said Mr. Smith, "that is just what we don't know yet. He may have been on the verge of a colossal bust-up. But, gadzooks, that's a crackerjack of a theory! That ought to be filmed! What a picture! The Blue Woman stalking her victim through the snow, marching round and round the beleaguered house, like Joshua round Jericho, looking for a breach in its defences, being foiled by charms and symbols, finding at last the weak spot on the roof; the mad rush up from inside of the trapped victim, the futile frantic attempts to bar the way—"

"You think I'm talking nonsense?"

"We-ell . . ." The inspector thrust his fingers through his thick dark hair and smiled disarmingly. "Well, you talk nonsense more plausibly than anybody I've ever met. You make it sound so feasible. But you leave a few gaps. For instance, considering this Blue Woman theory of yours, why was it necessary for her to walk all over The Rise and round about before coming here? Why not just —er—materialize here? It's for all the world as if she didn't know where Mason lived and had to go from house to house looking for him—which doesn't square with the theory."

"But, my dear Inspector, the answer is simple. She walked because she *does* walk. All the land round about here was, I expect, part of the original estate. The houses on The Rise might not have existed in her day. The Blue Woman haunts her earthly environment. For all we know she might do the same pilgrimage every time she walks."

"M'm . . . but until last night she never left a trace. And when she does leave traces—they're the marks of hooves!"

"Last night," said Miss Forbes sharply, "there was something to take and hold her traces. There was snow! Ghosts leave traces. Good gracious, of course they do! Have you never heard of Borley Rectory? The Blue Woman would leave traces of her passing when there was a medium to *hold* the traces. As for them being the impressions of hooves I have already suggested a possible explanation."

"We've had snow before," objected Mr. Smith mildly. "No hoof-prints."

"The two phenomena may not have coincided. But last night they did. The Blue Woman walked, and there was snow on the ground—Good heavens!" Miss Forbes jumped to her feet in a state of great excitement.

Mr. Smith was off the bed in a split second. "What's the matter? What's wrong?"

"*You're* wrong!" she cried, throwing out a hand at him. "We have had snow before, and there *have* been strange and inexplicable hoof-marks in the snow. *This has happened before!*"

"Oh? When?"

"I can produce irrefutable proof!"

"*What?*" It was the chief constable who exploded. All this time, while fairly seething with scepticism and impatience, he had held himself in with truly remarkable restraint. But that word "proof" had been the touchstone.

"Yes," said Miss Forbes, holding her hand to her head. "But not here, not now. I must get my scrap-book first. Colonel, can I see you again, all of you, say in your office?"

Colonel Gormsby fingered his neat little moustache and hesitated. "We-ell . . ."

"Oh, I realize you will be busy today. Postmortems, inquests and things," said Miss Forbes vaguely. "But tomorrow. Tomorrow morning."

"Humph! Well, all right, ma'am. Tomorrow morning in the superintendent's office at the police station, if you wish it."

*   *   *

Miss Forbes and Gregory Cushing pushed their way through a curious and baffled crowd back to the cross-roads. Croxley, Mayhew and Maltravers had gone on ahead of them, Croxley in a fret to get another roll of film and continue his photographing while conditions still permitted. The conditions at any time had not been of the best, for the sky was heavily overcast again and a further fall of snow seemed imminent. And the long clear trail of hoof-marks was now patchy, broken, smudged and entirely obliterated in places by the eager, hurrying feet of wondering and excited Winchinghamites.

The police had descended in force on the house and had begun a systematic investigation. Colonel Gormsby, Detective-Inspector Smith and Detective-Sergeant Poynter were up under the roof once more, about to open the skylight for a closer view of the prints on the roof. Down below in the study Superintendent Blackler was on the telephone to London and in earnest conversation with an inspector of the Metropolitan Police.

Miss Forbes, with her eye on the sky, expressed the opinion that more snow was due in the very near future.

"Yes," agreed Gregory limply. "Looks like it. . . . You know, I feel—wrung out."

"I know," said Miss Forbes sympathetically. "It's the reaction. This is the most amazing thing that has ever happened in Winchingham."

"Or anywhere else, I should say. It's a trite thing to say, but I came down here to try and forget. I came for peace and quiet. And what do I find? I find," he said gloomily, "an uncle whom I had previously considered merely a fairly harmless sort of recluse to be an eccentric and a drunkard; and not only that, but to be beset by a private ghost that scares hell out of him. And then I get myself tangled up in *this!*"

"You need some food," observed Miss Forbes sagely. "I suppose you've eaten nothing this morning yet."

"Now you come to mention it, I haven't. I've been, too busy. I've been—my God, what *have I* been doing? Following the footprints of Satan—or maybe some ghostly Blue Woman—leading to the body of a man who has hanged himself and so forfeited his soul to Satan. . . . Has the world suddenly gone crazy—or have I?"

"No, no," said Miss Forbes soothingly. "No one has gone crazy. Perhaps that unfortunate man—but who can fathom the secrets of the mind? For that is what you have been following, something in the mind."

"Yes, I know," said Gregory wearily. "You've been telling us that all morning. But that's where you do go crazy—in the mind."

They had reached the cross-roads and were turning the corner to climb to the top of The Rise when uncle Jake spotted them. Jake for some little while now had been in the Steeple Inn—in and out, depending upon the ratio of those who had been served by Honest George to those who were waiting to be served. He had woken up with a very thick and aching head, but a few hairs of the dog that had bitten him yesterday afternoon had worked wonders. He let out a yell when he saw Miss Forbes and his nephew, broke away from the throng outside the door and, tankard in hand, came lumbering up to them.

"Devil crumple me liver! Where've yer *been,* Greg?"

Gregory stopped and turned round and looked at him with frosty eyes. "If you've been in there for any length of time you know where I've been."

"Well, yeh, I've been hearin' some wild yarns. Devil-marks in the snow—saw 'em meself an' thought at first yer'd gone for a ride on Boomer—Mason found dead an' hangin' on a tree . . . that right?"

Gregory nodded curtly. "In a nutshell."

"Well, rot me!" cried old Jake indignantly. "Why didn't yer gimme a call before yer went clearin' off like that?"

"Give you a call! I like that! I tried to wake you, I did everything short of banging your head on the floor."

"Yer did no such thing!"

"You mean," said Gregory viciously, "you were still so damned drunk you have no recollection—"

"Hey!" said the old man, quietly and warningly. "That'll do, Greg. Y' may be me nephew, but no one says things like that to me. What I do with meself is me own business, an' even if I do take a wee drop too much now an' again overnight I always wake easy."

"Well, you didn't this morning. I tell you—oh, well, let it go." Some of Gregory's anger drained away from him. "Look, uncle, this is serious. What on earth happened to you last night?"

Jake looked at him slyly. "You should know that—don't yer?"

"I know I found you out cold on the floor of the bar in there, and I brought you home and put you to bed; but before that? That fellow Borwell says you went out but came rushing in again yelling the Blue Woman was after you, and then you passed out."

"Rot me!" said Jake, staring. "There y' go again. Blue Woman—what the . . .?"

"Popplewell!" broke in Miss Forbes in her cool, crisp voice. "The time has come when you can no longer be evasive about this. The police are already very interested in you, and they will want to know all about the Blue Woman."

"Sweet Fanny Adams! You, too! I tell yer, Miss Forbes, I haven't the faintest, foggiest, dimmest, damnedest idea—"

"It won't do, Popplewell. There are three witnesses to testify that you have, on more than one occasion, seen the ghost of the Blue Woman, and that it has upset you to the point of rendering you insensible: the innkeeper Borwell, a Mr. Silver, and your own nephew here."

Jake waggled the tankard feebly. "I dunno what to say. What *is* this? Give yer me solemn word, Miss Forbes, that I—" He broke off and was silent for a few seconds. Then he said seriously and a little unhappily: "If, be any mischance, I get to seein' things now and again—say like last night—I've no recollection. . . . Damme, Greg, I still think ol' Jim Silver's been pullin' yer leg."

But Gregory shook his head mercilessly. "I've heard you myself. That night you came home as if all hell was after you: you slammed the door shut and locked it, you threw your boots at the clock, and you said—you said, 'The Devil rot you, you blue-faced hag!'"

Old Jake looked piteously from one to the other of his accusers. "I don't remember," he muttered. "I don't remember. . . . But—but even if I do see a Blue Woman, what's it got to do with *this?*" And he pointed to the trail of hoof-prints in the snow that still, in places, remained visible and clearly defined.

"I'll tell you," said Gregory deliberately. "These hoof-prints be- gin suddenly a little way from your cottage—and *you* are the one who is plagued by her. They lead over the hill and down to here and along to where the dead body of Montague Mason was found hanging on a tree. He arrived here yesterday evening some time before the snow—the police found his car in the garage. And the police think he hanged himself because of what it was that left this trail. Mayhew thinks it was the Devil, Satan himself. But Miss Forbes thinks it might have been the Blue Woman, and has formed that opinion on more logical assumptions."

"Has the Blue Woman got hooves instead of feet?" asked Jake in a belligerent roar.

"Why not?" said Miss Forbes quietly. "She was reputed to have been a witch. Witches had power unknown to ordinary mortals."

"Rot my bones!" breathed the old man, staggered. "In this age an' day!"

"Is this age really any more advanced than that of the ancients? We study atomic physics, yes, but the study of the atom is still only the study of effects. We are as ignorant of causes as ever we were. The electron itself could be the maker of mind, and the cause of the effect that is the electron something that transcends even mind."

"I need another drink," grumbled Jake, staring dazedly into his empty tankard.

"No, you don't," said Gregory quickly. "You're not going back there again, you're coming home with us if I have to drag you.

Miss Forbes wants her scrap-book. Give me that mug!" He wrenched it from his uncle's hand and threw it high and far towards the inn, where some thirsty soul immediately snatched it up.

"Here!" began Jake angrily.

"So what?" demanded Gregory grimly; and for once in his misspent life old Jake capitulated.

"Well . . . Ha! Well, you tell me somethin', Miss Forbes: if this perishin' Blue Woman was layin' for Mason, why in the name of Sam Hill does she haunt *me?* Y' say she does."

Miss Forbes began to smile. "Yes, Popplewell, I have an answer to that. Two answers, perhaps. First, in order to see a ghost one has to attain a certain condition of mind where perception on the psychic plane is possible. In certain moments—such as yesterday evening, for example—you attain that state. Second, Mason's house and grounds are evidently what I might call the hub of the Blue Woman's environment, and you are addicted to wandering about not only in the environment as a whole, but in the hub. Speaking very loosely, you would be more of a familiar figure to her than any of us. . . . An impression on the psychic plane is the potential cause of an effect on the physical plane. By reason of your—ah—wanderings in her particular environment you have left an impression on the psychic plane; by reason of that impression a cause has been created, the effect of which you experience on the physical plane. In other words, you see the Blue Woman. To say you see the *ghost* of the Blue Woman is simply our way of endeavouring to state a psychic fact in physical imagery."

"Now you *are* going in deep," complained Gregory. "This is getting difficult."

But Jake seemed to know what she was driving at. "Whaddyer mean," he growled indignantly but sheepishly, "whaddyer mean, I wander about in the hub of her environment?"

Miss Forbes's smile widened, and she stretched out a hand in the direction of the thick belt of trees surrounding Mason's house. "There is wood lying about in there, plenty of it. And far more often than not the place is untenanted. As a question of purely academic interest, Popplewell, where do you get your firewood . . .?"

14

It was very cold in the cottage and Miss Forbes did not linger. She collected her precious scrap-book and departed. Jake, preternaturally silent, set about preparing a meal, while Gregory built

a fire in the parlour and set the table. This done, Gregory sauntered into the kitchen, fingering his chin.

"I could do with a shave."

"Y'll have to wait till yer've had yer dinner," returned old Jake
gruffly. "It'll be ready in a minute."

Still caressing his chin Gregory drifted back to the parlour and
stared down with unseeing eyes at the leaping flames. Jake came
in a few minutes later, dumped a couple of plates on the table and
went back for the teapot.

"Come an' get it," he rasped, and Gregory roused himself and
took his seat opposite his uncle. For awhile they ate in silence.
Through the diamond panes of the small windows figures could be
seen flitting past the low wooden fence.

"All Winchingham seems to be traipsin' up an' down outside,"
rumbled Jake irritably. Then he cleared his throat and his voice
rose to its normal aggressive bellow. "This damned blue hag that
seems to be followin' me around—what's it all *about?*"

"Well, if you don't know, I'm sure I don't," said Gregory moodily.
"But Jim Silver has a story, and Miss Forbes has a theory."

"I've heard Emmy Forbes's theory!"

"You've only heard part of it. There's a lot more to it, and the
farther she goes—I tell you, uncle, I don't know whether I'm on
my head or my heels!"

Jake put down his knife and fork with a clatter, and gloomed
across the table at him.

"Well, spill it! What the perishin' purple hades has been goin' on
round here? What possessed Mason to go an' do a thing like that?"

"The Thing. The ghost. The Blue Woman."

"Tchah! Anyway, how did he *get* here? I thought he was in
London."

"He drove down yesterday for some reason or another. Apparently he just beat the snow to it."

"What did he do that for? He never comes down here on his
own."

"Well, I don't suppose he's ever hanged himself before. . . . How
on earth do I know what he came down for?"

"Yer know a lot more than I know. These mysterious
hoof-prints—I wish yer'd tell me, Greg, y' seem to be in the thick
of it yerself."

"Yes," said Gregory unhappily, "and I wish I wasn't. It's only
because I happened to see them first—where they started from
this end, I mean. . . . Listen, uncle, I'll tell you everything we
found this morning, and everything that happened, and then *you*
can tell me who's crazy round here."

And he recounted in detail the discoveries and events of the morning, and the various theories advanced by Miss Forbes. By the time he had finished the meal was over, the dishes had been cleared away and washed up, and Jake was draping the dishcloth over the single tap above the tiny sink.

"Rot me!" exclaimed the old man, at the conclusion of the recital. "Emmy Forbes has been havin' the time of her life."

"We've all been having the time of our lives," returned Gregory wearily. "We've been wallowing in the fantastic and the incredible. What do you think of it, uncle Jake?"

"I dunno." Jake fumbled for his pipe, stumped back to the fire in the parlour and dropped heavily into the more decrepit of the two arm-chairs. He lit up and puffed noisily. "I dunno. The theory is—ain't it?—that this Thing, which Emmy Forbes now seems to think is the Blue Woman, was after Mason's blood."

"Well . . . yes."

"Um. It couldn't do anythin' in London, it had to get him here, on its own home ground, so to speak, where its influence was strongest. Where it was deadly, in fact. Ha! Yeh. Mebbe . . . I dunno. But there's one ruddy great fallacy in Emmy Forbes's theory."

"Is there?"

"Yeh. This Thing could pass through solid matter, couldn't it?"

"It certainly looks like that."

"Well, why didn't it?" demanded Jake belligerently.

"But it did!"

"Yeh—where it served no particular purpose. But where it *had* a purpose—when it was tryin' to get into Mason's house—it wasted time an' messed about at doors an' windows where it was baffled be charms an' symbols. It's illogical. Doors an' windows are things humans get through, because they're openin's in solid walls. But this Thing could get on all right without openin's. An' what I want to know is, why didn't it? Why didn't it just bung straight through the brick walls somewhere where there was no powerful ju-ju to stop it?"

"Are you asking me! Maybe it had a weakness for doors—Mason's wasn't the only front door it went up to. All the way along the trail, even at the Steeple Inn, it went up to various doors—for all we know it may have passed through some and wandered about inside. . . ."

"Or it may not. . . . An' there's another thing. At Mason's place it finally got up on to the roof. Theory is it got *through* the roof. Right?"

"I don't know. Miss Forbes wasn't too confident about that; that is more of a guess than a theory."

"Well, damme, consider it as a guess. The hoof-prints go round and round in a circle about the skylight: where did it *get* through the roof?"

"Through the skylight, I suppose. Mason's footprints in the dust inside show that he rushed up to try and bar the way."

"Through the skylight, hey? Just where there *are* no hoof-prints. What's the theory about that? Did the Thing rise up in the air an' do a power dive through the skylight?"

"I don't know," muttered Gregory, and put his hands to his head. "I don't know. . ."

They were still arguing and debating when Mr. Silver arrived. Old Jake greeted him with undisguised pleasure.

"Come in, Jim me boy. Come in an' make yerself at home."

Mr. Silver came in, and Mr. Silver made himself at home. Mr. Silver's rosy, relucent face was blank with mystification.

"Jake," he said breathlessly, "I've had the police at my place. They told me about Mason and—and other things, crazy, impossible things," said Mr. Silver, his voice going shrill, "and they wanted to know if I could tell them anything. *Tell* them anything? I didn't even know myself that anything had happened till they arrived—too busy looking after the stock in this snow. . . ."

Jake cackled rustily. "Tell him, Greg. Tell him what you told me. Tell him everything."

Gregory plunged into his recital once more, and at the end of it Mr. Silver was sitting on the extreme edge of his chair and his eyes were bulging out of his head.

"Now," Gregory wound up, "I've left something for *you* to tell, and that is the story or legend of the Blue Woman. You tell uncle Jake what you told me."

But Mr. Silver brushed that aside. Another matter had claimed his immediate attention.

"That rosary," he panted. "The rosary that was found in Mason's overcoat pocket—what was it like?"

Gregory described it as well as he could. "Just a cheap one. Must be thousands like it."

"Not round Steeple Thelming," said Mr. Silver energetically. "Why, dammit, that's my sister's! It must be!"

"Your sister?"

"Yes. She keeps house for me. But when Mason is here—when he was here—she used to go along and cook for him. That rosary's been missing for months."

"Since the last time Mason was here?" put in Jake.

"Well . . . yes. Now I come to think of it, it must have been about that time she lost it."

Jake turned to his nephew and grinned at him. "There's your answer to that mystery, me boy. Miss Silver must 'a' dropped it last time she was in Mason's house, an' he found it, mebbe lyin' on the floor somewhere, when he arrived last night. He picked it up and shoved it carelessly into his pocket. That's how it got there."

Gregory nodded agreement. "All right. That's simple enough. Now give me some of the other answers."

But at that the other two merely stared at him in silence; and then old Jake got up and made quite a ceremony of producing the whisky bottle.

*   *   *

Mr. Silver left the cottage again just before dark. He left somewhat hurriedly, because the snow that had been threatening all day had now begun to fall. It snowed in good earnest all that night, and in the morning a fresh and unspotted mantle of dazzling white covered the earth; a deep mantle that completely obliterated all traces of the multifarious eager, questing feet of the previous day—and every single trace of the unknown visitant. But hundreds of people had seen the "devil-marks" for themselves, and they had been photographed. And some of those same photographs stared up at millions of people from the pages of the evening papers on the Monday—there was also a brief account of the death of a prominent City business man, together with a small and villainous snapshot of the ferrety features of the late Montague Mason; but that was a bad second to the mysterious hoof-prints in the snow. One sub-editor, presumably with his tongue in his cheek, dubbed the phenomenon the "Footprints of Satan"—which an astonishing number of readers accepted at literal face value. And after that a swarm of journalists, spiritualists and ghost hunters, professional and amateur, descended locust-like upon Winchingham to make further and fuller investigation. By that time, of course, there was nothing to be seen. But there was always Miss Forbes to talk to, and to listen to. And Miss Forbes was only too ready to talk.

*   *   *

That indefatigable lady, with her scrap-book wrapped in stout brown paper and tucked under her arm, called at the cottage at ten o'clock the next morning. She was in a state of suppressed excitement, which six inches of fresh snow on the roads had done nothing to dampen. She dragged Gregory from the warmth of the parlour metaphorically by the scruff of his neck, and took him along with her to the police station in River Crescent in the heart of Winchingham. There they were conducted upstairs to the sumptuous office of Superintendent Blackler, where the chief constable, the superintendent and Detective-Inspector Smith awaited them, and were given chairs specially imported for the occasion.

Not that the chief constable was particularly enthusiastic about the visit. He wasn't: he didn't want any damn civilians messing about with his cases, and he was already a bit dazed by some of Miss Forbes's metaphysics. But she was an old friend of his, and friendship carries certain privileges. So he sat at the superintendent's desk in the superintendent's own chair and eyed her with a certain amount of trepidation.

She beamed on him. "Well, Colonel?" she inquired brightly.

The police had learnt a thing or two since Miss Forbes had last seen the three men, but the colonel wasn't giving anything away. He tugged at his little white moustache and replied unemotionally: "Well, ma'am?"

"Well," said Miss Forbes again, and began to undo the wrapping paper. "I said yesterday that this had happened before. I said there had been *another* occasion when, following a fall of snow, strange and inexplicable hoof-marks had been found in the snow. And I promised to produce proof of this. Well—here is the proof!"

She dropped the wrapping paper carelessly on the floor, and waved the book at him. Then she opened it at a marked place and, before anybody could anticipate her action, leapt up from her chair, bounded forward and placed the book open on the desk in front of him.

"Look at that, Colonel!"

Colonel Gormsby obligingly, but in somewhat pop-eyed fashion, looked at the page presented to his notice. The superintendent and Mr. Smith came forward and looked over his shoulders. Gregory didn't move—he had already seen it. On that page had been pasted some yellowing columns of an old newspaper, and centred at the top, its own familiar, unmistakable impress, was the name of the paper and the date of issue.

"Read it, Colonel. Read it aloud."

The colonel did so. "*The Times,*" he muttered. "Sixteenth of February, 1855. . . ."

"*The Times,*" repeated Miss Forbes gravely. "For the 16th February 1855." She retreated from the desk and bumped back on to her chair again. "You will agree with me that *The Times* is, and always was, the least sensational of newspapers. Yet it took the trouble to give an account of that other case, and that is what it had to say. Will you read it for us, Colonel?"

And Colonel Gormsby, after a preliminary clearing of the throat and smoothing of his clipped moustache, began to read from an issue of *The Times* that had been published thirty-one years before he had been born.

"EXTRAORDINARY OCCURRENCE

"Considerable sensation has been evoked in the towns of Topsham, Lympstone, Exmouth, Teignmouth and Dawlish, in the south of Devon, in consequence of the discovery of a vast number of foot-tracks of a most strange and mysterious description. The superstitious go so far as to believe that they are the marks of Satan himself; and that great excitement has been produced among all classes may be judged from the fact that the subject has been descanted on from the pulpit.

"It appears that on Thursday night last there was a heavy fall of snow in the neighbourhood of Exeter and the south of Devon. On the following morning, the inhabitants of the above towns were surprised at discovering the tracks of some strange and mysterious animal, endowed with the power of ubiquity, as the footprints were to be seen in all kinds of inaccessible places—on the tops of houses and narrow walls, in gardens and courtyards enclosed by high walls and palings, as well as in open fields. There was hardly a garden in Lympstone where the footprints were not observed.

"The tracks appeared more like that of a biped than a quadruped, and the steps were generally eight inches in advance of each other. The impressions of the feet closely resembled that of a donkey's shoe, and measured from an inch and a half to, in some instances, two and a half inches across. Here and there it appeared as if cloven—"

Here Mr. Smith uttered an exclamation, and glanced sharply across the desk at Miss Forbes.

"—but in the generality of the steps the shoe was continuous, and, from the snow in the centre remaining entire, merely showing the outer crest of the foot, it must have been convex.[1]

---

[1] It would appear that *The Times* has made a slip here, for ob-

"The creature appears to have approached the doors of several houses and then to have retreated, but no one has been able to discover the standing or resting point of this mysterious visitor. On Sunday last the Rev. Mr. Musgrave alluded to the subject in his sermon, and suggested the possibility of the footprints being those of a kangaroo; but this could scarcely be the case, as they were found on both sides of the estuary of the Exe.

"At present it remains a mystery, and many superstitious people in the above towns are afraid to go outside their doors after night."

That was the end of the account, and the chief constable laid down the scrap-book and knitted his brows at Miss Forbes, who smiled delightedly as if she had just pulled off some remarkable conjuring trick.

"There's more yet. No more clippings, I'm afraid—I was not allowed to retain them—but over the page you will find some comments and quotations."

15

Colonel Gormsby flipped over the leaf. the cutting from *The Times* was followed by some pages of typescript, the work of Miss Forbes herself, which was headed: "Further Notes and Comments on the Devonshire Phenomenon." The colonel took a fresh grip of the scrap-book and continued his public reading.

"Further information concerning the mysterious hoof-prints in the snow is to be found in the *Illustrated London News* in its issues between 24th February and 17th March 1855. Several points of interest are touched on, including exact details of the tracks. They are described as being exactly like the impression of a donkey's hoof, the size four inches by two and three-quarter inches—"

A mutter from Mr. Smith.

"—but instead of the marks being spread to right and left of a central line, as would have been the case had they been made

---

viously the word intended is "concave."—N. B.

by any normal creature, they were immediately one behind the other and approximately eight inches apart—"

"Ho!"—softly, from Mr. Smith.

"—The clergyman, the Rev. G. M. Musgrave, seems to have interested himself in the phenomenon to some degree, and to have made some discoveries for himself. In a letter to the *Illustrated London News* he writes: 'A scientific acquaintance informed me of his having traced the same prints across a field up to a haystack. The surface of the stack was wholly free from marks of any kind, but on the opposite side of the stack, in a direction exactly corresponding with the tracks thus traced, the prints began again—'"

"Gadzooks!"
Colonel Gormsby looked up at Mr. Smith in some irritation.
"Mr. Maltravers's pavilion," said the inspector quickly. "Mrs. Pendlebury's summerhouse."
"The comparison is obvious," said Miss Forbes severely.
"Yes, it is," barked the colonel, who had only just thought of it. "Confound it, Inspector, stop interruptin' me, you're puttin' me off. Where was I . . .? Humph—yeh. . . .

"—Mr. Musgrave lists the places where the hoof-marks were seen. He mentions Kinton, Dawlish, Newton, Exmouth, Withecombe, Raleigh, Lympstone, Woodbury, Topsham, Bicton and Budleigh. Other observers add Mamhead, Luscombe and, in one instance, Totnes. But Mr. Musgrave's list alone is enough to show that the marks covered a wide stretch of country.
"Various tentative explanations were, of course, put forward at the time, and others have been advanced at intervals since. I can divide these explanations or theories into two groups: those based on physical observations and experience, and those based on hyperphysical hypotheses.
"Those in the first group are all what may be called animal theories. A number of known animals, and one unknown, have been put forward as responsible. The known animals suggested are the kangaroo (by Mr. Musgrave), the badger, the otter, the rat and, for some reason or another, the raccoon. I cannot take the kangaroo theory seriously. It was, as a matter of fact, only suggested because a certain Mr. Fishe, of Sidmouth, owned a private menagerie which contained a pair of these interesting creatures. But there is no evidence whatsoever that either or

both of these kangaroos had escaped, and furthermore the mysterious hoof-prints cannot have been anything at all like the tracks that would have been left by a kangaroo.

"The claims advanced for the badger, the otter and the rat, merit perhaps a little closer attention. Stretching a point, the badger and the otter do leave prints *something* like the size and shape of those found in that Devonshire snow; but even so their four paws do not fall immediately one behind the other, they fall on either side of a central line.

"In the *Illustrated London News* for the 10th March 1855, a Mr. Thomas Fox suggested that the marks were those of a leaping rat. He drew a sketch to show that a mark left by a sitting rat would be similar to the marks observed, and he pointed out that those marks would be in a single line. An ingenious theory, perhaps, but it postulates a rat of most extraordinary behaviour.

"There are two major objections to any animal theory. The first is this: studying the list of places where the prints were observed, it can be seen that the minimum distance traversed by the animal would be something like 100 miles—and that in one night! The raccoon theory—which appears to have been not so much a theory as a wild guess—suffers not only from this objection, but also from the additional one that it is not even a native of this country.

"These objections were, of course, enumerated at the time; and a Mr. Richard Owen entered the arena with the assertion that the marks could not have been made by a single animal. A reasonable suggestion, but one that is not really very helpful. For even if a swarm of animals—"

And here the chief constable interrupted himself. "Swarm!" he snorted. "Animals don't swarm! Bees swarm!" Then he realized just who had typed down that word, and had the grace to look a little sheepish before hurriedly continuing.

"—For even if a swarm of animals had leapt or hopped about the snow-covered countryside that night it still leaves the second major obstacle to be contended with. Which is this. All reports show that considerable alarm was created by the discovery of the tracks, that many superstitious people were afraid to go outside their doors after nightfall, and that they went so far as to ascribe the marks to the Prince of Darkness himself. It is safe to say that by far the greater proportion of the superstitious would be country dwellers, rustics living in and around all those villages and towns concerned. But they are the very people who would be familiar with the tracks left by the little wild animals of the countryside: they would have had no difficulty in recognizing the marks left by a badger or otter, or any other known animal. The very fact that such consternation *was* caused is, to my mind, the best ground for ruling out any known animal.

"This leaves the unknown animal theory to be considered. And this may not be quite the indefensible theory it seems at first sight, for such theories have cropped up in our own time and have been given quite serious consideration—for example, the Loch Ness monster.

"The unknown animal theory was first put forward by a Mr. R. T. Gould. He reminded his readers that a somewhat similar set of footprints had been observed in May 1840 at Kerguelen Island by Sir James Clark Ross. These marks were traced in recently fallen snow for some distance, but were finally lost on rocky ground. Mr. Gould remarked that there was much in common between the two cases. In neither instance could the tracks be ascribed to any animal native to the country in question; but in both instances the place where they were found was near the sea. So, suggested Mr. Gould, the creature could have come from and gone back to the sea, where there may be creatures as yet unknown to science.

"This more or less exhausts the various 'explanations' offered based on physical or naturalistic theory. None, to my mind, is acceptable; none is anywhere near conclusive.

"So far as explanations based on hyperphysical or supernatural theory are concerned, they are really one and the same. Disregarding the first and foremost theory put forward at the time—that the marks were the footprints of Satan—and treating them purely and simply as objective phenomena, it is suggested that they were left by some supernatural entity: in other words, by a ghost or poltergeist.

"Now there have been *three* observed cases of this phenomenon of strange and mysterious footprints in newly-fallen snow: at Kerguelen Island in May 1840; in the south of Devon in February 1855—and at Borley Rectory at Christmas time 1938. Here again, at what has been described as that hotbed of haunting, foot-marks in the snow were found which corresponded to the Kerguelen Island and Devonshire marks. And here again they remained inexplicable. But as at Borley almost every known poltergeist effect was observed, the marks were taken as being part of the general phenomena; and there seems to be no reason to dispute this. But, therefore, if a supernatural explanation be accepted for the Borley phenomenon, surely it may be accepted also for the other two strikingly similar cases. Particularly in the Devonshire case, where the phenomena included apparent levitation and the passing of matter through matter (the haystack incident reported by the Rev. G. M. Musgrave), both of which are well-substantiated poltergeist phenomena.

"Admittedly this is only a partial explanation, since the question immediately arises: what *is* a poltergeist? But that is a rather pointless question, since all that is known of poltergeists are poltergeist *effects.* And it cannot be too strongly stressed that the study of effects does not necessarily lead to the discovery or knowledge of the cause."

Colonel Gormsby came to the end of the typescript, looked to see if there was any more, saw there was no more, dropped the scrap-book on to the desk and gave his larynx a rest.

"Rather an abrupt ending, I'm afraid," said Miss Forbes, "but there was really no more to be said. Anything further I might have added would only have been in the nature of a conclusion, and I was careful not to come to any conclusion, since I myself had had no first-hand experience of the phenomenon."

"Unlike yesterday's business," murmured the inspector, "when you did."

The colonel had turned back to the first page. "Look here, I suppose this really is a genuine extract from *The Times?* I mean—"

"Oh, yes," Miss Forbes told him confidently. "There is no doubt about that, Colonel. There are other copies of the same issue still in existence; in public libraries, for instance, and places like that—and, of course, in the offices of *The Times* itself. The same applies to the *Illustrated London News*—you could easily check up on it. . . . The subject," she added invitingly, "is now open for general discussion."

The colonel grunted dubiously; he didn't really care for this sort of thing. But Inspector Smith was not backward in accepting the invitation.

"By my home-made halidom," he said extravagantly, "I don't know when I've ever heard anything more intriguing! And now history repeats itself. Repeats itself with extraordinary fidelity. It's all there again, but on a smaller scale this time: the hoof-prints that begin and end without coming or going; the levitation; the passing of matter through matter. . . . I take it, Miss Forbes, that you look upon our own visitation as number four in the series?"

"Don't you think we have sufficient justification?"

"But this time, having had first-hand experience, you have come to a conclusion."

"I would rather you put it this way: that I have advanced for consideration what seems to me to be a likely explanation."

"Yes. Satan left those marks. Or else it was the Blue Woman. Miss Forbes, do you believe in the Devil?"

"What do you mean by the Devil?" countered Miss Forbes composedly. "That is a word, a tag, a label. To what mental conception do you attach the label—the Managing Director of Hell with horns, hooves and a tail? Or a Principle of Evil which may or may not exist independent of and beyond mind?"

"Well"—Mr. Smith scratched his head—"I can't quite see a principle leaving footprints in the snow."

"Then that leaves the traditional picture of the gentleman with the hooves, etc.; and you can jolly well answer the question yourself!"

"All right." He grinned at her. "Well, I rule out Satan, because that idea of him comes from the satyr of Graeco-Roman mythology; and if satyrs weren't purely and simply characters in a lot of fairy tales thought up by the ancients themselves, that is if they really did exist, then it is possible that they were merely convenient concepts of what in these times are known as poltergeists."

"It is possible. . . . You might as well rule out the other concept at the same time. For if the Principle of Evil exists in mind, what criterion have we that it does not do so *only* in mind, that it has no absolute existence but is merely a principle held by man for the convenience and benefit of society as a whole? Conversely, if it exists independently above and beyond mind, how can we, creatures of mind possessing only mind, test the truth of the assertion?"

The chief constable began to wave his hands about in a distressful fashion.

"Okay, okay," said Mr. Smith soothingly. "Old Nick, in any guise or form, is out of it. That leaves the Blue Woman. . . ."

Miss Forbes said thoughtfully: "Well, Inspector, we do seem to be on firmer ground here. This time—in what you call number four of the series—we have more data. We have direct mention, direct evidence, *of a* Blue Woman—"

"Yes," interrupted the inspector. "We also have a body!"

And after a moment, as Miss Forbes was silent, he went on: "You see, that's the part of it I don't like. Mason's death seems to be inextricably bound up with the phenomenon of the hoof-prints—" He checked himself suddenly and went off at a tangent. "By the way, have you noticed that *The Times* in its account of the Devonshire phenomenon never once uses the word 'hoof'? It speaks of footprints, tracks, impressions, steps—but never hooves. It uses instead the word 'shoe.' It says the impressions closely resembled that of a donkey's *shoe*. It says that in the generality of steps the *shoe* was continuous. But nowhere else is that word used. The *Illustrated London News* uses the word 'hoof.' It says that the tracks were exactly like the impression of a donkey's hoof, and it gives the size, four inches by two and three-quarter inches, which, for what the information is worth, happens to be the exact size of *our* mysterious prints.

"Well?" he asked pointedly. "Which was it? Shoe, or hoof? Was that Devonshire visitant shod, or unshod?"

"I don't know," replied Miss Forbes frankly. "There is not sufficient definite evidence. That is all I know"—pointing to the scrap-book on the desk—"that is all anyone knows now."

"M'm. . . . There is another little detail. On an average, according to the *Illustrated London News,* the distance between the Devonshire marks was eight inches. The average distance between our own marks is ten inches."

"Oh, Inspector, now you're splitting hairs! That is, after all, only a detail, and a very minor one at that."

"Well, yes, perhaps you're right. . . . But reverting to Mason's death, which definitely does *seem* to be part of the general phenomena and, I take it, is included in your theory: now I'll grant you that, like the Devonshire phenomenon, the Steeple Thelming phenomenon could have been the result of some playful prank by a poltergeist; I'll grant you that old Jake Popplewell does really see a Blue Woman, and that the Blue Woman might have been the poltergeist. But it's that dead body at the end of all this psychic phenomena that sticks in my gizzard. A dead man is a purely physical phenomenon."

"God bless the man!" cried Miss Forbes. "All phenomena is purely physical—how otherwise could we have cognizance of it? Psychic phenomena is really a meaningless term. But we are discussing the cause or reason for it. And I maintain that if the cause of the marks in the snow can be attributed to a psychic origin, then it is just as reasonable in the absence of any evidence to the contrary, to attribute the cause of Mason taking his own life to a psychic origin!"

"Meantersay," jerked the chief constable, following the argument with difficulty, "the ghost, the Blue Woman, pushed him into doin' it?"

Miss Forbes was calm again. "The ghost, the Blue Woman, has no *actual* objective existence; it exists *really* only in the mind. The verdict on Mason's death will almost certainly be suicide while of unsound mind. Now that doesn't necessarily imply a damaged brain—far from it. In a vast number of cases of suicide it means a deranged intellect. But what is a deranged intellect but a psychic disturbance?"

Superintendent Blackler laughed aloud. "No good, Smithy; Miss Forbes has all the answers. But I really think, in common fairness, we should let her in on the one or two things we've found out."

"Ye-es . . ." Mr. Smith stuck his hands in his pockets and began to drift about the office. "As the superintendent says, Miss Forbes, we have since learnt one or two things, rather odd things that don't seem to fit into your theory. I'll give them to you as we learnt them. We have found out from the Metropolitan Police that Mason came down here in response to an urgent summons—or, at least, some very important communication. The urgent summons took the nature of a telephone call from Steeple Thelming; and we have learnt from the girl at the Winchingham exchange who put the call through that it was made at 3.25 on the Saturday afternoon—and that it was made from Mason's own house!"

"But," exclaimed Miss Forbes, "Mason's house was shut up!"

"So it was supposed. Empty, closed and locked up. But we don't *know* that. We found the gate open and the side door unlocked yesterday morning: Mason also might have found the gate open and the side door unlocked—*and somebody inside waiting for him*—when he arrived the previous evening. It was a man's voice calling from the house, that much the exchange girl could tell us, but she couldn't tell us anything of the nature of the conversation, because once the connection had been made she ceased to listen. The rest we get from Mason's secretary. Mason himself took the call. After it, he was considerably agitated, he ordered his secretary to get out his car, told him that he would be going to Steeple Thelming almost immediately, that he would be going alone and that he would be staying overnight."

"I see," said Miss Forbes thoughtfully. "But surely this man must have given his name. Didn't the girl at the exchange—?"

"Yes. She asked for it. He gave the name," said Detective-Inspector Smith solemnly, "of Smith. John Smith."

And even Miss Forbes smiled. Then she asked: "And then what?"

"Then we don't know what happened—apart from the fact that Mason did come down in his car and that he must have arrived at the house some time before the snow—"

"And if some man *had* been there to receive him, then he must have *gone* before the snow. Otherwise he would have left traces."

16

Mr. Smith, who had been eyeing Miss Forbes earnestly, shifted his gaze to Gregory Cushing. "Well?" he said softly. "Let's have it."

Gregory, looking a little sheepish after his sudden irruption, muttered incoherently: "Well, I don't know . . . I'd forgotten . . . all this hoof-mark-and-Blue-Woman stuff had put it clean out of my head. . . ."

"What *is* it?" barked the chief constable testily.

"Well, sir, it's this: did you know there was another man staying at the Steeple Inn besides Honest George?"

The chief constable looked up at Mr. Smith, who exchanged glances with Superintendent Blackler over his head.

"No," said the latter. "We didn't. Tell us more, Mr. Cushing."

"Well, there is one. Or, rather, there was one. He was there that first day that uncle Jake dragged me into the inn, and he was there on Saturday afternoon when I collected the old man. At least," added Gregory thoughtfully, "if it's the same man. . . . I don't know anything about him myself, he's a very furtive sort of bloke. Uncle Jake and I heard him and Borwell talking together somewhere inside when we went into the bar that day I arrived here, but all we could get out of Borwell was that this mysterious type was a friend of his, and not a guest of the inn in the ordinary way. Then, on Saturday afternoon just before dark, when I went for uncle Jake, I caught a glimpse of this furtive bloke's back as he ducked inside. Well, of course, I had my hands full getting old Jake home, and then all this devil business happened, and it wasn't until you mentioned some unknown man just now that I remembered. . . . I'm afraid that's all I can tell you."

"Thank you," said the inspector crisply. "Thank you, Mr. Cushing." And went smartly to the door, wrenched it open and yelled down the stairs for Bill Poynter.

*   *   *

That was the end of the palaver. The inspector and Detective-Sergeant Poynter went away to the Steeple Inn—the police car, with chains on the tyres, took them to the foot of The Rise, but after that they had to trudge through the snow—and Miss Forbes and Gregory Cushing left almost immediately after. But it chanced that Miss Forbes saw the inspector again later that day, and she stopped him and asked questions.

"He wasn't there," Mr. Smith answered her simply. "The bird has flown."

"Oh?" said Miss Forbes, "and where has the bird flown to?"

"London. He left by the 9.30 train this morning. We learnt that from Honest George, who was so frank and cooperative that I'm wondering where the catch is. Honest George also told us his name—Cliff Sheldon—and gave us a description of him. Said he was a friend of his and had been staying with him for a little holiday. Said also that he could swear that Sheldon had not gone outside the Steeple Inn at any time after midday on Saturday."

Miss Forbes made noises indicative of doubt, and Mr. Smith smiled wryly.

"I know. How much reliance can we place on the word of the honest one? However, what with the snow and one thing and another, the 9.30 was four hours late in arriving at Paddington, and that gave us time to ring through to the Metropolitan Police. We gave them the dope, and they took Sheldon as he stepped off the train."

"Ah!"

"Yes; but this is where complications set in. The City police thanked us very kindly for the tip: they had been looking for Sheldon in connection with a little matter of robbery with violence—which would seem to account for his having gone to ground down here with his pal, the aforementioned honest one. Now they're going to hang on to him, which means that if I want to talk to him I'll have to go up to London to do it."

"But—but where exactly do the complications set in?"

Mr. Smith took off his hat and ran his fingers through his hair. "Well, as you know, the footprints in Mason's house were made by somebody wearing size 11 shoes. We have ascertained from the City police that Sheldon takes size 9 . . ."

*   *   *

Gregory Cushing also saw the inspector again that afternoon. He spotted him as he was passing the cottage on his way back from further cross-examination of Mr. Borwell, and from yet another hunt round in Mason's house and grounds. He also wanted to know about the man in the inn, and Mr. Smith told him more or less what he had told Miss Forbes.

"Bad luck," said Gregory sympathetically. "I'm sorry, Inspector, I should have told you before."

"No harm done. And anyway, the Metropolitan Police were grateful; you found a wanted man for them."

"I'm not worrying very much about the Metropolitan Police. You know, I could have told you something else this morning, but you went away in too much of a hurry. That rosary—or do you know about that?"

"What about the rosary?"

"Well," said Gregory almost apologetically, "it belongs to Miss Silver, Jim Silver's sister. Silver told us himself—he came round to see us yesterday afternoon. He told us he'd had a visit from you people, but apparently you didn't say anything about the rosary. Pity, because that was the one question he could have answered.

"You see, Inspector, Miss Silver used to go along and cook for Mason when he was at Steeple Thelming, and it was after his last visit that she missed the rosary. She must have dropped it in the house, or put it down somewhere and forgotten it, and Mason must have come across it and shoved it in his pocket."

"So," murmured Mr. Smith. "So that's how it got there."

"It looks that way, doesn't it?"

"It certainly does. It's easier to see Mason picking up a thing like that and dropping it casually into his pocket, than to see him carrying it around with him to tell his beads at prescribed intervals. We can easily check up on that. But," he sighed, "it doesn't help us much, does it? On the face of it, it's a sheer accidental detail—but it goes with the hoof-marks on the window-sill. It stopped the Thing that had hooves. . . . What about those hoof-prints, Mr. Cushing?"

"Good Lord, are you asking me? Have you read Miss Forbes's scrapbook?"

"No. Only what the chief constable read out this morning. By the way, where—?"

"We have it. Miss Forbes took it away with her again and left it here for us to have another look at it. I've been reading it all the afternoon while uncle Jake's been snoring in front of the fire. And, by Christopher, I'll believe anything now!" Gregory's eyebrows were half-way up his forehead. "The things that go on behind our backs, so to speak! Table-rapping and trances are kindergarten stuff! You browse through that book, Inspector, and you won't only be afraid of the dark again—you'll go about in the daytime looking over your shoulder!"

17

Monday night.

Old Jake Popplewell, once again in the bar room of the Steeple Inn, with his rakish tweed cap over one fierce little eye, his O.S. waterproof, windproof, thornproof greatcoat enveloping his stocky body, and his ancient but still active feet encased in heavy boots with soles an inch thick. Jim Silver, happily aglow, back against the bar, resting on his elbows, one heel hooked in the brass rail. Three or four minor characters, desultory "droppers in," vastly entertained by Jake. Honest George Borwell, filling tankards, automatically swabbing decks, listening uncomprehendingly. . . .

Jake had dozed all the afternoon and had woken up at tea-time, fresh as a daisy. Gregory, on the other hand, had been restless; alternately dipping into Miss Forbes's scrap-book and mooching from window to window in the parlour; going outside now and again for more wood for the fire; toying furtively with his portable wireless set. But tea over and cleared away, the seven devils of restlessness had gone out of him and apparently entered into Jake, for the old man had begun to fidget ominously. Relaxed and somnolent, Gregory had fallen asleep in front of the fire; and after a while uncle Jake had got up cautiously, collected coat and cap and sneaked out of the cottage for a constitutional.

Now, once more in the Steeple Inn with a skinful already inside him, he was at the top of his form. For his bosom pal was there to bear him company, and Honest George was there, and so were the three or four minor characters.

So also was the shade of William Shakespeare; and Jake was forcibly expressing both himself and the Bard.

"' A plague of all cowards, I say, an' a vengeance too! marry, an' amen! Gimme a cup o' sack, boy. Ere I lead this life long, I'll sew nether-stocks an' mend 'em an' foot 'em too. A plague of all cowards! Gimme a cup o' sack, rogue.'" He hammered on the bar with his empty tankard.

" 'Ere!" said Honest George austerely. "Give over, 'Amlet!"

"Fill 'em up again, George my boy," wheedled old Jake, lapsing into the vernacular. Mr. Borwell obligingly replenished the pewter tankard with the usual mixture. Jake took a deep drink, a deep breath, and burst out in a fresh place.

" 'Go thy ways, ol' Jack; die when thou wilt. If manhood, good manhood, be not forgot upon the face o' the earth, then I am a shotten herrin'. A plague of all cowards, I say still. . . .'"

"Listen, what's all this talk of cowards?" inquired Mr. Silver, grinning widely.

Jake skipped three or four hundred lines, and waggled his finger in Silver's red face.

" 'Two rogues in buckram suits. I tell thee what, Hal, if I tell thee a lie, spit in me face, call me horse. Thou knowest me old ward: here I lay, an' thus I bore me point. Four rogues in buckram let drive at me—'"

"You said two," objected Mr. Silver, paraphrasing, with admirable timing, the Prince's reply to Falstaff.

" 'Four, Hal, I told thee four. . . . These four came all afront, an' mainly they thrust at me. I made no more ado but took all their seven points in me target, thus.'"

And here Jake made a gesture as of one presenting a shield to an attack, and spilt a goodly portion of his beer-and-rum on the floor. He snarled a wicked word at this wanton waste, a word that in all his works Shakespeare does not seem to have used; and he used plenty.

"Never mind," said Mr. Silver soothingly—and mischievously. "Plenty more where that came from. These four rogues of yours. . . ."

"Seven," retorted Jake fiercely. " 'Seven, by these hilts, or I am a villain else.'"

As a matter of fact there did exist a parallel. You might almost say that history, even if fictitious, had repeated itself. Old Jake *had* been set upon by two men on his way to the inn, and that was probably what had set him going in this particular vein. But they had not worn buckram suits, nor were they rogues. They had been wearing a dark blue serge that was black at night time and rendered them practically invisible, and they were honest, conscientious police constables, who had been stationed there by Superintendent Blackler to keep watch and ward over Mason's house and its environment. They had stopped Jake, it is true, but they had made no attempt to detain him; they had grinned understandingly and let him pass by.

Jake hiccoughed, drank, and skipped several more hundred words of the *First Part of King Henry The Fourth.*

"Beware instinct," he said earnestly but somewhat irrelevantly to Mr. Silver. " 'Beware instinct; the lion will not touch the true prince.' " Then he swung round on the startled George. " 'Hostess,' " he cried in great good humour, " 'clap to the doors: watch tonight, pray tomorrow. Gallants, lads, boys, hearts of gold, all the titles o' goodfellowship come to yer! What! shall we be merry? Shall we have a play extempore—'Fill 'em up again, Georgie boy!"

The minor characters crowded round him. Only the last six words had made any sense to them, but even those that had gone before had seemed to carry a vague promise of free drinks. . . .

*   *   *

Back in the police station in River Crescent, Detective-Sergeant Poynter sat in his office-cum-workshop and pored over photographs and enlargements of photographs. He peered through a large magnifying-glass and muttered to himself. Presently he put down the magnifying-glass and sat back in his chair and rolled himself a cigarette, whistling dolefully the while. He ceased whistling to light the cigarette—for which the desk sergeant in the charge room adjoining was thankful. Half-way through smoking the cigarette he came to a decision; and he gathered up his photographs, carefully placing groups of them into different envelopes and marking the envelopes. He stowed these away in an inside pocket. Then he stood up, put his overcoat on his back and his hat on his head, dropped the magnifying glass into his overcoat pocket, and went out.

Early that afternoon the sky had cleared once more, but the snow still lay thick over the countryside, though on the paved streets of the town it was beginning to turn to slush. Ten minutes' walk took Poynter to his objective, which was the house of Detective-Inspector Lancelot Carolus Smith. Mr. Smith opened the door to him and gave him characteristic greeting.

"Gadzooks! Haven't you got a home to go to?"

"No," answered Bill Poynter calmly. "I haven't got a home. I don't dwell, I lodge. I thought you knew that."

"I do, I do. Well, come on in, for heaven's sake; it's perishing cold with this door open."

Poynter stepped smartly inside and removed his hat. "You haven't got visitors, have you?"

"What difference would that make?" asked Mr. Smith, closing the door.

"Well, if you have I'll go away again and see you in the morning. But if you haven't—I'd like to show you something."

"You've got something to show me?"

Poynter nodded. "Yes, I have. I've something to show you, but I want you to do the thinking about it."

"Oh," said Mr. Smith, staring at him suspiciously. "You do, do you? Well, hang your things up there and come into the living-room. There's a faint glow in the hearth there that Mary says is a fire."

Mary was Mrs. Smith, and she sat by the small fire in the living-room, knitting a sock. She smiled a welcome at Poynter. Then she stopped smiling and assumed an obviously artificial expression of severity.

"I know—business. Friends of mine tell me that being married to a doctor is pretty grim, and that being married to an author is worse. They don't know a thing; they ought to try being married to a policeman."

"Don't take any notice of Mary," said Mrs. Smith's husband. "She's turning the heel—that's always a trying time in the Smith household. Sit yourself down there and get it off your chest."

Poynter sat down at the table and produced his photographs and magnifying glass. "Pictures," he announced solemnly. "Pretty pictures."

"What about them?" asked the inspector morosely. "I've seen those damned things before."

"Look at them again," invited Poynter, "and let your uncle Bill show you a thing or two." He selected an envelope from the bunch and took out three photographs, which he passed to the inspector, who had sat down beside him. "Exhibits A1, A2 and A3."

"May I see?" Mrs. Smith jumped up from her chair, and came and stood beside her husband. "Ooh! Those are the mysterious hoof-prints."

"Yes," said Mr. Smith. "And if you promise not to lean your whole weight on my head, or dribble your knitting on the table, you may look over my shoulder."

"Thank you, dear."

"Exhibits A1, A2 and A3," repeated Poynter severely. "A1 shows the first half-dozen prints where they start at the bottom of The Rise. Not too clear, but the best that could be done under the circumstances. A2 is a close-up of the first print, A3 a close-up of the second. Let's try this on Mrs. Smith—do you notice anything, Mrs. Smith?"

"What am I supposed to notice?"

"Compare the two prints," suggested her husband.

"We-ell . . . they look slightly different. That one's thinner on the left-hand side."

"That's it," said Poynter approvingly. "That's the way it looks: the left half of the shoe that made the first print appears to be slightly narrower than the same half of the shoe that made the second print. The question is, is it really so, or is it a matter of imperfect photography, or the way the shoe struck the snow? Well, I think these will give us the answer." And he passed over three more photographs to the inspector.

"Marked respectively," he went on, "M1, M2 and M3. These, as you can see, are clearer, the detail is sharper. That is because they were taken at that gap in the hedge in Mason's garden, where the snow wasn't so thick, and where consequently the impressions were more clearly defined. M1 again shows some half-dozen prints—"

"It also shows something else," interrupted the inspector quietly. "See, Mary? See how the hoof-marks overlap Mason's own prints? Showing that the Thing was behind him—or *with* him. . . ."

Mrs. Smith saw, and shuddered involuntarily. Poynter went on unemotionally. "M2 is again a close-up of the first print in M1, M3 a close-up of the second—"

"That shoe," cried Mrs. Smith, "the left-hand side of it, is *definitely* narrower than the other!"

"Yes, I think so."

"And so do I," added Mr. Smith. "In fact, there's really no doubt about it. We can call that an established fact. All the same, Bill, I don't quite see—I never did think that this Thing hopped on one leg, you know."

"No, no. As you say, Inspector, the fact is established—I could show you more photographs, but it would only waste time. . . . But I particularly wanted it an established fact that the—the Thing did have two legs before I showed you *these.*"

And here Poynter produced another set of three photographs, labelled this time B1, B2 and B3.

"These were the second lot I took—you called me up from the bottom of The Rise to take them. They are the impressions that were on the Jacksons' hedge. B1 shows the two of them together, B2 shows the one on the left—the one you would naturally conclude to have been made by the left hoof—and B3 the one on the right—the one you would suppose to have been made by the right hoof."

"Oh, yes," said Mrs. Smith. "That's where the Thing stood on the hedge, isn't it? before it stepped down on to the road? Well, there you are; there are your right and left legs—"

She stopped abruptly. Mr. Smith had snatched up the magnifying glass and was studying the photographs intently.

"Odds blood!" he exclaimed. *"They're both the same!"*

There was a momentary silence. Mrs. Smith bent down for a closer view, and a stray lock of her still dark hair tickled her husband's cheek.

"Both the same—? You mean it's the same hoof?"

"Same shoe, anyway," amended the inspector cautiously. "The one with the narrower left half."

"Yes," murmured Poynter. "Yes. But I thought the theory was that the Thing had stood on that hedge with both feet. . . ."

"What else does anything with two legs do when it stands on anything?"

"Perhaps it didn't stand," hazarded Mrs. Smith. "Not like that. Perhaps it hopped up on one leg and overbalanced, and had to hop again, sideways, to steady itself."

But both men shook their heads.

"The impressions are too neat," pointed out the inspector, "too sharply defined. If there had been any overbalancing there'd have been some dragging, some slight disturbance of the snow. Bill's camera would have picked it up. But there isn't any. Those prints are as clear and clean-cut as a whistle. It *may* have hopped; but if so, it hopped cleanly and steadily. But in any case—"

"In any case," said Poynter, "it doesn't make sense. Why hop on one leg when you've got two to stand on? And there definitely *were* two. . . . Well now, leave those three on one side and give me back the others before they get mixed up. . . . Right. Now look at these."

It was a fat envelope that he passed over this time.

"Take them out one at a time in sequence. X1 to 17. Individual and consecutive prints from the circle on the roof round the skylight. Nearly half-way round, in fact."

"However did you take those?" asked Mrs. Smith.

"Climbed up the step-ladder through the skylight, and sprawled on my stomach in the snow. The inspector hung on to my ankles so that I shouldn't slide off the roof."

Mr. Smith was dealing out the photographs on to the table in front of him like a man playing a game of patience in slow motion.

"It went round there several times, didn't it, Bill? Still the last round, the ones on top, have come out pretty clearly. Um . . ."

"They're all the same again!" cried Mrs. Smith

"Yes," agreed Poynter heavily. "The narrow-sided ones again. . . . Well, Inspector, what's the answer? Did this Thing *hop* round that skylight, like a kid playing hopscotch?"

"Bill."

"What?"

"The window-sill."

"Oh, yes," Bill Poynter fumbled with his envelopes. "Here you are. S1, S2 and S3. S1, both together. S2, the left one—as the Thing stood. S3, the right one. Back to front this time, because, naturally, the photos were taken from inside the window, facing the prints, as it were, and not from behind them."

Mr. Smith studied S2 and S3 through the magnifying-glass. Still peering through the glass he asked for B2 and B3, the photographs of the impressions on the Jackson's low privet hedge. He laid the four photographs in a row and compared them carefully.

"Well, I'm damned!"

"They're different," pronounced Mrs. Smith, her head close to his. "I mean they're the same—but they're different. . . ."

Her husband knew what she meant. The two prints on the window-sill outside Mason's bedroom had been made by the one shoe, but it was not the same shoe that had made the prints on the Jacksons' hedge, or the ring of prints on the roof of Mason's house; it was the other shoe, the shoe that was the same width all the way round. . . .

*   *   *

About the same time that Poynter and the inspector were studying their photographs—about the same time that Gregory Cushing, in his uncle's cottage, woke up feeling cold and queerly deserted, and uncle Jake himself, in the Steeple Inn, was switching from the *First Part of King Henry The Fourth* to his beloved *Hamlet*—somebody else was mulling over the photographs *he* had taken that Sunday morning.

Mr. Croxley sat in the well-appointed drawing-room of his comfortable house on The Rise, with the light directly above him shining on his bald head and his blue jowls and his heavy horn-rimmed spectacles. Like Poynter, he was wielding a magnifying-glass; but, unlike Poynter, he was smoking a large cigar. His wife, a mousy, timid woman who lived only to minister to her lord and master, sat by the fireside and pretended to read a book.

Mr. Croxley had not the authority or standing of Detective-Sergeant Poynter, and so his series was not as complete. For instance, he had no photographs of the hoof-prints on the window-sill outside Mason's bedroom, nor of the circle of prints on the roof, nor of the marks under the tree where Mason's dead body had hung. But he had plenty of others, and a more leisurely and detailed examination of them had shown him just what they had shown Poynter: that whereas the impression of one shoe was the same width all the way round, the impression of the other shoe was narrower in its left half. The sharper the impression, the more clearly was this shown.

And he also had a photograph of the prints on the hedge, which showed beyond question that only the one shoe had left both impressions; the shoe with the narrower left half.

He studied this for a few moments, decided it was odd, put his cigar down very carefully so as not to break the ash, and hunted for the photograph of the tracks before his own front door. This showed two clear impressions side by side facing the door where, it was obvious, the Thing must have stood still, even if only for a second. It was also obvious that both shoes had made these marks: in other words, the Thing had stood there on both feet, or hooves.

Now, if Mr. Croxley had had Poynter's photographs of the prints on the windowsill, or the circle on the roof, he would not have hesitated a moment longer. But even so he did not hesitate for very long before he decided that his duty was clear. He picked up his photographs, stood up and said importantly: "Maud!"

"Ye—yes, dear?" answered his wife, giving a little jump.

"I am going out," said Mr. Croxley, practically in capital letters. "I must go to the police. It is possible I may be there for a little while, I can't say. Don't wait up for me; go to bed when the fire burns down."

"Yes, dear," said Mrs. Croxley submissively. Submissively, but not unhappily. Her actions had been ordered and her thinking done for her for so many years that she was now quite used to it.

Mr. Croxley put his cigar in his mouth, strode masterfully to the hall, wrapped himself up until only the tip of his pudgy nose and the cigar were showing, and set out for River Crescent to stir up the Police. . . .

18

"A man's a man for a' that," observed Mr. Silver gravely to the licensee of the Steeple Inn. "Robbie Burns said that."

"Ah!" commented Honest George, refusing to commit himself either one way or the other.

"An' that's about all he could say!" retorted Jake Popplewell crushingly, who burnt incense at the shrine of only one bard. "The Scotsman was a jinglin' rhymster, but the Man from Stratford was a poet an' a philosopher."

Fighting words these, but fortunately there were no Scotsmen in the bar.

"What," demanded old Jake rhetorically, "says the immortal Will on the subjec'? He says, an' this is only one small extract, mind yer! he says: 'What a piece o' work is a man! How noble in reason! how infinite in faculty! in form, in movin', how express an' admirable! in action how like an angel! in apprehension how like a god! the beauty of the world! the paragon of animals. . . .'"

Honest George sniffed disparagingly. " 'E ain't never met no coppers, that's plain! 'Ow about givin' us that bit about once more in the britches, dear frien's?"

"Ha!" snorted Jake approvingly, slamming his tankard down on the counter for the umpteenth time. "Fill that up agen, me lad, an' I'll oblige. . . ."

*　　　*　　　*

Inspector Smith hitched his chair a little closer to the table and asked for more photographs.

"Which ones do you want?" inquired Detective-Sergeant Poynter.

"Oh . . . Maltravers's wall, Mrs. Pendlebury's wall, doors of the various houses, under the tree. . . . Give me the one under the tree."

The methodical Poynter handed him not one but three more photographs. The first showed three or four hoof-prints leading up to and including the two together that marked the end of the long trail. Almost immediately above this point had hung the small dead body of Montague Mason; and here, it would seem, the Thing had stood and looked at it before dissolving into the nothingness from whence it had come. The second and third photographs were individual close-ups of the last prints. Round about these hoof-prints, and in two places partly obliterated by them, were some stray impressions of the human feet that had either preceded the Thing or been accompanied by it.

"Those foot-prints—" said Mrs. Smith in a low voice.

But just then the inspector wasn't interested in human feet. "Mason's," he said briefly. Then to Poynter: "Which of these is which?"

"O2 is the left hoof, as the Thing stood; O3 the right."

"Um. . . . Well, that settles it. There's your left and right, Bill—these are the marks of *both* shoes. The one that is narrower in its left half is the left shoe."

Poynter gave him two more photographs to look at. "Mrs. Pendlebury's low wall with the spiked railing. Maltravers's high wall. Prints coming at you."

"Uh. Well, it didn't hop along here, it walked."

Poynter poked another photograph at him. "Outside Croxley's front door."

"Both shoes again."

"Jackson's front door."

"Both shoes—"

"Maltravers's door. . . . Mrs. Pendlebury's door. . . . The Steeple Inn. . . ."

"Um," muttered Mr. Smith. "Both shoes all the way—except on that damned hedge. . . . One more, William: Mason's."

But Poynter shook his head. "I didn't take any there, they wouldn't have told us anything we didn't know then. It may have stood in front of both doors there, but if so the prints are lost under the others where it marched round and round. There's that spot at the gap in the hedge, the window-sill and the roof; and you've seen them all. . . . Well?"

"Well, it's crazy!"

"Yes," said Poynter drily. "So I have been given to understand."

Mr. Smith pushed the photographs away from him and waved a hand in an irritated, baffled gesture. "Oh, I know, the whole damn business is crazy. But it's inconsistent in its craziness. . . . I read the story these tracks in the snow had to tell us when we were standing under that tree—remember?"

Poynter remembered.

"Well, here it is again, briefly, brought up to date. And it's madness and moonshine.

"Some time early on Sunday morning something with hooves, and with shoes like small horse-shoes on its hooves, landed on this earth at the foot of The Rise. It walked up The Rise in and out of gardens, stood in two places close together on its *left* hoof on a low hedge that, by all the laws of nature, should have given way beneath it; apparently walked clean through Maltravers's pavilion and up on to his wall, jumped down to Mrs. Pendlebury's wall and walked along that to her gateway. It then walked down the drive to the front door and round the house to the summer-house, walked through that shut-up summer-house and on to the hillside beyond, and so on to the road again through a gap in the gorse hedge—

"Why bother to go for a gap, Bill? Why didn't it just push straight through that gorse as it had through the pavilion and the summer-house?

"Anyway, it walked on down to the Steeple Inn, turned away and went along to Mason's house where again it stood in two places close together—but on its *right* hoof this time—on that window-sill, and where, either before or after this, it *hopped* on its left hoof round and round that skylight on the roof. . . .

"And, of course, there's Mason. Is he part of that story? Or a different story? What made him go and take his own life like that?"

"The Blue Woman," said Poynter unemotionally. "Miss Forbes said so. He's part of the story."

"Then what about that telephone call—and the footprints we found in the dust up under the roof? The telephone call was made hours before it started to snow."

"What about it? That has nothing to do with the other business. In fact it may have had something to do with Mason's legitimate business—whatever that is; maybe legitimate is hardly the right word—he seems to have been a bit of a mystery man. Maybe the man who made the call was an agent or something, and something had gone wrong. It was hours after *that* that the Thing called on him and that he went out, under his own steam, into the snow and along to that tree."

"And that tree is part of the ghost story, yes. Part of Mason's death, not his life—not his ordinary everyday business life. And, as you say, the telephone call might have been. Um. . . . And the Thing went along to the tree either *with* him or *after* him, and it stood there right under that branch. Then—*zip*—it went. Went clean off the face of the earth and back to hell, or wherever it had come from. . . ."

"The psychic plane," said Poynter solemnly. "Where the Blue Woman lives. And I thought this Thing *was* the Blue Woman."

"Yes—with hooves on. . . . Bill, it's absurd. It's *silly.*"

Poynter flicked a photograph. "But it's there. It happened. We saw it."

"We saw marks in the snow. And between us we've let them tell us a medieval ghost story, an old wives' tale of witchcraft and black magic. An absurd story—with absurdities within the absurdity. And I can't swallow it."

"It's happened before."

"No."

"But *The Times*—"

"No," said Mr. Smith again. "Not this story. There's a dead man in the middle of all this witchcraft—or at least at the end of it. That never happened before."

"As a matter of fact," said Poynter calmly, "it has. People have suffered from hallucinations and visions and hauntings, and have committed suicide because of it."

"Echo of Miss Forbes," said the inspector bitterly. "Those hallucinations and visionings and whatnot didn't leave a physical trail a mile long."

He turned away from the table and stared into the fire. Mrs. Smith had long since gone back to her chair and taken up her knitting. Poynter began to gather up his photographs and juggle them back into their envelopes.

"Physical trail a mile long. What physical thing, what mortal thing, can hop about on roofs and second-story window-sills, and walk through locked and shuttered sheds and summer-houses, and walk *up* on empty air through them?"

Mr. Smith didn't answer him. He didn't appear to have heard him. He began muttering to himself. "Granting, for one wild and extravagant moment, that there was a demon loose on Saturday night, or Sunday morning, or a Blue Woman; and granting that it walked about the countryside in this eccentric fashion: that it hopped from the ground to a second-story window-sill and stood there on one leg with another hop three or four inches to the side, maybe for comfort or maybe to get a better view; and granting that, for some reason best known to itself, it hopped on the other leg up on to the roof and round and round that skylight . . . granting all these silly and impossible things, it's that damned hedge that I baulk at—it wouldn't support a well-fed wood-pecker—"

The rambling monologue suddenly ceased. Poynter said wearily: "I thought Miss Forbes had covered that ground. Weight, size, gravitation, don't mean a thing on the psychic plane."

"You and your psychic plane!" said Mr. Smith. But he said it without thinking. He said it without realizing he had actually spoken. He was still staring into the fire, but he wasn't seeing it any longer. He was seeing a little picture in his own mind: the picture of himself in the Jacksons' garden standing on one foot and lifting the other, placing it lightly on the hedge and leaving a clear impression on the crust of snow; and then bearing down a little more heavily, and his foot breaking through and sinking into the flimsy privet. . . .

But that was all he did see. It didn't tell him anything then.

*   *   *

In the Croxleys' drawing-room the fire was burning low. Mrs. Croxley shivered, roused herself, looked at her wrist-watch, put down her book and stood up and went to the window. She edged up the blind a few inches and peered out. She could, of course, see nothing in the darkness, but peering through windows while awaiting the homecomings of her lord and master was one of Mrs. Croxley's major entertainments in life. She dropped the blind and went out of the room, switching off the lights as she went, saw that the hall light was burning and went slowly and reluctantly upstairs to bed.

"Time, gennelmen, please!" announced Honest George Borwell.

If either Jake Popplewell or Jim Silver heard him they paid no attention. They were the last customers of the Steeple Inn; the minor characters and a few other desultory droppers-in had departed long since.

"Time, gennelmen, *pullease!"* bellowed Honest George again.

Jake turned at that. His legs were unsteady and his eyes were glassy, but his tongue was still in comparatively good working order. Sternly regarding the shimmering outlines of the central of the three Mr. Borwells appearing to confront him, he snarled thickly: "Time! What is time?

"The time o' life is short;
To spen' that shortnesh—*hic*—shortness bashely were too long,
If life did ride upon a dial's point—

"An' that," he added emphatically, clutching the edge of the bar for support, "is wash wrong with the worl' today. Ridin' on the poin' of a ruddy dial! Slave to a perishin' clock!"

"I can't 'elp that," countered the stolid George. "The law sez it's time—"

"Life, George," orated Jake solemnly, "is the fool o' time . . . Begod! the ol' maestro said that—

"But thought's the slave o' life, an' life'sh time'sh—*hic*
—life's time's fool,
An' time, that takes shurvey of all the worl'
Musht have a shtop. . . .

"The dyin' Hotspur," he explained for the benefit of Honest George. "A' the very end, seein' clearly an' with a flash o' genius—"

"I don't know nuffin' about any 'Otspur," growled Mr. Borwell sourly. "All I knows is the bar's closed an' you gotter go out. I ain't takin' no chances, there's two coppers out there—"

"Two rogues in buckram," interjected Mr. Silver brightly.

This stirred a chord in Jake's memory. He said nothing, but the light of battle flared up in his old eyes, and with startling suddenness he lurched away from the bar and stumbled through the door. Jim Silver, who was in much better shape than his friend, tossed a careless "'Night, George," over his shoulder and hurried out after him.

The two policemen were standing in the middle of the cross-roads; not because they had any particular interest in the inn, but because, being both cold and bored, they were endeavouring to lighten the tedium of their vigil and warm themselves a trifle by marching up and down between Mason's house and the cross-roads.

"Ha!" ejaculated Jake grimly, as he and Silver came upon them. He looked down at the snow, which seemed to occasion him some surprise, then up at the star-spangled sky, and then at the policemen.

" 'Tis now the very witchin' time o' night,
When Churchyards yawn an' hell itself breathes out
contage—contashe—*hic*—contagion to this worl'. . . ."

He extricated himself clumsily from Silver's supporting grip and waved his arms in horrific gestures. "Now," he thundered in bloodcurdling accents:

"Now could I drink hot blood,
An' do such bidder business as the day
Would quake to look upon. . . ."

Something, visible only to Jake, was gathering behind the grinning policemen; a dim shape was taking form. Jake's expression altered, his eyes widened and his beer-thickened voice faltered and sank.

"The witchin' time o' night," he repeated in a fearful whisper. "Churchyards yawnin'—an' hell. . . ."

The shape was now fully formed. It glided not so much between as *through* the two policemen; the shape, apparently, of a woman in a long dark loose dress with a hood over its head, and underneath the hood, in place of features, a blue void.

Jake let out a terrified yell. "Keep off, you hag!"

He turned to run, stumbled a few yards and fell headlong in the snow. Silver lumbered after him and helped him to his feet.

"What's biting him?" asked one of the policemen, using his flashlight.

"The Blue Woman," replied Silver shortly.

"The what?"

"The Blue Woman. It's a ghost he sees when he's like this."

Jake, keeping the stalwart body of his friend between him and that terrible faceless wraith, roared: "Away, you hag! To hell where y' came from, you slut, you trull, you carrion crow!"

"He's got a fine flow of language," commented the policeman disapprovingly. "If you ask me, it would 'a' been better for all parties if he'd left that pub a coupler hours ago—and what's struck *you*, Harry?"

The second policeman was shining his flashlight this way and that over the snow-covered road. "Well, I don't know—isn't that what's supposed to have made them hoof-marks the other night?"

"Eh?"

"This here Blue Woman. . . ."

"Ghosts!" scoffed the first policeman. "And do you see any hoof-marks?"

"No . . . I can't say I expected to, but all the same—"

"*There she goes!*" Jake pointed a quivering forefinger at the second policeman. "Behind yer—comin' this way—"

The policeman whirled round and flashed his torch, but of course there was nothing.

"You'd better take him home," said the first policeman austerely. "Get him inside quickly before we have to run him in—or before he chucks a fit!"

"I'm going to," said Silver curtly. And did so. . . .

He took Jake home over the hill and down to his cottage. But it was a fatiguing and a difficult task, for the Blue Woman went with them. The stars gave a pale glimmer of light, and Jake saw her flitting sometimes ahead, sometimes behind, and at the other times lurking in the hedges at the side of the road, keeping her at bay apparently only by the strength and richness of his vituperation.

Gregory, who for the past quarter of an hour had been half-heartedly trying to summon up enough energy to rise from his comfortable chair and go up to bed, heard them coming and made the mistake of going out to meet them.

"Full as a bed bug again, I see," he greeted Silver unpleasantly.

"Yes . . . and the Blue Woman's walking."

"Are you telling me!"

Once at the little wicket gate Jake struggled free of Silver's hands, uttered a final savage wordless snarl, and fled up the short brick path, bolting into the cottage like a terrified rabbit. Gregory heard the key being turned.

"That's a lot of use!" he said bitterly. "That's a fat lot of use! Now I'm locked out."

"What about the back door?" inquired Silver.

"He'll lock that too . . . unless we beat him to it."

"Then beat him. Get a move on."

But there was no immediate danger of the back door also being barred to Gregory: Jake, for the moment, was too busy alternately hurling defiance at the Blue Woman through the front door and throwing things at the clock in the parlour. Gregory went round to the back door and sneaked in through the kitchen and up the stairs to his own bedroom, leaving uncle Jake to his amusements downstairs.

While Jim Silver, the Good Samaritan, trudged away back over The Rise to his own home. . . .

19

Later that same Monday night—or, rather, Tuesday morning. . . .

Police-Constable Keyes stamped into the police station in River Crescent, strode across the charge room to the fireplace and spread his hands to the blaze. From his high desk opposite, Sergeant Perkins inquired: "And 'ow are the shock troops, Bert?"

By shock troops the worthy sergeant meant Constables Dempsey and Gimbel, the two policemen on sentinel duty outside Mason's house in Steeple Thelming. Sergeant Perkins was one of the old school. He was bald, fat, commonplace and unimaginative; but the Case of the Footprints of Satan had even him thinking along new and strange lines.

"They're all right," replied Keyes casually. He was much younger than Perkins and one of the new school. "But old Jake Popplewell's been at it again."

"What? Again?"

"Yes. If he keeps going like this he'll drink himself into the looney bin in no time. He's seeing things."

"What sort of things?"

"Blue Women."

Sergeant Perkins jumped a little on his padded stool. "Lumme! 'As 'e seen 'er again—tonight?"

"I don't quite know what you mean by again, but according to Dempsey"—and here P.C. Keyes began to grin—"as soon as Jake was emptied out of that pub he started yelling about a Blue Woman that was hovering about trying to get at him. He was scared stiff and using choice language. He was with a farmer who lives round there—chap named Silver. Dempsey says Silver saw Jake home, and he was fighting this Blue Woman all up the hill and down the other side."

"Lumme!" muttered Sergeant Perkins again, dabbing at his button of a nose. "Is she out again?"

"What do you mean by out again, Sarge?"

"Don'tcher keep yer ears open round 'ere, Bert? Don'tcher know old Jake Popplewell's Blue Woman was out the night Mason 'anged 'imself, and that she's supposed to have made them 'oof-marks in the snow?"

"What?" Keyes was frankly incredulous. "I thought," he said, mildly sardonic, "that it was supposed to have been Old Nick himself."

Perkins said nothing, but continued to massage his nose thoughtfully. Keyes was now grinning widely. "This is rich. . . . Is this Blue Woman a centaur, or something? How come she leaves hoof-prints?"

Sergeant Perkins was not quite sure of that word "centaur," and so contented himself with merely observing that the Blue Woman was supposed to have been a witch.

"Did you say 'witch'?"

"Yeah."

"Well, I still don't quite see the connection. . . . But you remind me, Sarge," added the young constable darkly, "you remind me of some women I have met in my time, concerning whom it would not have surprised me greatly if they had left *paw* marks instead of ordinary footprints. . . ."

*   *   *

Mrs. Croxley drowsily stretched out a hand and felt the other half of the wide bed. It was cold to the touch and still unoccupied. She made anxious clicking noises with her tongue. Mr. Croxley was very late; what could the time be now? She lifted herself on one elbow, switched on the bedside lamp and looked at her watch. Then her eyelids flew wide open and she gasped.

Twenty minutes past one!

Mr. Croxley couldn't be *still* at the police station. . . .

Mrs. Croxley began to worry. Mr. Croxley might have been taken suddenly ill—he might have been run over—he might have fallen in the river . . .

He might be lying hurt in the snow, unseen, unheard, needing help. . . .

True, he'd told her he might be late in returning home—but not as late as *this,* surely . . ..

Something must have happened. . . .

After ten minutes of this mental see-sawing, Mrs. Croxley slipped out of bed, put on a warm dressing-gown and slippers and went downstairs to the telephone.

Here she hesitated again. Then she took the plunge. She picked up the telephone and rang the police station.

A wheezing voice in her ear announced itself the police station.

"Oh!" said Mrs. Croxley, flustered. "Oh, it's Mrs. Croxley speaking. My husband, Mr. Croxley, left to go to see you earlier this evening . . . he should have been home *hours* ago . . . but he isn't—

"Croxley. Mr. Croxley, *Peacehaven,* The Rise. . . . Yes, yes . . . Oh, about nine o'clock—perhaps a little earlier. . . .

"*What* . . .?

"But he said—he told me . . .

"Are you *sure* . . .?

"Oh . . . oh, well . . . but I don't know what to do. . . .

"Oh, *thank* you . . . thank you. . . ."

"Ho!" observed Sergeant Perkins, clipping up his receiver. "Now, I wonder—"

"What was all that about?" asked P.C. Keyes.

"One of our most 'ighly respected citizens is missin'. Least-ways 'e 'as not yet returned to 'is 'ome from visitin' us 'ere at round about nine o'clock."

Keyes stared at him. "I didn't know anybody had been here."

"Nobody 'as," returned Perkins weightily. "That's what's rummy about it. Croxley's the sort of feller 'oo, when 'e sez 'e's goin' to some place, *goes* there—an' generally makes a noise about it. . . . Bert, I think you'd better go round there and see what it's all about. Go and talk to Mrs. Croxley. And make a lot of notes in yer little book—that generally calms 'em down and makes 'em feel better."

"Okay, Sarge," sighed Keyes. "What's the address?"

*   *   *

Mrs. Croxley stood in the hall at *Peacehaven,* clasping and un-clasping her hands.

Mr. Croxley had not been to the police station!

But he'd told her that was where he was going. He'd gone out with that special intention . . . and he'd taken his photographs with him. . . .

Perhaps . . .

Mrs. Croxley fluttered into the drawing-room and lifted a window blind. But she couldn't see anything outside; all she could see in the blackly shining glass were dim reflections of the room.

She pulled down the blind and went back into the hall. Without any clear idea in her mind of what she was doing, she went to the front door and opened it wide. The hall light streamed out and illuminated a few yards of snow-covered garden path. She peered out irresolutely, wringing her hands.

That was when she saw the hoof-marks. . . .

*   *   *

At Sergeant Perkins's elbow the telephone rang again.

"'Old on, Bert!" he called, and P.C. Keyes halted in the doorway.

"Yes?" said Sergeant Perkins tersely.

"All right, mum, all right. . . .

"*Whassat* . . .?

"Cor . . .! All right, mum, you leave it to us. . . . Yes, yes, we'll act at once. . . . Now, now, Mrs. Croxley, that won't do no good—there's nothin' to *be frightened* of, the police'll be there in a minute. . . ."

He slammed the telephone down on the desk and stared at Keyes.

"You were dead right, Bert—the Blue Woman *'as* bin walkin' again! She's bin walkin' in Croxley's garden! An' Croxley, 'oo was supposed to 'ave come in 'ere to see us at round about nine o'clock an' 'oo never turned up—is missin'!

"Cor lumme!" Sergeant Perkins blew out his fat cheeks and picked up the telephone once more. "This is somep'n for Smithy. . . ."

*   *   *

So Sergeant Perkins rang up the inspector, dragging him from sleep and a warm bed, and Mr. Smith listened to what Perkins had to tell him and then issued a few crisp orders. Then he did something he had never done before: he rang up Superintendent Blackler and dragged *him* out of bed.

And so it came about that some fifteen or twenty minutes later the police car, with P.C. Keyes at the wheel, came cautiously out along Old Chipping Road and stopped under the street light at the foot of The Rise a few yards on the town side from Jake Popplewell's cottage. Superintendent Blackler, Inspector Smith, Sergeant Poynter and Keyes got out, and all four produced flashlights.

"In line abreast," commanded the superintendent briefly. "Concentrate flashlights on the road. See if we can pick up any hoof-prints before we get to Croxley's gate."

But it wasn't so easy: there had been intermittent flurries of snow during the morning, but none since early afternoon, and all day, morning and afternoon, there had been traffic up and down The Rise. The roadway was a mess of footprints, and even under

134

the concentrated rays of four flashlights none of the searching eyes was able to spy so much as one hoof-mark. But Poynter spotted something else, and his flashlight hovered for a moment on a small brown object.

"What is it, Bill?" asked the inspector.

Poynter bent down and picked up the object. "Winston Churchill's been here," he mumbled. He rolled the little brown cylinder in his fingers, smelt it and added: "This is the size he smokes, and he's the only man I know who can afford to chuck away a king size cigar before it's even half smoked."

"Well?" inquired the superintendent patiently. "What about it?"

"I don't know, sir. Except that it's a lot of cigar to throw away, and I have an idea that it was thrown away not so very long ago."

Poynter, the human jackdaw, put it carefully away in a pocket, while on the other flank P.C. Keyes exclaimed suddenly: "Hullo!"

He was away out across the road and his flashlight had fallen on the gate that opened on to the rough cart track that led to the shed where Jake housed his donkey. The three other flashlights followed that of Keyes and the men came closer. It was a barred gate, and over it and through the bars they could see that the short cart track was a crazy quilt of tracks. Some were foot-prints, but the majority were the marks of hooves. There were scores of them, doubling and turning on each other.

The men crowded round the gate and their flashlights wandered up and down the track. Then:

"No," said Mr. Smith confidently. "No. That's Boomer, that's the donkey. . . . Hold back, everybody, let me have a closer look."

He opened the gate carefully and quietly and slipped through. He squatted down in the snow and studied the hoof-marks. He examined a dozen and more before he straightened up and came back to the gate.

"I guess that was the donkey all right, all those impressions, Bill, are the same width all the way round. It looks as if Boomer got tired of being inside all day and all night and came out for a walk, and somebody, either old Jake or his nephew, or maybe both, had a bit of a job persuading him to go back inside again. The donkey didn't get out on to the road. . . ."

The four flashlights, moved by the same impulse, swept the roadway round about the gate, and the wielders of them agreed that Boomer had not been on the road.

"Unless, of course," amended Superintendent Blackler, "his prints have been covered and obliterated by the drunken Mr. Popplewell and that man Silver, and maybe more. . . . If, by any chance, I've been pulled out of bed and into a freezing night just to look at some donkey tracks in somebody's garden. . . ."

"I'm afraid it's not as simple or as wholesome as that, Super," said the inspector in a low voice.

He closed the gate behind him, and the little party advanced again, the flood of yellow light sweeping the trodden snow ahead of them. But it wasn't until they were at Mr. Croxley's garden gate that they picked up the strange tracks; and the moment they saw them three of the party knew immediately that there had been another visitation. For here again was that odd single line of hoof-prints, one directly ahead of the other, approximately ten inches apart.

Superintendent Blackler muttered something under his breath. He stood at the entrance to the Croxleys' garden path, and the others clustered about him. The flashlights roamed in unison up and down the path from the gate to the front door, and Mr. Smith read their message in that same low, constrained tone of voice.

"Three lines of tracks. . . . The family's been inside all day. Some time ago Croxley came out—see?—to go to the station. He never went there. Why not? Heaven knows. But he *did* come back—see? those are his tracks returning—"

"Or *somebody's* tracks," interrupted the superintendent.

"Ye-es," said Mr. Smith. "I stand corrected. Somebody's tracks—Croxley's own, or somebody else's. But whoever it was, *something met him here and went in with him.* Either went in with him, or followed immediately after. . . ."

"Yes," agreed the superintendent a little breathlessly. "And caught up with him before he got to the door—or at the door. Otherwise he'd have gone in. Somebody would have visited Mrs. Croxley, or Croxley would be in there with his wife. . . . What happened at the door? *Because nothing's come out again; neither the man—nor the other thing. . . .*"

"Wait!" said Mr. Smith sharply. "Let's see where these hoof-marks come from first. Let's see where they start."

The beam of his own flashlight shone on the three sets of tracks curving in and out of the narrow gateway: Croxley's coming and, perhaps, going, down the hill, as was only to be expected; but the Thing's coming from *up* the hill. But only a little way up the hill, barely six yards, in fact, as the slowly travelling ray of light clearly showed. There, at the side of the road in untrodden snow, the hoof-prints began. They began, as they had begun farther down the hill two nights before, abruptly and inexplicably; as someone had observed, like a special act of creation. The nearest print to that sudden, mysterious beginning, an ordinary human foot-print, was four feet or so away towards the middle of the road, and was only one of scores spreading up and down.

"Oh, *Lord!*" breathed Superintendent Blackler.

"Yes," sighed the inspector. "Yes; same mixture as before. It materialized here—or something. . . . Well, let's follow."

Proceeding cautiously in single file, with the inspector leading the way, they went in through the little open gate and followed the tracks right up to the front door. And here the superintendent's question was, in part, answered. For, without any signs of hesitation, the two sets of tracks, the human and the unknown, turned sharply to the right and went on past the door to another gate set in a tall latticed fence. This was really part of the fence, and was closed: either Croxley, or some other man, or the Thing, had closed it again after passing through.

"Or," said Bill Poynter in his lugubrious sardonic voice, "Croxley closed it after him, and the Thing just walked right through it."

But nobody took any notice of him, for the trail this time was a short one and the end was now in plain sight. On the far side of this lattice-work fence was a rectangular lawn—hidden now, of course, under the snow. The lawn ran at right angles to the road, and save for those two lines of tracks leading, side by side, to the almost exact centre of it no foot had trodden there since the last heavy fall of snow.

The man's footprints led up the centre of this virgin mantle of snow, and there they ended.

The tracks of the Thing that had hooves led up to some four feet from the end of the footprints, and from that point they went round and round in a circle; a circle that was subsequently determined by physical measurement to have a mean radius of eight feet, one inch; a circle that had no beginning or end.

And in the middle of this circle, spreadeagled in the snow, lay Croxley. His hat had fallen off his head, and his bald pate shone like polished ivory in the concentrated rays of the four flashlights. But in one place just above the left temple it was dull and dark. There was a wound there, a semi-circular cut that had bled.

But it was bleeding no longer, for the life had gone out of the domineering and masterful Mr. Croxley.

The Thing wasn't there. There was nothing else there. In all that smooth expanse of snow there was not another mark.

PART THREE

The Lair of Truth

20

. . . After a few moments superintendent Blackler said in a hard, strained voice: "You're nimbler than I am, Smithy; hop inside that blasted magic circle and see if he's still alive."

Cautiously, like a ballet dancer, Mr. Smith skipped inside the ring of hoof-prints, squatted down beside that still, prone figure, and felt for a pulse.

"Dead," he said curtly. "And stone cold."

The superintendent grunted. "You wouldn't have to lie there very long before you grew cold. Oh, *Lord!* There'll be trouble over this."

"I know," replied the inspector with foreboding. "There'll be a reign of terror on The Rise after this." He stood up, and his eyes strayed from the dead body to the uneven circle of hoof-marks. "Because there was no suicide about this one—he's had a crack on the head. Violence, Super," he added very softly. "So at last we get—violence!"

"Yes, so I can see. . . . And Mrs. Croxley is waiting inside there, waiting for somebody to go in and give her news—and comfort. Comfort! My God—somebody's got to go in there and drag her out to identify the body. And I suppose I've got to go in and do the dirty work."

Three pairs of eyes rested on him, respectfully, but all saying the same thing. The inspector put it into words.

"Penalties of seniority, Super," he murmured sympathetically. "But let the identifying go for awhile. We know Croxley, there's no doubt about it. But there's a telephone in there—and we want Dr. Scott here just as soon as you can drag him out of bed."

"You shall have him," said the superintendent bitterly. He turned away and went slowly back through the gate in the latticed fence to the front door. Still standing like a statue, and moving only his eyes, Mr. Smith spoke to the others. "Stay where you are, Keyes, and don't move. Bill, can you take photos of this?"

"I can take flashlights," replied Poynter cautiously.

"Where's your camera?"

"In the car. I didn't know what we were going to run into, you know."

"Who did? All right, pop back and get it."

While Poynter went back down to the bottom of the hill for his camera and flashlight attachment Mr. Smith leapt away from the body and out of what the superintendent had called the magic circle and stood by Keyes, but that was all the movement he made.

When Poynter came back he said: "One comprehensive one, Bill. Body and that ring of prints, if you can get them in."

Poynter stood back and aimed his camera, and the inspector and Keyes blinked in the sudden blinding flash of light.

"Right. Now a few close-ups of those prints—and Croxley's own, where they end. . . .

"Good. That ought to be enough. Now I want at least two more, Bill. One at that front door, and one where the hoof-prints start a few yards up the hill."

"Okay," replied the unemotional Poynter, and went away to do the inspector's bidding. The inspector himself moved then. He went forward and foot by foot, with his nose only inches from the snow, he went round the complete circle of hoof-marks. P.C. Keyes, standing like a monument of patience, wondered a little at the procedure. The usual thing was to show a little more interest in the body.

"Keyes!" said Mr. Smith, when he had done the complete circuit.

"Sir?"

"There's a surveyor's measure—you know, a spool thing—in the car somewhere, either in the dashboard or in one of the side pockets. Hop down and get it."

"Yes, sir."

Keyes left smartly, and Mr. Smith took off his hat and ran his fingers unhappily through his hair. . . .

Poynter, coming in again, met Keyes on the way out. "And where are you going, my pretty maid? . . . Mind your big feet," he growled. "Don't get 'em all over those prints."

Keyes grinned at him. Like nearly everyone else in the Force, he knew his Detective-Sergeant Poynter. "You don't have to tell me that," he said mildly. "I'm watching it."

"Huh!" grunted Poynter with his eyes on the ground. Then he called sharply—and informally—after the constable, who had passed on. "Hey, Bert!"

"Hullo?"

Poynter was bent double and closely comparing two footprints in the snow, one that had been made by Croxley and one that Keyes had just made.

"Those clodhoppers of yours—what size are they?"

"A reasonable 10. Why?"

"Never mind why," Poynter told him haughtily. "On your way, lad, on your way."

Keyes grinned again in the darkness—he was young, and the late Mr. Croxley had meant nothing to him—and went on his way to the car. Poynter hurried to join the inspector.

"Inspector!"

"Yes, Bill?"

"Do that Douglas Fairbanks leap of yours again, will you, and have a look at the soles of Croxley's boots."

"Soles of his boots—?"

"Size," explained Poynter briefly.

"Oh!" Mr. Smith jumped again, squatted down and shone his flashlight on the soles of the stout brown boots on Croxley's feet; high up by the heel, on that little arch under the instep that never comes into contact with the ground.

"How did you know?"

"Size 11?" asked Poynter.

"Yes—but how did you know, Bill?"

"I didn't. Only Keyes takes a 10, and he'd planted one of his feet perilously near Croxley's prints—"

"Yes, sir," interpolated P.C. Keyes defensively, returning at that moment, "but not on them. I was watching that, sir."

"Well, of course you were," said Mr. Smith benignly, "—I hope. Got that measure?"

"Yes, sir."

"Good. Well, unwind plenty of slack—come up closer to this circle of prints—unwind enough slack and throw me the spool. Hold on to the end of the slack yourself."

Keyes executed the maneuver creditably, and the inspector caught the spool deftly and placed it on the middle of the dead man's back.

"Now, you hang on to that end, I'm going to wind it up taut. Hold your end immediately over the inner edge of the hoof-prints where they veer away from Croxley's. . . . That's it. But don't let it touch—I don't want any marring or marking of these prints."

Keyes held the end of the measure as directed, and the inspector wound in the slack until the tape was taut.

"Seven feet, ten inches," he murmured. "Now, Keyes, kindly emulate a perambulating frog. Or Miss Forbes's leaping rat. . . . I want you to go round this circle, three or four prints at a time, holding the end of the tape against the inside edge each time."

"Yes, sir," sighed Keyes, and the inspector wound and unwound the spool as the distances required. He called the measurements aloud.

"Seven feet, nine and a half inches—seven feet, ten—seven feet, eleven—eight, one—eight, three—eight, three. . . . M'm, widening out a bit. . . .

"Eight, two—eight, three—eight, two—seven, eleven and a half—seven, ten. . . . Ye-es. . . ."

"Well, Inspector?" inquired Poynter, when Mr. Smith had called the last measurement. "And what was all that clock-golf business in aid of?"

"Well—all right, Keyes, let go now, I'll take it—well, Bill, I was comparing circles, that's all: this, and the one on the roof round the skylight. They're both about the same size—this one might be slightly larger."

"Does that mean anything?"

"I'm damned if I know. . . . There is one slight difference; this is more uneven, it widens as it goes round. The shortest distance from the body is opposite Croxley's feet."

"And does *that* mean anything?"

The inspector shook his head wearily. "Once again, I'm damned if I know. They're the same prints, Bill. Same size, same distance between impressions, and while one is the same width all the way round the other narrows a little in its left half, looking at it from the direction it was going."

"Yes, I saw that. And somewhere along that circle the prints come to an end. Somewhere along there the Thing vanished, as it did under that tree."

"That's what the marks in the snow tell us."

"And what they tell us," said Poynter flatly, "is damn well crazy! Why the circle? Why does this Thing mooch round and round like this? Why does it hop round on the roof on one leg, and walk round here on two? It's just like last time. Once again it looks as though Croxley and the Thing came in together—until you come to this ring of prints, and then it looks as though the Thing came in afterwards, found Croxley lying here and walked round and round looking at him, and then buzzed off. . . ."

"Then what hit him?" demanded Mr. Smith. "Who killed him? Who else was here? Show me the marks of Croxley's killer—if it wasn't what everybody is now referring to in capital letters as The Thing—and show me how he got away!"

Poynter growled sardonically: "I suppose Mayhew would say the Devil threw a thunderbolt. What Miss Forbes would say I can't imagine."

"I can—vaguely. Some psychic force or influence, or something. And I think I've had enough of the psychic. Because this is a case of physical manslaughter, accidental or otherwise, or I'll eat my hat. This is the sordid physical crime that always seems to lie at the heart of these seemingly impossible, seemingly supernatural occurrences that have been plaguing us lately.

"You know, Bill," went on the inspector thoughtfully, "I have an idea that we've been looking at this business the wrong way round. We've been trying to work inwards from the outside, from the mysterious hoof-prints to the hidden inner cause. From the consequences to the effect is the usual way of working, the only possible way of working, I know; but the point is, which is the effect and which the consequences of that effect? On the face of it, it looks as though these two deaths were the consequences. That is to say they were the result of the visitation, the hoof-prints—the Thing walked, and two men died. But which way round is it *really?* Did the men die because the Thing walked, or did the Thing walk because the men died?

"I don't know. But I do know this, that here"—he flung out a hand at Croxley's dead body—"here is the core of this lot. Here is the inside physical *fact.* Now suppose we try working from that, from the inside—which is this dead man—to the outside—which is the peculiar and allegedly psychic phenomenon of the hoof-prints. . . ."

"Right-ho," agreed Poynter instantly. "Why was Croxley killed at all? Because he wore size 11 shoes?"

Mr. Smith was silent for a moment. Then he groaned and said bitterly: "I don't know. I can't even guess . . ."

*　　　*　　　*

Superintendent Blackler came back from the house looking harassed. "Somebody," he said to the inspector, "will have to stay here for the rest of the night, preferably inside the house. That woman's on her own, and she's on the verge of hysteria."

"How did you cope?" asked Mr. Smith.

"Brandy," returned the superintendent briefly. "And aspirin. I don't know how they combine. Now I come to think about it I don't suppose they do. I'll send the doctor in there when he gets here. Which reminds me—Keyes!"

"Sir?"

"Pop down to the car and look out for Dr. Scott. When he arrives bring him here, and see that he doesn't walk on those tracks."

"Yes, sir."

Keyes went away and the superintendent turned to Bill Poynter. "I did learn something in there. When Croxley left here about nine o'clock he was smoking a cigar. According to Mrs. Croxley it wasn't half-smoked when he went out. It was one of these—I snitched this from his cabinet. How does it compare with the one you found?"

He handed Poynter a long, fat cigar. Poynter dug into an inside pocket for the envelope containing the piece he had picked up in the roadway at the foot of the hill. He examined the two carefully.

"They're the same," he pronounced.

"You mean they look the same," amended Mr. Smith cautiously.

"Yes. But they're identical. And it would be altogether too much of a coincidence if this wasn't the one tossed away by Croxley."

"I'm inclined to agree with you," said the superintendent. "Point now arises, what made Croxley throw away as much as that? Cigar smokers aren't usually as wasteful as all that."

"I could put forward a suggestion," offered the inspector. "Boomer."

"Eh . . .? Oh! That donkey."

"The donkey," repeated Mr. Smith, and fell into a brown study. "Ye-es . . . that damn donkey . . . m'm . . ."

"What about the donkey?"

"It's so much in evidence," murmured the inspector abstractedly. "I mean it's *there*. . . . I know it couldn't possibly have had anything to do with these prints, but it's there, it exists. There *is* a donkey. . . ."

"But what the devil has Popplewell's donkey got to do with this cigar that Croxley didn't finish smoking?"

Mr. Smith came to himself with a start. "Oh . . .! Oh, yes. . . . Well, I was thinking. Boomer has been gallivanting up and down that path of his very recently, and somebody has apparently been with him—trying to get him to go back inside was my suggestion. Now he might have come charging up to the gate just as Croxley drew level with it, and startled Croxley into dropping his cigar."

"Possible," commented Superintendent Blackler. But Poynter objected.

"A herd of wild elephants could come charging up to a gate—providing I was on the other side of the gate—but it wouldn't make me abandon half a cigar as good as this one, even if I'd dropped it in the snow."

"We might be able to check up on that, Poynter. If there is any truth in the suggestion, then young Cushing might have been there also, he might have been the one who was trying to get the donkey back into its stall. In which case he might even have spoken to Croxley, and he might be able to tell us a little more."

"Could be, sir. But it would hardly be very important, what he might have to tell us, or he'd have told us already. Very intrigued by all this business, young Cushing, and practically lives in Miss Forbes's pocket."

"You know," muttered Mr. Smith, who had been staring in bemused fashion at the piece of cigar in Poynter's fingers; "you know, Super, I have a feeling that that cigar is not just an accidental detail but an integral part of the story. It's trying to tell us something, it could give us some of the answers. . . ."

"Getting fanciful, aren't you, Smithy? It's not giving me any answers at the moment, it's asking questions. It's a little question mark."

"But that's just it! I don't think it *is* only a little question mark—I think it's a mighty big one."

"Hullo!" said Poynter abruptly. "Here's the doc."

21

In appearance Dr. Scott was the conventional picture of the old family solicitor. He invariably wore a black coat and striped trousers, a wide-winged stiff white collar with a heavy black silk tie, and an Eden hat. Horn-rimmed spectacles gave him an air of gravity and wisdom, and he brushed his thinning hair straight back from an advancing brow. In appearance Dr. Scott was dignified. In speech and manner he was not. Now, escorted by P.C. Keyes, and somewhat sketchily dressed but with his hair neatly slicked back as usual, he was inclined to be irritable.

"What the hell," he demanded of no one in particular, as he came upon the body of Croxley lying within the circle of hoof-prints, "what the hell is going on in these parts? What the devil *is* this hoop-la stuff?"

Mr. Smith took it upon himself to reply. "You said it, doc."

"I said what?"

"You mentioned the devil. That," said Mr. Smith stonily, "is one of the answers. Old Nick done it."

"—!" snapped Dr. Scott coarsely.

"Well, then, the Blue Woman."

"Blue—!" grunted Dr. Scott, even more coarsely.

"Never mind the flowers of speech," requested Superintendent Blackler. "Tell us what killed him—and please avoid those hoof-prints, doctor."

The doctor snorted and hopped over the prints, squatted down beside the body and opened his little black bag.

"Well, he *is* dead," he announced unemotionally. "You can take that as official." And then he was silent for a long time, examining particularly Croxley's bald head. At length he stood up, and his keen eyes followed the trail of prints that surrounded him.

"Well?" prompted the superintendent.

"Well," replied Dr. Scott, and he was obviously puzzled, "he was hit with something."

"Thank you," said the superintendent with restraint.

"Yes. Something that was almost a perfect semi-circle in shape."

"Semi-circle?"

"You mean," asked Mr. Smith, pointing to the hoof-prints, "something in shape not unlike that?"

"That's just what I do mean. Something that shape—and size. . . . You can make what you like of this, but, not being able to think of any alternatives on the spur of the moment, it looks to me as if he had been kicked by a horse."

There was a short silence after this. The inspector broke it.

"Odd's blood! Here, let me have another look." He hopped into the "magic circle" and bent down beside the doctor.

"Look," said the latter. "Look at the wound, you can see it clearly now I've wiped the blood away. Not much blood at that, but there hardly ever is in cases of head injuries. You couldn't ask for anything plainer, it's as definite and incisive as if it had been made by a branding-iron. Only there was force with this, force that bashed his temple in and killed him instantly."

"Kicked by a horse," said Mr. Smith softly. "Or kicked by a donkey?"

"Horse or donkey—how the blazes should I know the difference? But that looks like the mark of a hoof, and a hoof with an iron shoe on it I should say."

"And he dropped in his tracks?"

"That's the hell of a cliché," sniffed the doctor.

"I know. I used it deliberately. But the answer—?"

"The answer is that the blow killed him instantly. You can put it your way if you feel like it—what's the matter?"

The inspector had taken off his hat and ruffled his hair and groaned. "I *don't* feel like it. As a rule those two statements mean exactly the same thing, but they don't in this case. They *can't.*"

Dr. Scott regarded him suspiciously. "Are you going to talk like a detective?"

"I'm going to try. . . . When you say that Croxley died instantly on being hit—or kicked—I accept that as a statement of true fact. You're the doctor. But when you say he dropped in his tracks you put us back among the bogeys and hobgoblins."

"You work that out with the superintendent," said Dr. Scott, rising. "All I know, without further and more detailed examination, is that that blow alone was enough to kill him, and to kill him on the spot."

"Yes," muttered the inspector, "but which spot?" He stood up in his turn and his voice grew urgent. "Wait a minute, this has got to be thrashed out now. You say he died instantly. I say that means he dropped in his tracks—"

"Well, dammit, of course it does! What are you harping on it—?"

"I'll tell you," said Mr. Smith grimly. "Look where his tracks *are!* Look where they end! Look where he's lying—his feet are four feet and more away from the nearest hoof-print—the only other marks in the snow. His head is more than six feet away. And those hoof-prints weren't made by any horse or donkey, or any four-footed animal! If he was kicked—by anything—where are the marks of the kicker? If he was assaulted by somebody, where are the marks of his assailant? . . . I know—there are only those damned mysterious impossible hoof-prints. So he was kicked by that? Kicked at a distance of four feet away by something that stands upright on two legs and takes a stride of ten inches?"

"Listen," said Dr. Scott heavily. "I don't *know* what hit him. I only said that the wound was made by something the same size and shape as that." And he pointed once again to the hoof-prints.

"Can you think of any weapon, anything four feet or so in length, that would leave a mark like a horseshoe?"

"Why four feet long?"

"Because—" The inspector hesitated. "Gadzooks, this is absurd. . . . Well, because if the Thing that made these prints hit him, or—blast it!—kicked him, and he fell dead on the spot, then the Thing was four feet away from him when it struck. . . . Or else he staggered forward a few paces after being hit."

The doctor pursed his lips. "He *could* have staggered a bit before he fell—but those footprints don't look like it."

"I know they don't," said Mr. Smith with a hint of desperation in his voice. "Not a stagger, not a waver. He went on walking steadily those last three paces, and then he fell. The Thing that was with him—"

"Or came after him," amended Poynter.

"—with him or came after him stopped short here and then went round in that circle. . . ."

Dr. Scott looked at him curiously. "You know, you asked me the same sort of question a long time ago."

"I remember," said Mr. Smith gloomily. "In that case the wound was triangular, and the triangle turned out to be the half of a rectangle. But in this case—"

"In this case the mark is whole, complete. It is *not* the half of a circle, it ends too cleanly on too flattish a surface. Dammit, Smithy, you can see for yourself. It's almost exactly like one of those hoof-marks."

"Inspector!" said Poynter urgently.

"Yes, Bill?"

"That cigar—where we found it. . . ."

Mr. Smith knew immediately what was in Poynter's mind, and he explained to the doctor: "Croxley, doc, was smoking a cigar when he left the house. Bill found it in the roadway opposite the gate that opens on to that cart track in Jake Popplewell's place. Now honest-to-God hoof-prints in the snow show that old Jake's donkey had been galloping up and down—"

"Ah!" crowed Dr. Scott.

"Yes?"

"Was that gate open?"

"We don't know. But it doesn't look like it. We found it shut."

"Suppose it had been open, and somebody closed it before you got here. Suppose the donkey had run out on to the road, run into Croxley, been frightened by him, whirled round and kicked out . . . caught Croxley with one hoof fair and square on the left temple . . . Croxley dropped his cigar—"

"And fell dead on the spot?"

"Um . . ." The doctor rubbed his long chin. "Well, he could have been carried here, and dumped. . . ."

"Oh, no. He walked here. Steadily and normally, on his own two feet. Right up to the point where he *did* drop. These are his own footprints—same size, same—"

Mr. Smith stopped abruptly, and his hand went to his head.

"Now what?" asked the doctor.

*   *   *

It was some little while before the inspector replied to this, and then his reply took the form of another and a most unexpected question.

"I suppose, doc, there's no doubt that Mason did put that rope about his own neck?"

The doctor blinked at him. "Good Lord! Why bring that up? Anyway, that's not for me to say, that's for the coroner's jury to decide."

"I know. And the inquest has been adjourned to allow us to find out more about the hoof-prints. I know—but . . ."

"All I can say is what I've already said. I don't make the decisions; I give evidence, and I *go* by evidence. The medical evidence is that Mason died of strangulation, and the strangulation was effected by that rope about his neck. And he'd been dead between six and twelve hours when I saw him. The rest is your department."

"Allow yourself plenty of margin for error, don't you?" said Mr. Smith gloomily.

"Yes. I'm a doctor, not a clairvoyant. We take temperatures, we flex the limbs, we guess at the general state of health, we guess at this, that and the other; then we put all the guesses together and make a final guess. And the final guess is the nearest we can get to the length of time the person's been dead."

"Well, Mason couldn't have been dead longer than seven hours or so, otherwise he'd have had snow on him. And the evidence in our department consists of his body being found hanging from the tree, the foot-prints leading from his house to the tree, and the foot-prints on that big knob sticking out from the trunk. And all that points to a rather bizarre suicide. But then, just to make things really complicated and mysterious, we have the hoof-prints."

Dr. Scott began to grin.

"What's the joke?"

"Are you getting some sort of idea in your head of Mason walking out there with the Thing, and the Thing obliging him by tying the rope round the branch and lifting him up and shoving his head into the noose?"

"I'm not getting any ideas in my head, unfortunately. But I'm thinking of the other man who was in the house that afternoon. The man who made the telephone call, the man who made those foot-prints in the dust up under the roof. Size 11 those feet were. Same size as these. And the same size as the foot-prints leading from Mason's house to his body—the foot-prints we didn't think to have photographed."

Superintendent Blackler cleared his throat. "Now wait a minute, Smithy, there's nothing to that. We knew the answer to that straightaway. Those prints were made by the gumboots Mason was wearing. The fact that the gum-boots were four sizes too large for him can only be explained by assuming that they were the only ones on the premises, and that they weren't his but were used by a gardener or some sort of servant."

"A very reasonable and logical assumption," said Dr. Scott approvingly. "But it seems to beg another question. How do you know it wasn't Mason in those gumboots who made the prints under the roof?"

"By the prints themselves. The soles of the gumboots carry a very close-ridged pattern. There were no such ridges in those particular prints."

Mr. Smith was gazing absently at the body lying in the snow at their feet, still lying there and waiting with the patience of death for the doctor's men to be called in to carry it away. "Maybe I'm stupid," he muttered. "Maybe I'm pig-headed, but the point is beginning to nag. When Mason went out to his death he didn't bother to put on his hat or his coat or his gloves. But he *did* put on a pair of gumboots that were four sizes too large for him and must have been uncomfortable—"

"Which explains the lurching and the wobbling of his prints to the tree," put in the superintendent in parenthesis.

"—uncomfortable to walk in. Now that seems a trifle illogical to me. Cold body, hands and head weren't going to worry him. Why bother about extra covering for his feet? He already had a pair of stout shoes on, and God knows cold or wet feet weren't going to worry him for very long. . . ."

"Smithy!" said the superintendent in a low voice.

"Yes?"

"Bring it to a head. What's in your mind?"

"Smog, mostly," replied Mr. Smith with a fresh access of gloom. "But what brought this up was what the doc said a minute ago—something about the body being carried here and dumped."

"Can't have been," said the superintendent shortly. "Look at the prints. They *end* here."

"I was thinking of Mason."

"But the same thing applies there. And more than that—if Mason didn't walk out there—if somebody else, who must have been wearing the gumboots, carried him out and hung him on that tree—then that's murder!"

"Yes."

"But, good heavens, it's impossible! It's doubly impossible! What happened to the other person who carried, him out? Where are *his* tracks returning, or going on somewhere else? Or did he also vanish like the Thing?"

"I don't know," said the inspector desperately. "I don't know." He raised a hand and let it fall hopelessly against his thigh. "I'm fumbling aimlessly, I admit it."

"You certainly are!" spoke up Dr. Scott with emphasis. "What was Mason doing while he was being carried out and hanged? I've done a p.m. on him, remember. He was a fairly fit little devil and he'd have fought like a wild cat. You can take it from me that he wasn't manhandled in any way. He wasn't hit on the head to knock him. unconscious, he wasn't bound or gagged, he wasn't doped, he wasn't drunk. There wasn't a mark on him, except where that rope had been round his neck. . . . I guess you're barking up the wrong tree, Smithy."

Mr. Smith said nothing.

Superintendent Blackler said briskly: "Come back to this one. More information from you, please, doctor. How long has he been dead?"

"Three—four—six hours."

"Vague enough, aren't you? Can't you get any closer?"

"Well . . . more like six than three. Sorry I can't give you a definite time, like ten and a half minutes past nine, but as I said before I'm a doctor, not a radio announcer."

"Um . . . good enough. He must have walked straight into it when he went out. Otherwise he'd have reached the station."

"Unless he was sidetracked," said the doctor helpfully. "Now can I take him away? I'm cold and tired, and I want to get back to bed."

"Super!" said Mr. Smith, coming out of his trance.

"Yes?"

"Can I try out something? I want Croxley's boots fitted against those prints."

"Good Lord! Are you still harping on that? . . . Keyes!"

"Yes, sir?"

"Hop in there and take those boots off Croxley's feet. Give them to the inspector."

P.C. Keyes, secretly glad of something to do, however grisly, leapt across to the dead man, squatted down and imperturbably removed the boots. Inspector Smith, taking them from him, fitted them into a number of impressions, while the others watched closely and interestedly.

"No doubt about it, I think," observed the superintendent. "They fit exactly, mathematically you might say. Are we all agreed? Smithy?"

"Oh, yes," sighed the inspector "They're his own prints all right. That's what makes it so impossible . . . Super!"

"What now?"

"Those two men on duty outside Mason's house—can I have them brought here?"

"Yes, if you want 'em. They don't seem to be doing much good there That's a good idea, they can stay here for the rest of the night."

P.C. Keyes breathed an inward sigh of relief. He had been afraid he was going to fall in for this.

"Keyes can go and get them," went on the superintendent. "Take the car, Keyes, if you can get it through the snow over the hill; otherwise I'm afraid you'll have to walk. . . . Was that the idea, Smithy?"

"Not altogether. I want to ask them a question."

"Eh? What about?"

"About the Blue Woman," said Mr. Smith.

The Blue Woman again. . . . Fumbling aimlessly, the inspector had said of himself. Yet he had come within an ace of hitting on the truth. But now he had shot away from it again.

22

Dr. Scott, somewhat belatedly, went into the house to minister to the distraught Mrs. Croxley, and Keyes went over the hill for Constables Dempsey and Gimbel. Mr. Smith stepped into the circle of hoof-prints and went through the dead man's pockets. Leaving everything else to be properly inventoried at the morgue he took out only the envelope containing the photographs, and these he glanced at quickly.

"More or less the same as yours, Bill. Including the prints on the hedge—it seems fairly obvious that he'd spotted what you had, and that was what was taking him to the station."

He handed them to the superintendent who had already been acquainted with the oddities of Sunday's tracks as disclosed by Poynter's own photographs. The superintendent looked through them and returned them.

"Put them back in his pocket. They don't seem to tell us any-thing we don't already know, and we can look at them later under a better light."

Then, Dr. Scott coming out again and rejoining them, Croxley's dead body was at last lifted from its bed of snow and taken away to the morgue. The doctor went with it, and Inspector Smith, followed by the superintendent and Poynter, worked his way slowly back along the tracks of Croxley and the unknown to the little garden gate. Here he stood still and glanced first down the hill and then up it.

"Why did he come back?" he inquired. "He set out with the de-liberate intention of going to the station—what sent him back?"

"Forgot something," hazarded Poynter.

"And came back to get it? Then why *didn't* he get it? Why didn't he go inside?"

Poynter said nothing to this, but pointed to the hoof-prints coming down the hill at the side of the road.

"Think so?" asked the inspector. "Then chew this over. For some reason or another he did come back. We don't know how far he'd got—you can't go by the length of that partly smoked cigar, because it doesn't necessarily follow that he turned back on dropping it or throwing it away. But—unless he was sidetracked, as the doctor so helpfully observed—he can't have been away longer than twenty minutes at the outside, or he'd have reached the station."

"Unless he was sidetracked," echoed Poynter sepulchrally.

"In which case he could have been away for perhaps two hours, going by the doc, who said with his usual vagueness—curse him!—that he'd been dead three to six hours."

"He couldn't have been dead longer than five hours at the most," said the superintendent. "He left the house at approximately nine o'clock—we found him at approximately two o'clock."

"That's so. But in any case, consider this. If he came back after a few minutes it wasn't to go inside the house again, for his tracks show that he went on without hesitation past the front door and along to the lawn. If some time elapsed before he returned, he still went straight to the lawn. There he met his death. And there, either already dead, or still alive *and walking steadily and normally,* he was overtaken by the Thing. But what on earth was he doing there? What was there in, on or about that bare, snow-covered lawn that brought him back after deliberately setting out for the police station?

"On the other hand, if he didn't come back in here alone, then look at what that implies! It implies that he met some Thing that walks upright on two legs, but has hooves instead of feet and, judging by the length of its stride, can be only about four feet in height, if that; it implies that here at his own gate he met and accepted this Thing calmly, without surprise or shock—look at the steadiness of his tracks!—went in with it round to the lawn, and was *kicked* by it at an impossible range. . . ."

Poynter opened his mouth and closed it again.

"I know," went on Mr. Smith. "Miss Forbes and her theory of a poltergeist or something. You would prefer to think, wouldn't you? that this Thing only walks; that it comes along afterwards, when people are already dead, and then, having done its little walk, dematerializes. Well, suppose it does. Suppose it did. Suppose

Mason was already hanging on that tree when it started walking. The charms and symbols that barred its way through the doors and window would still have been there—and it may have walked round the skylight on the roof just for the hell of it. Mason, in other words, could have been alone when he died. But Croxley couldn't! Something hit Croxley. Something killed him. Now, if something had been thrown at him, propelled from a distance, why didn't we find that something by the body? If he was hit at point-blank range by some human assailant, where are the tracks of the assailant? There aren't any. There are only the tracks of the Thing with hooves."

"In God's name, Smithy," said the superintendent in a hard, strained voice, "what *is* this Thing?"

The inspector shrugged his shoulders and made no reply.

"Can't anybody make *any* sort of a guess—other than a psychic visitant or a Blue Woman?"

Poynter made a guess. "Charlie McCarthy."

They stared at him.

"I'm told," said Poynter with sour humour, "they've learnt how to make him walk—and he'd take little short steps like that. You wind him up and put him down and he does a little walk. Then you pick him up again. Charlie McCarthy—with hooves on."

The others treated this with the contempt it deserved. The inspector was scratching his head and eyeing the superintendent in an odd manner.

"I have an answer—if you can call it an answer. If," he said gravely, "if it seems that something has happened that is utterly and completely impossible, then I will hold until the heavens fall that the thing never happened at all."

"Never happened at all?" cried the superintendent. "Are we dreaming this? Did we dream all that business of Sunday?"

"It cannot be too strongly stressed," replied Mr. Smith solemnly, "that the study of effects does not necessarily lead to the discovery or knowledge of the cause. I didn't say that, Miss Forbes said it. And by my disintegrating halidom, the woman is right!"

"Is she?" grunted the superintendent. "But she was talking philosophy or metaphysics or something then. The whole science of criminal investigation has been built on the study of effects."

"Ah, yes—but on the correct interpretation of those effects. And that's my whole point. We're studying effects. We're looking at marks in snow and reading the messages those marks seem to tell us. But, Super . . . I think we're reading them all wrong. . . ."

*   *   *

Flashlights bobbing down the road from the top of The Rise showed that Keyes was returning with Dempsey and Gimbel. Mr. Smith waited with what patience he could muster until the men reached him, and then pounced on Keyes.

"Well?"

"No, sir. Not a sign of any more anywhere."

"What's that?" asked Superintendent Blackler.

"I told Keyes to keep his eyes skinned for any more hoof-prints."

"Any *more?*"

"Just in case. Last time, remember? they appeared to stop suddenly in a couple of places, but they went on again after a little gap. This time it seems they don't."

The superintendent grunted. "We don't want any more."

"M'm . . . I want to ask these two some questions, Super."

"Go ahead."

Mr. Smith turned to the two policemen. "I suppose you know what's happened?"

"Yes, sir," replied Dempsey, acting as spokesman. "Mr. Croxley's been killed, and there's more of them hoof-prints."

"Succinctly put. All quiet at Mason's house?"

"Yes, sir."

"Um. . . . I understand that Jake Popplewell was in the Steeple Inn again tonight, and when he left he was in his usual sodden condition."

"Yes, sir. He was full. He was a bit noisy"—hastily and defensively—"but he wasn't doing no particular harm, so I told his friend—Mr. Silver, sir—to get him home quick."

"That's all right. What I want to know is, what's all this about a Blue Woman?"

Dempsey coughed deprecatingly. "I reckon, sir, he was seein' things."

"Yes, I know he was seeing things—but what about you two? Did you see anything?"

"No, sir," said Dempsey.

"No, sir," repeated Gimbel. "But . . ."

"But what? Go on."

"Well, sir, this here Blue Woman must have been very plain to old Jake. He pointed at her. He yelled at her. He said she was follerin' him about and trying to get at him. And from what Mr. Silver told us on his way back, she follered him over the hill and all the way home."

"But she didn't leave any tracks. She didn't leave any foot-prints—or hoof-prints?"

Constable Dempsey coughed his soft deprecatory cough again, but Gimbel replied instantly and confidently: "No, sir."

"How do you know?"

"I looked, sir. He cried out once, 'There she goes,' and I swung me torch but there was nothing there, and then I looked at the snow, silly like, I suppose, sir, but there were no marks. . . ."

"I don't think," said the inspector gently, "that the action was quite so silly as it might seem. Anyway, there were no marks. No hoof-prints anywhere?"

"No, sir."

"All right. What time was this?"

"Sharp on closing time, sir. Dead on ten o'clock."

Mr. Smith nodded and said to the superintendent: "Odd, isn't it, Super? An hour after Croxley leaves his house, maybe an hour after he dies, or maybe round about the time he died, old Jake Popplewell sees his Blue Woman. But when and where he sees her she doesn't leave any tracks. The tracks appear when and where he *doesn't* see her."

The superintendent grunted sceptically. "Does that tell you anything? And who said they were the tracks of this mythical Blue Woman?"

"M'm, yes, that's a point. Well, actually Miss Forbes said they were. But then she also said a lot of other things—everything's a myth, according to her."

"If you ask me," said the superintendent grumpily, "she said too damn much." He stabbed a thumb at Dempsey and Gimbel. "Finished with these two?"

"Yes, thank you."

"Right. . . . You two men are to stay here for the rest of the night. Go up this path and take up positions outside the front door of the house—and watch those tracks! Keep an eye on the lawn the other side of that fence thing, but mainly watch the house. Your job is purely and simply a nursemaid's one: Mrs. Croxley is alone in the house and she's upset and nervous, which is not to be wondered at. She's quiet now, but if she shows signs of becoming panicky again let her know you're there. You'll be relieved in the morning, but if there are any early snoopers keep 'em out. Keyes will keep in touch with you."

The policemen saluted and went in through the gate to take up their new vigil, and the superintendent sighed gustily and said to his inspector: "Now, I suppose, we'd better get over to Popplewell's cottage."

23

Gregory Cushing opened the door to them. Socks were on his feet and his overcoat was doing duty as a dressing-gown, his hair was on end and his eyes heavy with sleep; but the sleep quickly drained from them when he saw who the visitors were.

"Sorry to have to knock you up at this hour of the night, Mr. Cushing," said the superintendent suavely, "but the matter is important."

"Hullo! What's up? . . . Here, come in, it's pretty cold standing here." The four men stepped inside, and Gregory closed the door behind them and smoothed down his hair. "Now, what's up? If it's uncle Jake you want I'm afraid he's *hors de combat.*"

"We know."

Gregory grinned at him. "Oh, you do, do you?"

"Your uncle will wait," said the superintendent crisply. "He wouldn't be much use to us in any case. You're the man we want to talk to. Mr. Cushing, have you seen anything of Mr. Croxley tonight?"

"Croxley? No. What's he done?"

Superintendent Blackler didn't answer this. Instead he pressed the question. "Say about nine o'clock tonight. He must have been walking past here about then; you didn't see him—or hear anything?"

Gregory shook his head firmly. "Haven't seen anything of him all day. Why? What's happened to him?"

"Mr. Cushing," put in Inspector Smith quietly.

"Yes to you, Inspector?"

"What time was it when the donkey got loose?"

Gregory's eyes opened wide and he smiled again, briefly. "Hul-lo! This is real Scotland Yard stuff! How did you know? Got some spies round here?"

"Oh, no. But it was written in the snow plain enough for anybody to read. What time *was* it?"

Gregory wrinkled his forehead. "I don't really know. I was—Look here, what *is* all this? What on earth's happened now?"

"Tell us about the donkey first," requested the inspector smoothly.

Gregory frowned and searched his memory. "It's a bit difficult to give you anything like an exact time. Say half an hour before uncle Jake came home—perhaps a little longer than that. I'd fallen asleep in front of the fire. He woke me up—Boomer, I mean, not uncle Jake. I heard him padding and trotting up and down. . . . He didn't really get loose, you know, he's never tied up or locked in—the door doesn't lock in any case. But he knows how to nuzzle up a latch and push open a door or a gate. . . ."

"He didn't get out on to the road?"

"No—thank the Lord! That was what really took me out to him, I wasn't sure about that gate. But it was fastened all right, and Boomer hasn't yet learnt how to pull a bolt. And then I had the devil's own job to get him to go back into his stall; I don't know what got into him tonight."

"I wonder," said Mr. Smith softly. "Half an hour or so before old Jake came home. What time was that?"

"When he came home? When he was pushed out," replied Gregory significantly. "He arrived here about twenty past ten. His pal Silver brought him home. So that would make it tennish when Boomer and I were playing tag—say a quarter to, at the outside. And he was in a fine state when he did come home . . . howling like a ban shee—" He stopped suddenly and looked suspiciously at the inspector. "Look here, dammit, what *is* all this? Why the inquisition?"

"I'll tell you," said the inspector heavily. "The Thing has been walking again, the Thing with hooves. It walked into Croxley's garden and on to his lawn. So, some time or another after nine o'clock, did Croxley himself. The Thing went round and round in a circle, and then vanished—just like last time. We found Croxley, not up in the air like Mason, but lying on the ground in the middle of the circle of hoof-prints—with the side of his head kicked in. . . ."

"*What?*" Gregory almost shouted the word, and he stared at the men incredulously, his eyes darting from one impressive face to the other. "*Croxley . . .* Dead?"

"Very dead."

"Good Lord!" gasped Gregory, and after a pause repeated himself. "But I don't get it. Why the interest in Boomer? You're not going to tell me you think now that poor old Boomer—?"

"Oh, no! We don't think the donkey had anything to do with the kicking—or the walking—if that's what's in your mind. But, you see—" The inspector told him about Croxley and his cigar. "That's why we're interested in the time the donkey was careering up and down out there. But if it was only half an hour or so before old Jake arrived. . . ." He paused invitingly.

"Half an hour," repeated Gregory unhesitatingly. "Three-quarters at the very outside."

"Well, then, that means it was three-quarters of an hour after Croxley had set out from his own house. So—"

"So he couldn't have dropped his cigar because he was startled by Boomer. In any case—Hell!" he exploded. "This is crazier than that business of Mason! When you say kicked, you mean kicked by a—by a hoof?"

"Exactly. With, the doctor thinks, an iron shoe on it."

"But it's impossible! Boomer's out of it—he was never in it, anywhere! And even if he *had* been in it he wouldn't have kicked. He *never* kicks, you can do what you like to him and all he does is to flap his ears at you. . . ."

Mr. Smith said gravely: "I never thought Croxley was kicked by Boomer. Because he died instantly; the doctor is emphatic on that point. And that means he dropped in his tracks, and his tracks end in the middle of his own lawn. . . ."

There was a little silence after this, and then Gregory said slowly: "And the hoof-marks go round and round where you found him lying—and end there. . . . Inspector, you know uncle Jake was plastered again—*but do you know that he saw the Blue Woman again?*"

If he had hoped to create a sensation he was disappointed, for the inspector merely nodded his head wearily and replied: "Yes, we know that."

"You do? Oh . . ." Another momentary silence, followed by a long low whistle from Gregory. "You'd better take this up with Miss Forbes, this is beyond me."

Superintendent Blackler said, a little annoyed: "We haven't come here to take it up with you, or with anyone else; we came here to ask you a question and to see if you could give us any information that might have any bearing on Mr. Croxley's death."

"Sorry, but I can't. All the information I can give you is that Boomer wasn't out when Croxley must have been passing here, and that uncle Jake has seen the Blue Woman again. And you don't seem to think very much of that."

"You know," murmured Mr. Smith, ruffling his hair and gazing at the worn linoleum on the floor with a faraway look in his eyes; "you know, I'd like to have a look at that donkey."

"Certainly, if you wish it, but whatever for?"

Mr. Smith not answering the question but continuing to stare at the floor at his feet, Gregory added: "All right, half a tick till I get some shoes on."

He disappeared into the kitchen, leaving the others standing in the tiny passage that did duty as a hall, and Superintendent Blackler turned to his inspector and asked in a low voice: "Why do you want to see the donkey, Smithy? Don't you believe young Cushing?"

"Oh, yes. I see no reason to do otherwise. But I'd like to have a look at the donkey's shoes."

The superintendent could do no more than show his surprise before Gregory was back again, carrying his shoes in his hand. He smiled faintly and derisively at the inspector. "Though what you hope to learn by just looking at the moke. . . ."

Mr. Smith still maintaining his silence and his air of abstraction, Gregory gave it up and sat down on the floor and began putting on his shoes. While he was lacing up the one, the inspector absentmindedly picked up the other, glanced at it—a somewhat flimsy, dressy article—and appeared to go into a trance. Gregory waited patiently and a little curiously, and then held out his hand. But Mr. Smith didn't seem to notice. He turned the shoe round and round in his hands, and his eyes were as vacant as an idiot's.

"Are you going to tell my fortune?" inquired Gregory solemnly. "Or are you merely admiring a good shoe? Bit thin for this weather, I'll admit, but then I didn't know we were going to have this weather."

Mr. Smith came to himself with a start and dropped the shoe in the outstretched hand. "Sorry, I was thinking of something. . . ."

"Not about Boomer, I hope," said Gregory ironically. "Not about Boomer on two legs and walking over roofs and walls and kicking people on the head and then vanishing."

"No," said the inspector simply. "I was thinking about your uncle Jake. He's very quiet. And we've been talking for awhile and making quite a noise."

"That's nothing. He always is after a bash. You could bang a gong and he wouldn't hear it. You could drop an elephant on his head and I doubt if it would wake him. He won't stir until ten or eleven in the morning. Do you want to try? Would you like to go up and have a look at *him?*"

For the first time since he had left his home that night the inspector smiled. "Oh, no. No, thank you. As the superintendent has said, I don't think he'd be of much use to us. But if you'd take us out to Boomer's boudoir. . . ."

Boomer showed no surprise at the invasion, and only by the twitching of one long ear did he display even the faintest interest. A rope loosely knotted round his neck tethered him at comfortable range to his manger; it was long enough to allow him to lie down, if he felt so inclined. But apparently he had not as yet felt so inclined; he stood motionless on the flat of three hooves and the tip of the fourth, and his lower lip drooped apathetically.

"I thought you said he was never tied up?" queried Superintendent Blackler sharply.

"Well, he isn't—at least he's not supposed to be," replied Gregory defensively. He straightened the donkey's cover and took off the rope. "I did this just to persuade him to stay inside when I'd finally got him inside again. Uncle Jake would probably be very annoyed about it if he knew." He patted Boomer on the rump, and the animal half-turned its head, blew a sigh like a train letting off steam and resumed its drowsy regard of the empty manger. "Well, Inspector, there he is. The Pride of the Popplewells."

"Yes," murmured Mr. Smith vaguely. "But I'm more interested in his feet."

"Help yourself. I understand the procedure is to grasp the hock firmly and press on the back of the knee. . . . It's all right, Boomer won't object. He won't bite or kick or do anything like that—he probably won't even lift his hoof."

The inspector bent down, seized the near fore hock, pressed as directed, and the hoof was immediately lifted thus proving Gregory's gloomy prognostication incorrect. It came up almost automatically and apparently without Boomer being aware of any movement of his body. Mr. Smith scrutinized the shoe closely for some moments and dropped the hoof without comment. He went round the donkey, giving all four hooves and shoes the same intent examination, and still he said nothing. He backed out of the stall and waved his flashlight up and down the cart track. Then he began to walk forward towards the gate with his eyes fixed on the ground.

"What *are* you looking for?" asked Gregory, a shade irritably, closing the door after himself and the others. "They're Boomer's —what else can they be?"

"Oh, yes," sighed Mr. Smith. "They're Boomer's all right. And the footprints are yours"—glancing at Gregory's shoes—"you certainly seem to have had a job with him."

"You're telling me! I damn near broke my leg."

"Fall?" asked the inspector sympathetically.

"Yes. Over that thing."

"I saw that. I was wondering what it was."

"That thing" was a raised rectangle in the snow at the extreme edge of the track some five feet by four. It stood up three or four inches from the ground, a small plateau, and the snow that covered it was broken, pressed down and in places bunched up in ridges and heaps.

"That's the old well," Gregory told him. "When the water was laid on, which, I understand, was when those houses opposite were built on The Rise, uncle Jake boarded it up. There are two sort of doors there bolted together in the middle. You can't see the join for the snow, but you can see the bolt sticking up—that, needless to say, was what I fell on when I was charging down to head off Boomer from the gate."

"Bad luck. Hurt yourself?"

"Oh, nothing much, just a graze." Gregory pulled up one pyjama leg, disclosing a long lean shin, the skin of which was abraded and discoloured. "Bit painful in this cold."

"Ha!" said Mr. Smith suddenly and much more briskly, and ceasing to show any further interest in the track. "Well, we won't keep you out in it any longer. Sorry you couldn't help us, but thanks all the same."

"I'm sorry too. And, by golly, I don't mind admitting that I'm a bit, well—upset. I mean, Croxley and the hoof-marks again . . . this damn mysterious unknown practically next door. . . ."

The inspector grinned at him encouragingly. "If it will afford you any comfort, there are two policemen in Croxley's garden right now. They'll be there all night, and if you yell, they'll come running."

Gregory smiled back at him sheepishly. "It's not as bad as all that. Still, that is comforting to know." The smile vanished and he stared curiously at the inspector. "But tell me, do—what *were* you looking for along here?"

"I don't know," said Mr. Smith slowly, and weariness and depression enveloped him again like a heavy cloak. "I don't know. . . . I'm searching blindly for one sign of sanity in all this devilment."

"What sort of a sign?"

"I don't know," said Mr. Smith again, hopelessly.

"Huh! Well, if you find one, will you let me know? I could do with it too."

*   *   *

The four policemen walked, carelessly now, down the track and were let out by the gate by Gregory, who closed it carefully after them. He wished them good night and, as an afterthought, good luck and went back into the house and up to his room. But his bed was cold now, icy cold, and after shivering for some minutes he crawled out and put his socks on again and flung his coat over him as an extra cover. He felt slightly warmer after that, but even so sleep refused to return to him. Chaotic thoughts and fragmentary memories chased through his tired brain: little pictures of the hoof-prints in the snow, of Mason's dead body hanging under the dead tree, of Miss Forbes and her scrap-book and her theories, of his uncle Jake swaying in the bar of the Steeple Inn and quoting extensively and hoarsely from Shakespeare; incoherent and disconnected thoughts of the beer-begotten Blue Woman of that chronic inebriate, of Croxley lying in the snow on his own lawn, kicked to death, apparently. . . .

He tossed and turned and told himself he'd had enough of it. It was beginning to make him feel sick and scared—what was going to happen next? Literally and metaphorically he was in strange territory; this wasn't his country, he was a stranger in a strange land. Tomorrow he'd get out of it, leave it all behind him. He'd go back home and take up the threads—

But his heart sank again. Home. . . . An empty flat in Knightsbridge still haunted by his recently dead wife; that lovely, fascinating but wayward creature whom he had adored. She had left him for another man—and come back to him again like a hurt animal seeking shelter; and in an agony of jealousy and self-pity he had refused to take her in. She had gone away once more—and the river police had taken her sodden body from the contemptuous clutch of the dirty water below Blackfriars. "For each man kills the thing he loves. . . ."

In his own bed in the next room uncle Jake turned over and began to snore.

Outside, down below, Detective-Inspector Smith stood by the barred gate and gazed moodily over it at the cart track and the confused jumble of impressions in the snow. Superintendent Blackler, a man of vast but not unlimited patience, glanced at him solicitously.

"This track seems to fascinate you, Smithy. What's holding you here?"

"I don't know," mumbled Mr. Smith. "This is the worst yet, Super. This is hellish. This is the mark of the beast. . . . Somewhere in the last book in the Bible—which is Revelation—it says that the number of the beast is six-hundred and sixty-six. The mystic number in this mess seems to be eleven."

"Eh?"

Poynter shuffled his feet and said rather surprisingly: "It also says it's the number of a man. 'He that hath understanding, let him count the number of the beast; for it is the number of a man: and his number is six hundred and sixty and six.'"

" 'He that hath understanding,' " repeated the inspector bitterly. "I guess that's just what we haven't got."

"The significant thing about that number," went on Poynter reflectively, "is that it adds up to nine. Three sixes are eighteen, and one and eight are nine. Nine contains all the other digits, and there is a school of thought which takes this to mean that the number of a man is the number of all mankind."

And now the inspector raised his head, and he looked quizzically at his friend and right-hand man. "I didn't know you were a student of numerology, Bill—or of the Bible."

"Well, I'm not really, but you sort of pick up these things. You'll find a lot of that stuff in Revelation. It says also that some woman—which some people take to signify Eve—fled to the wilderness for a thousand, two hundred and threescore days. One, two, six, nought: there's your nine again. The walls of the new Jerusalem are to be a hundred and forty and four cubits—one, four, four: nine again. And the number of people to be saved, the number ` purchased out of the earth,' is one hundred and forty and four thousand. The Calvinists built a creed on that number, not realizing its esoteric significance; which is that the sum of its digits is nine, the number of the whole, referring to and containing *all* the sons and daughters of Eve."

Superintendent Blackler said a little sarcastically: "You must take this up with Miss Forbes some time, Poynter. Personally, and at the moment, I fail to see what it has to do with the inspector's own mystic number eleven. . . . And what did you mean by that, Smithy?"

"I don't know what I mean," responded the inspector dejectedly. "I only know that wherever you look in this appalling business the mark of a number eleven shoe stares you in the face. Where we find the mark of the beast we find, somewhere along the trail, the mark of a man apparently accompanying it: the hoof-prints—and the footprints of a size eleven shoe. . . ."

The superintendent's eyebrows twitched together. "I don't see—They're dead. They were the victims of it. They died of it—"

"Are they? Are they *all* dead? What about the man who was up under the roof in Mason's house?"

"Eleven," said Poynter *sotto voce*. "Another mystic number. One *and* one. Add them, they make a pair. But multiply them, and they're still one."

"You and your numbers!" growled Superintendent Blackler.

But the inspector had stiffened suddenly and was muttering to himself. "One *and* one. . . . One plus one. . . . One multiplied by one. . . ."

Very slowly he relaxed, his shoulders drooped slightly and he turned and walked blindly to the car.

*   *   *

Dr. Scott was still at the police station when they arrived back, but only just. He had completed a further and more detailed examination of Croxley's body and was on the point of leaving.

"Original diagnosis confirmed," he snapped at them. "He suffered only that one blow on the head—not another mark anywhere else on him—and it killed him. Killed him stone dead and on the spot. And it still looks like the kick of a horse to me, more than ever like it. I'll do a p.m. in the morning."

"Wait a minute," begged the superintendent, catching his arm. "Can you get any closer now to the time of death?"

"No. Three to six hours. But I'll say this, purely an opinion, of course, it was probably nearer six."

"Thank you," said the superintendent, and let go. "Good night—you cautious old devil, you!"

"Six hours," mused Mr. Smith. "Meaning five. . . . He came out of the house, went a little way down the road, turned back—and walked right into it. But why did he turn back? And why did he go in with the Thing so tamely and calmly? Why on to the lawn? And if he didn't go in *with* the Thing, or immediately ahead of it—what hit him?"

"Went back for another cigar," suggested Poynter diffidently. "Perhaps he's one of those people who will never relight a cigar once its gone out."

"Did he keep his cigars on the lawn?" inquired Superintendent Blackler, mildly sarcastic.

"No, but he might have seen something. He might have noticed the gate in the fence open and have gone to close it, or he might even have seen the hoof-prints—they might have been there already."

"How?" asked Mr. Smith tonelessly.

"Eh?"

"How would he see them—supposing they had been there? What would he use for light? He had no flash light on him. He'd know his way about, of course, and he wouldn't need any light to get him from his own garden gate to his own front door. And there'd be a faint glimmer on the roadway from the street light at the bottom of The Rise, but inside his garden it would be black as ink. . . . That's a point that everybody seems to have missed: this business, and all that of Saturday night, took place in darkness. The last street light is at the top of The Rise. Beyond that the Thing must have cavorted about in darkness—stood on that window-sill—walked away out to that tree—"

"If," interrupted the superintendent, "there was a light in that bedroom, the window-sill would be plainly visible. And Jake

Popplewell—and this man Silver—seem to have no difficulty in walking up and down that road in the dark."

"They're countrymen, and they probably know every inch of it backwards. But Mason—he had no lamp or flashlight with him, he walked away out through that tunnel of trees and across the bare paddock to the tree in intense darkness. Like Croxley, but not quite so steadily, he walked to his death in a black-out."

"Well, that could account for the unevenness of his tracks, the little lurchings and staggerings. And out in the open, with the stars shining overhead and that pale mantle of snow underfoot, it wouldn't *be pitch* dark."

"Were the stars shining when Mason set out? . . . The Thing, I suppose," said Mr. Smith, bitterly ironical, "doesn't need any light. Being a ghost, or a demon, it is independent of physical phenomena like light or dark—it sees by radar, or something. But it leaves physical phenomena behind it, it leaves a trail of hoof-prints." He added in the same heavy dead voice: "We're miles away from it, you know, Super. We're miles away from any of the answers; we're still reading the messages all wrong. . . ."

24

Mr. Smith went home. He had barely half a mile to go, but it took him a long time, for he walked all the way and he walked very slowly. He trudged along the slush-strewn pavements under the pale yellow lights, a silent and solitary figure, and the policemen on their beats glanced at him curiously as he passed by unseeing.

His mind was confused, his brain a battlefield where vague half-formed ideas and impulses, scarcely deserving of the name of thought, ran riot and slaughtered each other at birth. No matter where he started, no matter *how* he started, no matter what devious routes he took, what intellectual by-paths he strayed down, he was faced, not merely at the end, but right at the very beginning, with the blank walls of sheer impossibility. And not only at the beginning and end, but in between were other walls, not so massive but just as insurmountable.

There were, as isolated phenomena, the hoof-prints themselves, made, it was self-evident, by something that went on two legs and walked as one walks a tight-rope. There were, in both instances, tonight and on Sunday morning, those sudden incredible beginnings from nowhere, out of nothing, and the equally abrupt and incredible endings. There were those inexplicable gaps in the trail they had followed that Sunday morning; there were the prints on the low privet hedge that bordered the Jacksons' garden—not only an added impossibility, but an absurdity; the prints on the window-sill outside Mason's bedroom; the ring of prints surrounding the skylight in the roof where—the very height of absurdity—something had hopped round and round on one hoof. . . .

Such things simply could not be!

But such things *had* been; and the evidence had stared him and hundreds of other people in their blank bewildered faces.

And such things had been nearly a hundred years ago, when they had been seen by hundreds of the Devonshire folk of those times and vouched for by unimpeachable witnesses.

Yes—but there were differences. There were two main, two vast differences between that visitation and the visitation of tonight and of two nights ago; and the names of those differences were Croxley and Mason. Where the trails had ended, at those sudden blank and completely impossible endings, they had found the dead bodies of men. Now Mason could have taken his own life, and his suicide and the walking of the Thing could have been two separate and quite unrelated events. But Croxley couldn't have taken his own life, Croxley had been killed! Croxley had been hit with something, something the same size and shape as the shoe on the hoof of the unknown that had made those tracks—

The *shoe* on the hoof of the Thing. . . .

But the only other tracks beside his own were those of this mysterious, this absurd, this unbelievable Thing. . . .

It began to snow again. After nearly twelve hours of clear weather the clouds had massed and banked in the darkness overhead and the snow had begun to fall once more. This was to be the Great Fall that was to bury the countryside and tie up traffic throughout the land. But its onset was gentle and deceptive. The flakes, lighter than feathers, softer than thistledown, fell thinly and lazily, drifting and swaying on the still air, touching Mr. Smith's face with brief ethereal icy caresses. But he didn't feel them, never even noticed them. He plodded on unheeding, and the snow settled and gathered on his hat and his shoulders.

His thoughts turned on the men who had died, especially on the tracks *they* had left. Croxley had worn a size 11 boot, because that had been the size that fitted him. Mason had gone out to that dead tree wearing size 11 gumboots, because . . . Well, why? Because he had wanted to keep his feet dry even right up to the end, and those gumboots had been handy? Odd coincidence, that, the size in both cases being the same. And the marks of the feet that had trodden on those dusty boards up under the roof of Mason's house, immediately under the skylight—size 11 again. Another coincidence.

But *was* it all coincidence?

Well . . . what else could it be?

The foot-prints in the first instance had definitely been made by the gumboots that Mason had been wearing.

The foot-prints in the second instance had definitely been made by the brown boots that Croxley had been wearing.

But in the third instance—? There was no saying what boots or shoes had left those impressions, except that they had not been the gumboots.

Was it *all* coincidence?

Size 11. Number 11—one of Bill Poynter's mystic numbers. . . .

Mr. Smith walked even more slowly as his mind grew even more active. Vague incoherent ideas leapt and flashed in his brain like tongues of flame seen dimly through smoke.

One *and* one.. .. The hoof-prints—and the size 11 footprints. The mark of a beast—and the mark of a man. And there was a beast in Winchingham—but that was even more absurd than anything that had gone before, and he rejected the thought as soon as it was born. And yet—and to blazes with all this psychic stuff!—yet there *was* such a beast. It was inescapable. It was *there.* Boomer, the donkey—he had deliberately and carefully scrutinized the donkey's shoes. . . .

But, no! it was impossible. It was more than that, it was too ridiculous.

And he echoed Superintendent Blackler's heartfelt cry. What, in God's name, was this Thing that went on hooves and walked on two legs, but on odd occasions used only one?

Miss Forbes had postulated some mysterious Blue Woman, a spectre seen only by old Jake Popplewell, and then only when he was too drunk to remember it.

So it was a ghost, was it? The ghost of a woman that wore hooves!

Mr. Smith scowled savagely and uttered a wicked word to himself.

If there were no reasonable solution to the problem, no natural and logical explanation, then he had come to the end of the road. If it had come to supernatural visitations supervising or actively encompassing the deaths of mortal beings, then he was finished with police work. And not only he, but every professional criminal investigator in the country. They could only stand by and let the psychical researchers take over.

But this was unthinkable. This was simply too silly for words.

Well, then, what *was* this Thing that had made those hoof-prints, and made them in impossible places, left those tracks in the snow at the end of which death had been waiting?

Hundreds of people, simple, devout, religious people, believed it to be Satan; or a manifestation, or an emissary, of the Lord of Evil.

Bill Poynter, in a moment of ill-timed humour, had suggested Charlie McCarthy. A wooden puppet, a ventriloquist's doll that, by the genius of the ventriloquist himself, had acquired an almost human and considerably more magnetic and compelling personality than the man.

Satan—or one of his devils—in his medieval guise of half-fiend, half-goat . . . still wearing the shoes that had been tacked on to his hooves by the formidable and energetic Saint Nicholas. . . .

Miss Forbes's Blue Woman—or, rather, the drunken Jake Popplewell's Blue Woman—a ghost which, for reasons of its own, had changed its feet to hooves. . . .

A ventriloquist's doll, with the added embellishment of hooves. . . .

Archangels and atom bombs, what a selection! Poynter aside, of course, otherwise sane and intelligent people had advanced these suppositions in all seriousness.

The Devil—with hooves on. . . .

The Blue Woman—with hooves on. . . .

Charlie McCarthy—with hooves on—

*   *   *

Mr. Smith stopped dead. He halted in his tracks as if he had been shot. He stood stock-still; and the slowly falling snow floated and drifted past his unseeing eyes and all round him, lodging a little more thickly on his hat and forming epaulettes on the shoulders of his coat. For in his mind he had gone one step further. One short step, in retrospect an almost inevitable step—and what a gulf he had crossed!

Not one *and* one. Not one plus one. One *multiplied* by one.

One!

And by the plumes of Plantagenet he could give that one a name!

And then the moment passed. The wave of pure exhilaration that had suddenly drenched him receded, and doubt entered his mind. It rushed in; not just the little devil doubt, which is indecision, but the big devil doubt, which is cold hard scepticism.

No, it couldn't be. It was impossible. It was tempting—but it was impossible.

Or was it . . .? Hadn't he himself said they had been reading the messages in the snow all wrong? Suppose he tried reading them again in the blaze of that lightning flash of inspiration. . . .

But it was still impossible. Flatly, physically impossible.

He drew in his breath in a long shivering sigh. He moved on again, his feet falling blindly and carelessly on the slushy pavement. He forced himself to try to think calmly and rationally.

The hoof-prints considered merely as hoof-prints? Yes. The two impressions side by side on the low privet hedge that bordered the Jacksons' garden? Oh, yes. Easily, obviously—just as he himself had done. And yes! now to the prints on the window-sill outside Mason's bedroom.

His thoughts flashed to Mason. Then that meant—odds blood! it meant murder! Or at the very least some sort of suicide pact.

We-ell. . . such things had happened before, perhaps stranger things than that. It was damned unlikely, admittedly, but it wasn't physically impossible.

And maybe it wasn't—but something else was. Both sets of tracks, the man's and the beast's, had *ended* there. . . . And that ring of prints on the roof. . . .

Mr. Smith groaned and made a despairing gesture among the snowflakes. But the idea held him, nagged at him, it was too tempting, there must be some way over these seemingly insurmountable hurdles.

The prints on Maltravers's high wall and Mrs. Pendlebury's low one? Ha! But yes! Yes, of course; and probably in all Winchingham and the surrounding country only that—

No! Again, no. How did they get *on* to that six-foot wall? How get past, or over, or through Maltravers's pavilion, Mrs. Pendlebury's summerhouse? The gaps in the trail . . .?

Mr. Smith tried to comfort himself with the conviction that those seemingly impossible gaps, all that business of going in and out of gardens and standing in front of doors, the apparently thwarted attempts at entry into Mason's house—all that had been so much by-play, a smokescreen, confusion tactics to smother and bury the real objective, which had been—Mason. Montague Mason, deliberately inveigled—by that mysterious telephone call from his own house—into coming down to Steeple Thelming that very evening. For that special purpose? To put the rope around his own neck? *Or to have it done for him?*

But the tracks—again the tracks. . . . The hoof-prints, the foot-prints—they *ended* there. . . . The hoof-prints began from nowhere, ended in nothing. There were gaps in the trail inexplicable and impossible in the scheme of natural things. There was that ring of prints on Mason's roof, a circle without beginning or end.

It just simply could not be. There was too much against it. It was impossible—in that last instance doubly impossible.

But *still* he was loath to give up the idea. To give it up, to admit that the phenomena transcended the bounds of physical interpretation, was to stand aside and leave the field to Miss Forbes and her ilk. And if he did that, if the police did that, it would mean that Winchingham, and the world, had slipped back a thousand years to days of misty medieval thought and fearful belief in black magic and witchcraft. Miss Forbes wouldn't say that, of course; she would use polysyllabic Greek words, but that was what it would mean.

He turned the corner into his own street, frowning savagely and utterly ignoring the salute of a passing constable—who stared after him in pained surprise. His mind clung grimly to what he had called the inside physical *facts*—the dead bodies of Mason and Croxley.

Now Croxley had been *struck*; he had suffered an actual physical blow and had died instantly. But that only made things worse, for Croxley had, therefore, dropped in his tracks, and his tracks ended—

Momentarily Mr. Smith's own tracks ended.

Croxley's tracks had ended where the hoof-prints ended.

Mason's tracks had ended where the hoof-prints ended.

The foot-prints in the dust up under the skylight had been made by a size 11 shoe—shoe or boot, that was immaterial.

Mason, a little man with smallish feet, had been wearing size 11 gumboots.

Croxley had been wearing size 11 boots.

But naturally; that was the size of his feet—

Feet!

Boomer's hooves—Boomer's *shoes*. . . .

Croxley's feet—Croxley's *boots*. . . .

Somewhere in the depths of Mr. Smith's mind metaphorical wings began to flutter; the wings of truth struggling to rise and soar in the light of recognition.

Wait, now! Steady! Try your own prescription and work from the inside to the outside, from the known to the unknown. Work backwards from the dead bodies—

And suddenly he saw it!

Backwards!

*   *   *

Mr. Smith walked on again through the gradually thickening snow. He came to his own gate, opened it, walked up the little path to his own front door and went inside. He closed it gently and noiselessly behind him, he hung up his hat and coat—automatically, without seeing them—and stole upstairs to bed.

But not to sleep—not to sleep. To worry—worry—worry at his problem as a dog worries a bone.

When morning came to a white and snowbound world he had overcome some of the difficulties, perhaps most of them. But there were still some very serious ones left. There was still the problem of the gaps in the trail of Sunday morning. There was still the problem of Croxley's cigar—and the extraneous problem of motive—there wasn't the shadow of a motive. And, most serious of all, there was still the problem of the ring of hoof-prints round the skylight in the roof. That seemed to be insoluble; that didn't remain merely obscure, as perhaps the motive remained obscure, only waiting to be ferreted out; that remained physically impossible.

And yet he knew—he *knew*—he was on the right track.

During what had been left of the night, while he had tossed and twisted in bed to the discomfort and distress of his wife, he had thought of an added problem: the problem of where the Thing was *now*. But he had guessed the answer to this—admittedly a sheer guess, a hunch based on the killing of Croxley—and the recollection of it brought him out of bed in a tearing hurry and down the stairs to the telephone, where he rang up the police station and gave the sergeant on duty a hasty urgent order. Then he went back to the bedroom and, glancing out of the window, noticed for the first time that it was snowing. It was, as a matter of fact, still snowing, coming down now in great heavy multitudinous flakes, falling quickly and burying still more deeply a countryside that was already buried to a depth of eighteen inches to two feet. He shivered and dived back into bed to wrestle again with the master problem. The securely closed skylight. The foot-prints *under* the skylight. The hoof-prints on the steep roof above *round* the skylight, more than seven feet away from it at any point. The smooth even covering of snow *on* the skylight. . . .

It was no use. It *couldn't* have been done. . . .

But it *had* been done. . . .

His overtaxed brain began to function erratically. His thoughts grew muzzy and chaotic. He found himself once again standing on the stepladder and holding on to Bill Poynter's ankles while he wriggled around on his stomach on the steep snow-covered roof of Mason's house and photographed the circle of prints. Only somehow or another Poynter had turned into Croxley, and as well as using his camera he was lighting cigars and throwing them away. And round and round, just out of reach, some vague blue shape hopped on one hoof and jeered at him. . . .

When a slightly anxious Mrs. Smith brought his breakfast up to him, he was asleep.

25

"Snowbound, begod!" muttered Old Jake to himself, peering out of the window. He stood in his little kitchen, the whisky bottle in one hand and the other hand pressed to his forehead. Gregory, coming in a moment later, brushing snow off his trousers and shoes, inquired laconically: "Hair of the dog?"

Jake assented sadly. "Got a bit of a head this mornin'."

"Amazing!" commented Gregory sarcastically.

"Huh! Been out in it, have yer?"

Gregory nodded gloomily. "I've been talking to that policeman outside."

"Policeman? What policeman?"

"There's one out in the road."

"What the hades," demanded Jake caustically, "is a copper doin' out there on a mornin' like this—directin' traffic?"

"Keeping an eye on Croxley's place, I suppose." Gregory lounged against the sink-bench and looked pointedly at the bottle in his uncle's hand. "Your girl friend was out again last night."

"Hey? Whaddyer mean—gal friend?"

"Your Blue Woman."

Jake stared hard at him. Then, distrustfully, he eyed the whisky, corked the bottle and put it away with an air of solemn renunciation, and turned back to his nephew. "Somethin's up," he growled softly. "Somethin's happened—let's have it, Greg."

"Last night," said Gregory deliberately, "you saw the Blue Woman again. You had a lot of fun with her, you brought her home with you. Your pal Silver brought *you* home. Last night something walked into Croxley's garden, the something that has hooves. It walked through on to the lawn, went round and round in a circle and—well, then it vanished again. Last night, about nine o'clock, Croxley came out of his own house to go to the police station. He never got there, he never went back into his house again. The police found him about two o'clock this morning, stone dead—in the centre of that circle of hoof-prints. . . ."

Jake's little eyes widened to their fullest extent. "*Croxley!* Croxley, now!"

"Yes. Bit odd, isn't it, uncle Jake? A bit—queer. Every time you see the Blue Woman—someone dies!"

"Croxley!" repeated the old man, astounded and considerably alarmed. "God strike me—"

"Don't say it!" Gregory's frozen calm cracked, and his voice went high and shrill. "Don't *say* it!"

"Hey! Easy now—"

"Who's going to be next? That's what I want to know. When are you going to see her again, and who's going to be the next victim?"

"Now, now," said Jake severely, recovering himself. "No good thinkin' along those lines. That's senseless, leave that sort o' thing to Emmy Forbes—"

"All very well slinging off at Miss Forbes, but what other sort of lines have you got? What *other* lines can we think along?"

"Don't think at all. Leave the thinkin' to the police—that's what they're paid for."

"Easy enough to say that. Do you know what I was talking about to that policeman?"

"How the hades should I know? Lemme get at that stove, my boy, an' I'll get us a bite o' breakfast."

"Breakfast! I was talking to him about getting out of this place and going back home."

"Oh!" said Jake quietly, busying himself at the stove. "But have yer got a home to go to now?"

"Sort of. An empty flat."

"We-ell, suit yerself. But can yer?"

"No," said Gregory despondently. "That's just it, I can't. Not today, at any rate—unless I start walking. There are no trains running today. Nothing's moving, the whole country's tied up under this snow. . . . Uncle Jake, I don't want you to think me ungrateful, you've been very good to me, but I—I've had enough of all this, I didn't come here for *this*. . . ."

Jake nodded curtly but understandingly. "I wasn't thinkin' of that, the trains not runnin', I mean. I was thinkin' of the inquest."

"Oh . . . Oh, Lord! I'd forgotten about that."

"Yeh, I thought mebbe yer had. Adjourned till next Monday, ain't it? An' y're one of the principal witnesses. So even if yer did go away yer'd have to be back be Monday. Might as well stay on a bit longer, Greg. Might as well stay for the week, at least."

"Yes," sighed Gregory hopelessly, "I suppose I might as well. I suppose I'll have to. But, by heaven, *I've had this!*"

*   *   *

Detective-Inspector Lancelot Carolus Smith trudged through snow to his knees to the police station. By that time it had ceased falling and to all appearances had ceased for good. Detective-Sergeant Poynter was in his own office waiting for him.

"Good morning, Inspector. And eke good afternoon."

"Yes," said Mr. Smith absently. "What's been doing this morning, Bill?"

"The superintendent and I have been places. We've been out to The Rise interviewing Mrs. Croxley."

"What about?"

"What about?" echoed Poynter in some surprise. "Croxley, of course."

"I'll bet you learnt a lot. What could *she* tell you?"

"As a matter of fact she couldn't tell us anything we didn't know, which didn't surprise me particularly. But we did learn something."

"Oh?"

"Yessir! We learnt a little more metaphysics. Miss Forbes was there playing the Good Samaritan and looking after Mrs. Croxley. Miss Forbes hasn't exactly got a theory this time, but she's got ideas—psychic ideas."

"M'm . . . I've got some ideas myself—but they're not psychic ideas, they're very grossly material."

Poynter gazed narrowly at his senior officer. "The devil you have!"

"Yes. Some. Where's the super?"

"Upstairs. Waiting for you."

"Chief constable with him?"

"No, sir!" said Poynter sardonically. "The chief constable is snug in his own home. The chief constable is snowbound. But his telephone is still in good working order, and the chief constable is making noises like a baffled bull."

"I'll bet he is," said Mr. Smith unemotionally, and sped up the stairs to Superintendent Blackler's office. He tapped on the door and went in. The superintendent was sitting at his desk with his head in his hands.

"Hullo, Super! Thinking? Or praying?"

"Neither," returned Superintendent Blackler, and looked at him curiously. "Did you get any sleep last night, Smithy?"

The inspector shook his head. "The brain—such as it is—was too busy. But I dozed off just when it was time to get up again, of course! Sorry I'm late, Super."

The superintendent waved this aside. "Well, sit down and put your feet up. This is the hell of a snowfall. All traffic is held up, and most of the telephones north seem to be out of action—"

"Except the chief constable's."

"Yes, except the chief constable's," echoed the superintendent gloomily. "And the chief constable is—upset."

"Foaming at the mouth. I know."

"Er—yes . . . Smithy, I've just had a ring from Jamieson." Detective-Inspector Jamieson, of the Metropolitan Police, was investigating Mason's death from the London end. "Scotland Yard are getting interested."

"I'll bet they are," said Mr. Smith with conviction. "Tell me anybody in the country, policeman or civilian, who isn't. And the stuff that's creeping into the papers! Wait till they get this second lot!"

"H'm. . . . We're beginning to get a clearer picture of our Mr. Mason. He seems to have been a blackmarket operator in a big way. Dealt mainly in foodstuffs, direct from the source. You know what that means?"

"Yes, I know what that means. He operated in this district?"

"Apparently. And perhaps other districts. But Steeple Thelming was one of his main—er—action stations. Did you know he owned the Steeple Inn?"

"No! Did he? That junk heap!"

"Junk heap as an hotel, maybe, but apparently his headquarters down here. Borwell, of course, was one of his agents, a minor one. So was that man Sheldon. Only Sheldon had sidelines of his own that eventually led him into bad trouble—that's why he went to ground at that inn."

"I see," said Mr. Smith softly. "Well, that clears the air a little, but it doesn't get us much forrarder, does it?"

Superintendent Blackler grunted disconsolately. "It doesn't get us *any* forrarder. Why did Mason kill himself?—if he did kill himself—you seem to have doubts about that. His affairs were in order. The man was flourishing, making money hand over fist that the Commissioners of Inland Revenue didn't know anything about—it wasn't until after his death, and because of it, that his affairs were blown upon. . . . That man Sheldon still swears black and blue that he never left the Steeple Inn after midday on Saturday until he cleared out by the 9.30 yesterday."

"I believe him," said Mr. Smith easily. "He takes a size 9 shoe."

"What?" The superintendent drew his eyebrows together. "These damn sizes and numbers of yours! Look, Smithy, if it wasn't one of Mason's agents who put that call through to him from his own house on Saturday afternoon, if neither Borwell nor Sheldon did it—who did?"

Mr. Smith told him.

"*What?*" shouted the superintendent, sitting up and staring at him.

Mr. Smith repeated the name. And then he began to talk rapidly and earnestly, and he talked for some time. But when he finished he did so not on a period but on a question mark, on several question marks.

"Yes. . . ." muttered the superintendent. "My aunt! My sacred, swivel-eyed aunt! Yes. . . . But those are the biggest stumbling blocks, and unless you get over those. . . . And then we've got to prove it. . . ."

"I know," groaned the inspector. "You don't have to tell me. And there's the question of motive. There doesn't seem to be the shadow of a motive—unless your friend Jamieson can ferret something out his end."

"Well . . . we can try it. We can put it up to him."

"As for proof," went on the inspector thoughtfully. "I have a hunch. It's really a double-barrelled hunch and it works both ways. I have an idea that Croxley was killed because of that proof, and just because he was killed I have a vague idea that, if we are very lucky, we might be able to put our hands *on* the proof."

Mr. Smith left the superintendent and went downstairs again to Bill Poynter's room. Poynter was trying to open a cupboard door that had stuck, and was cursing it in a lugubrious undertone.

"Put your bonnet and shawl on, Bill," commanded the inspector, coming in briskly. "We're going for a walk."

"Are we?" returned Poynter, still struggling. "Well, we've got a nice day for it. Where are we going?"

"Out to The Rise. We're going to study architecture."

Poynter stood away from the cupboard and gloomed at it. "Have a heart, Inspector. I've already been out there once this morning."

"Well, you're going again. With me. And then we're going on to Steeple Thelming."

"Steeple Thelming!" repeated Poynter indignantly. "Walk! You don't know what you're saying! We'll get frozen to death! We'll fall in a snowdrift and get buried alive and then the robins will come and cover our innocent bodies with leaves."

"Your King and country," said Mr. Smith solemnly, "need you. . . . What *are* you trying to do?" For Poynter had attacked the cupboard door again.

"Trying to open this ruddy door."

"How about unlocking it first?"

"It is unlocked. It's stuck—warped, or something."

"What do you want it open for?"

Poynter gave it up, stood back from it and scowled at the unyielding panel. "I've got a pair of goloshes in there, I know I have. I put 'em there last summer."

"Goloshes! What do you want with goloshes? You've got a pair of good stout boots on—tuck your trousers into your socks. And come on, you slothful devil!"

"Very well," said Poynter with dignity. "If I get chilblains, I get chilblains. And if I perish in the blizzard, my untimely demise will be at your door."

Still grumbling he put on his hat and coat, and the two of them set out along River Crescent, into Old Chipping Road and along to The Rise. And as they went the inspector told him some of the ideas that had come into his head during the night; and at the end of it Poynter slapped his forehead and said he was hornswoggled.

"If you're right it's the craziest, most outlandish thing we've ever struck!"

"People will try to be clever, Bill. People are always trying to go one step farther. It's complicated, but it's not necessarily crazy. Look for a complicated mind, William, and you'll find the Devil."

"That's a pearl of philosophy. But a bit double-edged, isn't it? I mean, with all due respect to my superior officer, how about your own? You've evidently followed some if not all of the complications—"

"Mine? But I've got a simple mind! I don't make mysteries—only the complicated minds do that—I unravel them, or try to. That's the mark of the simple mind. My mind is too simple to believe what my eyes seem to tell me, so I look for the simple truth."

"And in this case you've found it."

"I believe I have."

"Yes . . .some of it. But I dunno about this simple mind of yours, Inspector. I think you're kidding me. The really simple-minded people still think it was the Devil."

"And in one sense," said the inspector thoughtfully, "they may be right."

"Eh?"

"In the sense," said Mr. Smith seriously, "that a man may sell his soul to the Devil. Or, if we don't believe in souls, in the sense that he gives himself up to evil."

Poynter grunted noncommittally. "But there's a lot of guesswork to it, isn't there?"

"Of course. It's all still guesswork. But what will you have in its place—Miss Forbes's supernatural visitation? Jake Popplewell's supernatural Blue Woman?"

"Um. . . . How are you going to get over those gaps in the trail at that pavilion thing of Maltravers's and Mrs. Pendlebury's summerhouse? *And* the circle of prints on the roof? *Nothing* with any weight could have stood on that roof, Inspector."

"I know, Bill. And nothing did stand on it. Only. . . . There are answers to those questions—there *must* be. . . ."

And after that they plodded along in silence for awhile, and then Poynter asked: "What put you on to it? What made you suddenly think—?"

"Oddly enough you did."

"*I* did?"

"Yes. Your little discourse on numerology—that was very helpful. Speaking of the number eleven, you said that it consisted of two ones. And there are two ones—the hoof-prints, and the size eleven foot-prints. You said one plus one made two, which narrowed the field slightly but didn't seem to help much. But then you said that one multiplied by one still left only one—and that was the answer! And then there was your brilliant inspiration that it was Charlie McCarthy who—"

"Oh, here!" protested Poynter feebly. "You can't expect me to believe that! It was a damn silly thing for me to say, and I don't know why I said it."

"And yet I assure you, Bill, that it pulled a trigger in my mind that should have been pulled long ago. It was the third step in a chain of four steps that jolted me on to the truth. . . . And, of course, there is the clear evidence that one of the Thing's shoes is narrower in its left half than the other, and that it appeared in illogical, not to say absurd, sequences in certain places along the trail."

Whereat Poynter stared at him and said he was horn-swoggled again.

And so they came to The Rise.

At the foot of it Mr. Smith had a brief word with the policeman who had been posted there at his urgent request.

"Well, Sutton?"

"Nothing to report, sir. Nobody's been near it."

"No, I don't suppose anyone is likely to now. But you know what to do if anyone does?"

"Yes, sir."

"Good. Anybody stirring?"

"People have been popping in and out of their gates to have a look at the snow, but that's all, sir."

"No particular interest shown in the Croxley house?"

"No, sir. Of course, there's nothing to see now."

"Yes, and probably just as well. Thanks, Sutton. Keep on with the good work, you'll be relieved in another hour."

26

"Smartly now, Bill!" urged Mr. Smith. "up to Maltravers's place—and I hope to heaven we get past Croxley's without being ambushed by Miss Forbes."

Poynter, floundering along behind him, grinned at his back. "Not interested in her theories any longer, Inspector? Not interested in the psychic any more?"

"I am not!" Mr. Smith was firm. "If it hadn't been for Miss Forbes and her mysticism—" He broke off abruptly and his footsteps slackened a little. It was heavy going in the deep snow; one raised a foot high, like a thoroughbred pacer, and sank it again to the knee. "Scrap-book," mused Mr. Smith. "Ha! Yes—of course. . . ."

They passed Croxley's gate without running into any ambush, and climbed on up the hill to Maltravers's house.

"Common courtesy," mused the inspector, "demands that one should seek out Mr. Lionel Maltravers and beg formal admission to his property. But I think we'll dispense with it. There's nothing he can tell us, and I don't know that I want an audience. We'll take the risk. Come on, Bill."

Followed by the faithful Poynter he entered the wide gateway into the drive, turned sharply right, cutting across the long hump in the snow that marked the bordering flower-bed, and walked along the edge of the croquet lawn under the wall to the pavilion in the far corner. Snow lay thickly on the tops of the walls and the roof of the pavilion.

"Pretty, isn't it?" commented Poynter admiringly. "Like a fancy wedding cake with all that icing on it. Or something out of the *Blue Bird*."

"Yes," said Mr. Smith grimly. "A fairy cottage in a fairy tale, inhabited by a goblin. And our job is to smash the fairy tale and destroy the goblin."

He turned his eyes upwards to where the roof curved suddenly but gracefully outwards to the gutter that ran round all four sides. The roof projected some eighteen inches beyond the walls, and immediately beneath this overhang, at regular intervals, were carved wooden brackets; placed there, it would seem, not so much for additional support for the roof as for decorative purposes, to break and soften the hard angle where roof and wall met.

The inspector's eyes narrowed thoughtfully as he gazed at these brackets, and motioning Poynter to stay where he was he went into the narrow space between the back walls of the pavilion and the six-foot brick walls that, in the one instance, faced the road and, in the other, divided Maltravers's property from Mrs. Pendlebury's. He walked right round the pavilion, coming to a halt at the point where the tracks of the Thing had ended so suddenly and inexplicably that Sunday morning, and he looked up.

"Well?" inquired Poynter, watching him closely. "Destroyed your goblin?"

"Um," said Mr. Smith unsatisfactorily. "We saw it before, I suppose—we *must* have seen it—but, of course, we didn't know what we were looking for then."

"And do we now?"

"Vaguely, vaguely. . . . I'd like to get up on that wall, Bill."

"You'll break your perishin' neck!"

"Oh, I don't think so. I can push that snow off out of the way first."

"Is it absolutely necessary?"

"Well . . . perhaps not—but I'd like to satisfy myself."

"Hum! Does that mean I brace myself against the wall while you spring off my lumbago?"

Mr. Smith smiled fleetingly. "No, Bill. I think I'll get up the way the Thing got up."

"You definitely will break your neck!"

Mr. Smith made no answer to this, but took Poynter with him back out of Maltravers's garden and on to the road again, and up past the high brick wall to where it gave way to the three-foot wall of Mrs. Pendlebury's. He eyed both walls speculatively for a moment, and then he hopped up on to the lower one, balanced himself, and lifted his right foot to the top of the higher wall. But though he could place his foot on it, he could not give himself enough impetus to rise high enough to stand on it.

"Ho!" muttered Poynter from below. "Snag number one."

"No-o, I don't think so," returned the inspector meditatively. "I fancy you've forgotten something, Bill. Two things: the hooves—or shoes—that would give added height; and the fact that I'm not

as young as I used to be. And there's a third thing, a very significant factor that I learnt from Miss Forbes—I don't think you
know about it yet. . . . Oh, well. . . ."

He cleared a space of wall free from snow, placed his foot on the
lateral between two of the spikes in Mrs. Pendlebury's railing, and,
gripping the top of Maltravers's wall with his hands, stepped easily
on to it and crouched there like a frog. Then, cautiously, he stood
up and began to walk slowly along it.

Poynter closed his eyes. "If I hear a dull sickening thud I'll know
what it is."

"Child's play, Bill," said Mr. Smith proudly. "This wall is thicker
than you'd think. Anyway there's plenty of snow down there if I
should fall." And then he squatted down on his heels with his nose
only a couple of feet or so from the edge of the pavilion roof, and
was silent for awhile.

"Stalled your engine?" asked Bill Poynter at length.

"Um . . ." Mr. Smith stood up again and descended from the wall
the same way as he had ascended.

"Slay your dragon?" asked Poynter.

"Eh?"

"*Have* you destroyed your goblin?"

"Yes, I think I have. This particular one, at any rate."

"Well, that's good. I suppose you'll tell us all about it when you
feel like it. What next?"

"Mrs. Pendlebury's summerhouse. And we'll go right round and
attack it in the rear—more than ever I don't want an audience."

They plodded up to the summit of The Rise and down the other
side to the first gap in the ragged gorse hedge. The scene spread
before their eyes was one that normally would have halted the
inspector in silent admiration, but though now he was silent he
was not in a mood to appreciate the beauties of Nature. And not
until they were through the gap and advancing across the hillside
up towards the summerhouse did he lift his eyes from the ground.
Then he said quietly: "Bill!"

"Yes, Inspector?"

"Pray for a miracle. We'll need one here. There's nothing about
the summerhouse that I can remember. . . ."

But the miracle was there, if you can call it a miracle. And it was
not in the inspector's memory, because he hadn't noticed it before.
But now, looking for something, something at once vague and
specific, he saw it. The boards that closed the summerhouse all
round during the winter months did not fit quite flush up under the
roof; there was a little space between, a space through which you
could have pushed, say, a fountain pen. And clambering over the

cutback part of the privet hedge he saw that it was the same all the way round. And remembering where the snow had lain that Sunday morning, and where it had *not* lain, he destroyed the second goblin, the one that had been dwelling in this summer-house.

He had solved one of his two major problems. He had closed the gaps in the trail.

He came back and rejoined Poynter on the other side of the hedge. "God is good," he said simply.

"What you might call a self-evident proposition," observed Bill Poynter drily. "Though at the moment I can't say I see—"

"Thus showing that it is not always a self-evident proposition," retorted Mr. Smith. "The goodness of God isn't always apparent. Sometimes you have to look pretty hard for it, and to pass through agony of mind and spirit before you find it."

Whereat Poynter glanced at him queerly and was silent.

They went on. They retraced their footsteps out on to the road again and trudged on down to the crossroads at Steeple Thelming and along to Mason's house where the snow, smooth and as yet unmarked, seemed to be even deeper. They entered the house, went upstairs to the little box room and ascended the step-ladder to the space under the roof. And underneath the skylight, dark now under its heavy mantle of snow, Mr. Smith halted and ruffled his hair and sighed.

"I know before we start we're wasting our time. And yet. . . . You know what the real problem is now, Bill. How did the hoof-prints get on the roof without the snow on the skylight being disturbed."

"I don't know that I do altogether," said Poynter diffidently. "I know I've said it before, but I'll say it again; nothing could stand on a roof as steep as this one and walk round—"

"Gadzooks!" The inspector stared at him. "But I thought you'd seen it now! Nothing *did* stand on the roof. Nothing stood on the Jacksons' hedge, or on that window-sill. . . . I know *what* was done here; what I want to know is *how* it was done!"

Poynter shrugged his shoulders. The inspector, gazing up at the skylight only inches above his head, went on: "The only way on to this roof—other than by ladder from the ground, and there is no ladder long enough on the premises, neither is there the slightest evidence that any such ladder was used—rather and most decidedly the reverse . . . the only way on to this roof is through this skylight, and, it seems obvious, by means of that step-ladder. That's if you want to climb out on to the roof. But if you merely want to open the skylight, say to air the place, you prop it open with that pole. But in any case, if I open it, what will happen?"

"The snow on it will fall off," replied Poynter promptly, "same as it did last time." After a moment he added: "But last time we threw it wide open and let it lie back flat on the roof. Try it gently, how far can you go?"

The inspector tried it gently. The wooden frame of the skylight rested on narrow wooden ledges in the roof, which prevented any chance of it falling downwards on to your head when you pulled the bolt, and swung upwards and outwards on two hinges. The inspector drew back the bolt and pushed upwards cautiously.

"Hand me that pole, Bill," he requested; and Poynter gave him the slender seven-foot-long pole that was still lying there. He placed it in position and pushed the skylight a little higher. But before the pole could be propped upright, the snow began to slide off the glass.

"Not far enough," he muttered, answering Poynter's question. "Nowhere near far enough."

Poynter said nothing. There was nothing to say, except to labour the obvious. Mr. Smith let the skylight fall to again with a little thud, and absently held out the pole for Poynter to take from him.

"We're wasting our time," he said again. "It can't be done, that's all. It's impossible."

Poynter still said nothing.

"So," went on the inspector, mumbling to himself, "if it's impossible it wasn't done. . . . Yet it was done all right, for the prints were *there*. So it wasn't done *that* way. . . ."

At that Poynter opened his mouth. "What other way is there?"

Mr. Smith waved his arm in a despairing gesture. "I don't know, Bill! I can't think. . . ."

*   *   *

That amateur nurse, Miss Forbes, seizing a moment when her patient was sleeping, slipped out of the house and across the road and down to Jake Popplewell's cottage. She had already seen and exchanged courtesies with P.C. Sutton, and now she paused and regarded him thoughtfully.

"I wonder," she mused, "if you have any idea of what you are looking for?"

The policeman, who had a very definite idea of what he was there for, smiled at her and replied diplomatically: "Just anything, ma'am. Anything out of the ordinary."

"H'm! And I wonder what exactly is meant by that?"

"Don't quite know myself, ma'am," said the young policeman cheerfully. "That's as far as I go."

"Yes," said Miss Forbes shrewdly, "that's as far as any of you go. It's not very far, is it?" And nodding to him in friendly fashion she continued on her way. Jake opened the door to her.

"Ah, Popplewell."

"Mornin', Miss Forbes. Come in an' sit yerself down, the parlour's warm."

"Thank you. . . . Parlour—a delightful old word, you hardly ever hear it now. A room for conversation. People have no conversation these days, and the parlour has given way to the lounge—very expressive word—and the living-room, which means nothing. . . . Ah, good morning, Mr. Cushing."

She sat down in the chair proffered by Gregory. "I can only stay a minute—I suppose you've heard . . .?"

"Croxley?" inquired Jake gruffly. "Yeh, we've heard."

"A dreadful thing. A terrible thing. Poor Mrs. Croxley, I'm so sorry for her. How much do you people know?"

Gregory told her. Miss Forbes sat up and stared at him. "*Kicked?* I didn't know that. I didn't know exactly what had caused his death, I imagined perhaps he'd fallen or been struck down somehow—not by a *physical* blow, I mean—and had frozen to death in the snow. But kicked!"

"Yeh," grunted old Jake. "Be a hoof with a shoe on it. That's a physical enough blow, ain't it?"

"I don't know. The *effect* is that of a physical blow, yes, but the *cause*. . . . Was there anything that pointed to a physical cause?"

Gregory shook his head. "The hoof-prints, beginning again from nowhere and ending at nothing, that's all."

"First time I ever heard of a ghost *killin'!*" muttered Jake.

"They can kill," said Miss Forbes seriously. "Oh, yes, they can kill. By subtle devious ways. But however it may be accomplished, death is still a physical phenomenon. I think I know what is in your mind, Popplewell: you are still thinking on the surface, your mind is still in the grip of the illusion that the physical is—well, solid, substantial. It is not. It is hollow, a shadow, an evanescent creation of mind. Actually, in terms of the Absolute, it is non-existent. But both the physical and the psychic are merely different aspects, or emanations, of some transcendent Force; and we are its creatures."

"Yes," said Gregory hastily. "But Croxley—have you any ideas, Miss Forbes?"

The lady hesitated. "One idea does enter the mind. It is not very helpful, but it persists. Mr. Croxley was very interested in the phenomenon of the hoof-prints. He took a number of photographs of them, he *perpetuated* them, as it were—"

"So did that police photographer. He took even more, and by reason of his job is even more interested and investigated more deeply."

"No! That doesn't follow. He took photographs, and is taking part in the investigation, yes. That, as you say, is his job. But that doesn't necessarily imply that he is more interested. What counts, you see, is not the actions of the man, but the mental state behind the actions. Now Mr. Croxley was—well, highly enthusiastic. And there is an added detail that, to my mind, simply cannot be altogether without some significance."

"Is there?"

"Yes. In its passing that night," said Miss Forbes solemnly, "Mr. Croxley's garden was the first to be entered by the Thing, his door the first to be approached—and contemplated. . . ."

"Rot me!" exclaimed Jake. "That's a cheerin' thought!"

"What did I say to you this morning?" cried Gregory, bounding up out of his chair. "Who's going to be next? Who's next on this Thing's list?"

Uncle Jake let out a fierce bellow. "Now, wait a minute! Calm down, Greg, y' fathead! This cheery little thought of yours, Miss Forbes: why Croxley? Why the Jacksons? An', Powers above, why *you?*"

"Who knows?" posed Miss Forbes sombrely. "Who knows what is in our past lives?"

Jake grinned his hyena grin. "Shady spots every where, yeh. Kept secret an' buried an' crushed down. Croxley, the Jacksons, an' Mister Lionel Maltravers—that retired bloodsucker!—but you yerself? Now, now, Miss Forbes! Anybody more God-fearin'—to use an old-fashioned phrase—anybody more intellectually honest, more morally courageous—"

"You flatter me!"

"I never flatter anybody. But what on God's good earth—or on His psychic plane—could there be in your blameless existence to interest a homicidal ghost?"

"Murder."

"*What?*" Gregory positively leapt in the air.

"Murder," repeated Miss Forbes calmly. "Oh, I didn't do it, Mr. Cushing—nor my sister. But some time ago our gardener was brutally murdered on our own property. . . . You remember the case, Popplewell."

"Yeh. Yeh, vaguely. I remember—what the papers called the Bishop's Sword case."

"My God!" breathed Gregory, staring at his uncle. "What's in *our* past lives?"

Jake, the agnostic, the reprehensible, grinned again. "I don't think y' need start worryin' yet, me boy. We're a long way down the list. We weren't even visited. We were passed by, ignored. . . ."

*　　*　　*

Detective-Inspector Smith and Bill Poynter, the former in a rather dejected frame of mind, arrived back at the police station as Superintendent Blackler was on the point of going to lunch.

"Before you go, Super," begged the inspector, "give me a minute."

"Two, if you like," replied the superintendent obligingly.

"Well," said Mr. Smith, and hesitated.

"Well, what?"

"I'm right. I *know* I'm right. I've got everything now, except that last mystery. I can show you exactly how the Thing passed through matter without leaving traces—the pavilion and the summerhouse, Super—I know how the hoof-prints come to start and end in that apparently impossible manner—I could do it—*you* could do it—"

"Thank you. But you don't know how they came to be on the roof?"

"No," said Mr. Smith. "No," he said angrily, "not yet. And yet there must be some simple explanation, only I'm still damn fool enough not to be able to see it. But I've got enough without that—and we might be able to *force* that. . . . Super, I think we'd better act on my hunch!"

Superintendent Blackler stroked his jaw. "H'm. . . . This snow—that'll give the game away."

"We'll have to take that risk."

"Well . . . when? *If* you're right, and if you do it in broad daylight. . . ."

"Tonight. At dead of night. I'll take Bill Poynter and Keyes with me."

The superintendent meditated a little longer. "Well, all right. But suppose what you're looking for isn't there?"

For a moment or two, in his turn, the inspector was silent. When he answered the superintendent his voice sounded troubled. "If we don't find proof of the truth, Super—if we never find it—then I'm afraid we're sunk. The spiritualists and the psychical researchers will smother us, and we'll never lay the ghost, we'll never—blow up the Thing with hooves. . . ."

*   *   *

Superintendent Blackler went on to his lunch. Mr. Smith turned into his own office, sat down and held his head in his hands. Presently he became aware of sounds in the next room, which was Poynter's; rasping, shaking sounds, and mutterings from Poynter himself. He stood up and strolled in to see what it was all about.

"What the blazes are you trying to do, William?" he demanded testily.

Poynter was on his knees at the cupboard door, tugging at it and cursing in a lugubrious undertone. "I'm trying to open this—door!" He stood up suddenly, darted to his table, wrenched open a drawer, rummaged about in it and brought out a screwdriver. "I'll fix the swine!" he said savagely.

"Here! You mustn't damage government property like that!"

"I'm not going to damage any government property!" retorted Poynter, plumping down on his knees again. "I'm going to take the blasted thing off its hinges."

He poised the screwdriver and squinted closely at the door. Then he became aware of a sudden silence in the room, a dead, empty silence, and he glanced over his shoulder. Mr. Smith had gone.

*   *   *

That afternoon the inspector shut himself up in his office with a large sheet of paper and a pencil.

And that night, some time after midnight, he rang up Superintendent Blackler. The superintendent, dragged once again from his bed, thought his voice sounded tired but triumphant.

"No!" said Superintendent Blackler.

"Yes!" said Mr. Smith.

And then there was a long discussion, and some argument, and as a result of the discussion and argument. . . .

27

As a result of it there was a kind of "at home" in the police station the following morning. It was held in the superintendent's office above the charge room, and the guests numbered five. They were Miss Forbes, Mr. Mayhew, Mr. Maltravers, Gregory Cushing and, to his own surprise and sardonic amusement, old Jake Popplewell. But Jake's amusement didn't last very long. The five of them sat in a rough semi-circle on one side of Superintendent Blackler's massive polished desk, and the superintendent himself sat opposite. Flanking him were Detective-Inspector Smith, and, looking preternaturally solemn and wise, Detective-Sergeant Poynter. On the desk, in front of the inspector, stood a smallish brown bag. It looked something like a doctor's little bag, but actually it was one in which Superintendent Blackler used to keep bowls.

The chief constable wasn't there. The chief constable was at his own home confined to bed with a shattering cold. And perhaps, from Mr. Smith's point of view, this was just as well; for the chief constable was inclined to be distrustful of what he called his inspector's "dramatics" and might have vetoed the whole thing.

Superintendent Blackler, notoriously a man of few words, opened proceedings after the manner of a chairman. "Lady and gentlemen," he said formally, "I must thank you for your attendance here this morning. We have asked you to come here because, with one exception, you are the people who first discovered the mysterious hoof-prints in the snow—"

"Yeh," old Jake interrupted him. "With one exception. Me! An' why? Why have I been dragged here to hobnob with coppers?"

"But you haven't been dragged here," protested the superintendent mildly. "You were invited to be present, and you are here of your own free will. And you were invited because . . . well, because it's your donkey and it seems only fitting—"

"Donkey? What the perishin' purple hades," roared Jake, "has poor old Boomer got to do with it?"

The superintendent sank back in his chair and regarded him almost benevolently. "Everything, Mr. Popplewell. The donkey has everything to do with it. If it hadn't been for your donkey, specifically your donkey's shoes, there would never have been any mysterious hoof-prints in the snow."

Jake stared at him suspiciously. Miss Forbes asked sharply: "What do you mean, Superintendent?"

"I mean," said Superintendent Blackler deliberately, "that we have at last discovered the truth."

There was a sudden tense silence in the room. The superintendent went on evenly: "And having discovered the truth we think it right that we should pass it on to you people, who, in a manner of speaking, have been most closely concerned, and who have—er—attempted to give us material assistance"—with a sidelong glance at Miss Forbes—"so that you may pass it on to the world, and so scotch all these silly superstitious rumours that are flying round. And now I leave it to the inspector here to tell you all about it."

Nobody spoke. Nobody broke the silence that followed. And Mr. Smith, with his eyes fixed on the bag in front of him, said almost casually: "As the superintendent has intimated, we have laid the ghost. We have actually caught the Thing and are holding it in custody. It's in the bag. That bag. . . ."

He lifted his gaze then and looked at them. He gave them each a long slow deliberate scrutiny. Miss Forbes returned his stare frankly, with open-eyed candour. Gregory Cushing, next to her, knotted his brows and switched his own eyes from the inspector's face to the brown bag. Mayhew moved uneasily on his hard, straight-backed chair, and with difficulty suppressed a nervous titter. Maltravers produced a large white handkerchief with a flourish and blew his nose resoundingly. While old Jake scratched his chin-whiskers and glared back with even deeper suspicion.

Mr. Smith's steady searching gaze rested finally on Jake, and stayed there. "Where do you think we found it, Mr. Popplewell?"

"What?" asked Jake gruffly. "The bag?"

"No—the truth. Come, now; where does Truth lie?"

Jake said nothing. He sat back lowering, and waited. Mayhew said with a diffident titter: "There's a saying, Inspector, that Truth lies at the bottom of a well."

"And that's just where it was." The inspector's eyes were still fastened on Jake. "That's exactly where we did find it. At the bottom of a well. *Your* well, Mr. Popplewell. . . ."

Silence. But in the silence the sound of someone drawing in breath sharply.

"*Your* well," repeated Mr. Smith softly. "*Your* donkey. *Your* Blue Woman. . . . The answer must be obvious now."

He hesitated a moment, and then he pounced. He tore his eyes away from the little old man sitting hunched up at one end of the semi-circle of people facing him, and suddenly and sharply threw out an accusing finger at the other end.

"Mr. Cushing! I have a very good idea why you killed Alfred Croxley. But why did you kill Montague Mason?"

And at that Gregory Cushing's nerve broke. He leapt up from his chair, stared wildly about him and then made a bolt for the door, upsetting his chair in his flight. He wrenched open the door and flung himself through—and two uniformed policemen on the other side swooped on him ungently.

28

Mr. Smith, with his hands deep in his pockets, half leant back against, half sat on, the superintendent's desk and stared at his feet. Gregory Cushing had been taken away downstairs and order had been restored in the room. The four civilians—old Jake a little apart from the other three—sat and faced him expectantly: gaped at him like so many codfish, was the way Poynter put it to himself. Superintendent Blackler had vacated his chair and was standing in his favourite position by the window, gazing absently out across the little river Winch immediately below, and over the snow-covered residential area of the town.

"The difficulty," said Mr. Smith to his feet, "is to know where to begin. There was never any 'Thing,' of course; there was never any supernatural visitation; there was only a man. One man with murder in his heart. . . . I think I'll give it to you the way it struck me last night.

"Last night we found a trail of mysterious hoof-prints stretching from just outside Croxley's garden gate to the middle of his lawn, where we found his dead body. On Sunday morning we found a trail of mysterious hoof-prints stretching from the foot of The Rise away over the hill and down to a tree in a field on Mason's property, where we also found *his* dead body. Note," he added emphatically, raising his head, "that I use the word 'stretching,' not 'leading.' And ever since Sunday we have been asking ourselves what manner of created thing could have left those trails. Various guesses were made. In the nature of things that's all they could be, guesses, since only experience is knowledge, and these trails were outside all experience. Actually three guesses were made, and while the third was obviously not meant to be taken seriously, yet it must be considered, because—and this is the point—in my mind those three guesses were something in the nature of stepping-stones that led me to the fourth. And I may say here that that fourth step—which was the truth—was the one we *should* have thought of first, only we had been cleverly and systematically led away from it, first, deliberately, by the maker of the trails, and second and all unwittingly by—Miss Forbes.

"Well," he went on hastily, "these were the three guesses.

"One—the Devil, or one of his imps, with hooves on.

"Two—the Blue Woman, with hooves on.

"Three—Charlie McCarthy with hooves on—"

"*Who?*" demanded Miss Forbes.

Mr. Smith told her. "Now, in arriving at that fourth guess, which was almost inevitable, it is *my* mental attitude you must consider. I knew it was no animal. I knew also, of course, it was no ventriloquist's doll. I didn't believe it was any supernatural agency; in my bones I *knew* it wasn't any supernatural agency. It wasn't the Devil, it wasn't the Blue Woman, it wasn't a 'Thing.' It wasn't

Charlie McCarthy, which is an *imitation* man. So it was the only thing left—it was a *real* man."

Mr. Smith took his hands out of his pockets and stood up straight. "There were other things that led me, or, rather, jolted me to that conclusion, and one of these I must tell you about now. A trail, or spoor as the chief constable calls it, is a sequence of two or four impressions of foot, hoof or paw marks, depending upon how many feet, hooves or paws the trail-maker possesses. In this case it was obvious that the trail was a sequence of impressions of two shoes *exactly the same size as those on the hooves of Boomer the donkey.* Photographs taken by Detective-Sergeant Poynter and the late Mr. Croxley show that one of these shoes was slightly narrower in its left half than the other; and it is this fact that shows us that the sequence of impressions forming the trail was oddly broken in three separate places.

"First, the marks on the Jacksons' hedge. At first sight it appeared that the 'Thing ' had stood there on both hooves. But closer investigation showed that those two marks had been made by only the one shoe, the shoe with the narrower left half.

"Second, the prints on the window-sill outside Mason's bedroom. Again it looked as though the 'Thing' had stood there on both hooves, but again closer examination showed that the impressions had been left by only the one shoe, this time the shoe that was the same width all round.

"And third, the ring of prints round the skylight on the roof. And here we discovered that all those impressions were those of the shoe with the narrower left half.

"Now nothing on two legs stands or walks like that. How, therefore, did those prints come to be made? Well, I showed you myself that morning when we were all in the Jacksons' garden. I lifted my right foot and placed it lightly on the hedge, where it left a perfect impression. If I had done the same thing again a few inches farther on there would have been two impressions of my right foot side by side, just as there *were* two impressions of the 'Thing's' right shoe. . . ."

Poynter interrupted him. "Left, you mean, don't you, Inspector?"

"No, Bill. Right. Think it over."

"Eh . . .? Oh! Yes, of course—I see it. Sorry."

Mr. Smith turned back to his audience.

"As for the prints on the window-sill, once you get the picture of a man *using* horseshoes that size it is then easy to see him using one of these shoes to leave those impressions. He merely opened the window from the inside, pressed one of the shoes down on the snow on the window-sill, pressed it down again beside the first print, and then closed and re-latched the window. . . ."

The inspector held up his hand. "Wait! All objections and obstacles will be dealt with in their turn. Let me tell it in my own way, you can ask the questions afterwards. . . . You should have by now in your minds, as I had then, a vague picture of a man walking on some contraptions that would leave the impressions of a pair of shod hooves exactly the same size as Mr. Popplewell's donkey. Three questions then immediately spring up.

"One: where would such a man procure such a pair of shoes? Answer, in the place where the donkey lives. And the donkey belongs to, and lives in a shed that is on the property of, Mr. Popplewell. And in that shed there are some cast-off donkey-shoes.

"Two: what man would have easy access to Mr. Popplewell's shed and would know just where to lay his hands on a couple of those shoes? Well, at first sight it seems we have two alternatives, Mr. Popplewell himself, or his nephew. But a little reflection rules out Mr. Popplewell. Even if his—er—indisposition of Saturday night had been assumed it still could not have been he, for a man cannot move about in snow without leaving traces—*and the only marks in the snow from his cottage to the hoof-prints were Gregory Cushing's footprints!* Freeze on to that point," said Mr. Smith earnestly. "And freeze on to this one as well, for it is the answer to a good many puzzles. *Gregory Cushing takes size* 11 *in footwear!*

"So now we can give the man a name. We have now answered where and who. Third question—why? Why did Gregory Cushing go through this peculiar performance? Briefly, *(a)* to disguise his own foot-prints, and *(b)* to try and make it appear that something inexplicable, if not positively supernatural, had been abroad. But why did he do *that?* Well . . . what was at the end of the trail on Sunday morning? A dead man who had been hanged from a tree. And what was at the end of the much shorter trail on Monday night? A man who had been struck down and killed. . . ."

Mr. Smith, tired of standing still, began to roam about the office. "And now perhaps a fourth question arises. Where did Gregory Cushing get the idea from, the idea of disguising his own foot-prints by means of the donkey's shoes, the idea of creating the spoor of something absolutely unknown in the physical world? And the answer is—from Miss Forbes's scrap-book—"

"Good patience!" ejaculated that startled lady.

"Yes, Miss Forbes, that's where he got it from. From that scrap-book you had lent him—or perhaps I should say lent Mr.

Popplewell—a week before: the scrap-book that contains, amongst other queer and intriguing things, such an interesting account of the mysterious hoof-prints that were discovered in the snow in Devonshire one morning in 1855. And although there was no snow on our ground then it was a fairly safe bet that we were bound to have some at some time or another during the winter—we did have one fall, you remember, a week later, and then, three days after that, we had another, the first of this lot"—nodding his head at the window—"and when that came we had twelve hours clear warning that it was on the way. And twelve hours was plenty long enough for Gregory Cushing—it only took four hours to bring Mason down to his house at Steeple Thelming after Cushing had put through that telephone call. . . . But I'm getting a bit ahead of myself. Briefly and in a nutshell, Gregory Cushing deliberately re-created, in part, the Devonshire phenomenon of nearly a hundred years ago to disguise murder—"

Old Jake moved sharply on his chair.

"Yes—murder! And he very nearly got away with it. If it hadn't been for the fact that Mr. Croxley had been an ardent amateur photographer he *might* have got away with it. And incidentally Mr. Croxley would have been alive today—"

"Got away with what?" rasped Jake. "Whaddyer mean, murder? Mason hanged himself."

"Mason did not hang himself," replied the inspector deliberately. "Mason was murdered and his dead body hung on that tree by Gregory Cushing!"

Jake rose from his chair in a state of tremendous indignation. "God clot me blood!" he roared. "Why should Greg 'a' murdered Mason? He didn't even know the feller—"

"Sit down!" said Mr. Smith quietly, and Jake sat down. "I admit that, at the moment, the question of motive is the one question I can't answer. But I can show you that the only possible solution of the puzzle of those suddenly ending tracks in the snow under that tree is that Mason was strangled in his own house and his dead body carried out there and hung up." He paused to let this sink in, and went on: "I have shown you where a man could have got the whole idea from. I have shown you where he could have laid his hands on a couple of cast-off shoes of Boomer the donkey, and so have made himself something in the nature of clogs or pattens that would leave the impressions of the donkey's shoes wherever he walked on them—on *how* he walked, of course, would depend the character of the trail he left behind him. I have shown you the most likely person to have been that man—as we go on you will find evidence being piled on evidence until there is no room for doubt—and presently I shall show you the actual contrivances that Gregory Cushing made, and on which he left those trails. You already know where we found them; later I'll tell you how we came to make that lucky hit."

He turned round and stretched out a hand for the bag on the desk, and as he did so the telephone beside it rang sharply.

*   *   *

Superintendent Blackler came quickly away from the window. "I'm half expecting that," he murmured, "you carry on, Smithy." He picked up the telephone and slid into the chair behind the desk, and Mr. Smith carried on. He opened the brown bag, took from it a stiff roll of paper and closed the bag again.

"In speaking of those trails a few moments ago I asked you to note that I used the word 'stretching' in preference to the word 'leading.' You'll see why in a minute. I also promised you that all objections and obstacles would be dealt with in their turn. Well, now, let's deal with some of the main obstacles.

"The hoof-prints appeared suddenly in the snow at the foot of The Rise thirty-seven feet from the nearest habitation, which happens to be that of Mr. Popplewell. They ceased equally abruptly and impossibly under that tree in the open field beyond Mason's house, and at a point where Mason's dead body hung from the tree. From the side door of Mason's house to the tree two sets of tracks ran side by side, the hoof-prints and the series of impressions made by the gumboots that Mason had on his feet over his shoes. Here are those trails in diagrammatic form."

Mr. Smith unrolled the paper and held it across his body so that the four people sitting facing him could see what was on it. Across the paper, from one side to the other, he had drawn in ink a line of very blunt arrowheads representing the hoof-prints. There were twists and turns in this line corresponding to the twists and turns in the actual trail itself, and in two places were two small gaps. From the last turn a line of dashes accompanied the arrowheads, and this the audience understood to represent the tracks left by the gumboots.

"Enumerating the main problems," continued the inspector, "they are these. The sudden beginning. The two gaps in the trail. The circle of prints on Mason's roof. And the sudden ending.

"Now, either we solve these problems along natural and logical lines, or we return to what the superintendent has been known to refer to as the witches and the warlocks. This is unthinkable; so let us try using our brains intelligently. Well, we have a number of hints or pointers, and I'll also enumerate these for you.

"One: at the end of the trail we have, accompanying it, the tracks made by those size 11 gumboots.

"Two: inside Mason's house we have those foot-prints in the dust up under the roof. Admittedly this is a detail extraneous to the prints in the snow, but the significant thing about it is that those prints were also made by a size 11 boot or shoe.

"Three: a hint which I borrow, legitimately, from the second case: from the confused mess of impressions in the snow outside Croxley's gate, and accompanying the hoof-prints, to the spot on his own lawn where they ended in that circle that went round his dead body, we have the impressions of Croxley's own boots, which again were size 11.

"Four: Gregory Cushing takes size 11 in footwear.

"And, five—and this can definitely be taken as truth and not just theory—five, which is the most significant and enlightening of all, the donkey's shoes made those tracks—*but not the donkey's hooves!*"

Maltravers suddenly sat bolt upright and gave a low whistle.

"Aha!" cried Mr. Smith approvingly. "You begin to see things in a different light now, eh? Look at the diagram again. At one end of the trail of hoof-prints we have the trail of the size 11 gumboots, those gumboots that were four sizes too large for Montague Mason—but just the right size for Gregory Cushing! At the other end we have—"

He paused invitingly. "Well, what have we?"

"We haven't got anything," said Miss Forbes, frowning. "There was nothing that end, only the hoof-prints—"

"And how do you know that? How do you know there was nothing else there?"

"Mr. Cushing said—" Miss Forbes stopped abruptly.

"Oh, yes," said the inspector softly. "Mr. Cushing said so. But we don't *know* that, we have only Mr. Cushing's word for it and Mr. Cushing has become suddenly very suspect. . . . Mr. Mayhew!"

The startled Mayhew jumped in his chair and jerked his eyes up to the inspector's face.

"Mr. Mayhew: tell us again just what you saw when you looked out of your wife's bedroom window on Sunday morning."

"I saw the hoof-prints—stretching up The Rise—there was nothing else. . . ."

"Oh, but there was! There *was* something else. Perhaps you didn't notice it at the time, but you did notice Gregory Cushing?"

"Well, yes, he was there. He was standing there looking down at the marks—"

"That's it, Mr. Mayhew! That's the whole point—Gregory Cushing was already there! So there *was* something else at that end of the trail; there were Cushing's own foot-prints stretching from the cottage to that sudden beginning. I know he said he'd come out to have a closer look at the marks in the snow, had gone back to try and rouse his uncle, and had come out once more—thus accounting for those three separate sets of his own tracks that you found there when you went out to him—but how much notice can we take now of *anything* that Cushing may have said?"

He was silent for a moment, then he went on: "Now, I wonder if you see it? Do you see what we've done? We've closed the trail at both ends. We no longer have an impossible set of tracks beginning from nothingness and ending in nothingness; we have instead a sequence of impressions stretching from Mr. Popplewell's cottage to Mason's house! Which may still be mysterious, but is no longer impossible—"

"I don't see that," said Miss Forbes sharply. "What you've got is three separate and distinct sets of tracks!"

"Yes—but those three apparently separate and distinct sets of tracks make up the one long sequence! They're an unholy trinity, a three-in-one. . . . You see, Miss Forbes, what we have been doing—and *all* we've been doing—is studying marks in snow. Those marks tell a story, they spell out messages to us. But we've been reading the messages all wrong, and so we've gathered a completely impossible story. It's up to us now as intelligent human beings to read the messages aright and so gather a comprehensible and rational story. And—"

"And you think yer've got the right story, hey?" interrupted old Jake.

"Yes," said Mr. Smith simply.

"Then that's just where yer ruddy well wrong!" retorted the old man crushingly. "I guess I know what's in yer mind now, an' it's all back to front. Greg walkin' out from the cottage back along the road a little way, then puttin' those things on his feet, whatever they were, an' walkin' over the hill, goin' into Mason's place an' stranglin' him an' carryin' his body out an' stringin' it up . . . some-thin' like that?"

"Perhaps," said Mr. Smith gravely.

"Huh! An' then what? That's where yer story goes phut! *How did he get back to the cottage?* He couldn't 'a' got back, not without leavin' more traces!"

"I agree with you wholeheartedly," said Mr. Smith equably. "He couldn't have got back. It's impossible."

"That's what I'm tellin' yer!"

"And yet he *was* back—no doubt about it. So, as no man can achieve the impossible, he *must* have left traces. And so, as the only traces visible were those we have already considered, it would seem that we are still reading their message wrongly. So—what's the answer?"

Jake made no reply to this. He sat staring at the inspector out of slitted eyes, with his whiskers thrust up in the air at a challenging angle. Mr. Smith regarded him quizzically.

"Come, Mr. Popplewell! What *is* the answer? You've already said it was all back to front. . . . What? No answer? But that *is* the answer. You used a phrase almost accidentally, just as a similar phrase came into my own mind last night. The answer is, not that we are exactly reading the message wrongly, but that we are reading it *wrong way round.* We're reading it back to front! Read it the other way round, and see what happens! Look!"

He turned his diagram upside down.

"That's the direction the trail really runs. It stretches either way, but it leads only one way; it leads from Mason's house back to Mr. Popplewell's cottage. That means it actually ended where it seemed to begin—which means that Gregory Cushing didn't have to get back from the tree in Mason's field, but only from a spot in the road a mere thirty-seven feet from his uncle's cottage. And *that* gap has already been closed by his own footprints—"

"Wait—a—minute!" said Maltravers slowly and sceptically. "That would mean he walked backwards all the way from the tree—I can't swallow that."

"Neither can I," retorted Mr. Smith promptly. "For in that case it would not only have been a tricky and exhausting business, it would have been a physical impossibility for him to have made those other two gaps in the trail in the way he did. But why should you conclude that he must have walked backwards? Remember what he was walking on—some sort of gadgets made out of a pair of the donkey's cast-off shoes—wouldn't it have been far more simple and convenient to have fastened those shoes on to their bases *back to front?*

"And that, Miss Forbes and gentlemen, is just exactly what he did do—as I shall now definitely prove to you. . . ."

29

Inspector Smith dropped his diagram on to the desk and opened the bag again. From it he took out two articles, which he balanced one in each hand.

"These are the things that left those mysterious hoof-prints in the snow. These are the gadgets that Gregory Cushing made from odds and ends lying about in his uncle's shed. These," said Mr. Smith solemnly, "are the Feet of Satan."

He held them out for everybody to see and examine. The Feet of Satan, to use his own picturesque phrase, had been fashioned from the footplates of a pair of ice skates, two blocks of wood and a couple of Boomer's cast-off shoes. The blades had been shorn away from the skates, presumably with a hacksaw, and a number of screw-holes had been drilled in the centre parts of the footplates. The blocks of wood had been chiselled and planed to the same shape and size of the donkey's hooves, but deeper, being some eight inches in depth, and were firmly held to the iron footplates by screws. But they had been screwed on the wrong way round, in the reverse direction to the way the footplates pointed. The "hooves" were shod. In other words, the shoes had been nailed to the undersides of the blocks of wood.

Jake stared at these things and growled something under his breath.

"You recognize them, Mr. Popplewell?" asked the inspector.

"Yeh," grunted Jake unhappily. "Yeh. Those bits o' skates—they're off a pair of old ice skates that 've been kickin' around in me shed for donkey's years. Missed 'em the other day, but a'course didn't think anythin' of it."

"Donkey's years," murmured the inspector. "Very appropriate. . . . Well, there they are. There's our bogeyman. And I shall now give a demonstration of how easy it is to walk on these things."

The footplate of each "hoof" carried a pair of straps, one tying across the instep from behind the ankle, and one across the toes. Mr. Smith placed the contrivances on the floor, strapped them on to his feet, immediately increasing his height by eight inches. Then he began to clump about the room on them.

"Simple, isn't it? Now, supposing there were snow on this floor, but not deeper than eight inches, I would be leaving a trail of hoof-prints behind me. And if I took little short steps—like this—and was careful to place one foot immediately in front of the other—like this—you would see exactly similar tracks to those you saw in the snow last Sunday morning. Only the tracks would appear to be coming towards you, not away from you. Is that clear?"

That, it seemed, was now perfectly clear.

"Right," said Mr. Smith with satisfaction. "Continuing the demonstration, supposing I want to make it appear that the hoof-marks come to a sudden and apparently impossible end, what do I do? I'll show you. I stop—like this—I balance on one foot while I remove the gadget from the other"—with some difficulty the inspector suited the actions to the words—"and then I jump sideways, or even longways for that matter, and land on my own natural foot. And," he added meaningly, "a jump of four feet or so would be no trouble to me—if I were Gregory Cushing, *who is a notable exponent of the athletic feat known as the hop-step-and-jump.* . . .

"Aha! Yes! That's something that perhaps you two gentlemen didn't know. But Miss Forbes knew, she'd got it from Cushing himself in the course of casual conversation and in a similar casual conversation with myself she passed it on to me. That was another hint, another little pointer to the truth.

"And now," said Mr. Smith, taking off the other "hoof" and placing both on the desk, "I think the time has come for me to tell you in the form of straight narrative, without any more messing about, just exactly how Gregory Cushing did the things he did. You might remember," he pointed out modestly, "that I didn't know the nature of these imitation hooves then, didn't even know, as a matter of fact, that they actually existed. I held merely a theory, and I had to work it out the hard way."

"Either before he came to Winchingham to stay with his uncle, or while he was actually here, Gregory Cushing decided to murder Montague Mason. He thought up and worked out a plan based on that extraordinary Devonshire case of nearly a hundred years ago. He familiarized himself with the geography of The Rise and Steeple Thelming, made these 'hooves' for himself at odd times while his uncle was absent from the cottage, and also made—or perhaps found—a key that would unlock the side door of Mason's house. Then he sat back and awaited his opportunity, perfecting and adding to his plans while he waited.

"His opportunity came last Saturday. All day the radio had been warning us that snow was on the way. We all *knew* it was creeping down from the north and that it would be only a matter of hours before it reached us. And so he set his plan in motion.

"The first thing was to get Mason down here. This he did, as you know, by telephoning him at his London house from his own house in Steeple Thelming. There was no difficulty about that. Cushing's uncle was—er—occupied that afternoon, and Cushing had the key to the side door. It was the simplest thing in the world for him to stroll over The Rise and down there, enter the house, put through that 'phone call and be back at the cottage again before his uncle returned. It is fairly safe to say that he knew perfectly well where his uncle was and how he was—er—occupying himself. Just exactly what Cushing said to Mason to bring him flying down like that we don't know—not yet—but the fact remains that he did come down, and when he arrived, which was just ahead of the snow, Cushing was waiting for him. . . . Before that, of course, he had brought his uncle home from the Steeple Inn and put him to bed—"

"Supposing," interrupted Maltravers, "supposing Mr. Popplewell hadn't been so obliging as to have been—er . . ."

"I think," said the inspector drily, "that Cushing would have then seen to it himself that his uncle *was* what you diplomatically refer to as 'er,' Mr. Popplewell being notoriously obliging in these matters—"

Jake, looking singularly impenitent, merely snorted at this.

"Frankly," said Mr. Smith, "it was a pretty safe bet, safe as the weather conditions anyway. Putting it in a nutshell, if the coast hadn't been cleared for him, he would have cleared it himself.

"Well, there we have him that Saturday evening just before the snow began to fall; inside Mason's house waiting for Mason, with his uncle safely tucked up in bed in his own cottage a mile away and oblivious to everything. And likely to remain oblivious for some considerable time. Mason arrives. He opens the gate—thus resolving a minor mystery for the special benefit of Miss Forbes—drives up to his garage, puts the car away and hurries to the side door of the house, which is the nearest to the garage. And my guess is that Gregory Cushing met him there just inside that side door and strangled him immediately with that length of rope. I know he was strangled in the house, because that rope, once tight about his throat, was never removed again until we took it off the next morning when we found him hanging from the tree. That factor, more than anything else, I think, had the effect of making us, in the early stages, *sure* that Mason had committed suicide.

"Cushing then begins his vigil. He doesn't have to wait very long before the snow begins to fall, and fall in satisfactory volume, but he has to wait a long time before it stops again—"

"Supposing it hadn't stopped at all that night?" posed Maltravers.

"That was a risk that had to be taken. But as a rule it does not continue to snow for very long in this part of the country, a few hours at most. But if it hadn't stopped before dawn I presume Cushing would have waited until the last possible moment and then stepped out and hoped for the best. Possibly he was lucky with the weather; but he wasn't so lucky with his 'hooves'—as you will see. . . .

"Well, shortly after one o'clock in the morning it did stop snowing, and the sky cleared. And what Gregory Cushing did with himself, and what his thoughts were during the passing of those long, slow hours, only God knows. But when he saw that the snow had finally ceased he set to work in earnest. He had already taken Mason's coat and hat and bag up to the bedroom to make it appear that Mason himself had been up there, and he had slipped that rosary—that he had actually found himself, by the way—into Mason's overcoat pocket, for no particular reason, except to get rid of it. And perhaps he had thought up a couple of extra details to add to the general mystification he was about to create. For before he left the house he opened the bedroom window and, with one of the 'hooves,' made those prints on the window-sill. And in doing so, all unconsciously made his first big mistake. How? In using only one of the 'hooves'! But then that, of course, was a perfectly natural action, and how was he to know, without close inspection, that one of the shoes on these 'hooves' was slightly narrower in its left half than the other? Then, having made those prints, he closed the window again, re-latched it, and went up to the skylight."

And here Mr. Smith, who had begun to drift about the office again, halted and ran his fingers through his hair in a rueful gesture.

"It is strange how sometimes the simplest things stump you. My biggest problem, the thing that nearly wrecked my whole theory, was to discover how Cushing had managed to push open the skylight, in order to make that circle of prints on the roof, without disturbing the snow *on* the skylight. The answer was so simple—and yet I couldn't see it until Detective-Sergeant Poynter, quite unconsciously, showed me how it could have been done. Well, the answer is that Cushing *didn't* push open the skylight; he drew the bolt at one end of the frame, and took off the hinges at the other! Then, very carefully, he worked it down inside and laid it on the floor-boards where, with its covering of snow unmarked, undisturbed, it stayed while he made that ring of prints. And how did he do that? Well, it so happens that a seven-foot-long pole is kept up there, possibly to prop open the skylight, or for some specific reason or another, and he fastened one of these 'hooves' sideways on to the end of that pole, stood on the step-ladder with his head and trunk sticking up through the skylight opening, held on to the other end of the pole—is it necessary to add that he wore gloves all the time?—and solemnly plonked the 'hoof' round and round in a circle. And so made the devil-circle—and his second big mistake. Because this time it chanced that he had picked up the other 'hoof', the one carrying the normal shoe that was the same width all the way round. . . .

"Well, having done that, he untied the 'hoof' and put the pole back on the floor where he had found it. Then—very carefully again, for this was a ticklish job—he worked the skylight frame up through the opening, settled it back into position, screwed the hinges on again and shot the bolt. And that was that.

"Now came a very grim and cunning piece of work. In order to make it appear that Mason had committed suicide, Cushing had to make it appear that Mason had himself walked out to that tree; and that's where the gumboots come in, those size 11 gumboots that he had previously found somewhere in the house and which belong presumably to somebody in Mason's employ—this is another of the minor details that we shall settle very shortly. For while it is impossible for a man with size 11 feet to leave size 7 tracks, it is both possible and feasible, under those given conditions, for a man with size 7 feet to don a pair of gumboots that happen to be handy, and so leave size 11 tracks. And that is what we were meant to think, and did think; that Mason had walked out there under his own steam. Actually, of course, Cushing put the gumboots on his own feet over those rather flimsy shoes of his, slung Mason's body over his shoulder and carried it out to the tree. It was a fair step and the going wasn't too smooth, and I don't think we should now be surprised at the little irregularities that we noticed in that otherwise almost dead straight line of gum-boot tracks.

"Well, he reaches the tree. He has Mason's body slung over his shoulder, he has the 'hooves,' probably tied by their straps about his neck, and he is carrying a flashlight—obviously, since he couldn't have done these things in the dark. He is pretty well burdened, you see, and without any false moves, or leaving any betraying traces in the snow, he has to get the body hanging from that bottom branch.

"Now, in order to make it appear that Mason has hanged himself, he has to make it appear that Mason stood on something, tied the end of the rope to the branch, put his head through the noose and stepped off—obviously his feet must not touch the ground. Well, there is something there for Mason to stand on; there is that large wart-like excrescence on the trunk of the tree. Cushing can stand on that and so leave the impressions of the gumboots for us to find later on—but he can't do it with Mason's body on his shoulder! There just simply isn't room.

"So what does he do? He does this—you must remember that Mason has been dead for hours now, with the rope still about his neck. Mason would not have been tall enough to have tied the other end of the rope round the branch while standing on the ground. But Cushing is tall enough, and he can and does. He ties it there close to the trunk of the tree, and eases the body off his shoulder. Then he stands on that knob on the tree trunk and leaves those impressions for us to find later. And that accounts for the disturbance of the snow lying on the branch close to the trunk, for which I put forward a quite fallacious explanation on Sunday morning—"

"Why," inquired Maltravers, interrupting once more, "why didn't he leave it there? Why move it again?"

"Because it *was* too close to the trunk—it must have been touching it. And, supposing Mason really to have hanged himself, in his death agonies, when reason and purpose would have left him, he would have grabbed at the trunk and his feet would have found a resting-place. The suicide would have defeated his own object—gadzooks! do I have to elaborate?"

"No!" said Miss Forbes, loudly and firmly.

"All right, then. Standing on that excrescence Cushing moves the body a little farther along. Now, follow closely. The trail of the gumboots has been left from the house to the tree, and no more gumboot impressions must be left; for, of course, that excrescence is the last point on this earth where Mason, had he really committed suicide, would have set foot. So, balancing on one foot on that knob—and don't forget that an outstanding exponent of the hop-step-and-jump would have an outstanding sense of balance—balancing on one foot, Cushing takes off the other gum-boot, puts it on Mason's foot, and straps a 'hoof' on to his own foot.

"Now, consider the situation. One gumboot on and firmly planted on the knob, one 'hoof' on and held up in the air. The next foot-print in the snow *anywhere* must be that of the 'Thing,' and it must be left so as to appear to form part of a trail from the house. And there is that gumboot to be placed on Mason's other foot. Quite a tricky little problem.

"But the diabolically ingenious Mr. Cushing has it all worked out, and this is what he does. He jumps. He turns as he jumps and lands on the 'hoof with his back to Mason's body. Uncomfortably close, as it happens, but it is a very tricky jump. He *has* to turn round as he jumps, because the 'hoof' being back to front he must make it appear to be the *end* of the trail, not the beginning which it *really* is. He, you remember, faces the opposite way to the 'hooves.'

"Well, he lands safely enough on the foot with the 'hoof' on it, takes off the other gumboot and, twisting his body round a little, places it on Mason's other foot, straps the second 'hoof' on to his own other foot and brings it down in the snow beside the first. You see now why the hoof-prints had to end so close up to Mason's body? It was because of the necessity of placing that other gumboot on the dead man's foot without leaving a single extra out-of-place betraying mark.

"So there he is, standing there with his back touching Mason's dangling body—I tell you it was a grim business!—all ready to move off on his 'hooves.' The only marks in the snow so far are the tracks made by the gumboots *that Mason is wearing*, leading direct from the house to the tree and ending logically where Mason has himself—well—ended. The only other marks that are going to be in the snow will be the hoof-prints of some strange unknown 'Thing' beginning at the foot of The Rise a mile away and leading *away* from the cottage where Gregory Cushing is living with his uncle; leading, with erratic inexplicable gaps and leaps on to walls and a roof and a window-sill, to that spot under the tree, there to end most illogically and with such bewildering finality as to smack of the supernatural. . . .

"And, placing one foot immediately in front of the other, taking little short steps in imitation of those tracks left in the Devonshire snow a century ago, he sets out to make that trail."

30

Mr. Smith paused and cleared his throat. Tiring, apparently, of being on his feet, he hitched himself up on to the superintendent's desk and sat there between the two "Feet of Satan," resting his elbows on them and interlocking his fingers across his diaphragm.

"He sets out," he repeated solemnly. "Those mincing little straight-line steps—it must have been a fairly arduous business even for him, and it's no particular wonder that he put a 'hoof' down now and again slightly off centre. . . . He deliberately walks back alongside the gumboot trail in order to create an idea of association in our minds; which, in my opinion, was unnecessary and a mistake—I think he over-played his hand there, but these too-clever people always do do that—and he follows it back to the house presumably to tie-up with those prints on the roof and the window-sill. And there, for good measure, he marches round and round the house.

"Now, I very much doubt whether all the things were in his mind that came into Miss Forbes's mind the following morning. The Cross on the shield in the glass above the front door, the horseshoe nailed up above the side door, the rosary in Mason's overcoat pocket that he had carelessly tossed on to that chair under the window—I don't think any of Miss Forbes's highly ingenious theories regarding these things ever entered his mind at all—until she put them there later, when he capitalized on them and, at a moment of climax, or perhaps anti-climax, deliberately brought up the story of the Blue Woman. . . . Incidentally, Miss Forbes, you may remember how, in this office on Monday morning, just when I was getting interested in a *man* who had been in Mason's house on Saturday afternoon, he very cleverly produced a man. The man, Cliff Sheldon, who had been hiding in the Steeple Inn. He *said* he'd forgotten all about him, but had he really?

"Anyway, having gone round Mason's house several times, Cushing proceeds out through the now open gate and on to the road. He walks down to the door of the Steeple Inn—no reason for that approach, except to give us something extra to think about—turns away again and begins to walk up the hill. Two-thirds of the way up he cuts through a gap in the gorse hedge and proceeds diagonally across the hillside to Mrs. Pendlebury's summerhouse. For here again there is to be another special act of mystification. Here it is to be shown that the 'Thing' apparently possessed the power of passing through solid matter.

"So we come to one of the two gaps in the trail that we have to fill in. How did he get through or past that summerhouse without leaving traces in the snow that lay on and all round it? Well, he did it by a little athletic feat that was probably quite easy for him. You all know that Mrs. Pendlebury's summerhouse is boarded up to the roof during the winter. What may possibly have escaped your notice is that it is not boarded up quite to the roof; there is a small gap at the top all the way round through which you could thrust your fingers—*and hang on by them*. And that is what Gregory Cushing did. He thrust the gloved fingers of both hands into that narrow aperture, hung there gripping the top of the boarding, with his feet clear of any surfaces, and worked his way round by his hands until he came to the door at the front. Then he let one hand go, twisted his body round, let the other hand go and dropped the few inches down on to the snow, landing on one 'hoof.' . . ."

Maltravers opened his mouth.

"I know," said Mr. Smith quickly. "How did he get up there from the other side of the hedge? Simple. He hopped up on to the portion of ledge at the back protruding from under the boarding—which was not a very difficult feat when you remember that the 'hooves' on his feet had increased his already considerable height by another eight inches. And don't you remember that that one particular ledge right at the back by the hedge *had no snow on it!* The snow hadn't lain there; that ledge, and that cut-back portion of hedge, had been protected by the body of the summerhouse. . . . Clear, now?"

"Clear," grunted Maltravers.

"Only too clear," added Miss Forbes in a kind of groan.

"Well," continued the inspector, "there's another miracle, there's another touch of the supernatural to add to what has already been planted; and on his merry way he goes. Through the rose garden and round up to Mrs. Pendlebury's front door and up the drive to the gate. And now for another piece of poltergeist phenomena. He steps up on to Mrs. Pendlebury's low brick wall, and from there hops or steps up on to Mr. Maltravers's higher one. Considering the man's height—six feet, two inches—and the added eight inches that the 'hooves' would give him, I think he could have stepped up there: I don't think the feat was actually as dangerous as it might seem—in fact, I very nearly did it myself yesterday.

"So now we have him on Mr. Maltravers's wall about to perform another miracle. Again he is going to make it seem that something strange and apparently supernatural has passed through solid matter. . . ."

Mr. Smith broke off and grinned ruefully at them. "Odds blood! I could kick myself. It was so simple, so easy. Once you realize he was travelling in reverse, so to speak, you wonder how you missed it. You wonder how you ever came to let yourself be so thoroughly taken in.

"There he is, standing on Mr. Maltravers's wall with the roof of Mr. Maltravers's pavilion near enough to step on to—"

"He didn't step on to that roof!" jerked Maltravers quickly and emphatically. "There wasn't a mark on the snow!"

"No. No, of course not. But what's *under* the roof, immediately below the eaves?"

"Oh!" said Maltravers. "Oh, my word. . . ."

"Yes. You see it now. But the others haven't. They weren't looking there that morning; they weren't looking in the one place where there *wasn't* any snow, which was right up under the eaves of the pavilion. And so they didn't see those ornamental brackets—or if they did their eyes simply slid over them without taking note. Me, too, I was in the same boat with the rest of you. But I've had another look since then. . . .

"Yes; those brackets. Cushing squats down on the wall, reaches out, grips the nearest bracket and lets himself down off the wall, and hangs there by his hands with his feet clear of the ground. Then he swings from one bracket to the next, which is well within arm's reach, and so on until he works his way round to the side of the pavilion. And then, as before, he drops on to one 'hoof' and sets off across the snow to your front door, leaving behind him an *ending* hoof-print up against that blank wall, and a *recommencing* one on the top of the high wall beyond. . . . You see?"

"We see," said Miss Forbes in a peculiarly subdued voice.

"Good. Well, it's practically all over now bar the shouting. From Mr. Maltravers's door he goes up the drive and out on to The Rise. Down The Rise to the Jacksons' low hedge. You know now how he made those prints on that hedge, and having made them he steps over it and across the lawn to their door. For no special purpose, merely to add unreason to unreason. Out on to The Rise again, in and out of Mr. Croxley's place, and then straight down to the foot of the hill and a little way past Mr. Popplewell's cottage. A little way past it purely and simply for safety's sake; I suppose he felt it wouldn't have done to have that long trail ending—or rather beginning—bang outside his uncle's gate. And now we have to consider how he finished off that night's work.

"The last hoof-print—which is to appear to be the first, the beginning of the trail—is to be left at that point, thirty-seven feet from the cottage gate. Theoretically, therefore, Cushing has to get from that point to the cottage without leaving traces. Practically, that is obviously impossible, and so the traces that he cannot avoid leaving must be misleading ones. So this is what he does.

"Balancing on one foot he unstraps the 'hoof' from the other, jumps, landing on that other foot, takes off the second 'hoof' and then walks normally and naturally back to and into the cottage. And so ends his night's work.

"But the job is not quite finished yet. For consider: the first witness on the scene in the morning is going to come upon a series of foot-prints showing that somebody has gone into the cottage without having first come out of it. It is therefore necessary that Cushing himself be first on the scene in order to apply the finishing touches. Now, if he merely comes out again it will still leave that ingoing series of foot-prints to be accounted for; and the only way he can account for them is for him to say that he has come out and gone in again to tell his uncle what he has seen. In that case there must be *two* sets of outgoing foot-prints. That clear?"

"Yes," said Maltravers impatiently. "Yes. Go on—how did he do it?"

"I'll tell you. I don't suppose he went to bed at all that night, and with the dawn he keeps his eyes peeled for the first signs of movement on The Rise. Specifically in the danger section of The Rise, which is where the mystery hoof-prints appear to begin. From his bedroom he sees the first sign of movement, which is the lifting of the blind on Mr. Mayhew's bedroom window, announcing to anybody who knows Mr. Mayhew's habits—*as Cushing himself does now*—that he is about to dress to attend early Communion. And so Cushing then applies those finishing touches.

"He goes out to the first hoof-print; but he goes out, in a manner of speaking, twice at the one time. He takes a pace forward from his own door, landing, say, on the right foot. Still on the right foot he hops to one side, thus making the first two impressions in the two sets of tracks he intends to leave behind him. Then he takes a pace forward, landing on the left foot; and still on that left foot hops back to the other side, thus leaving the second impressions in the two sets of tracks. And in this manner—step, hop—step, hop—he makes his way out to that first hoof-print.

"Hops," said Mr. Smith reproachfully, with his eyes on Miss Forbes. "Steps. And jumps. He practically left his sign-manual on the whole box of tricks—only we couldn't see the material fire for the supernatural smoke that blew up and rolled all over it."

Miss Forbes blushed faintly, but said nothing. Maltravers observed: "He took a risk going out like that—in the daylight. . . ."

"Well, yes," admitted the inspector, "but it was a risk that had to be taken. To a certain extent, of course, he could guard against it—apart from Mr. Mayhew here you people on The Rise don't seem to be particularly early risers, especially on a Sunday morning—which was probably why he picked a Sunday morning. And Mr. Mayhew couldn't see, from his own room, the beginning of the trail; and by the time he entered his wife's room and looked out of her window Cushing was there, standing in the snow, gazing down at the mysterious hoof-prints, curious, baffled, *innocent*. . . . And that, as they say of the movies, is where we came in. . . ."

31

Upon which Detective-Inspector Smith fell silent and slipped to the floor again. Maltravers, who had been following him intently and intelligently, brought up a point that was beginning to occur to the others.

"Wait a minute, Inspector. Where does the Blue Woman come in all this?"

"Don't ask me," replied the inspector, grinning at him. "Ask Miss Forbes—she brought the Blue Woman into it."

"No, I didn't!" protested Miss Forbes quickly. "That is, not altogether. She was there already. The Blue Woman, in a sense, already existed; and, in the same sense, still exists—"

"Yes; but apparently, only in Mr. Popplewell's mind."

Everybody looked at Jake. Jake stared back at them unmoved, and refused to open his mouth.

"There certainly does seem to be some story or legend of a Blue Woman," added Miss Forbes tentatively.

Superintendent Blackler, at the window, broke his long silence. "I don't pretend to be anything of a psychologist, but I could put forward a suggestion. There is a story of a Blue Woman. There is Mr. Popplewell, once a married man but now long divorced and a fierce misogynist. And there is a certain physical and *mental* condition into which Mr. Popplewell frequently and lamentably falls. It is perhaps possible that, when in this lamentable condition, Mr. Popplewell's psychosis—as I believe the psychologists term it—manifests as the Blue Woman."

"Hum!" commented Maltravers dubiously. "But she has nothing to do with the—ah—the Case of the Foot-prints of Satan?"

"She has nothing to do with the Case of the Footprints of Satan," repeated Mr. Smith gravely. "Except to add bulk to what I called a few moments ago the supernatural smoke cloud. . . . But let's get on with the actual facts, otherwise we'll be here all day.

"We now have to consider the murder, or perhaps I should say manslaughter, of Alfred Croxley. Croxley, as you know, had also taken photographs on Sunday morning; and last night he, also, noticed what we had noticed in our own; that there was a slight difference in the widths of the horseshoes, and that the one shoe only had made those marks on the Jacksons' hedge. And he set out last night to come here to tell us all about it. He didn't get here. Instead of him coming to us, we had to go to him. And we found him lying dead in the middle of his own lawn, circled by the mysterious hoof-prints, and with a mark on the side of his head that indicated that he had been kicked by something that wore horse-shoes exactly the same size as the prints—the other details you already know.

"But *now* we start off with the tremendous advantage of knowing how those hoof-prints could have been made by a man, and of realizing that, once off the foot, one of these things"—dropping his hand on one of the "hooves"—"could have been used as a club. And now we know—or at any rate have postulated as a logical and reasonable theory—that the hoof-prints apparently leading up to Croxley's body must actually have *started* there; and it therefore follows that the only way Cushing could have got to that point without apparently leaving his own tracks was by apparently leaving Croxley's tracks. In other words, by repeating his previous performance. In still other words, by putting Croxley's size 11 boots on his own feet, carrying Croxley's already dead body on to the lawn, there dropping it and replacing the boots. Which he did, and I shall show you how.

"But first, for a moment, consider these Feet of Satan. What did Cushing do with them after he had laid that long trail on Sunday morning? I don't know. Hid them somewhere in his room, I suppose. But then what? Well, the obvious thing to do would be to dismantle them as soon as possible, and so destroy or get rid of damning evidence. But when was his earliest opportunity? That same night? No. Because if he had gone out to the shed to work on them, there would have been some very awkward foot-prints in the snow on Mr. Popplewell's path the next morning to explain away. And then there was the noise to consider.

"Sunday afternoon then? No. His uncle was there, his own man again. And Mr. Silver was there. Sunday night? Again, no. Mr. Popplewell was still there, there was a fresh fall of snow that night and so the conditions were again as they had been the previous night.

"Monday morning? No. He was here. Monday afternoon? Still no. His uncle stayed with him in the cottage all that afternoon. Well, then, Monday evening? And Monday evening it was.

"The conditions must have seemed ideal for him. His uncle was again in the Steeple Inn; a few more foot-prints in the already well-trodden snow on the path and round about the shed were neither here nor there; it was conveniently dark and The Rise reassuringly deserted. So on Monday evening, at round about nine o'clock, he went out to the shed and set to work.

"And a few minutes later Mr. Croxley came out of his house, walked down to the foot of The Rise—and either heard him or saw him in the shed, and stopped to see what it was all about. . . .

"Here I must add two extra details to the picture. One *may* have been in the picture then, but the other wasn't. But I must tell you about the second detail, because it was in the picture when *we* saw it. The first is the little detail of Croxley's half-smoked cigar being found in the roadway just outside the gate, and the second—well, the second is this. When we arrived there some time later we saw a great number of hoof-prints in the snow on the cart track from the gate to the shed, which seemed to indicate that Boomer had been out of his stall galloping up and down there. I questioned Cushing about this, and he substantiated my guess—or my deduction, if you like. He also added that he didn't know what had got into the donkey, which seemed to imply that Boomer didn't make a practice of this sort of thing. In fact, the animal had never been known to behave like this before. . . . Am I right, Mr. Popplewell?"

"Yeh," grunted Jake. "Funny thing, that—I'd 'a' thought the moke had more sense."

"I believe he has, Mr. Popplewell, I believe he has. And I know just why he galloped up and down that path at that time of night. Because he was taken out of his stall by Cushing—whose foot-prints were also there in quantity—and *made* to.

"Now, why should Cushing have done this seemingly senseless thing? Well, what happens to snow when a man and a donkey go charging up and down in it? It gets marked, churned up, covered with foot- and hoof-prints. But why should Cushing have wanted that particular stretch of snow, at that particular time, churned up and covered with *fresh* prints—?"

"I know!" interrupted Maltravers. "Yes; I know! I can see it now. To obliterate other marks that were already on that same stretch of snow."

Inspector Smith smiled faintly and eyed him approvingly. "It rather jumps at you, doesn't it? Those other marks being . . .?"

"*Croxley's* foot-prints. He saw or heard Cushing in the shed as he was passing the gate, so he opened it and went up the path to have a word with Cushing—and caught him red-handed."

"Yes, I think so. I fancy that is what happened. He saw Cushing with the Feet of Satan actually in his hands. And perhaps he said something, or perhaps he didn't; and perhaps Cushing struck him with one of the 'hooves' with the deliberate intention of killing him, or perhaps he merely lost his head and struck blindly and wildly. Whatever the way of it, I am certain that Croxley was killed there, in that fashion, by Cushing.

"For see what happened next—it was all written in the snow for us to read, and this time we are reading it correctly. How long it took Cushing to work it out, I don't know; but this is what he did when he realized that Croxley was dead. He took off Croxley's boots, and he took off his own shoes. The shoes he stuffed into his overcoat pocket, the boots he put on his feet. Then he picked up Croxley's dead body, slung it over his shoulder and carried it down the track and out on to the dark and deserted roadway. Once there his foot-prints were lost in the general confused mess of prints and other traffic marks. He walked up The Rise to Croxley's gate where, turning in at it, his footprints appeared again clearly defined—as he meant them to. He walked up the path to the house and past it on to the lawn, and there he dropped the body, where we found it. He also remembered to place Croxley's hat where it would give the impression of having fallen from his head as he pitched forward.

"Then—and this was tricky, but quite possible—he put the dead man's boots back again on his feet. None of you ever saw those foot-prints this time, but the last two were one directly ahead of the other, exactly as if the man had fallen headlong in his stride. Left foot, right foot—that way. Cushing, drawing back on to his left foot after he had dumped the body, took the boot off his right foot, and put on his own shoe. Then, placing his right foot carefully and accurately in the impression already made, he put the boot on Croxley's foot. Balancing on that right foot, he took off the left boot and put it back on Croxley's left foot, and put on his other shoe again.

"Then, still balancing on his right foot, he strapped a 'hoof' on to his left foot and jumped away from Croxley's body as far as he could, landing *on* the hoof. He jumped, as it happened, a matter of four feet or so to make that first hoof-print. Then he strapped on the other 'hoof' and began to leave the trail of hoof-prints. He started off by walking in a circle round and round the body—just for sheer general mystification, of course—and then he walked back off the lawn, considerately closing the gate in the fence behind him—more mystification; maybe we were expected to think that the 'Thing' had walked clean through it without opening it—and back down the path to the garden gate. Here he turned *up* The Rise to make it appear that the 'Thing' had come from that direction, keeping close to the side of the road, where there was a strip of untrodden snow.

"At a convenient spot he stopped, stood once again on one foot while he took off the other 'hoof', and jumped sideways, landing in a place where the snow was already trodden on and where his own natural foot-print would merge indetectably into the general mess. Balancing on that foot, he took off the second 'hoof', walked naturally and normally back to the cart track, closed the gate behind him, and went on up to the shed.

"But along that track Croxley's footprints were plain to see. So he brought out Boomer and ran him up and down until none of those telltale prints remained—I suppose he thought it was the most convincing and realistic way of obliterating them—"

*   *   *

The inspector's words had been coming faster and faster, as if he were anxious to have done and rest his tongue, and for some moments past Maltravers had been stirring impatiently in his chair, trying to interrupt. Now he succeeded.

"But I don't see—!" he burst out. "All that complicated business of changing boots and shoes—using Croxley's boots. . . . I don't see the necessity for it—they both took the same size. . . ."

"Yes," replied Mr. Smith equably, "but size wasn't enough. The impressions that Croxley's boots make are very slightly different from the impressions that Cushing's thinner shoes make. And Cushing had heard me say that it had been evident to us that the foot-prints in the dust on those boards up under Mason's roof had not been made by the gumboots found on Mason's feet. They had, in fact, been made by Cushing's shoes; and this time he was not going to repeat that mistake. He was not going to run even the semblance of a risk of duplicating those identical impressions."

Mr. Smith paused and thrust a hand through his hair. "It's rather odd, looking back on it. I actually tested those foot-prints myself by fitting Croxley's boots into them. But the very two I *didn't* test were those last two inside the circle of hoof-prints. And that was because I was outside the circle at the time and the boots were taken off Croxley's feet and handed to me by somebody else. Even so I doubt if I'd have detected any difference, in that snow. . . .

"But let's get back to what Cushing did next. I have to admit that this was an inspired guess on my part, but it was a guess that turned up trumps.

"While running up and down that track with Boomer, Cushing had fallen over a disused and boarded-over well, the covering boards of which stick up some inches above the level of the ground. He actually told us of this accident himself, and showed us a graze on his shin as evidence. Afterwards I began thinking about this well, and it struck me as being an ideal place to swallow up the 'hooves' holus-bolus, without having to take the trouble—and risk—of dismantling them. So last night, when the rest of the world was asleep, Detective-Sergeant Poynter, Constable Keyes and I went fishing for them—and there they were. . . ."

"Ha!" exclaimed Maltravers. "And supposing they *hadn't* been there?"

Mr. Smith shrugged his shoulders. "Then we should have looked somewhere else for them—and kept on looking."

"You might never have found them."

"It's possible. But we *had* to find them. We had to find these imitation hooves, or some evidence of their manufacture, or we might never have had a case; for, until we had actually laid our hands on them, the theory I had worked out was still only theory. But don't forget it was that theory that led me to look for them, and to find them in that particular place, and not vice versa. And, though I say it myself, the theory was eminently logical and satisfactory in that—with all due respect to Miss Forbes and Mr. Mayhew—it gave the only possible explanation of the whole series of mysteries. So the 'hooves' had to be *somewhere,* and we looked in the most likely place first, and there they were."

"That policeman," put in Miss Forbes. "The one at the foot of The Rise all day yesterday. . . ."

"He was there to keep an eye on the well, of course, just in case Cushing had dropped them in there—or hidden them somewhere else in the immediate vicinity—as a temporary measure. He was there to see that no one went fishing before we did. We had to wait until dead of night so as not to disclose our hand to Cushing. . . . Another point about that, Mr. Maltravers: if Cushing had gone outside the cottage garden or grounds to hide the 'hooves'—dismantled or otherwise—his traces in the snow would have given him away.

"Now, there's one last little detail, and you can exercise your own choice in this. That half-smoked cigar of Croxley's. It could be that he had tossed it away when he opened the gate to go down the cart track to the shed when Cushing was about to work on his imitation hooves. But Detective-Sergeant Poynter here won't have that. He says that no connoisseur would throw away unsmoked so much of such a choice cigar. If he is right then it would seem that the cigar was actually dropped on the spot where Croxley was struck and killed, which must have been on the threshold of the shed. In that case it is therefore reasonable to suppose that Cushing, noticing it perhaps later and realizing just exactly what it would mean to us if we found it there, picked it up and threw it away over the gate out into the road. In which case he made another and a bad mistake in not throwing it somewhere else, say down the well after the 'hooves'.

"But it's easy enough for us to talk now. That diabolically ingenious brain of Gregory Cushing's must have been under tremendous strain then, and . . . well, you know, considering all the things he has done since Saturday night, I am not surprised that his nerve gave way just now when I directly and deliberately accused him. . . .

"Well, that's the story; the full and complete account of the killing of Montague Mason and the killing of Alfred Croxley, and of the mysterious hoof-prints in the snow. And now we want you to go out and put an end to all those other silly stories of devils and Blue Women and ghosts and whatnot."

There was a little silence in the office, a silence that was akin to applause. Three of the four people sitting facing Detective-Inspector Smith stared at him in admiration, digesting what they had heard. But the fourth—old Jake Popplewell—gazed unhappily and unseeingly out of the window.

"Greg," he muttered. "Me own nephew. Me own sister's boy— thank God she's dead. He did all *that?*"

"Yes," said Mr. Smith softly. "I'm afraid he did."

The old man stared at him full. "But why?" he demanded passionately. "In the Name o' God, why did he kill Mason?"

Superintendent Blackler came sharply away from the window. "Perhaps I can answer that now. That telephone call a little while ago: that was from Inspector Jamieson of the Metropolitan Police, who have been investigating Mason's affairs from the London end. We heard from your nephew's own lips that Mason had an unsavoury reputation where women were concerned, and we asked Jamieson to look into this for us. Well, he looked, and he found plenty. He gave me a list of Mason's girl friends—Mason's mistresses, to put it bluntly. The man seems to have collected women as another man collects butterflies. He enticed them one by one to go and live with him—oh! I expect he gave them a marvellous time while it lasted. But it didn't last very long. One by one they succeeded each other; and one by one they superseded each other.

"Jamieson gave me a list just now. I stopped him at the fourth name—there was no need to go any farther. Because the third name he gave me was that of Mrs. Pauline Cushing. . . ."

Jake stared at him sombrely. "Pauline. . . . Greg's wife. . . . The gal who liked pretty an' expensive things an' livin' luxuriously. . . . An' when he'd tired of her there was only one thing for her to do, an' that was to go back to Greg. Only Greg wouldn't have her after. . . . Y' can't blame him. By Heaven, Mason deserved to die!"

"I'm afraid, Mr. Popplewell," said the superintendent gently, "that that is a matter of opinion, of judgment. And we are not judges, we are only policemen."

"What will happen to him?"

"He will stand his trial. A fair trial at the hands of his peers."

Jake stood up. He seemed to sway a little. He said in a strangely subdued voice: "Greg. . . . Can I go now?"

And the superintendent nodded sympathetically. And Maltravers and Mayhew followed soon after. Miss Forbes lingered behind, and not until she was alone with the three policemen did she break her silence. Then she said to Mr. Smith: "So that's the truth of it?"

"Yes, Miss Forbes. That's the truth. I don't know much about Truth being Beauty, and Beauty Truth. It seems to me that Truth can be pretty sordid at times."

"And the Devonshire case?"

"Oh, I don't know about that. I wasn't on that job you know," he said, striving to speak lightly.

"Yes," murmured Miss Forbes. "Ye-es. . . . I said you were an intelligent man, Inspector." She was silent a moment, fingering the edge of the desk. Then she went on: "Twice while you were speaking to us you used a certain phrase. Twice you referred to that unfortunate young man as being 'diabolically ingenious'. Perhaps you were right."

"Eh?" Mr. Smith stared at her. "Exactly what do you mean by that?"

"What," asked Miss Forbes, still in that same serious, hesitant voice, "made Gregory Cushing kill Mason?"

"Why, revenge, of course. People will do these things—"

"Revenge, yes. A very human failing. But what made him *kill?* What put it into his head to *kill* for revenge? What good did that do him? Did it bring back his wife? Did it wash out the past? . . . That's the whole point, Inspector. It was useless. It was futile. It was diabolic.

"Diabolic," she repeated. "Of the Devil. . . . Perhaps, in a certain sense, the common people, the superstitious as you call them, were right after all. Perhaps they *were,* in that sense, the Footprints of Satan. Perhaps it *was* the Devil. . . ."

Mr. Smith said nothing to this. His daily work chained him to the solid and the earthy, but even he could sense vaguely the deeps beyond. He said nothing. He gazed thoughtfully and curiously at the Feet of Satan for some moments. Then he picked them up and put them back in the superintendent's brown bag.

THE END

RAMBLE HOUSE's

HARRY STEPHEN KEELER WEBWORK MYSTERIES

(RH) indicates the title is available ONLY in the RAMBLE HOUSE edition

The Ace of Spades Murder
The Affair of the Bottled Deuce (RH)
The Amazing Web
The Barking Clock
Behind That Mask
The Book with the Orange Leaves
The Bottle with the Green Wax Seal
The Box from Japan
The Case of the Canny Killer
The Case of the Crazy Corpse (RH)
The Case of the Flying Hands (RH)
The Case of the Ivory Arrow
The Case of the Jeweled Ragpicker
The Case of the Lavender Gripsack
The Case of the Mysterious Moll
The Case of the 16 Beans
The Case of the Transparent Nude (RH)
The Case of the Transposed Legs
The Case of the Two-Headed Idiot (RH)
The Case of the Two Strange Ladies
The Circus Stealers (RH)
Cleopatra's Tears
A Copy of Beowulf (RH)
The Crimson Cube (RH)
The Face of the Man From Saturn
Find the Clock
The Five Silver Buddhas
The 4th King
The Gallows Waits, My Lord! (RH)
The Green Jade Hand
Finger! Finger!
Hangman's Nights (RH)
I, Chameleon (RH)
I Killed Lincoln at 10:13! (RH)
The Iron Ring
The Man Who Changed His Skin (RH)
The Man with the Crimson Box
The Man with the Magic Eardrums
The Man with the Wooden Spectacles
The Marceau Case
The Matilda Hunter Murder
The Monocled Monster

The Murder of London Lew
The Murdered Mathematician
The Mysterious Card (RH)
The Mysterious Ivory Ball of Wong Shing Li
   (RH)
The Mystery of the Fiddling Cracksman
The Peacock Fan
The Photo of Lady X (RH)
The Portrait of Jirjohn Cobb
Report on Vanessa Hewstone (RH)
Riddle of the Travelling Skull
Riddle of the Wooden Parrakeet (RH)
The Scarlet Mummy (RH)
The Search for X-Y-Z
The Sharkskin Book
Sing Sing Nights
The Six From Nowhere (RH)
The Skull of the Waltzing Clown
The Spectacles of Mr. Cagliostro
Stand By—London Calling!
The Steeltown Strangler
The Stolen Gravestone (RH)
Strange Journey (RH)
The Strange Will
The Straw Hat Murders (RH)
The Street of 1000 Eyes (RH)
Thieves' Nights
Three Novellos (RH)
The Tiger Snake
The Trap (RH)
Vagabond Nights (Defrauded Yeggman)
Vagabond Nights 2 (10 Hours)
The Vanishing Gold Truck
The Voice of the Seven Sparrows
The Washington Square Enigma
When Thief Meets Thief
The White Circle (RH)
The Wonderful Scheme of Mr. Christopher
   Thorne
X. Jones—of Scotland Yard
Y. Cheung, Business Detective

Keeler Related Works

A To Izzard: A Harry Stephen Keeler Companion by Fender Tucker — Articles and stories about Harry, by Harry, and in his style. Included is a compleat bibliography.

Wild About Harry: Reviews of Keeler Novels — Edited by Richard Polt & Fender Tucker — 22 reviews of works by Harry Stephen Keeler from *Keeler News*. A perfect introduction to the author.

The Keeler Keyhole Collection: Annotated newsletter rants from Harry Stephen Keeler, edited by Francis M. Nevins. Over 400 pages of incredibly personal Keeleriana.

Fakealoo — Pastiches of the style of Harry Stephen Keeler by selected demented members of the HSK Society. Updated every year with the new winner.

RAMBLE HOUSE's OTHER LOONS

A Shot Rang Out — Three decades of reviews from Jon Breen
The Time Armada — Fox B. Holden's 1953 SF gem.
Sideslip — 1968 SF masterpiece by Ted White and Dave Van Arnam
The Triune Man — Mindscrambling science fiction from Richard A. Lupoff
Detective Duff Unravels It — Episodic mysteries by Harvey O'Higgins
Mysterious Martin, the Master of Murder — Two versions of a strange 1912 novel by Tod Robbins about a man who writes books that can kill.
The Master of Mysteries — 1912 novel of supernatural sleuthing by Gelett Burgess
Dago Red — 22 tales of dark suspense by Bill Pronzini
The Night Remembers — A 1991 Jack Walsh mystery from Ed Gorman
Rough Cut & New, Improved Murder — Ed Gorman's first two novels
Hollywood Dreams — A novel of the Depression by Richard O'Brien
Six Gelett Burgess Novels — *The Master of Mysteries, The White Cat, Two O'Clock Courage, Ladies in Boxes, Find the Woman, The Heart Line*
The Organ Reader — A huge compilation of just about everything published in the 1971-1972 radical bay-area newspaper, *THE ORGAN*.
A Clear Path to Cross — Sharon Knowles short mystery stories by Ed Lynskey
Old Times' Sake — Short stories by James Reasoner from Mike Shayne Magazine
Freaks and Fantasies — Eerie tales by Tod Robbins, collaborator of Tod Browning on the film FREAKS.
Five Jim Harmon Sleaze Double Novels — *Vixen Hollow/Celluloid Scandal, The Man Who Made Maniacs/Silent Siren, Ape Rape/Wanton Witch, Sex Burns Like Fire/Twist Session*, and *Sudden Lust/Passion Strip*. More doubles to come!
Marblehead: A Novel of H.P. Lovecraft — A long-lost masterpiece from Richard A. Lupoff. Published for the first time!
The Compleat Ova Hamlet — Parodies of SF authors by Richard A. Lupoff – New edition!
The Secret Adventures of Sherlock Holmes — Three Sherlockian pastiches by the Brooklyn author/publisher, Gary Lovisi.
The Universal Holmes — Richard A. Lupoff's 2007 collection of five Holmesian pastiches and a recipe for giant rat stew.
Four Joel Townsley Rogers Novels — By the author of *The Red Right Hand: Once In a Red Moon, Lady With the Dice, The Stopped Clock, Never Leave My Bed*
Two Joel Townsley Rogers Story Collections — Night of Horror and Killing Time
Twenty Norman Berrow Novels — *The Bishop's Sword, Ghost House, Don't Go Out After Dark, Claws of the Cougar, The Smokers of Hashish, The Secret Dancer, Don't Jump Mr. Boland!, The Footprints of Satan, Fingers for Ransom, The Three Tiers of Fantasy, The Spaniard's Thumb, The Eleventh Plague, Words Have Wings, One Thrilling Night, The Lady's in Danger, It Howls at Night, The Terror in the Fog, Oil Under the Window, Murder in the Melody, The Singing Room*
The N. R. De Mexico Novels — Robert Bragg presents *Marijuana Girl, Madman on a Drum, Private Chauffeur* in one volume.
Four Chelsea Quinn Yarbro Novels featuring Charlie Moon — *Ogilvie, Tallant and Moon, Music When the Sweet Voice Dies, Poisonous Fruit* and *Dead Mice*
Four Walter S. Masterman Mysteries — *The Green Toad, The Flying Beast, The Yellow Mistletoe* and *The Wrong Verdict*, fantastic impossible plots. More to come.
Two Hake Talbot Novels — *Rim of the Pit, The Hangman's Handyman*. Classic locked room mysteries.
Two Alexander Laing Novels — *The Motives of Nicholas Holtz* and *Dr. Scarlett*, stories of medical mayhem and intrigue from the 30s.
Four David Hume Novels — *Corpses Never Argue, Cemetery First Stop, Make Way for the Mourners, Eternity Here I Come*, and more to come.
Three Wade Wright Novels — *Echo of Fear, Death At Nostalgia Street* and *It Leads to Murder*, with more to come!
Four Rupert Penny Novels — *Policeman's Holiday, Policeman's Evidence, Lucky Policeman* and *Sealed Room Murder*, classic impossible mysteries.
Five Jack Mann Novels — Strange murder in the English countryside. *Gees' First Case, Nightmare Farm, Grey Shapes, The Ninth Life, The Glass Too Many*.
Seven Max Afford Novels — *Owl of Darkness, Death's Mannikins, Blood on His Hands, The Dead Are Blind, The Sheep and the Wolves, Sinners in Paradise* and *Two Locked Room Mysteries and a Ripping Yarn* by one of Australia's finest novelists.

Five Joseph Shallit Novels — *The Case of the Billion Dollar Body, Lady Don't Die on My Doorstep, Kiss the Killer, Yell Bloody Murder, Take Your Last Look.* One of America's best 50's authors.

Two Crimson Clown Novels — By Johnston McCulley, author of the Zorro novels, *The Crimson Clown* and *The Crimson Clown Again*.

The Best of 10-Story Book — edited by Chris Mikul, over 35 stories from the literary magazine Harry Stephen Keeler edited.

A Young Man's Heart — A forgotten early classic by Cornell Woolrich

The Anthony Boucher Chronicles — edited by Francis M. Nevins
Book reviews by Anthony Boucher written for the *San Francisco Chronicle,* 1942 – 1947. Essential and fascinating reading.

Muddled Mind: Complete Works of Ed Wood, Jr. — David Hayes and Hayden Davis deconstruct the life and works of a mad genius.

Gadsby — A lipogram (a novel without the letter E). Ernest Vincent Wright's last work, published in 1939 right before his death.

My First Time: The One Experience You Never Forget — Michael Birchwood — 64 true first-person narratives of how they lost it.

Automaton — Brilliant treatise on robotics: 1928-style! By H. Stafford Hatfield

The Incredible Adventures of Rowland Hern — Rousing 1928 impossible crimes by Nicholas Olde.

Slammer Days — Two full-length prison memoirs: *Men into Beasts* (1952) by George Sylvester Viereck and *Home Away From Home* (1962) by Jack Woodford

The Golden Dagger — 1951 Scotland Yard yarn by E. R. Punshon

Beat Books #1 — Two beatnik classics, *A Sea of Thighs* by Ray Kainen and *Village Hipster* by J.X. Williams

A Smell of Smoke — 1951 English countryside thriller by Miles Burton

Ruled By Radio — 1925 futuristic novel by Robert L. Hadfield & Frank E. Farncombe

Murder in Silk — A 1937 Yellow Peril novel of the silk trade by Ralph Trevor

The Case of the Withered Hand — 1936 potboiler by John G. Brandon

Finger-prints Never Lie — A 1939 classic detective novel by John G. Brandon

Inclination to Murder — 1966 thriller by New Zealand's Harriet Hunter

Invaders from the Dark — Classic werewolf tale from Greye La Spina

Fatal Accident — Murder by automobile, a 1936 mystery by Cecil M. Wills

The Devil Drives — A prison and lost treasure novel by Virgil Markham

Dr. Odin — Douglas Newton's 1933 potboiler comes back to life.

The Chinese Jar Mystery — Murder in the manor by John Stephen Strange, 1934

The Julius Caesar Murder Case — A classic 1935 re-telling of the assassination by Wallace Irwin that's much more fun than the Shakespeare version

West Texas War and Other Western Stories — by Gary Lovisi

The Contested Earth and Other SF Stories — A never-before published space opera and seven short stories by Jim Harmon.

Tales of the Macabre and Ordinary — Modern twisted horror by Chris Mikul, author of the *Bizarrism* series.

The Gold Star Line — Seaboard adventure from L.T. Reade and Robert Eustace.

The Werewolf vs the Vampire Woman — Hard to believe ultraviolence by either Arthur M. Scarm or Arthur M. Scram.

Black Hogan Strikes Again — Australia's Peter Renwick pens a tale of the outback.

Don Diablo: Book of a Lost Film — Two-volume treatment of a western by Paul Landres, with diagrams. Intro by Francis M. Nevins.

The Charlie Chaplin Murder Mystery — Movie hijinks by Wes D. Gehring.

The Koky Comics — A collection of all of the 1978-1981 Sunday and daily comic strips by Richard O'Brien and Mort Gerberg, in two volumes.

Suzy — Another collection of comic strips from Richard O'Brien and Bob Vojtko

Dime Novels: Ramble House's 10-Cent Books — *Knife in the Dark* by Robert Leslie Bellem, *Hot Lead* and *Song of Death* by Ed Earl Repp, *A Hashish House in New York* by H.H. Kane, and five more.

Blood in a Snap — The *Finnegan's Wake* of the 21st century, by Jim Weiler and Al Gorithm

Stakeout on Millennium Drive — Award-winning Indianapolis Noir — Ian Woollen.

Dope Tales #1 — Two dope-riddled classics; *Dope Runners* by Gerald Grantham and *Death Takes the Joystick* by Phillip Condé.

Dope Tales #2 — Two more narco-classics; *The Invisible Hand* by Rex Dark and *The Smokers of Hashish* by Norman Berrow.

Dope Tales #3 — Two enchanting novels of opium by the master, Sax Rohmer. *Dope* and *The Yellow Claw.*

Tenebrae — Ernest G. Henham's 1898 horror tale brought back.

The Singular Problem of the Stygian House-Boat — Two classic tales by John Kendrick Bangs about the denizens of Hades.

Tiresias — Psychotic modern horror novel by Jonathan M. Sweet.

The One After Snelling — Kickass modern noir from Richard O'Brien.

The Sign of the Scorpion — 1935 Edmund Snell tale of oriental evil.

The House of the Vampire — 1907 poetic thriller by George S. Viereck.

An Angel in the Street — Modern hardboiled noir by Peter Genovese.

The Devil's Mistress — Scottish gothic tale by J. W. Brodie-Innes.

The Lord of Terror — 1925 mystery with master-criminal, Fantômas.

The Lady of the Terraces — 1925 adventure by E. Charles Vivian.

My Deadly Angel — 1955 Cold War drama by John Chelton.

Prose Bowl — Futuristic satire — Bill Pronzini & Barry N. Malzberg .

Satan's Den Exposed — True crime in Truth or Consequences New Mexico — Award-winning journalism by the *Desert Journal*.

The Amorous Intrigues & Adventures of Aaron Burr — by Anonymous — Hot historical action.

I Stole $16,000,000 — A true story by cracksman Herbert E. Wilson.

The Black Dark Murders — Vintage 50s college murder yarn by Milt Ozaki, writing as Robert O. Saber.

Sex Slave — Potboiler of lust in the days of Cleopatra — Dion Leclerq.

You'll Die Laughing — Bruce Elliott's 1945 novel of murder at a practical joker's English countryside manor.

The Private Journal & Diary of John H. Surratt — The memoirs of the man who conspired to assassinate President Lincoln.

Dead Man Talks Too Much — Hollywood boozer by Weed Dickenson

Red Light — History of legal prostitution in Shreveport Louisiana by Eric Brock. Includes wonderful photos of the houses and the ladies.

A Snark Selection — Lewis Carroll's *The Hunting of the Snark* with two Snarkian chapters by Harry Stephen Keeler — Illustrated by Gavin L. O'Keefe.

Ripped from the Headlines! — The Jack the Ripper story as told in the newspaper articles in the *New York* and *London Times*.

Geronimo — S. M. Barrett's 1905 autobiography of a noble American.

The White Peril in the Far East — Sidney Lewis Gulick's 1905 indictment of the West and assurance that Japan would never attack the U.S.

The Compleat Calhoon — All of Fender Tucker's works: Includes *The Totah Trilogy, Weed, Women and Song* and *Tales from the Tower,* plus a CD of all of his songs.

RAMBLE HOUSE

Fender Tucker, Prop.

www.ramblehouse.com   fender@ramblehouse.com

318-455-6847   10329 Sheephead Drive, Vancleave MS 39565